"You might as well give up.
I'm a lot smarter than you think.
I know what you're about.
You can't seduce me."

"Then you have nothing to worry about, have you?" His lips were in her hair, kissing the soft fringe that edged her face, his breath stirring more than the curls that nestled there. "You are immune to this sort of thing, aren't you? So strong. So capable. So determined to resist. Nothing I do has any effect on you, does it?" His breath was even and warm, the touch of his lips gentle as they moved in a slow circular pattern across the smoothness of her troubled brow, down the straight, dainty line of her nose, to brush faintly across her surprised mouth. "This," he said in the softest of tones, "is something you hardly notice."

She knew nothing about intimacy, but she was gathering some mighty strong clues from the places where her blood ran thick and warm. She was hot. She was cold. She wanted to say *yes*. She was thinking *no*. She must stop this. Now. Weakly she said, "Stop it, some more," and heard his soft chuckle. . . .

Elaine Coffman

Somewhere Along the Way

A DELL BOOK

Published by
Dell Publishing
a division of
Bantam Doubleday Dell Publishing Group, Inc.
666 Fifth Avenue
New York, New York 10103

ISBN: 0-440-20800-9

Printed in the United States of America

Published simultaneously in Canada

September 1992

10 9 8 7 6 5 4 3 2 1

RAD

For my grandmother,
whose shadow has danced through my life.
Maude Tatum Davidson
1881–1952

I always knew I was deep in your heart; now I can tell you, you are still twined around mine. You were life's anchor. *Remember* was your magic word. Whatever I've become, whatever I've managed to do, it was all because of you. How often I've wished I could see you once more, if only to say, thank you. I loved you then. I love you now.

No one is a light unto himself, not even the sun.
—Antonio Porchia, *Voces* (1968)

The moment I heard my first love story
I began seeking you,
not realizing the search was useless.
Lovers don't meet somewhere along the way
They're in one another's souls from the beginning.
—Jalal Al-din Rumi, Persian poem

I
THE
WOMAN

What one beholds of woman is the least part
of her.
—Ovid, *Love's Cure* (C.A.D. 8)

Prologue

Dornoch Castle, Scotland, 1848

The trouble all began when her mother named her after a horse.

Thinking about her best friend back in England, and how she must be enjoying the last of the season in London right now, Lady Annabella Stewart shifted uneasily from one foot to the other. Resentment and humiliation seethed within her. Everything had looked so bright and promising that day a few months ago when she left Saltwood Castle and journeyed to her family's town house in London. She had just turned seventeen, it was to be her first season, and she had considered herself the most fortunate of women.

Oh, how the world had turned upon her! *You should have known, Bella. You should have known. Anyone named after a horse . . .*

Shortly before she was born, her mother had attended a horse race, and had watched a beautiful dapple-gray filly named Lady Annabella cross the finish line first to win.

"But, Bella," her mother had often said since, "it was a very *beautiful* horse. And it did come in first."

Only when a glass of champagne was thrust in her hand did Annabella pull her thoughts away from England and the past to Scotland and the present. *Over,* she thought. *My life will soon be over.* This couldn't be happening. Not to her. She stared at her father, feeling the panicked pounding of her heart, the choking fingers of fate tightening around her throat. Feeling sick and desperate, she let her eyes do her pleading. The Duke of Grenville narrowed his eyes slightly and cleared his throat. He did not speak.

Annabella closed her eyes, shutting from her sight the vision of her father's grim face. *He's going to do it,* she thought. *He's really going to go through with this.* She would be betrothed coldheartedly, and without feeling, to a man she had just met, a man who had been twenty years old when she was born.

Humiliated, Annabella felt the chill of the castle reach out to her from the far corners of the room. This was a celebration, a gathering of family and clans to seal a bargain and honor a betrothal. It should be a happy occasion.

But instead, it was a day of sadness. Annabella's mother tried to look cheerful, but her eyes sparkled a bit too brightly to be anything but tears. Upstairs, Bettina the maid was crying. Jarvis, the duke's valet, had something in his eye. Outside, the rain poured down. Even the candles in the candelabra dripped.

"Here's tae us and to hell with the English!"

The loudly flung toast sliced through the soft tones of conversation like a thunderclap, leaving nothing but the eerie silence of a tomb behind.

Anyone in the great hall of Dornoch Castle could have shouted it. At any other time that toast would have been enough to raise the hackles on any red-blooded English-man, but Alisdair Stewart, the Duke of Grenville, simply looked at his daughter, Annabella, and John Gordon, the Earl of Huntly, her betrothed, and raised his glass. "May you enjoy a long and happy life together."

He looked at his wife and smiled. The duchess raised her glass, and smiled, looking at their daughter. But Annabella did not smile. She did not look at anyone. Instead, she stared at a fixed point in the tapestry across the room, her breathing uneven, and tried to hide the outrage she felt at being betrothed to this Scot.

She prayed for a sudden shot of courage, but all she felt was shame—shame for being such a coward; shame for wanting to cry instead of resist; shame for being the shiver-ing, quaking thing that she knew she was. Why could she not think of the hundred things a woman of spirit could say or do at a time like this? Why could she merely tremble and go pale, or look heartbroken and wretched? It was a painful thing to see herself as she was—meek, obedient, green as grass; a malleable young woman submissive to parental au-thority with no more spunk than a sleeping babe and very little optimism.

"To my betrothed," Huntly said with an edge to his voice that stirred terror within her.

Knowing she must look at her husband-to-be, she turned to face him, smiling to cover a growing wave of hysteria. Cold and terrified, she blinked to hold back tears and prayed her thoughts would take their prodding elsewhere. In a blur of misery, she thought again of Emily, her best friend back home in England. How Emily must be enjoying the last of the season in London right now. Annabella shifted uneasily from one foot to the other. She had never felt so lonely, or so wretched. She wanted to cry. She wanted to go home.

She had said as much to her mother only that morning. "I want to sleep in my own bed and wake up to a real *English* breakfast. I want to have tea at Aunt Ellen's. I want to paint pictures of the caravans in Peasholme Green during Martinmas Fair. I don't care if I never put another foot in Scotland for as long as I live. I don't like seaweed jelly. I don't like eels. And I *hate* haggis. I don't know how anyone could like it. I don't understand these people. They're insulting and intimidating. They talk strangely. They look at me strangely. They don't even like me." She swiped at the tears dripping onto her bodice. "I hate the thought of being married. I don't want to spend the rest of my life eating all this horrible food with a man I don't even like. Why are things like this always happening to me?"

"Oh, Bella," her mother had said, enfolding her in her arms. "Would that I could do something to make you happy. I feel so helpless. All I can think to do is send for the hartshorn." The two of them stood together and cried.

"I shall never be happy again," Annabella had said at last.

Even now, here at this gathering several hours later, she felt the same way. She would never be happy. Never, never, never.

Across the room, Annabella's uncle, Colin McCulloch, studied her thoughtfully. She stood pale and still as a pine, her eyes so full of unshed tears it was impossible to tell their exact color. Unlike Annabella and her mother, he didn't look particularly sad, but he also didn't look too pleased with the way things were going. As if sensing that Annabella could do with a little cheerful humor, he raised his glass for another toast. "May old Douglas Macleod loan you his Fairy Flag for your nuptial bed," he said, looking directly at Annabella. And then he did the strangest thing. He winked.

The wink would have been enough to send a spot of color to her cheeks. But the mention of the nuptial bed turned her entire face red. She looked at her uncle Colin, wondering what he meant. Colin McCulloch was the Earl of Dornoch and her mother's eldest brother. He was head of the McCulloch clan and as boisterous and redheaded as they came—a Scot from the red pom-pom on his bonnet to the *sgian-dubh* in his stocking.

"I'll be loaning them my Fairy Flag all right, but judging from the looks o' the wee lass, this betrothal isna sittin' too well with her," said Douglas, called the Macleod by his kin.

"Aye," Colin said. He studied her gently. "She may be wishing for it to bring herring into the loch instead o' bairn to her belly."

While the laughter was at its loudest, the duchess looked at Annabella, wondering how to soothe her sad, bewildered youngest child. Leaning closer, she whispered, "the Fairy Flag is a Macleod treasure that supposedly came from the Crusades. It has three properties—carried into battle, it increases the number of Macleods; placed on the marriage bed, it ensures fertility; and it brings herring into the loch."

Annabella felt her mother's arm around her waist. She longed to drop her head on her mother's shoulder, as she had so often done as a child, as if that simple action could somehow act as a mighty stick in the spoke of wheels that had already been long in motion. Trying to still her panic, she looked up at her mother. "Uncle is right," she whispered back, unable to keep the apprehension from a voice that was breathy and unsteady. "I'd rather have herring in the loch."

"Perhaps," her mother said, giving her a pat on the arm,

"you will be blessed with both." The pat was bracing, but the voice quivered too much to offer comfort. And with good reason. The duchess was feeling mixed emotions herself. Her heart went out to Annabella for the grief she knew she was feeling, and it hardened toward her husband for his lack of understanding, for the ease with which he seemed to forget what it was like to be young and so influenced by the ways of the heart. She had tried to explain this to Annabella the day before by saying, "Your father simply has a sort of unruffled practicality that would drive a sober man to blue ruin." She would have gone on to say more about feeling the urge to take a nip or two of gin herself, but about that time the duke walked into the room—which was always an effective curb to any conversation.

Whatever the duchess was going to think next was interrupted by the pouring of another round of champagne. She patted her daughter's hand, offering consolation in the only way she could. "The Scots aren't such a bad lot. Their ways just seem a bit strange at first, but soon you'll learn to love them."

Annabella attempted to stifle a gasp. "Love them? I don't see how anyone could love them. I've never seen such mean, ill-mannered people in my life. Father was being kind when he said they were 'half-tamed.' A wilder lot I've never seen."

Her mother smiled, leaning closer to whisper, "That's because you've been around my family. Not all Highlanders are so unruly. Take your betrothed, for instance. He's quite the gentleman, even by English standards." Seeing the frown on her daughter's face, she added, "Don't be forgetting that more than half of your blood is as wild as the Highlands where Colin and I were born. Now smile, Bella, and try to look happy."

Annabella didn't want to smile. Happy looks were for happy people; and all in all, this was a very negative day for her. She didn't want to be here in Scotland. She didn't want to be attending this betrothal celebration. And she most certainly did not want to be betrothed to anyone. Not to any of the endless parade of men her father had considered back in London, and absolutely not to Lord Huntly, the man he had eventually decided upon. Most assuredly she did not want to be betrothed to a Scot. And what Englishwoman would? *Here's tae us and to hell with the English,* indeed.

Annabella stole a look at the man she was destined to wed one year hence. How could her father, a man she had always adored, have done this? All five of her sisters were married to refined, smooth-speaking men, English men. Men who would live in a civilized place like London, or Kent, or even York. How well she could remember her sisters' reaction upon hearing their father had promised his youngest and last daughter to a Scot:

"A Scot?" repeated Judith. "He must be daft!"

"How could father be such a fool?" asked Jane.

Coming to her feet, Sara said, "Every unmarried duke in England has begged for Annabella's hand. Why didn't father settle on one of them?"

To which Margaret replied by asking, "Why is Father shipping her off to Scotland as if he couldn't find a good English husband for her? And why would any Scot want an English wife? They don't even like us."

Elizabeth answered that one in her most pretentious Scottish brogue, "Because the deaf man will aye hear the clink o' money."

On any other occasion they would have laughed. But this day was different. "I'm sure Father has his reasons, and to him it seems quite the thing to do. It's simply that men have such an odd way of looking at things," Jane said, sliding her arm around Annabella. "Still, I can't believe he would do such a thing to his own flesh and blood."

And neither could Annabella.

Never could she have imagined her father would settle upon anyone for her husband other than a man from her own country, an Englishman. "But, Bella, the Scots *are* English," her father said.

A point that caused her mother's Scottish blood to run a little warmer. She sent the duke a peevish look. "No, Alisdair," she said with perfect calmness. "The Scots aren't English. They won't ever be English any more than the English will ever be Scots."

The duke looked skeptical—something he did a lot around his wife and daughters. "What do you mean, they won't ever be English? They've been part of England for over a hundred years," he said.

"They're part of Great Britain, but that doesn't make them English." The duke opened his mouth as if to strengthen his position, but the duchess cut him off with a wave of her hand. "You're bested and you know it, Alisdair. One man against seven women . . ."

"I manage to prevail, Anne," he said.

"Yes, you do—*occasionally*."

"Scot or English, we're all one," the duke said in his defense. "It's the same with families."

"Perhaps. As long as you don't forget that the clan is stronger than the chief."

"And don't you be forgetting that I h'ae a bit o' Scots blood in me."

His wife said something that sounded like "*humph,*" then added, "Your Scots blood is too watered down with English tea to do you any good."

"His blood isn't watered down, it's cold," Sara said, glaring at her father.

Wishing she had the fortitude to say something like that, Annabella stiffened her spine and tried not to look beseeching as she said, "Why do I have to marry a Scot when none of my sisters did?"

The duke looked at Anne with a question in his eyes. "Should we tell her?"

"Tell me what?" Annabella asked. She looked past her father to where her mother was standing. "Am I being bartered to the highest bidder like a prize sow at the fair?"

"No, dear, you aren't being bartered," Anne said. "And don't refer to yourself in such common terms."

"Has Father gambled away our fortune at White's?" Bella asked her mother. "Are we destitute? Is that it?"

The duke scowled. "I rarely go to White's anymore, and when I do, it isn't to gamble. More importantly, I am not a man to sell my daughter for thirty pieces of silver."

"Thirty-one pieces, perhaps," Elizabeth said.

It was the first time they found something to laugh about —everyone save Annabella, that is.

Refusing to be distracted by anything, not even humor, Annabella drove her question home. "Why are you and Father being so secretive?"

Anne sighed and looked at her husband, who looked as if he would rather be anywhere else at this moment than standing here in the library with his family. "I suppose we owe it to her," he said.

"Owe me what?" Annabella almost shouted, but the words came out in a flustered, disjointed voice that made it sound as if she was having second thoughts. Before she lost all her nerve, she said hastily, "Do you intend to tell me, or tease me to death?"

"Do you want to tell her?" the duke asked his wife.

Anne looked at Annabella and shook her head. The perfect picture of wifely submission, she said in the meekest of tones, "No, dear, you go ahead."

All hell was breaking loose in the back of Annabella's mind—where she was imagining the worst—which was probably what prompted her to throw up her hands and say without thinking, "I've never had so many people talking circles around me."

Her mother made a big to-do about straightening a few books on the bookshelf beside her, her cheeks suffused with bright red color. She did not look away until the duke cleared his throat and said, "It's a bit complicated."

Annabella lowered herself into the nearest chair. "Something tells me I'd better sit down."

In a small, apologetic voice Annabella hardly recognized, her mother said, "I think I'll join you."

Distracted by the pillar of meekness her mother had suddenly become, Annabella found her attention momentarily diverted from the catastrophe at hand. She almost smiled at the novelty of it.

The duke took advantage of this unexpected lull and bolted for a finely made wine cellarette and opened it. Taking out an elaborately gilded decanter inscribed BURGUNDY and removing the cut spire stopper, he poured himself half a glass. A second glance at his wife made him hastily fill it to the brim. He finished that glass and half of another before he spoke. "When I fell in love with your mother and wanted to marry her, her father wasn't too keen about marrying his daughter to an Englishman, regardless of the fact that I had Scottish ancestors."

"He must have warmed to the idea," Annabella said.

Then looking suddenly horrified, she sprang to her feet and asked, "Don't tell me you aren't married."

The duke laughed and regarded his youngest with loving fondness. "Of course we're married."

Relieved, Annabella sat back down as her father continued. "Old Donald McCulloch agreed to the marriage, because he was a shrewd old buzzard and knew uniting his family with such an illustrious English family as mine was a wise decision. But he made one stipulation: If we had only one daughter, she was to marry a Scot."

"You have six daughters," Annabella put in.

"There's more to it than that," the duke said. "If we had several daughters, the youngest one had to marry a Scot."

To be singled out to suffer by her very own grandfather was a fate she didn't deserve, and she cursed the solitary event that would change the course of her life. How unfair it was—but there was nothing she could do except ache for what might have been and hate the callousness of her unfeeling grandfather—which did nothing to endear anything connected with Scotland to her.

"Donald McCulloch is dead now. What difference does it make whom I marry?" Like a mouse in a trap struggling to free itself, Annabella felt her emotions go from anger, to desperation, and back to anger. "You aren't afraid of a dead man, are you?" The moment she uttered the words her head flew up and her eyes widened. She wondered if it was fear or anger that drove one insane, for surely she must be so to speak so to her father.

But if he was offended by her pinprick of a challenge, he took no notice. "No, I'm not afraid of a dead man," he said thoughtfully. Then, shaking his head with disbelief, he added, "although I do feel that if anyone could make it back from the hereafter to haunt me, old Donald McCulloch could. He was a superstitious man, a believer in bogeys and warlocks, kelpies and monsters. And all this was sprinkled with a daft streak." The duke glanced at his wife, and seeing Anne wasn't taking any of this too badly, he went on. "You were born at midnight and Donald believed any child born in the *wee sma' oors* was destined to be different."

"Different," Annabella repeated. Then as if it had suddenly become apparent, she added, "And he made certain that I would be different, by forcing you to such an agreement." A sudden afterthought made her eyes widen. "You don't have to keep your promise," she said meekly. "He's been dead for a long time. Probably no one remembers such a promise."

"He had it written into our marriage contract, so he could rest easy. If you don't marry a Scot, Bella, we would be guilty of breaching the contract."

"Isn't there any way we can get out of my being forced to obey? What if I never married?"

"You don't have that choice," the duke said, looking away from her.

"And if we refuse? If we breach the contract, what happens?"

"Our marriage could be invalidated and all of our children declared illegitimate."

Rising to her feet with a swish of ruby red Chinese silk, Annabella walked to the ornately carved library doors and paused. "I wish Grandfather were still alive," she said to her mother. "So I could tell him just what I think of him and his stipulation." Then Annabella did something she had never done before. She slammed the door behind her.

The duchess released a long-held sigh. "Dear me," she said to the duke. "Do you suppose we have a rebellion on our hands?"

"No," the duke said. "It's just some of that wild blood from your side of the family that's boiling. But don't worry. Annabella has been reared with a firm hand and a strong understanding of what is expected of her. Good breeding and discipline will carry her through when common sense won't. She'll come around."

His wife was still staring at the door. "I'm not so sure," she said.

"My love, our daughter is an English lady through and through. She won't let us down."

"I know, but she reminds me so much of my father. Every so often I feel that wild Highland spirit lives on in Annabella."

"Your father was dead before she was a year old. She's never even been to Scotland."

"That doesn't matter. My father always said it took two generations to breed Scots blood into a man and two to breed it out. Annabella is only the first generation."

"I still say we just need to give her time. She'll come around and see things our way."

Over the weeks that followed, Annabella hadn't warmed to the idea, nor had she begun to see things their way, but she had accepted it, as she did all dictates from her parents. She might be half-Scot, but she was, just as her father had said, all English lady. She had been reared to fear the Lord, honor her mother and father, and exhibit the suitable qualities of a gently born English lady, behaving with well-bred appropriateness at all times. The proper upbringing of the daughters of the Duke of Grenville was of prime importance, and great care was taken to see that all six of the duke's daughters learned to display, by their restraint, their superior birth and breeding. For all of her young years, Annabella Catriona Stewart had behaved, not as she pleased, but as was expected of her. Never, not even once, had she been a disappointment to her parents in that regard.

And now, several weeks later, she was far from the civilized life she had known at Saltwood Castle, or even at the Duke of Grenville's town house in London. Here she was at Dornoch Castle, a place of bleak landscapes and swirling, dark waters, where even the roar of the sea couldn't drown the harsh echoes of the Scottish tongue. Even in her bitterness, she tried to remind herself that this was her mother's home, the place of the duchess's birth.

Reminding herself of this fact, Annabella looked at the gilt-framed paintings that lined the damp stone walls. Her own history stared back at her. Within these cold gray walls lay part of her past. But her future? What of that?

Annabella looked at her mother's concerned face and felt her legs tremble. What had her mother said? *Smile, Bella, and try to look happy.* Looking happy was impossible, but knowing how important it was to her mother, she did her best to smile. Smiling was difficult. Especially when one was crying inside. Never had she felt so helpless or so hopeless. She had been given no time to adjust to the horrible shock, to the surprise revelation that she was to marry a man of her father's choosing—and close to her father's age —when the next thing she knew, her father had announced she would marry a Scot.

Never to live in England again? She felt her eyes burn with repressed tears as she stole a look at her betrothed once more. What a travesty. What an insult. She would never be ready to marry him, this man they called John Gordon, the Earl of Huntly.

She had known it since yesterday, from the moment she had first set eyes upon him. Perhaps it was only the difference in their ages that made her think of him more as a father figure than a lover, but after Colin McCulloch had introduced them, Annabella could only stare, her eyes huge with alarm and disbelief. Through a bleary haze Huntly had cupped her chin in his hand and turned her face to the light.

For a moment he stared down into her pale green eyes, seeing something one could call only hopeless resignation in their depths. He released her. A cold hardness settled within her heart.

"So you're Colin McCulloch's niece," he said, glancing at Colin, as if to see if there was any resemblance.

"Yes," Annabella said, feeling tortured by her own misery.

"No one bothered to tell me you were such a bonny lass."

And no one bothered to tell me you were so old. Despair welled within her.

After a miserably long dinner, they had parted. Annabella offered her hand and felt a shiver as his cold lips pressed against it. At that moment, she knew this man would never be capable of "igniting a fire within her and bringing the slumbering coals of passion to life," as she had overheard her father say to her mother. The Earl of Huntly didn't look as if he could ignite a trail of gunpowder with a blazing lucifer.

With sublime effort, Annabella forced herself to give her attention to yet another toast. At least all this champagne was dulling her senses and quelling the desire to cry. She listened to more comments and wishes for married bliss. Her head ached and she felt strange, as if she were watching all of this from some place far away. Surely this was all a dream—a nightmare from which she would soon awake. Trying to shut out the reality, she closed her eyes, remembering, wishing, knowing even as she did it was all fruitless. Everything was lost to her now. Her future was sealed. Last night she had slept in Dornoch Castle for the first time. Just one night ago she had fallen into a deep, troubled sleep and heard voices—voices that made her remember the tales told at dinner, tales of how the McCullochs had always been known for their courage, and how they would ignore the opinion of the world and risk death and damnation for what they believed in.

She had opened her eyes. She wasn't at Dornoch Castle, or even Saltwood, but a strange place, a place of swirling mists with the crashing sound of the sea nearby. She was standing at an altar beside her betrothed, when a strange, dark mist began to fill the room and the sound of bagpipes saturated the air. And then she saw him, tall and straight as a Scottish fir, his hair as black as midnight and eyes as blue as a bonny loch, his strong body wrapped in yards of plaid and swirling mist.

Suddenly he was between them, taking her hand from her betrothed. Shouts erupted. A dozen swords were soon at his throat. Yet the sound of his laughter rent the air. His plaid drifted like the mist, all about her, and Annabella felt herself lifted and borne away. She fought against the plaid that covered her face, tried to see his face, to ask his name.

Then she awoke.

The memory of that dream brought the rise of emotion to the back of her throat. Maintaining her composure was difficult, but she called to mind all she had been taught, remembering who she was and what was expected of her. With firm resolve, she began to take hold of herself. She wasn't a child who believed in fairy tales. Lord Huntly was her reality, her betrothed; there was naught she could do about it, short of dying, and she wasn't quite ready for that yet. Her dark brows drew together. As Huntly turned to speak to her mother, Annabella looked him over.

As far as gentlemen went, she could do worse, she supposed. He was handsome enough—for an older man—but nothing about him or his manner stirred any feeling to life within her. At least he wasn't fat, or ugly, or illiterate and uncouth. At least he looked very much the English gentleman, with his sandy blond hair and pale blue eyes. And he dressed very much in the manner of an English gentlemen. As far as manners were concerned, he was as proper as any English lord, and that was just it. Everything about him was proper and dull, and she couldn't shake the feeling that her life with this man stretched before her as bleak and barren as these windswept moors. In Annabella's opinion, Lord Huntly was plain as English pudding.

Gordon, as if sensing her study, turned toward her and smiled fleetingly. But Annabella knew all about practiced smiles. Hadn't she spent hours herself in front of a mirror under the tutelage of her governess practicing a smile, a flutter of eyelashes, or the opening of her fan with a flick of her wrist? Women of the English *ton* would give up a London season for such a man. The thought distracted her, and she immediately found fault with not only his appearance but everything about him. *How odd*, she thought, *that in a place overrun with wild, unruly men I should find his genteel appearance, his gentrified manners, his very Englishness, so annoying*.

And then again, perhaps it wasn't any of those things. Perhaps it was only the fact that she was being forced to marry him that she found so distasteful.

Annabella shivered, as if a cold hand had brushed over

her. She glanced around the room: nothing was out of the
ordinary, yet she felt another presence. She pushed the
feeling away and returned Huntly's smile. Although her
smile was frozen and weak, he looked pleased by it. She
sensed concealed mysteries behind his light-colored eyes.

Suddenly, and without warning the doors to the hall
broke open and a great wind filled the room, swirling and
moaning and gutting the candles. Two servants quickly
closed the doors and an eerie silence followed as the candles were relit, one by one. The wind howled down the
chimney, then was still. A light knocking was heard. *Tap.
Tap. Tap.*

"A raven," Colin said. "Tapping at the window."

"A sign of death," someone behind Annabella whispered.

"Come, my lady," Huntly said. "Let them fall victim to
their silly superstitions. It's naught but a tree branch scraping against a windowpane."

Annabella's benumbed mind reacted dumbly and she
blinked in confusion at the man standing beside her. The
earl held out his arm. "Shall we go?" he asked.

Annabella nodded and placed her trembling hand upon
his arm, her touch whisper light. Together they led the way
to dinner, Annabella's mind not upon the meal they would
share, or even the lifetime they would spend together.

As they walked slowly toward the great dining hall of
Dornoch Castle, she was thinking how she wished everything had been different. If she were going to be forced to
marry a Scot, why couldn't it have at least been one like the
famous Highland chiefs of old—the clan leaders she had
always heard so much about—a man who would risk ruin or
death for a dream of passion as wild as the Highlands, a
bonny fighter with an adventurous spirit who would invade

her life and conquer her heart, a man as passionate as he was reckless?

A man like the man in her dream. A man who would risk death and defy the world for what he believed in. A man who would laugh in the face of danger.

II
THE
MAN

A handsome man is not quite poor.
SPANISH PROVERB

Chapter
1

Texas, 1848

"Open up, you bastard!"

Ross Mackinnon broke the kiss and stared down at the face of the woman beneath him.

"I know you're in there, Mackinnon. Open up before I break the door down."

The choice of words, each disturbed tone stressed by a fist that pounded like prophecy against the door, went over him like a cold blue norther, and he froze.

"Oh, Lordy, Lordy! It's my pa," the woman wailed, clutching pathetically at his arm. "He's caught us for sure."

"Don't bet on it," Ross said, prying her hands loose and pulling away.

The woman grabbed his arm. Her voice sounded alarmed, frantic. "You can't go! Not yet! I'll be ruined!"

His laugh was deep and rumbling. "Sweetheart, you were ruined long before I stumbled into this neck of the woods." Giving the woman a quick kiss, Ross rolled off the bed. "I sure hate to miss the little reception you had planned, but I'm not much for shotgun weddings."

Ross made one quick grab for his clothes, which lay across the caned bottom of a fiddleback chair, and tucked them under his arm. He snatched his boots and tossed them out of the window ahead of his clothes, then looped his gun belt over his arm. He had just reached for his hat when the voice boomed again, this time backed up by a hard kick against the pitifully thin door of a two-bit room in the cheapest hotel in Corsicana, Texas.

"You might as well open up, Mackinnon. I've caught you red-handed this time. I've got witnesses that saw Sally Ann come in here with you."

Sally Ann sat up in a hurry and pulled the sheet upward, holding it pressed against her generous breasts. Seeing what Ross intended, she leaped from the bed, dragging the sheet with her. "Wait!" Then turning toward the door, she shouted, "Papa, don't shoot!"

"Sally Ann, you stay back away from the door, honey."

With a groan of defeat, Sally Ann pressed herself flat against the watermarked wallpaper that covered the wall behind her. She clapped her hands over her ears as three shots put three neat holes in the door and shattered the glass chimney on the hurricane lamp across the room. She screamed, not out of fright but from the supremely frustrating sight of the best-looking hindquarters she'd ever seen on a man going through the window and out of her clutches.

Outsmarted, outmaneuvered, and outfoxed. *Damn! Damn! Damn!*

"Come back here!" she shouted, stamping her foot in vexation. "Come back, you hear? You can't do this to me, Mackinnon!" But the only response was the bedeviling sound of Ross Mackinnon's deep, rolling laugh drifting through the lace curtain to settle over her, where his body had pressed only moments ago. Her fists doubled with aggravation, she turned against the wall and pounded it repeatedly. Her father had messed things up good and proper this time. He could be the most irritating man—always having to be the first hog to the trough. Couldn't he have waited and given her time? Frustration mounting, she pounded her fists again. "Damn! Damn! And double damn!"

The irritant kicked open the door and stepped into the room, looking around. "Where is he?"

Sally Ann stamped her foot again, then wailed, "He's gone, of course. I told you not to come until I turned out the light. Now we'll never catch him." In the depths of despair, Sally Ann fell across the bed and collapsed in a fit of tears.

A few miles out of Corsicana, Ross eased his running horse into a walk. This one had been a close call. A *real* close call. Closer than all the others. He wondered why it always happened to him like this, why he couldn't get a decent job and settle in a place for more than a week or two before some gal started getting ideas in her head. As Sally Ann had done. He wasn't made of cast iron. Just what was a man supposed to do when he came in bone tired and crawled into bed, falling asleep only to be awakened some time later with a woman's soft, coaxing hand wrapped around him? Spit in her eye?

Every town had a Sally Ann, and Ross felt as if he had seen them all. Sometimes he felt he was running out of time. And towns. Perhaps he was. He wondered if he shouldn't head on back to the family place on Tehuacana Creek and let things cool down a bit. The good Lord knew he liked women. He really did. But just now, he was a bit tired of them. His oldest brother, Nick, always said, "That pretty face of yours is gonna get you in a passel of trouble, little brother," and it looked as if Nick was right. Only Ross couldn't see that all this trouble could be over a face. Certainly not one like his. Whenever he looked in the mirror, he just saw the same face he'd been seeing for years—certainly nothing for a woman to get all riled up over. But something sure as the devil riled them up, and caused more than one woman in every town he drifted into to set her cap for him.

Right now his horse was as tired as he was, but something told him to keep on moving. He wouldn't put it past that crazy old man of Sally Ann's to have the law after him. Ross laughed at that. Not at the thought of being chased by the law—something he was growing accustomed to—but simply at the irony of it: being chased for making love to a woman he'd never made love to. 'Course, he would have, if Sally Ann's pa hadn't shown up when he did. Ross grinned. Wouldn't it be funny if this one time, when he was innocent as all get-out, he would get caught?

He stopped grinning. It could end up changing the direction of his life—and for the worse.

He couldn't help remembering the way Sally Ann had screamed like a scalded cat for him to come back. It made him feel good to remember the way he'd laughed and kept right on going while her pa was making threats and blasting holes through the door. Ross wondered what it was in him that prompted him to get into one scrape after another.

He didn't know, but it was a damn good way to get his head blown off.

The next morning, Ross rode into Groesbeck to pick up a few supplies before heading out to the Mackinnon place. Old Herb Catlin, who ran the post office, chased him down, hollering and waving a piece of paper in his hand. At first

Ross simply waved and continued on his merry way. And why not? He was never on the receiving end of any mail, so it never occurred to him that the piece of paper Herb was waving like the dickens might be a letter—or two.

"Mackinnon, dad-blast your ornery hide! Hold up there a minute, will you?" Ross paused just outside the General Store and turned to wait while Herb—his face red and his glasses fogged over—caught up with him. "What's your hurry, Mackinnon? You're moving like someone rinsed your drawers in turpentine."

"What drawers?" Herb laughed and Ross said, "What's all the ruckus about?"

Herb had to breathe a spell before he could answer. His breathing slowed somewhat, he pulled his handkerchief out and wiped his face. "I'm glad I saw you come into town. You've got a couple of letters here. They've been waiting here for quite a spell." Herb handed the letters to Ross, saying, "One of them has been here for a *real* long spell. It's from Scotland."

Ross eyed the envelope. "Have you read it?"

"Nope," Herb said, "only what's on the envelope. I'm honest as the day is long."

Ross nodded and touched the brim of his hat. "Thanks, Herb."

Herb turned away, then checked himself. "You in town for good?"

"No. I just dropped by to check on the old place. I won't be hanging around more than a week or two, then I'll be shoving off again."

"Well, it's good to see you. We don't see much of you Mackinnons since you boys all hightailed it."

"No," Ross said, running his fingers along the crease in the yellowed envelope. "I don't suppose you do."

"I'll be seeing you, then," Herb said.

Ross waved the envelopes at him. "Thanks for holding the mail."

"No trouble. No trouble atall."

The next evening, after a supper of cold beans and undercooked potatoes, Ross picked up the letter. Without opening it, he studied the envelope, remembering another letter that had come from Scotland a while back; that one had been addressed to his older brother, Nicholas.

He tossed the envelope on the table and stared at it for a few minutes. It had been quite a spell since he'd heard from Nick and Tavis, or from the twins either, for that matter. He reflected for a moment. His brothers were as scattered as last year's leaves. He looked around the kitchen, trying to remember the way it had looked back then, back when he was just a little tyke and his mother was still alive. But the image shimmered in the darkness, faint and elusive, just beyond his recall.

Maybe it was just as well. It always made him a little sad to think about his mother. He knew if she were alive, he would be seeing disappointment in her eyes. He was a hellraiser and a heartbreaker and folks said no woman was safe around him. That wasn't exactly the kind of testament to make a mother proud of her boy. He looked at the envelope again. It had come a long way, all the way from the land of his parents' birth.

His father, John Mackinnon, had been the traditionally ignored second son of a duke, and consequently he was a man of noble birth with no title and no fortune to inherit. In his younger days, John Mackinnon had been a bit of a hothead, and after a falling out with his father, he lost his temper completely. He left Scotland at the age of eighteen, sailing to America with nothing more than one battered old trunk, a few dollars in his pocket, and no future. In time he married the daughter of another kindred soul who had traveled to America on the same ship. After two years in North Carolina, John left, bringing his wife Margaret and his son Andrew to Texas. Another son, Nicholas, was born on the way.

The young family had settled in Limestone County at a place not far from Waco called Council Springs, on the banks of Tehuacana Creek. Life was good to them there, the black land rich for farming, the grass up to a horse's belly and good for grazing. By 1836, John and Margaret had a fine spread and seven growing children.

Little did they know it would all soon change.

In May of 1836 the Comanches raided Parker's Fort, carrying off five captives, one of them the Mackinnons' only daughter, six-year-old Margery. A year later, when John and five of his six sons were away from home, searching for Margery, the Comanches struck again, this time killing Margaret and their son Andrew. A year after that, John Mackinnon was scalped, leaving behind a legacy of five young, orphaned sons.

The boys made a real effort to farm their land after their pa died. After a few years of trying to make it on their own, the Mackinnon boys began to give up. One by one, they drifted away from the old family place and Texas.

Nicholas, the oldest, was the first to go; going north to find their mother's brother, who owned a shipping line in Nantucket. When he announced his intent to leave, Tavis, who was a few years younger, decided to go with him. Not long before they left a letter came, asking Nicholas to come to their grandfather's home in Scotland to inherit a title.

Nick laughed and tossed the letter to Tavis. "Are you interested, Tavis?"

Tavis wasn't much of a talker, but he shrugged a lot. "It's your letter," he said with a shrug. "You go."

"I'm more interested in the sea than any title."

"Me too," Tavis said, tossing the letter back to Nick.

Nick answered the letter, declining for himself and explaining that the next oldest Mackinnon, Tavis, had declined as well. A few months later, the youngest brothers, the twins Alexander and Adrian, left to join the Texas Rangers. Ross, who always felt left out, was left behind. He didn't know what he wanted to do.

It was about this time that Ross discovered he had something that women liked. Something they wanted. That was when his troubles began.

Ross wasn't always to blame. All the Mackinnon men had been blessed with good looks, but Ross was blessed a little more than the others. He was tall and black haired, with the bluest eyes this side of heaven, and there was a certain roguish magnetism about him that made women take notice right off. Yet there was a strength and independence of spirit that was a legacy from his ancestors. And like his forefathers, he was a combination of grit, guts, and determination; he was possessed of a certain resilience, a streak of resignation and pitiless ferocity—a hard shell that hid a sentimental soul with an undying loyalty and love for family.

He was easygoing and good-natured and a bit of a tease, and when he laughed, women wondered if it was the sound of the laugh that attracted them or the overall effect of that enchanting sound coupled with his beautiful smile. More than once he had hightailed it out a bedroom window with his pants slung over his shoulder and his boots tossed out ahead of him. But only once had he had to ride off without time to pull on his clothes. He had decided then and there that it was the last time he would ever ride a horse without his pants on.

A man could go lame doing that.

He always made the mistake of thinking each new town would be different, but before long an irate husband or a matrimony-minded papa would come looking for him. Up to now, he had always managed to stay one jump ahead of them, but it was just a matter of time. He knew that.

There were times he felt his fast-paced life was catching up with him. Pleasures had a way of being paid for with peril and pain. Sooner or later, even the best cowboy was tossed on his backside by a gentle horse. His time was coming. He knew that. The question was, what would become of him when it did?

Something will turn up. It always has. Ross let out a long sigh and reached for the letters. The first one was an offer to buy the Mackinnon place. He tossed it aside and picked up the second letter. He opened it and read the same request that Nicholas and Tavis had both refused—a request that he come to the home of his grandfather on the Isle of Skye to inherit a title that was his by right of lineal descent, since his father was dead and his two older brothers would not come to Scotland.

Ross's first reaction was to laugh. A moment later, he leaned back in the kitchen chair and crossed his long legs, propping them on the table, not mindful of the way his spurs were gouging the tabletop as he looked the letter over again, lingering for a moment on the note scratched at the bottom. "If your destiny lies in Scotland, you will come. *Fate leads the willing, and drags along the reluctant.*"

If your destiny lies in Scotland . . .

He pondered that for a moment. Did his destiny await him there?

It was such a strange, far-off place, unknown yet familiar because he had heard his parents speak of it so often. Funny how the mind worked. He couldn't recall his parents' faces too sharply, yet he could distinctly remember the soft Scottish burr, their use of such words as *lass* and *dinna,* words Ross and his brothers still used from time to time.

Scotland. So familiar, yet so unknown.

The more he thought, the more he decided there wasn't much reason for him to go traipsing off to a foreign place. It was his parents' home, not his. His place was here. In Texas. He put the letter back into the envelope and laid it on the table. He didn't know where his destiny waited for him, but he didn't think it waited in some far-off place halfway around the world.

Ross picked up the letter. Walking to the fireplace, he was about to toss it into the flames when he heard the sound of horses thundering into his front yard, running as if they were in a powerful hurry. From somewhere outside a voice cracked out and penetrated the silence like a rifle shot.

Silence followed. Then a voice broke through the stillness. "Mackinnon, this is Hank Evans. You better come on out here. I've got the preacher and the sheriff with me, and I aim to see that you right the wrong you've done to my Sally Ann. You come on out now, nice and peacefullike, and there won't be no trouble."

"Shit!" Ross said. He wasn't exactly in a marrying mood right now, and if he had been, it wouldn't be to no gal picked out for him by some angry, lead-packing papa. Ross might not have bedded Sally Ann Evans, but he knew for a fact that even if he had, he wouldn't have been her first.

"Mackinnon, you've got five seconds to make up your mind, or we're coming in after you."

Putting the letter in his pocket and not bothering to pack

up any belongings, Ross climbed out the back window and silently made his way to the barn. A minute later the barn's back doors burst open and he rode out, his horse's hooves skimming over the soft earth as if he were shod with fire. Ross heard the shouts behind him, the sound of horses in pursuit, but he knew they wouldn't catch him now. He was in Mackinnon territory and he knew this land as well as he knew his own face.

Ahead of him, he saw a full moon hanging in the sky, its mellow light glistening white in grasses stirred by the wind. From behind him came shouts and the pounding of many hooves. Digging his spurs into the sorrel's flanks, he leaned low over his horse as a shot whizzed over his head. Down, down, down into a narrow ravine he rode, the sound of his laughter drifting behind him like a flaming arrow, pointing the way.

He was a bonny fighter with an adventurous spirit, a man as passionate as he was reckless. He was a man who would risk death and defy the world for what he believed in, for the woman he loved. A man who would laugh in the face of danger and quietly slip away.

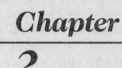

Chapter
2

New Orleans was steamier than rice pudding and hotter than a biscuit. In town only an hour, already Ross felt as wrung out as an old cow's teat. Nothing seemed to disturb the calm that comes with such heat—nothing save a volley of Creole curses that drifted his way now and then. He looked down at his shirt. It was wet with perspiration and plastered to his skin. He'd seen fish that were drier.

He walked along narrow streets with odd names and strange little houses that were nothing more than plastered walls and ornate iron railings. He was wondering if these New Orleans folks had something against yards, when he saw through an open door a courtyard draped in lush foliage and cooled by a large fountain. It was something a woman would like. As for Ross, he had to have a little more elbow room. He'd be running into himself in a place like that. No wonder these Creole men were so small.

He ducked into The Absinthe House and had a drink, more to get out of the sun and cool off than from any real thirst. He eyed the green anise-flavored liqueur and wondered why it was so popular. A good shot of whiskey was more to his liking. Finishing the glass of absinthe, he reread the letter from his grandfather he had folded in his pocket and copied down the name and address of the lawyer he was told to contact in New Orleans. He tossed a coin on the table, pausing to watch it spin on its edge, then left, heading up Bourbon Street—the first sensibly named street he'd come across—in search of one Mr. Pinckney.

CHARLES THEODORE FREDERICK PINCKNEY III, ATTORNEY-AT-LAW

Ross studied the name etched in fancy script on the brass door plaque, trying to see if he could get any hunches about a man with a fancy name like Charles Theodore Frederick Pinckney III. After a moment or two, the only thing Ross could come up with was that a man with a name like that had to have a lot of patience. With that he opened the door and went in.

Charles Pinckney was almost as old and massive as the intricately carved oak desk he sat behind. Judging by the plush furnishings, Ross figured old Charles Theodore to be quite successful, and rich as raisin pie.

Ross stepped farther into his office, and Charles Pinckney looked up to make a thorough appraisal of the young, dark-haired man standing before him. "My assistant tells me you have identified yourself as Ross Mackinnon. Do you have any proof that you are who you say you are?"

"No. All I have is this letter." Ross tossed it on the desk.

Charles looked at the letter. "I forwarded that letter to you months ago. What happened to you and the letter during all that time?"

"The letter's been sitting in Groesbeck. I've been away from home for quite a spell."

"Doing what?"

"Working."

"Where?" Charles asked.

"Here and there."

"Move around a lot, do you?"

"You could say that," Ross said.

"Why is it that you don't seem to stay in one place?"

"I have my reasons."

"Isn't it true that you have an itch for the ladies that tends to get you run out of town on a regular basis?"

Ross grinned. "Well, now. You might say that's partly true. I've been known to leave town a little sooner than I expected to a time or two. Maybe that's due to an itch. Maybe not." Ross shifted his weight to the other leg. "Either way, I don't think you could say it was necessarily *my* itch that prompted it."

Charles pushed a piece of paper across the desk toward Ross. "Are you familiar with any of the women listed here?"

Ross read the list of names—ten or so women he had known intimately over the past couple of years. "I guess you could say that, although 'familiar' isn't exactly how I'd put it."

"With which women were you, er . . . familiar—for lack of a better word?"

Ross laughed. "All of them."

Charles Pinckney folded his hands tentlike in front of him. He came close to smiling. "I see. And in what way are they familiar to you . . . that is, what is the relationship of these women to you?"

"Bluntly?"

Pinckney nodded.

"You could say we've shared a poke or two."

"Where?"

"In the usual place. What do you think I am?" Ross was

feeling just a little put out. He wondered if ole Pinckney had any Indian blood in him. His face sure was red.

"I mean where—as in the actual location, not what part of the . . . er . . . body."

Ross shrugged. "In beds. Mostly."

Charles coughed and cleared his throat. "Perhaps I should have said, in what towns?"

"Well . . . different ones."

"Give me some names. For instance, in what town, specifically, did you encounter one Phyllis Whitehead?"

"Waco, I think."

"And Caroline Archer?"

"Fort Worth."

"Molly McCracken?"

Ross thought a minute. "Somewhere near Mexia."

"Rebecca Harper?"

"Hard to remember. Gatesville, I guess." Ross was more than irritated now, but before he could utter a protest, Mr. Pinckney, apparently satisfied, changed the direction of his questions.

"You have five brothers, I understand. Tell me where they are now—what they're doing."

"Actually, I have only four brothers living. My oldest brother, Andrew, is dead."

"And the others?"

"Nick and Tavis are in Nantucket, building ships. Alex and Adrian were with the Texas Rangers for a spell. God knows where they are right now. The last letter I had said they left the rangers and had signed on with General Zach Taylor to fight in the war with Mexico."

"Your parents?"

"Dead."

"No other immediate family members?"

"No." Seeing the doubtful look on Pinckney's face, Ross sighed and said, "Unless you are referring to my sister, who was taken during a Comanche raid about fourteen years ago."

"Where is she now?"

"Still with the Indians, as far as I know. Or dead. All our searches turned up nothing."

As if declaring this discussion over, Charles leveled a penetrating pair of deep blue eyes on Ross, then swallowed and rose to his feet. "All right, Mr. Mackinnon, I'm satisfied. Let's get down to business, shall we?"

Ross nodded. "That's what I'm here for."

Charles cleared his throat again.

"You got the croup or something?"

"No, just a little catch in my throat." Pinckney looked at Ross. "I'm sure you're just a little curious about what all of this means, and while I'm not at liberty to reveal too many details, I can tell you that your grandfather, Lachlan Mackinnon is the Duke of Dunford and Chief of Clan Mackinnon. He lives in the family castle, Dunford, near Kyleakin. Your late uncle, Robert Mackinnon was in line to inherit. It might interest you to know that your grandfather has already gone to considerable lengths to enable you to inherit the title Duke of Dunford upon his death."

"What do you mean, considerable lengths?"

"Legally your brother Nicholas inherits the title, whether he wants it or not. In England it would have been nigh impossible to alter this, but fortunately for your grandfather, Scotland, although part of Great Britain, is not England. Many of the old Scottish ways still exist, and that goes for the Scottish legal system as well. English law isn't the same thing as Scottish law." Charles paused, as if thinking something over. "What I'm saying is, it cost your grandfather considerable time and money to make you his heir."

"What made him so certain I wouldn't refuse like Nick and Tavis did?"

"Your grandfather is a very wise man. He allowed his youngest son—your father—to come to America, but he always knew what was going on in his life. His files on your father, as well as your brothers and yourself, are quite extensive." Charles opened a file in front of him and studied it for a moment, his face flushed as he spoke. "Your grandfather has known for some time that you are considered to be a rather headstrong and reckless sort of man, that you have a . . . er . . . knack for getting into trouble, usually always over a young woman, and that you are, for lack of a better word, a bit of a hell-raiser, sir."

"Go on," Ross said with a faint smile at Charles's apparent discomfort.

With a nod, Charles tugged at the collar that had suddenly grown tight. He pulled out a white handkerchief and wiped his brow. Folding the handkerchief, he tucked it into his pocket as he said, "It has also been brought to your grandfather's attention that you are fairly well educated—by Texas standards—and while considered a bit rebellious, you are reputed to be both honest and just. It is also noted here, that you, more than any of your brothers, carry on the Mackinnon tradition of being quite handsome, and that this may have some bearing on all the trouble you seem to have with the ladies."

"He knows all of that?" Ross asked.

"He does."

"You seem to be very thorough, Mr. Pinckney."

"It's my job to be thorough."

"And it's mine to be cautious."

"If all the things I've read about you are true, Mr. Mackinnon, I can certainly understand why you should be."
This was said with such an expressionless face that Ross
couldn't help throwing back his head with a hearty laugh.

Then he said, "Does that report say anything about my
having a mole on my left hip, or a scar beneath my left
arm?"

Mr. Pinckney flushed. "Indeed . . . that is, we know
about the scar, sir."

Ross laughed, rose to his feet, and walked to the window.
Pulling back the curtain, he was able to glance over the
rooftops to the Mississippi. He stared at the muddy stretch
of water, wondering what it would feel like to live on water
for the next few weeks.

Crossing his arms and leaning his shoulder against the
window frame, he kept his thoughts on the water as he
considered what might be the most important decision of
his life.

After a moment, Charles cleared his throat. "I don't mean
to rush you, but have you reached a decision, Mr. Mackinnon?"

Wordlessly, Ross turned and walked back to the desk.

"I've a curious feeling you've decided to accept," Charles
said.

Ross grinned. "You're a sly old weasel, Mr. Pinckney. I
have a feeling you knew I'd accept before I did."

Mr. Pinckney laughed. "To be perfectly honest, the moment I read those reports on you, I knew you'd accept.
Eventually."

"And how did you know that?"

"Your past life-style made it inevitable, Mr. Mackinnon.
Absolutely inevitable. There are just so many towns to be
run out of, you see."

Ross was still grinning. "Is there anything else I need to know?"

Charles handed him an oiled leather pouch. "This contains quite a bit of information on your father's family and the Clan Mackinnon. Your grandfather thought it would help things along a bit if you would study it and learn as much about the history of your family and the land as you could before the two of you meet."

Ross took the pouch, bringing it to his forehead in a salute. "Well, here's to my first meeting with old Lachlan," he said, and started to turn away.

"As chief of the Mackinnon clan, your grandfather is referred to as *'the Mackinnon,'* not Lachlan."

"That's all he's ever called?"

"When the occasion warrants it, he is also referred to as 'your grace,' or 'the duke.' "

Ross nodded. "As long as I don't have to curtsy."

The corners of Mr. Pinckney's lips twitched. "A handshake will suffice," he said. "Even in Scotland."

"I can handle a handshake."

"I have a feeling you can handle almost anything you set your mind to."

"From what I hear, that seems to be a Mackinnon trait."

"It's also a good way for you and your grandfather to lock horns."

"If my grandfather is anything like the other Mackinnons I know, he was born with a contrary spirit."

Charles Pinckney slapped Ross on the back. "He has long been known to harbor the spirit of opposition, if that's what you mean."

An hour later Ross was wrapping things up with Charles Pinckney and signing the last of the documents placed be-

fore him. "Are you sure all of this is necessary? I'm not
signing my life away, am I?"

Charles laughed. "No, of course not. It's just that everything must be validated, so we can establish that you are
who you say you are, Mr. Mackinnon. The others are re-
ceipts for the files and information I've given you." Charles
Pinckney pushed one more paper in front of Ross. "Sign
this one and that should be the last of them."

Ross studied the document. "What, exactly, am I signing
now?"

"It's simply a receipt stating that I relinquished the sum
of eight hundred dollars to you for the purchase of your
passage to Scotland and your traveling expenses."

"Eight hundred dollars?"

"Your grandfather intends that you should want for nothing."

"And here I grew up thinking 'Want' was my middle
name."

Mr. Pinckney laughed and Ross signed. He handed the
paper back. "I never dreamed my signature would be worth
eight hundred dollars," he said.

"It soon will be worth considerably more than that."

After checking the document over, Charles went to his
safe and removed three envelopes, handing two of them to
Ross. "This one contains the money. The other contains the
necessary information about your final destination and directions to your grandfather's estate. There is also the name
of his solicitor in Edinburgh, in case anything should happen to your grandfather before you get there." Charles
paused, looking down at the third envelope he still held in
his hand.

Ross looked at the envelope and then at Charles. "Is that
one for me as well?"

"My instructions were to give this one to you to be opened only if you ever questioned the rightness of your decision."

Ross laughed "I've been doing that since I signed the last paper."

Charles raised both eyebrows, but said nothing. He handed Ross the envelope.

Ross studied the three envelopes but didn't open any of them. "If there isn't anything else, I'll be on my way."

Charles Pinckney studied Ross as the young man turned and crossed the room. Although he guessed Ross to be no more than twenty-five, his eyes had the look of a man with much more experience than one could collect by twenty-five. His steps had a sort of vigorous purpose that said he was a man accustomed to activity. But it was difficult to tell, from the clothes he wore, just what that activity might be, regardless of what the reports said.

"Oh, Mr. Mackinnon," Charles Pinckney said as Ross reached the door, "there is more than ample money provided for you to purchase proper attire."

Ross turned a questioning eye in his direction and looked down at his clothes. "What's wrong with what I have on? Isn't this proper enough for you?"

"It isn't for me, Mr. Mackinnon. I was thinking of your grandfather. The old gentleman is a duke, don't forget, and, from what I hear, quite a stickler for propriety. He doesn't ask, he expects. And because he is a duke, he can get away with it. I only thought you might save some time by purchasing some clothing here, while you're waiting for accommodations on a ship."

Once again, Ross leveled a pair of penetrating blue eyes on the solicitor, and Charles stepped back behind his desk.

"Is there anything else?" Ross asked.

"No," said Charles. "No, I believe we've covered everything."

Ross nodded and swept his hat from the hat rack as he stepped through the door and closed it quickly behind him. Once he was outside, he opened the third envelope. There was nothing inside except an old crumbling piece of parchment with five lines of flowing script, the ink faded to a pale brown.

> O Caledonia! stern and wild,
> Meet nurse for a poetic child!
> Land of brown heath and shaggy wood,
> Land of the mountain and the flood,
> Land of my sires!
> > —Sir Walter Scott,
> > "The Lay of the Last Minstrel"

Ross walked the few blocks to the river and stood on the quay, watching the swiftly moving currents of brown water rush by as if in a hurry to reach the sea. He followed the course of the river for as far as his eye could go. Out there somewhere, beyond the swirling currents of the muddy Mississippi, beyond the warm waters of the Gulf, lay Scotland, a strange land of brown heath and shaggy wood, the land of his sires.

He closed his eyes and felt its pull.

Sometime later he opened his eyes, his hand moving to touch the old piece of parchment gingerly folded in his pocket. He had never met his grandfather, but already he had learned one thing about him: The old man was a master at exerting his influence.

Two days later, Ross Mackinnon set sail for Scotland aboard the clipper, *Charity.* He stood on the deck, watching

New Orleans fade from sight, then opened the piece of parchment, and noticed for the first time that something was written on the back. Something from the Book of Joel.

Your old men shall dream dreams, your young men shall see visions.

III
THE
WELCOME

Chance makes a football of a man's life.
—Seneca, *Letters to Lucilius* (1st. c.)

Chapter
3

Scotland

When Ross Mackinnon stepped on Scottish soil for the first time, he felt that he was home. A strange thought, when he considered he had never even been to Scotland, but it was a feeling that continued to plague him, a feeling he could not shake. He had come home. Home to the land of his fathers. Home to Scotland.

He knew so little about this raw, wild land, this place of rugged mountains and crystalline seas, of mirrored lochs and soft green hills that called out to him to fulfill his destiny. It was a country as stern and demanding as a father's pride, as enduring and nurturing as a mother's love. He had done much reading on the ship during his crossing and had learned that Scotland had an incredible history for such a small country—a history as bittersweet and sorrowful as the mourning of a dove, a story of struggle and daring and desperation against the fist of fate that was slowly closing.

Scotland. He had learned so much. He knew so little. Yet
the very name Scotland sang in his blood like warm brandy.
Scotland. A land of glory, ghosts, and intrigue. Land of the
wild, unconquerable Picts, who forced the Romans to claim
them too barbarian to civilize and build Hadrian's Wall to
hold them back. Home of trows and wee folk, of holy trees
and magic mounds, habitat of Celtic guerrillas and pagan
druids, place of barbarous Nordic plunder and pleasant peat
hearths. Scotland. A land of pride and determination that
prompted Robert the Bruce to say, "For so long as a hundred of us are left alive, we will yield in no least way to
English domination." Scotland. A land of war and little
peace, of gentle Lowland folk and wild, kilted Highlanders,
a proud people broken and beaten but never brought to
their knees. A place of blood and defeat, of sadness and
maudlin song, a land lashed by man as well as by the elements, a land of swirling Scottish mist and blinding snow, of
demon wind and banshee serenade, and home of the bonni-
est banks that ever lined a whispering river. Scotland. A
forgotten jewel set in the crown of history.

At first glimpse, the windswept Isle of Skye made him
feel as if he had just read a long, mournful passage that left
him feeling reflective and humbled. His first sight of the
gray stone walls of Dunford Castle evoked a feeling that was
sadder still—for there it stood, huge and ancient and crumbling, a fortress of dead dreams and a glorious past, a
flower, wild and sweet, that pierced the flesh and bled from
the heart.

Ross had been in Scotland only one week, but already he
knew his life would never be the same.

He spent a few days in Edinburgh after leaving the *Charity*—something not as easy as it sounded, for the moment
he tried walking on solid land after weeks at sea, his knees

buckled and he stumbled. It was a mighty embarrassing situation for a man known in six counties for his ability to ride wild horses and even wilder women. A ride on a ship took longer to recover from than a ride on a horse, or a woman either, for that matter. It took a full day for him to get his land legs back.

From Edinburgh he had taken the train to Mallaig, where he hired a boat to take him to Kyleakin on the Isle of Skye. Kyleakin, he learned, was pronounced *Ky-lakkin* according to John MacLeod, the owner of the boat.

John MacLeod was an odd sort, a man of dour wit and Calvinistic cheer who was as stingy with his words as the thrifty Scots were reputed to be with their coin. One of the few times Ross heard him talk at all was as they passed a gap-toothed old ruin that caught his eye. When he inquired about it, MacLeod seemed to take pleasure in giving a reply. "Maoil Castle. Goes all the way back to the Middle Ages, it does, when a noblewoman from Denmark called Saucy Mary owned it. Some say she was a Norman princess, but you canna believe everything you hear. They say she stretched a chain from the castle to the mainland and demanded a toll from those that passed." He fell silent once more, not saying another word until he asked for his coin when they reached Kyleakin.

Kyleakin was a tiny waterfront village where the people weren't any friendlier than John MacLeod. After asking directions to Dunford from several people, Ross was about to lose his patience, along with his temper, but persistence paid off. He finally found someone who would answer him, a young, ruddy-faced boy loading milk cans in a pony cart. It was this humble milk cart that delivered Ross Mackinnon to his ancestral home, Dunford Castle, or at least relatively close to it.

The cart pulled up at a fork in the road. "I canna take you any further. But dinna fret. 'Tis only a wee bittie way down that road to Dunford," the boy said, pointing to the deeply rutted trail.

"Thanks for the ride." Ross flipped the lad a coin and turned, starting down the trail, not waiting for the boy to drive off.

It was a longer walk to Dunford than he had at first imagined. Ross noted that a *wee bittie way* in Scotland was much farther than either a *hoot and a holler* or a *just a little piece* was in Texas. When he reached the castle, he sent the huge brass knocker crashing against the door. A moment later a white-haired woman with bright blue eyes and a blank expression opened the door. She didn't say a word, but simply stared at him.

"Is this Dunford Castle, home of Lachlan Mackinnon?" Ross asked.

"Have you any particular reason for wanting to know?"

That took Ross back a bit, but he composed himself, remembering how the ship's captain had warned him that the Scots weren't all too eager to warm to any strangers. "I suppose I do," Ross said, smiling. The woman's expression turned sour. The smile vanished from Ross's face. "My name is Ross Mackinnon."

"I dinna ken any Ross Mackinnon," she said and began shutting the door.

"Wait!" Ross said, shoving his foot out to stop the door. "I've just come from Texas."

"Then it canna be a problem to find yer way back." She gave the door another shove.

"Hold on now. Give me time to state my piece."

"Dinna fash yerself with me. I had to call the dogs on the

last puir laddie that wanted to state his piece. Now, get on with you."

But Ross held his ground. "I've come a long way to see Lachlan Mackinnon. I believe he's my grandfather and I don't suppose he would take too kindly to your sending me away, considering all he's gone through to find me."

The woman gave him an appraising stare. "You say the Mackinnon is yer grandfather? I dinna ken that to be possible, but come along wi' you, then. His Grace will send you on your merry way soon enough." The woman stood back, motioning for him to enter, her sharp little eyes clamped on him in a none-too-friendly manner.

As Ross was ushered through the door of this inhospitable-looking Scottish castle, he was thinking folks in this part of the world spoke a strange brand of English. The accents here were different from even those he had heard in Edinburgh. And as far as manners went, the entire Scottish race must have been standing behind the door when they were passed out. After being here several days, he was already becoming accustomed to it. That was why this woman's clannish and unfriendly behavior didn't particularly chap him. But he hadn't exactly adjusted to the rude stares, and as he followed the short woman down a dim, winding corridor, he couldn't help noticing how the servants stopped what they were doing to stare as he passed, making him wonder if he might have ripped the rump out of his britches.

Because his mother died when he was young, Ross hadn't been taught a lot of things, but he did know it was not polite to stare—something folks in this neck of the woods had obviously never learned. "Is this the way folks welcome a stranger in these parts?" he asked. "By staring?"

"They dinna stare at you," the woman replied, "but at yer strange clothes."

Ross looked at himself in the next mirror they passed. He didn't see anything particularly wrong or strange about what he was wearing: a decent pair of buckskin breeches, his best pair of boots, solid silver spurs (won in a poker game), a blue cambric shirt, and his Texas hat, which he had pulled off and tucked under his arm the minute he stepped inside. He did notice that no one he had passed wore a gun. Perhaps it was the sight of the Colt strapped to his hip that caused these openmouthed stares.

His spurs ringing against the stone floor, he was ushered into the library, a darkly paneled room with an impressive collection of leather-bound books. On the walls were maps of Scotland, England, and the world. Tiny compartments were stuffed with manuscripts, papers, and more books. In the center of the room, an enormous table was littered with maps and papers, inkwells, scissors, seals, a pair of scales, a rule, a compass, and a pair of gold candelabra. A huge desk sat between two oriel's.

The man sitting behind the desk seemed nearly as old as everything else in the room. The light streaming through the windows absorbed all the color from his hair and turned the gray to white.

"Your Grace," the woman announced, "this gentleman says he is yer grandson."

"Thank you, Mary. That will be all." The man stood, the light from the window streaming around him in shafts of brilliance, and Ross felt a sense of both awe and reverence as if he were standing in the presence of someone holy.

So this was his grandfather.

It occurred to him what a good feeling it was to know a sense of family, something he had not felt for a long, long time. He didn't say anything, but simply stood there, looking at the lordly old man, trying to put out all the little fires of feeling that seemed to be erupting all over his insides. Ross couldn't remember the last time something had twisted his guts with emotion the way being ushered into this man's presence had. He was so excited he couldn't think of anything to say. Maybe the old man felt that way as well. Maybe that was why he didn't say anything either. All Ross knew was he was being stared at with such intent that it made him feel plumb stupid, like a big lumbering ox, clumsy as all get-out.

All of a sudden he had two hands and two feet that he couldn't seem to find a place for. He was afraid to move, afraid of his legs that had gone weak and trembling on him, yet he felt awkward as the dickens just standing there. "Are you *the* Mackinnon?" he asked, knowing he sounded a bit simpleminded, the way his voice broke just as he said "*the*," giving it more emphasis than he intended.

The old man's brows lifted in amusement. "Aye," he said in a voice that crackled like dry paper. "I'm the Mackinnon, although it surprises and pleases me to hear you address me so."

He had pleased the old man, and hearing those words sent a whisky warmth shooting throughout his body. "I wish I could claim it was all my doing," he said, "but the truth is, your friend in New Orleans set me straight about a few things before I left there."

"I ken advice given isn't always heeded. The light in which a man receives advice tells a lot about him."

The two of them were still staring at each other across the distance that separated them. Ross couldn't tell too much about his grandfather's features from this distance, but he was impressed with his height and all-around physical shape. He was still a formidable-looking figure of a man, and Ross had an inkling he was as feisty as they came.

"Come over here lad," the Mackinnon said. "Here. In the light of this window, so I can have a better look at you."

Ross went to the window and stopped, feeling suddenly breathless and at a loss for anything to say. The Mackinnon was tall and lanky, with a face as bleak and weathered as the alkali flats that ran along the Rio Grande, but there was something proud and yet touching about him that reminded Ross of a sad song. Only one word could he use to describe the old man and that was *noble,* the way a seasoned bear could be called noble, or a wise old buck that had seen too many long winters and survived too many duels for dominance.

Ross might have continued his thinking along those lines, if it hadn't suddenly struck him that something mighty peculiar was going on here. Something was happening, something so unbelievable, he couldn't help wondering if the Mackinnon had been touched and left as speechless by the discovery as he was.

Ross was seldom moved by uncanny things, but looking at the man who he knew now, without a doubt, was his grandfather, it was as if he were looking into some sort of ghostly mirror that shimmered and grew cloudy and gray. Then he seemed to see the image of himself fifty years into the future. The grayness shifted and the image began to clear, and he saw that he wasn't looking at himself, but at his grandfather, and then he understood. It was his grandfather, but it was also his own face fifty years hence. The resemblance between the two of them was as amazing as it was surprising—even to a man accustomed to surprises.

The Mackinnon was about the same size and build as Ross, and unless he missed his guess, the old man's eyes, like his, were such a dark blue they looked almost violet. Ross felt both dazed and foolish, knowing how intently he stared, yet unable to do anything about it. He had known only one other person who shared his cleft chin, and that was his brother Nicholas. He knew now just where it had come from. Ross swallowed as dryness was sucking the residue of moisture from his throat.

The Mackinnon's eyes were piercing and direct and they stared hard into his. Ross could see in his grandfather's face that the striking resemblance between the two of them had touched him and left him shaken.

"He . . ." The Mackinnon's voice, overflowing with emotion, broke, but he regained his composure enough that the only sign that he was moved at all was the watering of his eyes. "He is my grandson. You may leave us alone, Robert."

"Your grandson, Your Grace? Are you sure?"

"Aye," the duke said so brokenly that Ross wondered if he would be able to continue. "I'm sure. 'There is little liking where there is no likeness.' The lad is my grandson. There is no doubt of that."

Until that moment, Ross hadn't noticed a tall, slender man standing across the room. The man nodded and left, taking a different door from the one used by the woman called Mary.

"Sit down," his grandfather said. "We have much to talk about."

Ross approached the chair, but he didn't sit down. "What makes you so certain I am your grandson?" he asked. "I could be lying."

"Aye, you could be. I knew who you were the moment you entered, even before Mary spoke of you."

"How? How did you know?"

"Many Mackinnons come through those doors. Their presence gives light but no heat, like the sun in winter. You gave not only light, but heat, like . . ." His voice faltered again.

Without thinking, Ross said, "Like the sun in summer."

"Aye, like the sun in summer."

The old man's words left Ross with a tightness in his throat. He decided it was no more unusual than the absence of the thoughts that should be forming in his mind about now—thoughts that would express the way he was feeling. Thoughts he could never remember having so much difficulty collecting.

Perhaps that was because there were no words to describe the way he felt. All these years he had been an orphan, and now he had a family, something to inherit besides poverty and no direction. For the first time in his life he had a purpose, something to work for, something to count on besides always being on the run. A trembling weakness enveloped him. He held the back of the chair for support, but he did not sit down.

The duke said, "I understand my son . . . your father . . . is dead."

Ross nodded. "Several years ago."

"And your mother and eldest brother as well."

"They were both killed at the same time, about a year before my father."

"And your sister—the one taken by Indians? No word of her?"

"No. Nothing."

The Mackinnon was silent for a long time. Then he leaned back, the massive leather chair creaking. "Tell me everything you can remember about your family. Begin with your earliest recollections. Leave nothing out."

Ross sat down. He was silently thinking, his mind going far, far back to his childhood. "This may take some time."

"Something I am fast running out of, but as long as I'm breathing, you may keep talking."

Ross told him as much as he knew, as many things as he could remember about his father and mother, up to the time of their deaths, and what had become of him and his brothers since that time.

"I knew most of this," his grandfather said. "I have quite a bit of information on you and your brothers. You, for instance, because of your undisciplined ways, would have been my last choice."

"Then we think alike," Ross said, rising to his feet, "because coming here certainly was mine."

"You're honest. As well as outspoken."

"I have no reason not to be."

The Mackinnon nodded. "You can sit down. I said you weren't my first choice. I didna say I was right."

Ross sat down and his grandfather began to tell Ross the story of his three sons, Angus, Robert, and John, his three daughters, Mary, Elizabeth, and Flora. Ross stopped him. "I thought you only had two sons."

"I had two sons that outlived the others. My firstborn, Angus, died when he was four. Robert, his wife and four daughters all drowned when their ship ran aground during a storm. My wife Catriona and my daughter Mary died in a fire in a crofter's cottage, where they had gone to nurse the sick. Elizabeth died in childbirth. Flora was the youngest. She was only twenty when she was raped. Two days later she hung herself. We never knew who violated her. She never spoke a word after it happened, but something about it all made me think she knew the man who violated her . . . knew and preferred death to facing the humiliation of

what happened, the pain of revealing the name of the man."
The Mackinnon paused, his eyes going to a miniature painting of a young woman on his desk. "She would be thirty-one
now, not too many years older than you. I see that surprises
you. My wife was considerably younger than I was. Flora
was born much later than my other children, and was quite
a surprise to all of us. Perhaps that's why she was so dear to
me—the child of my middle years. *'Mo nighean donn nam
meall-shuilean—'* " His eyes grew misty and he turned
away. "It's a Gaelic song I used to sing to her: 'My brown
haired girl with the alluring eyes.' "

"You've had a hard time of it," Ross said. "That's something I understand. It seems we have that in common, at
least."

"Aye, we have that," the duke said softly. "That and
more." He took a gold watch from his waistcoat pocket and
wound it thoughtfully. He dropped it back into his pocket.
"Like most Highlanders, the Mackinnons have learned to
live with sorrow, even to wallow in it on occasion. It's part
of our history to relive the glory and bewail the tragedy,
something we do with a wild sort of independence. We
cherish our past, lad, but we don't know what to do with it."

"Maybe that's why my pa loved Texas so much—because
it reminded him of the Highlands. He used to say we were
part of the prideful poor."

"You're very much like your father," the Mackinnon said.
" 'Tis something I wondered about for years—which of
John's get would be the most like him. Perhaps I knew all
along. Perhaps that was why I thought of you as my last
choice—because your wildness, your defiant nature was so
like the painful memory of my break with him." The Mackinnon paused, looking at Ross strangely. "They say wisdom
grows from the ashes of folly and that reflection sharpens

understanding. I've had time for both. I was wrong about your father. I stood too close to him. I shadowed him and slowed his growth."

He stopped talking and Ross had a feeling he was about to say something about him, something he wanted to think through. Ross watched the old man take a deep breath and noticed also how he seemed to grow in stature. "I was wrong about you," his grandfather said, his voice strong, his tone full of conviction and meaning. "I said you weren't my first choice. I didna ken that was because you were the only choice. Mistakes," he said, his eyes glistening with remembrance, "brood a nest of sorrows."

A heaviness seemed to settle over Ross. He found this sort of talk sad, even gloomy. It carried too many reminders for him, brought to the forefront of his mind too many things he had tried to forget. Yet he couldn't keep from looking at his grandfather and wondering how much of what he was feeling the older man sensed.

"You've had a difficult time of it, lad."

"No more difficult than my brothers."

"Aye," the duke said. "I know their stories as well." The sparkle seemed to go out of his eyes, and Ross thought he looked tired. "I have often regretted not sending for the lot of you right after I learned about John's death." The corners of his mouth lifted with a weak smile. "At times I feel like John found a way to get back at me. Here he fathered six boys, and his brother Robert, who was to inherit the title, fathered none." The Mackinnon looked very much the old man now, battle weary and worn, but there was no sign of defeat. He sighed and leaned back in his chair. "And now they are both dead." He shook his head and the smile grew broader, his eyes sparkling like a youth's. "Six boys he fathered, and which one do I get to come back here? The one that's just like him. I ken he's found a way to get even with me after all."

"Or a way to let you go back."

"Aye, a way to go back, a chance to start over." The duke paused, then said, "God help me if I dinna make a better go of it this time."

"You will," Ross said, with a boldness that surprised even him.

The Mackinnon laughed. "Have you the Lord's confidence then, lad, or do you have the gift of sight?"

Ross looked at his grandfather, at the way his coat fit his broad shoulders, at the proud arrogance of his white head. "I know myself. I won't let you down."

"Aye, I ken you won't, lad." His smile was full of pride. "You're a Mackinnon, aren't you? And your father's twin?"

"I'm nothing like my father. Everyone says so."

"No, you're all me on the outside, lad, but inside, you're like your father." The Mackinnon drew a deep breath. "I've wondered about you since I sent the letter asking you to come—wondered if you would, if I'd done right by asking you."

"I'm here," Ross said, "as for the other, I can't speak to that."

The Mackinnon chuckled. "The future looks to be entertaining then. I only hope I keep a sober head and remember misfortune can make or break a man."

"It hasn't broken me, and it won't. No matter how hard it tries," said Ross.

"That's because you're a Scot," his grandfather said. "And a Mackinnon."

That came as a bit of a shock to Ross. It was the first time he could ever remember being called a Scot, or being considered anything but a wild, rowdy Texan.

"There was a reason the fates decided upon you, lad. I've been busy plotting ways to get the Mackinnon clan on its feet, to see a strong, healthy young leader at its head. I'll not see another clan claim what has long been ours."

The duke must have sensed that Ross was watching him closely, for he paused and pulled his watch out of his pocket. "God's whiskers!" he said cheerfully. "I'm carrying on like an old woman, and I've let my impatience override my manners." He knew the lad had been given a lot to absorb today. It was time to let the blood clot. "We'll make a go of it," he said, getting to his feet, "if I have to strangle every man who gets in our way." The Mackinnon looked at his grandson sharply from beneath white, shaggy brows. "At times I think it will be my own eagerness that will be my undoing. I dinna always remember the man who waits at the ferry will get across sometime. There's no need to fash myself by jumping in to swim."

He went to a table and filled a glass with what Ross guessed to be wine from a tall cut-glass decanter. "Drink this. It'll remove some of the travel weariness and replace your apprehension with clear-thinking calm."

"That's the first time I've heard of a glass of wine giving a man a clear head."

"Tisna wine, lad, but whisky, *uisgebeatha*, a Scots *water of life*." The duke poured himself a glass and returned to his chair. "To my grandson," he said, "the next Duke of Dunford and chief of Clan Mackinnon."

Ross lifted his glass in response and both men took a drink at the same time. Once he had finished half the glass, his grandfather sat back, sinking more deeply into the leather of his chair. He held his glass up, looking at its pale amber color. "How this reminds me of the old days," he said, "when a man got his whisky from a little mountain hut called a *bothy*. They canna build them like that anymore, but back then, they were cozy and snug, with sturdy stone walls and thatching so tight not a drop of water seeped through. I can still see the way it was on the inside—filled with casks and tubs, with so many pipes carrying the cold spring water into the stillroom a man could get dizzy looking at them." His look turned wistful. "It's rare now to see a *bothy* like they had back then. Most of them have been torn down with the crofters' huts." He swirled the liquid in his glass. "But the taste isna far from what it used to be, God be praised."

The Mackinnon rose and moved to the wall, pulling a silken cord. A few minutes later the door behind him opened and a draft of wind blew into the room. Mary reappeared. She moved to stand halfway into the room. "You rang, Your Grace?"

"Mary, I'd like you to meet my grandson, Ross. This is one of John's sons."

"He isna the one you wrote to the first time."

"No. John had six sons, five of whom survive. Ross is the fourth son . . . and the best," he added with a wink in Ross's direction.

Mary snorted, obviously unimpressed. "The other four must be puir laddies, indeed," she said.

Ross couldn't help laughing, and he noticed that it was only with great control that his grandfather managed not to join him.

"Take Ross into the kitchen and tell Cook to fill him to bursting. While he's stuffing himself, you see to his room. I want him to have John's old room. And have a bath sent up with plenty of hot water." To Ross, the Mackinnon said, "Go with Mary now. I'll see you at dinner."

Ross nodded and turned toward Mary. She made a quick

curtsy, her stiff skirts skimming the cold gray stones of the floor. "And, Mary," the duke called out, "tell Robert to see what he can do about some clothes."

Ross paused, turning back toward his grandfather. "I have clothes."

The Mackinnon's expression was unreadable. "You dinna like our way of dressing, I take it?"

"They're fine . . . on you." Ross studied his grandfather's appearance. His clothes—a pair of trousers and coat of dark blue, a waistcoat of pale gray, beautifully embroidered—looked perfectly suitable on him, but Ross knew that didn't necessarily mean they would look that way on him. "I'd feel like a fool in a getup like that," he said.

He turned to follow Mary, who said, "I'll tell Robert, Your Grace."

"I didna think you wouldn't," the old duke said, a ripple of laughter in his voice.

"Go ahead," Ross said. "It won't do you a bit of good."

"Aye, it may not. *It's ill wark takin the breeks frae aff a Heilandman,*" his grandfather said, the ripple giving way to a full blown laugh.

Mary led Ross back down the long winding corridor, then turned off in the opposite direction from the way he had come. Ross followed her down a narrow staircase into the kitchen. The cook was a large, robust woman with a respectably large meat cleaver in her hand. Ross kept his distance. "His Grace says you are to stuff his grandson and heat him some water for a bath." She turned from the room, saying over her shoulder, "When he's satisfied, send him to the north wing."

The cook nodded and indicated a table with a wave of the cleaver. Ross seated himself at the long stone table, keeping it between himself and the cook. He wasn't too trusting of these tight-mouthed Scots—at least not yet. A second later he heard the door behind him close and figured Mary was unhappily on her way to make his room comfortable.

He ate a meal of cold mutton and potatoes, wondering what it was going to be like to live here in this crumbling, drafty old place. It had been his father's home, and now it was his. Would it ever *feel* like home? Ross couldn't think much further than that. Tomorrow would be time enough to think.

Over the next week, Ross spent considerable time with his grandfather, most of the time doing what Ross called locking horns. It didn't take Ross long to learn that he and his grandfather were more often than not on opposite sides of the corn bin. One of the biggest issues they exchanged words over was the way Ross dressed. And on that point, Ross did not waver one bit. He was born a Texan and raised as one, and that meant he dressed as one. He wasn't about to wear those uncomfortable fancy clothes with their stiff collars and uncomfortable coats of the kind his grandfather wore. He saw no reason to.

Over the course of time his grandfather had decided that Ross needed to remain in seclusion at Dunford to give ample time to see to what he termed "Ross's enlightenment," at least for the next several weeks before they began traveling to inspect some of the lands he would inherit from his mother and grandmother once he received the title. It was more than obvious that this wild, unrefined lad from Texas wasn't anywhere near being ready for introduction to the polished Scottish society, which included many English nobles.

Ross, on the other hand, hadn't given much thought to that sort of thing. He figured you inherited a title much like you bought a section of land. Once you had the bill of sale in your back pocket, it was yours to do with as you saw fit.

He soon learned that was not the way things went, at least for the Scottish temperament. There were a few things he would have to agree to, according to his grandfather. None of them were to his liking.

And neither was the needle-nosed man his grandfather had put in charge of his enlightenment, one Lord Percival.

The first time they met, Ross took one look at Lord Percival and decided this man couldn't enlighten anything. After he heard him speak, he was convinced this was true. "He speaks worse than either one of us."

"Lord Percival is English," his grandfather said. "He is an old friend, and he has graciously agreed to leave his home in England for an indefinite period of time, in order to be your teacher, tutor, friend, and guide. I've placed him in charge of furthering your education."

"What?" Ross said, then he dug his heels in. He wasn't about to be pushed, prodded, or led anywhere. Not by this man. "What in the hell is that supposed to mean? Further my education, my ass. There isn't anything wrong with my education. I finished school," he boasted, jabbing a finger at his chest. "I'm literate."

"Barely," said Lord Percival, his thin lips curling in disgust. He sighed and pinched his nose. "You must be tutored, nevertheless. You are quite ignorant when it comes to anything pertaining to either Great Britain or Scotland. You know nothing of the history of the clan you are to lead, nothing of the ways of a Highlander. More importantly, you can't possibly expect to be a duke and take your place in society, looking and acting the way you do."

"There's not a thing wrong with the way I look," Ross said through clenched teeth. If this had been Texas, he would have already loosened the man's front teeth. Nobody talked to him like that. Nobody. Ross scowled, giving that Percival fellow the eye. Let him think him uncouth, uneducated, or unmannerly. He didn't care. As long as the man saw Ross as someone he didn't want to tangle with.

"First we will start with the way you walk," Percy went on, as if he hadn't heard Ross at all, and looked down his nose at him with an uppity expression.

"The hell you say!" Ross missed the uppity look. He was halfway out the door.

"Or, if you prefer, we could start with that hair of yours," Lord Percival called after him. "It's much too long and ill kept."

"Go to hell." Ross slammed the door on his way out.

Lord Percival had his work cut out for him, that much was certain. But Lord Percival had a lot more stamina than Ross figured this skinny foreigner could possibly have. The little man was everywhere, and nothing seemed to deter him from his duty. For a while, Ross wondered why in the Sam Hill they bothered to even try making him over. Nothing about him seemed to be right: not the way he walked, or talked, or dressed, or wore his hair; not his table manners, or any other manners, for that matter.

"What have you got against my manners?" Ross almost shouted.

With perfect calmness, Percival said, "I can neither like or dislike something I have never seen." While Ross glared at him, the undaunted Lord Percival went on to say, "I will be more than happy to pass judgment on your manners when I've had the opportunity to observe them."

"You're hollering down a rain barrel."

"Beg pardon?"

"You're barking up the wrong tree," Ross said, close to snarling.

"Are we talking about the same thing here?"

"*I'm* talking about an education," Ross said. "I don't know where you got off." He dug his fist into the ruffled front of Percival's shirt. "Don't call me uneducated. You wouldn't do half as good as I'm doing if we were doing this to you, in Texas." He gave him a shake. "Let's just see just how educated you are, Percy. Do you know what it means to spill the beans? Do you know what it means to be madder than a wet hen? Or to fling a Joe Blizzard fit? Or to be faster than a chicken on a june bug? Do you know what a blue norther is? Or the name of the president of Mexico? Can you name the river between Mexico and the United States? Do you know what *Tejas* means?"

Before he could go on, the sound of laughter coming from behind him reached his ears and Ross turned, not bothering to release Percy.

His grandfather stood in the doorway.

Ross let go of Percy, and while Lord Percival put his shirt back in order, the duke said, "Lord Percival, are you experiencing some difficulty with my grandson?"

"Yes, Your Grace, I am."

"Leave Ross and me alone for a while, Percy."

"With extreme pleasure," Percival said, heading for the door. "He's all yours."

Ross scowled, his eyes hot on Lord Percival's back as the man exited the room as if his pants were on fire. "Percy missed his calling. He should be working in the dungeon, turning the screws on the torture rack."

"Come with me, Ross. I have something to show you."

Ross followed his grandfather into the library. Standing in front of the desk, he watched the duke shuffle through a stack of papers on his desk. Finding one that apparently satisfied him, the older man grunted and handed the paper to Ross.

FIVE—THOUSAND—DOLLAR REWARD

FOR INFORMATION ON THE WHEREABOUTS OF

ROSS MACKINNON

WANTED FOR RAPE

CONTACT SHERIFF OF CORSICANA, TEXAS

Ross tossed the paper on the desk. "That's a lie."

"I believe you, of course. But would they? More importantly, do you have any means for defending yourself?" He sighed. "If you refuse the title and the requirements that go along with it and return to Texas, this," he said, thumping the paper, "is what will be waiting for you. I'm an old man. I don't have much longer to live. It is imperative that I secure my title before my death. There is no point in wasting either your time or mine if this isn't what you want. I understand how difficult it must be for you. If it's more than you can handle, I understand."

Ross scowled. "I can take anything you or Lord Percival can deal out."

"Can you now? Are you certain about that, lad?"

"I can take it. It just goes against my grain, is all." Ross's scowl was gone, and so was most of the anger from his voice.

"Then, do you suppose you can be a little more agreeable? Lord Percival isn't here in the capacity to torture you. He's only doing his job—as a favor to me, I might add."

In the end Ross agreed to being tutored, primarily because his grandfather gave him the option of being tutored or returning to Texas, "to stand trial for rape," as the Mackinnon so eloquently put it.

"I told you that was a lie. I never raped a woman in my life," Ross said, coming up out of his chair and banging his fist on his grandfather's desk. "I never had to."

The duke looked as if he were about to smile, but he cleared his throat instead. "Not according to Tess Cartwright."

"Tess Cartwright couldn't get a corpse to sleep with her. And I've never been that desperate." This time when he coughed the Mackinnon's cough was real.

Ross cooled down a bit and agreed to keep trying with Lord Percival, but he wasn't fully convinced his grandfather didn't have something to do with those trumped-up charges. Tess Cartwright? Jesus, Mary, and Joseph. A man couldn't get drunk enough to crawl between her legs. He knew beauty was only skin deep, but Tess Cartwright's ugliness went clear to the bone. He had about as much use for a woman like that as a hog with a Sunday hankie.

He looked at his grandfather, not missing the gleam in his eyes. He had learned a couple of things about the old man since coming here. One, that he was a man to be reckoned with, and two, that he would stop at nothing to get what he wanted. Absolutely nothing.

Once his tutoring was under way, Ross amazed everyone with how fast he learned. He also amazed the old duke with how much he already knew as far as women were concerned. Once his grandfather called him on the carpet for dallying with a parlormaid and said, "It appears you are giving considerable attention to furthering your education of women."

"I already knew enough," Ross said. "I was just making sure I didn't forget any of it."

Chapter

4

Lord Percival held his glass toward the lamplight and stared distractedly at the prism of color reflected in the deeply cut crystal. He was listening to the old duke's words as he shared a whisky with the Mackinnon. Their topic of conversation, was, as it had become of late, the duke's grandson.

The duke gave a short, sardonic laugh and said in an explanatory way to Percy, "God's love, Percy, he's so much like John that I find myself hard-pressed to call him Ross at all."

Percy joined in with a laugh. "That could be his biggest asset . . ." The laughter faded, his face turning serious. "Or his worst trait," he said in rather doleful tones.

"Aye. It could make him or break him," the Mackinnon added a second later, his expression somber as well, his words coming deep and rasping in his throat.

At this moment the thought gradually permeated Lord Percival's slow-moving mind that the old man seated on the other side of the partner's desk was a different old bird from the one he had been talking to only months ago. Right before his eyes his old friend had changed. Not long ago his eyes were dull and lifeless, his gait slow and wobbly, but now his walk was sure and strong, and his eyes reminded Percy of hope. *If Winter comes, can Spring be far behind?*

As he studied the duke, the dark blue eyes gazing at him over an aristocratic nose seemed to sparkle with vitality, their look filled with the light of sudden, unanticipated insight—the result of which was something Percy could only liken to humorous understanding.

"I'll tell you something else," His Grace was saying, his voice light and spruce. "He's a wee bit like me when I was a lad. Impetuous. Full of more answers than there are questions—with a tendency to leap before he looks."

Percy had learned some time ago that the Mackinnon's grandson bore the old man more resemblance than mere physical attributes. He knew also that it would merit him nothing to mention it, and that the Mackinnon would come to recognize the way of it in his own time. Apparently that time had arrived.

Percy smiled. "As you're so fond of saying, he's a Mackinnon through and through. There's no denying that," Percy went on to say. "The lad is coming along, faster than I anticipated. He's smart, and has a strong desire to please you which makes him try all the more, but I do worry that we won't have him ready before Colin McCulloch arrives with the Duke of Grenville and his family." Percy shook his head. "I'm not one to fret unnecessarily, but there's still a lot of the uncivilized American in him, and our ways don't come easy or natural to him."

"They will in time," the duke said.

"Yes, but time is the one thing we don't have much of—if we're going to keep to the original schedule. You will be having that horde of houseguests arriving sooner than we'd like, unless . . ." His voice trailed off, his expression frozen in thought. "It's not too late to postpone the ball, you know —or to beg off completely. After all, you planned it before your grandson materialized. Everyone would understand."

The Mackinnon came to his feet and faced Percy with hard, angry eyes. "What do you mean, beg off? Mackinnons dinna beg . . . for anything. What would be the wisdom in that? Do you want me to teach him it's all right for a Mackinnon to go back on his word? Or that he can grovel his way out of his obligations?"

Percy shrugged. "Very well. I know when I'm surrounded. I surrender. I don't know why I suggested that. I knew before I said it that those words would ride about as smoothly as a poorly gaited horse with you."

"Aye," the Mackinnon said, "it would." His voice softened, but the look in his eye was as determined as ever. "We'll proceed as planned. Ross is my grandson. He'll be ready."

The old duke walked back to his chair and settled himself in it, leaning his head back and closing his eyes. Without opening them, he said, "The Stewart lass will have her betrothal ball, but I'm wary of the match she's made."

Percy raised his brows and waited, his interest piqued.

Opening his eyes, the duke caught Percy's amused look. "I know what you're thinking, and it's nae because Huntly didna choose to wed a Highland lass," he said. "A Highland lass would have had more sense than to be forced to marry a man like Huntly."

"A Highland lass wouldn't be so complaisant. She would want to do her own choosing," Percy said.

"Aye," the Mackinnon said, but it was obvious to Percy that his old friend was still bothered. "I didna ken Colin

McCulloch for a fool," he went on. "He couldna be too happy about his niece's betrothal to a man like the Earl of Huntly."

Those words surprised Percy. "Why? Huntly is considered a good match . . ."

". . . To those who dinna know him well," the Mackinnon finished. "I've nae trusted Huntly. The man galls me, and it's no mystery why. Misery seems to follow in his footsteps."

As he spoke, the duke was thinking of his beloved daughter, Flora, and how her infatuation with Huntly years ago had given her naught but the stinging slap of rejection. At the time he thought Flora better off for it, but she never seemed to be herself after Huntly spurned her for another —turning his back on Flora to marry the daughter of the Duke of Corrie, who was held in such high favor by Queen Victoria.

"There's more here than you're telling me," Percy said slowly. "The problem isn't the Stewart lass, or the fact that she's English. It's Huntly, isn't it? What has he done to you? Why do you dislike him so?"

"Dislike? Ha! 'Tis too mild a word to describe the way I feel about Huntly." The Mackinnon looked suddenly tired. He rubbed his eyes. "I dinna ken hate would even do justice to my feelings." He looked up and saw the way Percy was looking at him. "I ken you'll give me no rest until you've wrung the last dram of information from me."

Percy laughed. "Is it that obvious?"

"Aye, it is." He thought for a moment, wondering where he should begin. "You never knew my youngest daughter, Flora."

"No." Percy's gaze rested upon the miniature portrait of Flora on the duke's desk. "She was lovely."

"Aye, she was lovely and when that portrait was painted she was in love."

"The man was fortunate."

"The man was the Earl of Huntly."

"Huntly? I never knew. I heard he came close to marriage with one of Argyll's daughters."

"Aye, but Argyll wasna foolish enough to sell his geese at such a poor market, so Huntly married another wealthy lass."

The face Percy saw was hardly the face of the Chief of Clan Mackinnon he knew. He looked suddenly older, and tired, his face strained and withdrawn, as if he had gone back, retreated into something painful. There was no humor in him now, no laughter, only a grimness that comes from pain too sharp and too deep to be borne. "Three months after she was cast aside by Huntly, Flora was raped. Brutally. And she was with child. I ken she knew the man who did it—knew him and preferred death to revealing his name. She hung herself two days later."

"And you never learned the identity of the man she protected?"

"No. Flora was dead. It no longer mattered."

"Something about it still matters, or you wouldn't feel such hatred for Huntly."

"He broke Flora's heart and ruined her life. After what that did to her, death was a kindness. For that reason alone I'd like to meet him with the business end of a claymore. Other than that, I have no feeling for the man, although I'd wager my title that there's something evil about him."

"Perhaps the Duke of Grenville hasn't heard about Huntly's faults. I know him. He wouldn't do that to his daughter if he had. He's an honorable man, and a just one.

He's a loving father, completely faithful to his wife and devoted to his family."

The duke's face grew seriously intent. He took another swallow of his drink, his heavy-lidded eyes studying Percy's face. "I ken all about Grenville. I'm certain he hasn't heard anything about Huntly. Few people have. Huntly isn't what he seems. He covers his tracks well. He hides behind a mask of false virtue and passes himself to the whole of Scotland as a wealthy and influential man. Even in the eyes of the kirk he is just and upright—a benefactor who pays in gold coin from a sullied purse."

"You make Huntly sound like a man who would skewer his own mother if it profited him," Percy said.

"Aye," the Mackinnon said. "That he would."

"And you're having a ball to honor his betrothal?"

"It would be a slap in the face for me not to have a ball for the Stewart lass. Colin McCulloch and I have family ties —and we've been friends for a long, long time. I knew the lass's mother, Anne." With a frown he added, "I fancied myself in love with her at one time. She was too bonny to be married to an Englishman."

"You make it sound like punishment," Percy said, and laughed. "Anne is still a beautiful woman, and I've seen her daughter, Lady Annabella. Like her mother, the girl's a beauty. More so than her mother, I think. She has a look about her—and a face that draws a man's breath from his body and turns his reason to ash."

As soon as he spoke these words, Percy felt the oppressive weight of uneasiness settle about him. Ross was a wild one, and a bit unscrupulous when it came to women. He glanced at the duke and saw the gleam of similar understanding in his eyes.

"It seems we have a potential problem here," Percy went

on to say. "Lady Annabella isn't one to go unnoticed, and we both know Ross has an eye for the lassies." He was shaking his head. "I can only hope . . ."

The Mackinnon laughed. "Hope. If my memory doesna fail me, *'Hope is a prodigal young heir, and Experience is his banker.'*"

Percy looked sick. "I'm aware of that quote, Your Grace. I simply chose to ignore it." He could tell the duke was enjoying this, but Percy wasn't about to be deterred. "It's the latter part of that quote I'm worried about. History repeats itself . . . Will you stop laughing, Your Grace? God knows the lad doesn't need additional experience. That's reason enough for me to think it might be wise to keep the lad out of sight a while longer—prolong his teaching . . ."

"And shorten his experience?" the duke said with a tone that was light and lively.

Percy stiffened. "There will be other balls, Your Grace."

"Aye, and other lassies as well." The duke stood, returning to the silver tray and pouring himself another drink. "I'll give some thought to what you've said, Percy, but I'll warn you now, you've just handed me a very interesting reason for seeing that Ross is at his polished best when Huntly arrives."

Percy came to his feet, his face pale. He placed his glass on the tray next to the whisky decanter. "It would be disastrous to even mention your grandson's and Lady Annabella's names in the same breath. You know that. I suspect he's already stolen the virtue of every bonny maid within five miles of Dunford. You can't afford to take that risk."

"Cornering a milkmaid in the hayloft isna the same thing as going after Huntly's betrothed. What makes you think the Stewart lass isna safe around him?"

Percy's expression was dour. "He fishes on who catches one."

The Duke of Dunford regarded his longtime friend with a furtive smile and nodded, a thoughtful expression in his eyes. With bearing that could only be called regal, he did not speak, but sat with almost stony dignity as Percy crossed the room and opened the door, then closed it quietly behind him as he left. Keeping his eyes focused on the massive carved doors, the duke leaned back in his chair and folded his hands thoughtfully across his chest. His gaze traveled across the room and settled upon an ornately carved frame, gilded with gold. The granite features softened as his eyes rested upon the portrait of his daughter. He lifted his glass, the glow from a nearby lamp striking the crystal and shattering the light into a thousand rainbow fragments.

"For Flora," the Mackinnon said calmly, and downed the contents of the glass.

Chapter

5

"Percy! Where in the hell are you?"

The library doors rattled on their hinges and banged open. Like a shot from an overheated pistol, Ross Mackinnon burst into the room. "I've been obliging for all the things you've thrown at me up till now," he said, "but this time you've gone too far. Tell me one good reason why I need to learn Gaelic?"

Percy lowered his head and peered at Ross over the top of his glasses. With a labored sigh, he laid the *Glasgow Free Press* aside. He had been quietly engrossed in an article discussing the morality of anesthetics in childbirth—a major issue since the discovery of chloroform. He looked at the young man who had just barged into the room like a runaway locomotive with steam pouring from beneath his collar, and thought of yet another use for chloroform.

"I never said you had to *learn* Gaelic, Ross. I said you needed to *familiarize yourself* with it. It *is* the language of your forefathers. It is still spoken extensively in some parts of Scotland—but even I'm not such an ogre as to demand you learn to speak it. That could take years."

Ross relaxed somewhat, even going so far as to look a bit sheepish.

"You've got a lot to learn, lad, if you're ever to wear the mantle of clan Mackinnon with the same dignity as your grandfather," Percy said. "You're too impetuous and too sure of yourself. Sometimes that makes you appear uncaring. A rash young chief is what you'll be called, and ill-qualified is the reason they'll give to back it up."

Ross remained silent and Percy stared hard at him, thinking to label the lad as such would be a great underestimation of his ability. True, he was young, and at times rash, but that was a deceptive barn that hid a war-horse inside. Scotland had need of strong, young leaders such as this, men who would come in the wake of her fast-spreading fame in the civilized world. A movement begun by Robert Burns and Sir Walter Scott that had already begun to transform the image of the uncivilized barbarians of the Highlands into fearless heroes with their hearts in the right place. It was men like this young firebrand standing before him who would help restore to the Scots the self-confidence and self-respect that the past century had so devastatingly destroyed. Scotland would be given back her history and her pride, and it would come through young men such as this one.

"You've a lot to change about yourself, lad, or you'll find yourself in charge of nothing. The men won't follow someone they don't respect."

Ross clenched his fists at his sides. "They'll respect me when I'm Chief of the clan."

Percy resumed his upright position and rubbed the bridge of his nose. "Do you think the moment your grandfather passes the title to you that it will simply happen? That all the clan members will suddenly hold you in high esteem?"

Percy could tell by his expression that that was exactly what Ross thought. He shook his head. "Why is the highest mountain always the one covered with mist?" he whispered. "It won't happen that easily. They're *Scots*, lad, and Scots never do anything without a bloody good reason. If you think you'll immediately hold the loyalty and friendship of every clan member, you are bloody mistaken. Why would they become devoted to a man who won't even *try* to understand them and their ways? Would you respect them if they did? Whether you learn their ways or not, you will be tried. You can count on it. The first time you meet the clan members as chief, you will find a reception about as warm as yesterday's porridge. You'll have to *earn* their respect and loyalty, lad. It's no easy task for any man, and you'll have a harder go of it than most."

"Why?"

"Because you're a foreigner."

"I've got as much Scots blood in me as any man born here."

"Men don't follow blood. They follow men—men who are leaders. Your balking every time you're asked to learn their ways and customs, or told to familiarize yourself with their ancient language and traditions will serve you ill. Continue to hold yourself separate and apart and they will see to it that you stay that way."

Ross didn't say anything, but his scowl was deeper than before, his mood suddenly subdued by introspection.

Percy clapped him on the back. "Be of good cheer, lad. Wisdom often comes when we're low as a pine marten, not when you soar with eagles. You were born green; now is the time of ripening. Your hour in the sun will come. Time will correct your mistakes and teach you what I cannot. Time is the rod of God, the rider to tame the ways of youth."

Ross sat down. "You said yourself that I don't have much time to learn the things I need to learn."

"The butterfly has but a season, but it's enough." Percy saw his words were getting through.

"You know how to make a man feel lower than a snake's belly," Ross said. "Everytime I open my mouth, I find my boot in it, spurs and all."

"Then remain silent. It too, can be a teacher. Many a man has come to regret his words; few regret their silence."

Ross leaned back in the chair, the leather creaking comfortably as he looked at the man sitting across from him. How different he seemed now from that man of his first impression. Here was a man who could go where swords could not, a man whose ammunition was swifter and more certain than bullets. All his life, Ross had lived by his fist or his gun and his ability to dig in his spurs and hit the road in a cloud of dust when the odds were stacked against him. He now gazed thoughtfully at Percy's fragile frame. Here was a man the wind could buffet, a man whose strength lay not in sinew and muscle, but in wisdom and wit.

For the first time in his life, Ross found something he envied in another man, something that could not be his by force or demand, something that would come to him, only through patience and waiting—two things Ross knew he didn't possess in abundance. For the first time since his father's death, he felt cheated, not just of a father's love, but cheated of the things he would have been taught, the things he could have learned.

So deep in thought was Ross that he did not notice Percy get up and move to stand in front of the window. After lengthy introspection, Ross, feeling infinitely lower and smaller than he had moments ago, grunted and pulled the sheaf of papers toward him. He did not hear Percy move, but he felt his hand ruffle his hair. "Obedience is a good sign, lad. If you can't obey, you can never lead."

Ross looked over the list of words: *lochd cadail,* a wink of sleep; *meirghe,* a banner; *tacar,* produce; *sealbh,* possession; *clais,* a ditch or furrow; *gartlann,* cornfield. He would never be able to make anything of words like these. It should have been a tremendous relief to know he wasn't expected to learn the language, but his rashness, his jumping to conclusions left him feeling uneasy. He felt as lost and without direction as he had the day the sheriff had ridden out to the Mackinnon place on Tehuacana Creek and told the five Mackinnon boys that their father was dead.

Percy watched Ross lose himself in the pages before him. Soon he would teach the lad to pronounce some of the words he was so studiously humped over; soon he would teach him—through the Gaelic writings of his ancestors—about wisdom and pain and suffering. But for now, he would sit back and enjoy the lad, for there was nothing like watching an illumined mind at work.

Ross was at his pinnacle now. For him the whole world sparkled and glistened with the light of understanding—a rare stone to be picked up and put into the pocket. Percy folded his hands over his stomach and leaned back. Just as he was about to close his eyes, he caught a glimpse of the old duke standing in the doorway, the carved features of a weathered old man suddenly appearing years younger, his skin radiant with the sparkle of pride. But it was in his eyes, misty with the feeling, that made Percy know what the old man saw when he looked at Ross. He wasn't seeing his grandson. He was seeing himself.

When the Mackinnon left, Lord Percival rose from his chair and followed him into his private study. Moving to the window, the Mackinnon looked out across the lawn and could not help thinking of his own youthful follies, the way he had with the lassies, and the striking similarity between them and those of his grandson. The lad was something to be proud of, a bright ray of hope after a long and bitter darkness. The duke had lost two sons, but he had gained a grandson. Ross was everything he could have hoped for in a son: strong and determined, eager, with a sense of fairness. He was a wolf's whelp, orphaned young and turned off the teat too soon. Still, he had learned, on his own, many of life's lessons. Lessons that would serve him well later on.

The Mackinnon felt his spirits lifted to heights they had not attained in years. The lad had given him something to look forward to, a reason to live. He hadn't done so badly after all. Hearing someone come in, he turned, and seeing Percy, he said, "Seems the lad is having a hard go of it. He's wild and unruly as they come, I can see that much. Are you worried about him?"

"I'd be more worried if he were grave and quiet. He's a lot like Scotland, as I see it, wild and barbaric, quick to anger, slow to forgive, loyal to the death to those he loves, but a man you can count on and one you can trust behind your back." Percy shook his head. "Faith! I find I can't stay angry at the lad for long. He has a way about him, he does."

The old duke's face brightened. "The lad is blessed with that old Mackinnon charm. It can soothe the beast in a man's breast faster than a shot of Mackinnon Drambuie." The duke turned pensive. "Faith! 'Tis like walking on eggs, Percy. I want to curb the lad, but I dinna want to break him."

"I don't think that will happen. There's a bit of magic that surrounds him. One day the Mackinnons will come to worship him," Percy said. "I can feel it."

"If they dinna kill the puir laddie first."

"Aye," Percy said, imitating the duke's burr. "If they dinna kill him first."

The duke laughed and clapped Percy on the back. "What fools men are," he said, pouring them each a glass of Drambuie. "A hundred years from now none of this will make any difference."

"That's what they said after Culloden," Percy said. "Do you think it's true?"

"I dinna ken there will ever be a time when that's true," the duke said, "so long as there's an ounce of Scots blood flowing in any of our veins."

Over the next few days, Ross familiarized himself with Gaelic and the Gaelic translations of Scotland's poets. He learned Percy was not a man to be long appeased, for Ross would no sooner give in on one issue than old Percy would thrust another one at him. Only this time it was something they had been over time and time again.

"My clothes are clean and they cover everything personal," Ross said, "and those are the only two requirements I care about—aside from the fact I like them and they're comfortable."

Percy was always relying on that most irritating of English traits: the tendency of wanting to be involved in the turning of the world by shaping the ways, character, and lives of men and countries alike. Ross figured that was what prompted Percy to say, "If you are going to be the Duke of Dunford, you must learn to dress like a Scottish gentleman. I have taken the liberty of sending for a gentlemen's clothier. He will be here this afternoon to take some measurements."

"When hell freezes over!" Ross said. "I never agreed to dress up like some dandy."

"A gentleman is a long way from a dandy. And it was your grandfather's request, lad. If you've a problem with it, I'll send for him and the two of you can talk it over." With uplifted brows, Percy said, "Shall I send Robert to find His Grace?"

Ross knew as sure as the sky was blue that his grandfather would come in waving that damned WANTED poster in his face. And that would be a waste of time, for whenever he waved that paper at Ross, Ross gave in. "No," he said at last.

Ross drew himself up ramrod straight and looked at Percy with fire banked in his eyes, his face clouded with suspicion. "What kind of gentlemen's clothes?"

The sound of Percy's laughter rolling along dark corridors and through long silent rooms was talked about for days afterward.

Douglas Alison, gentlemen's clothier, arrived with all the pomp his profession would allow. Robert, wearing his most baffled expression, announced to Lord Percival, "There is a man to see you wearing clothes that defy description. He said his name was Douglas Alison."

Percy laughed. "Bring him into the lad's study."

When Douglas walked in, Ross was talking to Percy. Immediately Ross looked at the newcomer, who was strutting like a rooster. His brows snapped together in a frown.

In a typical lapse of awareness of what was going on around him, Douglas began talking the moment he spied the two men. "Lord Percival! I can't tell you what an honor it is for me to clothe the duke's grandson. Why, only last week . . ." He broke off with a horrified gasp at the sight of the tall, scowling man across the room. "Oh, dear me," he said, then ever so slowly he approached Ross and began examining his clothing. Over and over again, he murmured, "Mmmmmm," or "Oh, dear, this will never do," or "God's eyeballs! What have we here?"

With unabashed skepticism, he eyed Ross's breeches. "Animal skin," he said with a shudder. "My, my, these will have to go."

Douglas ran his hand over the leather pants and Ross let fly with a bellow of rage, followed by a backhand that sent Douglas tumbling. "Slap me for a fool," Ross said. "The man acts like a woman! Or a pederast!" Then he grabbed Douglas by the lapels and slammed him against the paneled wall, thumping his head against the wood with each word he spoke. "You'd better be careful where you put your hands, fancy man, or I'll take that greedy little prick of yours and use it for fish bait. Do I make myself clear?"

Douglas rolled his eyes in desperation toward Lord Percival. "P-p-perfectly clear," he said weakly.

"Here now," Percy said. "Douglas didn't mean it as an insult, Ross."

"Like hell!" Ross bellowed. "The man is misfixed and you're defending him?"

Percy pulled Ross's hands away and straightened the lapels of Douglas's coat as Douglas slid weakly down the wall. Pulling Douglas to an upright position, Percy went on talking. "When you have clothes tailored, it is understood that the tailor is going to have to touch you now and then."

"He can touch," Ross said harshly, his eyes burning into Douglas, "but he better be damn careful where he puts his hands, or he'll be eating those chattering teeth of his for lunch."

"Douglas is the best gentlemen's tailor in England," said Percy.

"That ain't all he's good at, I'll wager," said Ross.

"He knows what he's doing," Percy said.

"You sure couldn't prove it by me," Ross said, giving Douglas the mean eye. "He doesn't look like he could grow pole beans in a pile of horse shit, to me."

Percy cleared his throat and forced back a smile. "Texans have a way of speaking in the vernacular," he said to Douglas's horrified expression. Then to Ross he said, "May Douglas continue?"

Ross stepped back. "He can take a stagger at it." To Douglas he said, "Watch those hands, fancy man."

Douglas blinked with each word Ross said, then looked at Percy. "Carry on," Percy said. "Carefully."

With an audible swallow, Douglas dropped down to his knees and pulled up the leg of Ross's pants, poking at the boots, touching the rowels of his Mexican spurs. "What an odd set of spurs—terribly out of fashion, I'm afraid." He studied the spurs thoughtfully. "If they were ever *in.*"

"Percy . . ." Ross said, and Percy smiled blandly at the warning.

As for Douglas, he was submerged in tailor's thoughts and took no notice. "In order to outfit you properly as a gentleman of your class, I must take some notes on your current wardrobe."

"That won't take long," Ross said.

Pencil and notepaper in hand, Douglas began firing questions. "Do you have any of the following: frilled shirts for evening wear, tucked or pleated for daytime?"

"No."

"Drawers that are knee-length or shorter?"

"Drawers?" Ross glanced at Percy. "I don't wear drawers —of *any* length."

Percy coughed. Douglas looked aghast. "You don't wear drawers? 'Pon my word, what *are* you wearing beneath those dreadful animal skins?"

"More animal skin," Ross said with a snarl. "Mine."

Douglas jumped a mile and sputtered. "Nothing? You mean beneath your trousers you are n-n-naked?"

"As in 'stark,' " Ross drawled, enjoying this at last.

"Oh, dear me, this is dreadful—dreadful indeed. Much worse than I thought." Douglas took out a handkerchief and mopped his glistening forehead. "Well, let's move on. Now, where was I?" he said, checking his list. "Here we are . . . cravat. Do you have cambric or linen, or do you prefer the newer, smaller necktie?"

"Well, I don't reckon I have a cravat," Ross said, drawing the word out so that it sounded like *craaaaw-vat.* "Seeing as how I don't even know what one is. *Craaaaw-vat,*" he repeated, testing the sound of the word. "Sounds like some part of the body." Ross grabbed his back and began limping around the room. "If I ain't got the worst pain settlin' down in my craaaaw-vat. Somebody call a doctor."

Douglas glanced at Percy who was suddenly taken with something outside and stared intently out the window, his cough acting up again. Scribbling a hasty note on his paper, Douglas went on, his voice suddenly going all wobbly and high-pitched. "Coats," he said, then cleared his throat. "Do you have a good double-breasted tailcoat with knee-length tails?"

"No."

"How about a short coat?"

"No."

"Mr. Mackinnon, do you have *any* suitable dress clothes for evening wear?"

"Mr. Alison, where I come from people don't have the time or money for much socializing in the evening, and when they do, they don't wear clothes that are much different from those they wear during the day—just a little cleaner, is all. In my case, I was on the move a lot. Everything I owned could be packed in a couple of saddlebags. I have three choices when I dress: Sunday best, everyday, and work. Take your pick."

Turning to Lord Percival, Douglas said, "I believe we need to outfit him completely."

"That is the same conclusion I reached," said Lord Percival.

Over the weeks that followed Lord Percival and Ross settled into what could be called harmony—the two of them working with such good humor that Percy was actually amiable and Ross, at times, could even be accused of being called obliging.

After the initial round of tutoring, being fitted for clothing, and taking up the pleasures of a Scottish gentleman, which included riding, hunting, fishing, and a sport the Scots seemed to love—something they called golf—Ross spent several hours a day with his grandfather and a few of his closest advisors, clansmen all, who worked hand in hand with the Mackinnon to see that everything ran smoothly around Dunford.

Under the relentless tutelage of Lord Percival and the rigorous training of his grandfather, Ross began to slowly warm to the idea of becoming a Scottish duke, partly because he was growing to love Dunford and all it stood for, and partly because he was coming to admire and love his grandfather. There was another reason as well, a reason that was deeper, something that went beyond his love for Scotland and his grandfather.

His grandfather had once said, "There comes a time in a man's life when he wants something badly enough that he will pay any price to have it."

Those words stayed with him. For the first time in his life, Ross Mackinnon realized he wanted something badly enough to pay any price to have it, just as the old duke had said. What he wanted was to be a part of something, to feel he was important, to feel he had put down roots someplace. All his life he had wanted this, and all his life he felt he had been left out in the cold. Growing up without a mother or father, he had always felt empty and alone; always felt like the orphan he was—even with the company of his four brothers. He was the one caught in the middle, the one with no one, the one with two older brothers and two younger ones. As to be expected, the older two, Nicholas and Tavis, were close as the bark on a tree, while the twins, Adrian and Alexander, were too busy fighting to pay him much mind.

And so he became a loner and a drifter, a man who stuck to himself, moving from town to town, woman to woman. A man who showed the world he needed no one. Now he was in another country, making a new start, but the lonely feeling was still with him. For this reason he was willing to endure anything—anything at all—to find his niche and have this thing Percy called his hour in the sun.

IV
THE
MEETING

In love, there is always one who kisses
and one who offers the cheek.
FRENCH PROVERB

Chapter
6

Annabella sat in the garden behind Dunford Castle listening to the Ossian-like notes randomly plucked by an afternoon breeze from the strings of an Eolian harp suspended from a low-sweeping branch of an ancient pine.

The entire Grenville party—that consisted of her two coaches, an embarrassing amount of baggage, her mother, father, brother, four coachmen, her father's valet, who served both Gavin and her father, and two maids: her mother's and her own—had arrived that morning.

The ride in the family coach was exhausting, not because the coach was uncomfortable, which it was, and not because the journey from her uncle Colin's was a particularly long one, which it was not. She had been seated next to Gavin, the two of them facing their parents, and the topic of conversation for six hours had been Bella's wedding, something discussed in exhaustive detail.

Her father, commenting upon her silence, said, "Bella, aren't you in the least excited about the wedding? Think of all the clothes you'll need to have made."

"I am trying to be excited. Truly. I know you must find me very rude," she said, desolately wringing her folded hands. She glanced at Gavin and the thought hit her swiftly, mercilessly. *They'll separate me from Gavin. They'll keep him in England and leave me here.* "It all happened so fast . . . the betrothal and all, I mean. I haven't had much time to . . ." She felt a stinging, burning pressure building in her eyes and she blinked as one determined tear escaped, to meander in an aimless path across her pale cheek.

"Bella, don't cry," Gavin whispered in her ear, his voice gentle and full of compassion.

Gavin's concern unleashed a flood. "I've tried to be happy about the wedding, but I can't. I don't want to be married. Please. Can't you change your mind? Can't we go back home?"

Her father studied her face for a moment, and then sighed wearily. "We have discussed this before, Annabella. I thought you understood completely why this marriage must take place."

"I understand it, but I don't want it."

"I understand that as well, but the betrothal has been announced. The wedding must proceed as planned. Your persistence only makes things more difficult for your mother and me. It isn't our objective to see you miserable and unhappy."

But that's what you're doing, making me miserable and unhappy. Tears of rage glistened in her eyes, but she guided herself away from sounding defiant. "Isn't there anything you can do, Papa?"

Ever the mollifier, the balm of the family, the one most likely to interject humor at a time when it was sorely needed, Gavin said cheerfully, "There is one thing," and three pairs of eyes focused on him immediately. "I could strangle Huntly."

The memory of that brought her mind back to Huntly and the present. Huntly, a man she found both horrid and distrustful. He was also something she did not want to think about, especially since she did not have to. Since he had not yet put in his appearance at Dunford—something Annabella found quite pleasing—she found it perfectly reasonable to cut him completely from her thoughts, in spite of the fact that it was quite the rage in London to cultivate a little unhappiness. As the paperweight in her father's study was inscribed, IT IS THE WISE MAN'S PART TO LEAVE IN DARKNESS EVERYTHING THAT IS UGLY. And that was where she intended to leave Huntly: In the dark—at least as much as possible.

The garden was, much to her liking, deserted. This fact meant there was no one about to disturb her solitary concentration, for her parents were taking tea with the duke, whom everyone strangely persisted in calling "the Mackinnon." Her brother, who could be quite pestiferous at the times she wanted to be alone, was last seen plying his charm on a coy milkmaid in the dairy.

As for Annabella, she was still wearing her dark blue carriage dress. Her heavy black hair, perfectly dressed, was swept back into a gleaming coil and tied with a blue grosgrain bow. Her appearance suggested a fragile cameo: lavender and lace with a delicate constitution. She was a small girl, dark haired, fair skinned, with cheekbones set high in a heart-shaped face. It was an unusually warm afternoon, yet it never occurred to her that removing a petticoat or two or loosing a few of the buttons on her high-necked gown might make her more comfortable and less hot. And taking her shoes off was something she would have never imagined anyone did, outside of the bedroom, that is. It would have sent a flush of color to her cheeks even to think of such a thing. Still, she did pause a moment to reflect upon the casual dress of the milkmaid Gavin had cornered. She remembered the way the girl's hair was coming loose from its knot, the low-necked dress and cool, cotton skirt she was wearing.

Bella looked down at her notepad, open and in her lap. Her face was pensive as she thought of the lines she would write. So far, she had only the title: "Ode to an Eolian Harp."

She was about to write the first line, "Half-stirred to passion, embraced by the wind," when her brother Gavin interrupted her tranquillity.

She had expected no one to disturb her here in the garden at this time of day, so when she heard footsteps approaching and looked up to see Gavin burst between the glossy green foliage of a hedge of holly, she was startled.

"Ho! There you are, Bella. Come! Put away your letter writing. Lord Percival showed me the most splendid green —perfect for a game of croquet."

Annabella looked at her brother. "Gavin, if that *splendid* green is anything like the roads coming to this place, there will be potholes large enough to lose a carriage in." It was perfectly clear from her tone that leaving her poetry to play croquet was not something she found particularly appealing.

"I've seen the green, Bella. It is splendid. Truly." Then with a cajoling grin, he cuffed her on the chin. "Come on, brat," he said, taking her notepad and pen from her. "You'll have a good time once you're playing. Or would you rather go fishing?"

"I'm not such an ogre that I have to be beguiled into

playing a game of croquet," she said, ignoring the offer to go fishing.

"Then you'll play—or fish?" he asked with a wide grin.

"Of all the bounders," she said, clucking her disapproval; then, smiling fondly at him, she added, "I'll play, but I ought to change my slippers, I suppose."

"You look quite the fashion," he said. "We're just going to play croquet."

"But if I ruin them—"

"You won't. The grass isn't damp at all. They'll be fine." He pulled her to her feet. "Come on. I'll show you the green."

Brother and sister set off down the gravel pathway. A large black dog ran across their path, following a rabbit he had spotted turning up the lane. Annabella followed the chase until they turned the corner of the castle and saw a sloping green meadow. "Is this the green?" she asked.

"Of course. I told you it was splendid."

"Splendidly full of lumps and bumps. We can't play croquet on this," she said.

Gavin gave it a critical look. "Of course we can. Percy said they play here all the time. See, the wickets are already set."

An hour later they had played three games—which Gavin won. "One more, Bella," he pleaded.

"Why? So you can trounce me again?"

"I'll let you win, then. Come on, one more. Please?"

"Let me win? Oh, thank you very much. You're cajoling me again."

"Whatever it takes," he said, grinning.

"One more game," she said emphatically. "One . . . and no more."

"And I let you win."

"Fair and square," she said.

Gavin won the next game as well. "Be a sport, Bella, and play one more."

"No."

"Come on, what else have you got to do?"

"We can't play another game," she said.

"Why not?"

"We don't have enough balls." Before he could respond to that, she drew back her mallet and smacked the wooden ball lying nearest her foot. It left the ground and sailed across the green before bouncing twice and rolling into the trees.

"We will in a minute," Gavin said, laughing, and giving chase.

As soon as he ducked into the trees, searching for the ball, Annabella located the second ball, and as she had done before, she brought her mallet down, sending it sailing in the opposite direction.

Like its predecessor, the ball lifted off the ground, but this one skipped over the stone fence before coming down on the other side.

A moment later a loud bellow pierced the air.

"What in the hell?"

Annabella's mouth dropped open, but no sound came forth. Whatever she wanted to say was frozen somewhere between her lungs and her throat. Her first instinct was to seek sanctuary behind the thick stone walls of Dunford Castle. But what if she had injured someone—injured them badly? Without a moment to waste, she cast a quick look toward the trees where she had last seen Gavin. He was nowhere in sight, which was precisely the way she wanted it. It wouldn't do to have Gavin know she had turned an

intellectual into the village idiot with one whack of her croquet ball. He would never cease to remind her of that.

Racing across the green, she paused inside the gate for a
moment, then with a fortifying gulp of air, she opened it
and stepped out into the lane, looking the perfect picture of
composure. She looked to the right, and then to the left.
And then she saw him.

For the second time in a few short minutes her mouth
dropped open.

Ross had been standing in the lane, just beyond the gate,
rubbing the rising bump on his head and holding a croquet
ball in his other hand when he saw her step through the
gate. He saw the croquet mallet in her hand and was braced
to receive a second bash on the head, when he received a
jolt of another kind—one that was just as leveling.

She stood just outside the gate, framed in a bower of
yellow roses that arched over her head. Her eyes were as
green as the meadow she had just left and she was looking
at him in a startled, surprised way. She looked small and
shy and so terrified that he was for a moment distracted. He
forgot about the rising goose-egg on his head and was content to look at the exquisite delicacy of the lady standing a
few feet away, the lady with the raven's-wing hair and the
heart-shaped face. Her lips were full and soft, and bowed
with surprise. Her lashes were long and thick and dark as
her hair.

From the first moment he laid eyes upon her, Ross felt
struck by the all-over loveliness of her, the way her yellow-
green eyes held a gleam of shy hesitancy that seemed to war
with the picture she obviously went to great lengths to present. When she looked at him and saw the flare of interest
in his eyes, she lifted her head. Ordinarily he would have
thought the upward tilt of a woman's chin meant haughti-

ness, but in her case he felt otherwise. For a moment he had a fetching vision of what she would look like naked.

As for Annabella, she had not moved, not since she stepped through the gate and saw the giant who looked both destructive and all-consuming. A hurricane followed by wildfire. She had never seen a man such as this. Had he stepped from the pages of her history book? Was he one of the legendary figures of her schoolroom years—a pagan Viking, or a barbarous Hun, or perhaps a pirate, brandishing steel with his shirt opened down to the waist? Surely there was something wild and untamed and undisciplined about him—he was a man completely her opposite in every way, and more than attractive because of it. He was a man of both legend and nightmare, the kind of man the parlormaids in London whispered about. The kind chaste women like herself dreamed about.

His expression was angry, and mindful of an ink drawing she had seen at the museum, one of a furious Zeus shooting thunderbolts at a fleeing Hera. His hair was as long and black as a pirate's. There was an aura about him—an air of relaxed self-possession, an air that gave him a sort of lazy indifference that made her think he did exactly as he pleased, regardless of propriety or convention. It was this suspicion that sucked the breath from her lungs and drew moisture from her body to pool in tiny dots across her forehead. It was this suspicion that branded her mind with the warning: stay away from this man.

She had known from the first instant that he was unlike any man she had ever known or seen, for surely if she had innocently passed him riding in Hyde Park or walking down St. James's Street, she would have noticed him, would have had the same feelings. It wasn't the setting.

It was the man.

That made her wonder if he had been born with a special brand of appeal that gave him such an air, or had it come as a trophy is given by those who loved and admired him—obviously in his case, women.

He was literally the most handsome man she had ever seen, in a raw-boned, rugged sort of way. He was wearing, without a doubt, the strangest clothes she had ever seen as well. Tall and well built, he was all hard flowing muscle that filled out the rough-looking fabric of breeches that seemed, on closer inspection, to be made of some sort of animal skin —appropriate, she thought, for a barbarian.

His shirt was as blue as his eyes, and he wore a pistol strapped low around his hips in the oddest fashion. Even his speech was odd. And right now he looked frightfully angry at someone.

That someone turned out to be herself.

"Do you always stare like a cornered fox whenever you encounter someone?" he said like a snap of the fingers, pulling whatever scrap of her dignity that remained from under her feet.

Startled, she looked at the croquet ball in his hand.

"Yours?" he asked.

Unable to speak, she nodded.

"Are you mute?"

She shook her head.

"Do you speak English?"

Yes, but I'm not certain you do, she wanted to answer, but instead she said, weakly, "Yes, I speak English."

He looked at the mallet in her hand, then rubbed his head. "In case you're interested, which I doubt you are, you came damnably close to cracking my skull."

Annabella didn't answer at first. She was too busy thinking her mother would boil her in leek soup if she found out about this. She shuddered to think what her father would do. "I'm sorry, sir. Is it terribly painful? Can I get you a posset? Some herb tea? Would you like to sit down?"

Ross listened to the music that was her voice and forgot all about his anger. He tossed the ball over the fence and gave his full attention to looking her over. Slowly. She was small and green-eyed, with the blackest hair this side of hell and the whitest skin that blushed rose-petal pink in all the right places. He thought of a few things he could do to make her blush all over.

To her surprise, his face softened. She was so relieved she felt her knees go weak, and she reached out to brace herself against the fence.

The man swore and stepped toward her. "I'm the one that gets whacked on the head and you go all weak-kneed and faint. Are you all right?"

She nodded.

"You're pale as a sheet."

She raised her hand up to her face and touched her cheek, cringing at the warm clammy way it felt. Shame ate at her for the cowardly way she stood here, terrified to speak, even more terrified to run. She knew she couldn't spend the rest of the day standing here in the lane quaking in front of this towering, angry man and knowing she had to display something that resembled good manners. She could inquire after his welfare. *You've already done that.* She should excuse herself then. Intending to do just that, she took a deep breath and opened her mouth to speak. Then she looked into his eyes.

That was a mistake.

For all her tutoring and education, nothing had prepared her for what she was experiencing now. For some strange reason, the only thing she could think of to say was, "Fancy meeting you here," which besides being terribly inappropriate, was also ridiculous. Doing her best to rephrase the thought, she managed to whimper, "Who are you?"

Ross gave her a brief and not too reassuring smile and said, "I think that's my question," he said, and her eyes became as wide and challenging as his answer.

He was much closer than he was before, and his hand came out to close over hers where she gripped the croquet mallet.

He looked down at the white knuckles, the small hand frozen in place. "Do you mind?" he asked softly.

It occurred to her that he looked a great deal more amused than he should, when one considered his numerous references to his injured head. She pulled back quickly—a little too quickly—and stumbled backward into a prickly holly bush. Before she fell too far, she heard a rich oath and felt a steely grip on her upper arms as she was yanked forward.

"Here," he said, "let me have that before you hurt yourself." He held out his hand and she put the mallet into it. *Foolish, foolish,* she thought. *If you had an ounce of mother wit you would've given him another whack on his head, and a knot to match the other one.*

He frowned and ran his hand through his hair. "Don't bust your drawers, girl, I'm not going to hurt you," he said, laying the mallet aside. It was the first time she felt terrified of something other than the fact she had cracked his head.

"I'm not afraid of you," she announced and regretted it immediately, because the words had no more than left her lips than a flicker of interest began to smolder deep in his eyes.

Feeling a rush of tenderness, Ross watched the enchanting way her cheeks flushed the palest peach. "Are you sure?" he said softly. He rubbed his palm over the soft curve of her cheek and touched a narrow red welt. "You've scratched yourself."

"I don't care. It doesn't hurt. Don't touch me."

He smiled. "I take it you haven't spent much time alone with a man."

"I've *never* been alone with a man," she said, recovering her tongue along with her anger. It was a much more welcome feeling than the terror she had felt a moment earlier. She thought that was a good sign.

"Somehow, that doesn't surprise me, sweetheart."

"Don't call me that! I'm not your . . . I don't even know you."

"Ahhh, but you could."

"No! No, I couldn't. I'm not what you think I am. You've made a mistake."

He looked her over. "You don't look like a mistake," he said. "Not in the least." He stroked her face again, his fingers curling beneath her chin and lifting her face to his. "You don't feel like a mistake." His voice was husky now. She gasped and took a step backward, prepared to feel the prick of holly bushes, but instead found herself in his arms. While her mind was catching up to the fact that she was indeed in this man's arms, he kissed her so swiftly she was caught completely off guard.

His mouth took hers with surprising tenderness, moving slowly and filling her with a sort of lethargy that prevented her from pulling away. Standing stiff and clumsy, she felt herself jerked from artless innocence to a higher plane of awareness. With every nerve in her body responding to the insistent pressure of his soothing kisses and questing hands —which had spread to the narrow confines of her back— she felt him draw her closer to him, and she felt herself drowning in the warm sunlight that surrounded them, her ears buzzing too loudly to be the droning of bees. And then she was kissing him back with every ounce of strength she had, as if no part of her could get enough of him.

She had no way of knowing if it was the heat from the sun, or the hot blistering of his passion that left her a smoldering heap, with no more will than to melt against him.

"Do you live near here? Is there somewhere we can go to be alone?" he asked.

It took only a moment for her to realize he wasn't kissing her any more, that he now had other things on his mind. Naïve she might be, and inexperienced too, but it didn't take much to know what he was asking.

Just then a voice on the other side of the fence broke the long stretch of silence. "Bella, where are you?"

Her brother was there, on the other side of the stone fence, looking for her. Relief swam in rainbow hues all about her.

"Bella, can you hear me?" Gavin called again, his voice louder now. He would come bounding through that gate in a moment, and there was little doubt that he wouldn't settle for anything less than a full, complete, and unabridged account of what was going on.

Dear, sweet Gavin. She could hear his concern for her in his voice. The thought of his being worried had a calming effect upon her, and along with the calm came the churning uneasiness of guilt. How many people trusted her? Gavin, of course. And her parents, too. Not to mention her betrothed, the Earl of Huntly. The shock of it all hit her. How could she have been so wicked?

"Who is that? Your lover?"

The stranger smiled wickedly at her horrified whimper.

"You don't have enough time to beat the answer from me. I'll never tell you."

"Why would I consider it? There are other ways, you know. More effective ones. How far do you think you would have let me go before you started telling me the things I wanted to know?"

Calling her brother's name, she pushed at him and whirled around, darting through the gate, leaving nothing behind but a shower of yellow rose petals and a croquet mallet lying on the ground.

Ross didn't have much time to think about his encounter with the lovely one in the lane, for Percy was waiting impatiently for him the moment he returned to Dunford Castle.

"There you are, you rounder! You had me worried that you wouldn't be back in time to bring you up to date on a few things before the duke's ball. You do know, of course that you must be dressed early. Your grandfather expects you to stand beside him in the receiving line."

"What receiving line? To receive what? What in the hell is a receiving line?"

Lord Percival, a man of infinite patience said, "It's a line of ladies and gentlemen of the house and those being honored by the house. You will stand in the line next to your grandfather and be introduced to the guests as they arrive."

"All three hundred of them?"

"Unless some have to beg off at the last minute."

"Then why was it so important for me to learn all those dances if I'm going to stand in line all evening?"

The corners of Percy's lips lifted in spite of his intent to hold them stiff. "So you could dance, why else?"

"There won't be time . . . three hundred people. Saint Sebastian! I don't think I've ever even *seen* three hundred people, at least not at one time. We used to have about thirty-five or so at church on Sunday when I was a kid—and I thought that was a crowd. Once in a while the saloon in Ft. Worth would have up to sixty or seventy people. But three hundred?" Ross shook his head and headed for the door.

"Where are you going?" Percy inquired.

"I'm going riding."

"Be back by five."

"Yes, *Aunt* Percy." Ross curtsied and dropped a kiss on top of Percy's head, then darted through the door. Lord Percival laughed outright, calling after him. "Keep a tight check on the time."

Ross was late.

The moment he entered the hallway, he saw Lord Percival was waiting for him, pacing back and forth in front of the door to his bedchamber like a hungry wolf. "Hello, Percy."

Percy grabbed him by the ear and gave it a twist. "Never mind the greetings, you rogue. Save that for tonight." Percy opened the door to Ross's room. "You're late and we haven't much time." After following Ross into his room, Percy informed him that the duke had decided Ross should wear the "traditional Scottish attire" for this ball.

Ross had a feeling something was up. He didn't like the way the hackles were rising at the back of his neck, or the way the words *traditional Scottish attire* grated on his nerves. He turned and crossed his arms over his chest, his eyes leveled at Percy. "*What* traditional Scottish attire?"

About that time someone knocked on the door and Lord Percival opened it. Robert was standing on the other side. Percy nodded at him and he led in a man wearing a short plaid skirt. Ross had seen this outfit before, of course. The great halls of the castle were lined with pictures of Mackinnon ancestors wearing this garb. But Ross had never seen a live man in a kilt. He had been told it was, at one time, the traditional dress of Scotland, but had been outlawed by the English after the battle of Culloden. He hadn't been told people still wore them—or worse yet, that *he* might be asked to wear one.

"Oh, no," Ross said, holding his hands up to ward off any sudden attacks. He began backing toward the door. "You aren't going to get me into one of those. Don't even start trying."

"Ross . . ."

"Not no, but *hell* no!"

"Will you listen to reason?"

"Listening to reason is responsible for all this in the first place."

"Your grandfather will be wearing one as well."

"I don't care if the King of England is wearing one," Ross bellowed.

"We don't have a king," Percy said. "We have a queen."

"No," said Ross. Before Lord Percival could say a word, Ross said, "Where's my grandfather?"

"He's in the music room, receiving some of the out-of-town guests before the ball."

Ross eyed the door.

"Ross," Percy said firmly, "you can't go there right now—not dressed as you are, and unannounced."

"The hell I can't." He stopped momentarily at the door. "You watch me."

The merry ring of Ross Mackinnon's spurs against the cold stone floors was the only thing cheerful about the way he strode down the corridor toward the music room, his mind clamoring with all the things he planned to say to the Mackinnon.

Both doors to the music room burst open and crashed back against the wall. Five or six guests turned to stare as Ross walked in, Lord Percival trailing apologetically behind him, Robert and the man in the kilt bringing up the rear.

The duke's face turned red as he drew himself up to his full height. "What is the meaning of this?" he asked, his words more civilized than he looked.

"I've just been told something and I've come to see if it's true."

"And what is that?" asked the duke.

"That I'm supposed to wear a kilt tonight," Ross said. "Is that true?"

"It is."

"I won't do it," Ross said.

"We'll discuss this later," the duke said.

"No, we won't. There's nothing to discuss. I won't wear a kilt and that's that. You can threaten me . . ." At that moment, Ross caught his breath and looked away. He promptly lost his breath again. Standing next to and slightly behind his grandfather was the most breathtakingly beautiful woman he had ever laid eyes upon.

She was also very, very familiar.

A moment earlier Annabella had been standing between her parents and the Countess of Stoneleigh when she heard the woman draw in a sharp breath and say, "My God! *Who* is that?"

Annabella turned her head to follow the direction of the woman's gaze. The man who had caused her dramatic reaction was walking with a determined gait into the room. He was tall and well built—a powerful figure of a man, and quite a romantic one—and then Annabella had a jolt of sudden awareness. She knew who he was.

She felt a ripple of unease, knowing that any moment he

would see her and recognize her and remember their meeting earlier. Her pulse quickened and she felt a coiling tension sing along her nerves. If he mentioned their meeting this afternoon, how would she explain it to her father?

The man had stopped talking now and was staring directly at her. There was no doubt that he recognized her. The blood drained from her face as someone whispered who he was. The name echoed like a gunshot through her head. Lord Leslie Ross Mackinnon. The Duke of Dunford's grandson.

She braced herself for what was to follow, for the words he would utter that would cause her father to send for her as soon as this gathering was over.

She must have given herself too much significance, placed too much importance on their chance meeting, for the moment she thought he would speak of it, he did not. Instead, she saw a glimmer of recognition, then a relaxed smile. Without saying a word, without giving any indication at all that he had ever made her acquaintance, he looked away.

He looked at Lord Percival and then at the man in the kilt. "What's he wearing under that?" he asked, and Annabella almost swooned from relief.

If he had looked at her, he would have seen her smile of gratitude, for there was no doubt in Annabella's mind that his diversion had been intentional. But why? She wasn't privileged to linger on the answer to that, for Lord Percival cleared his throat and said:

"That isn't a question to be discussed in front of the ladies."

"If you will excuse me for a moment," the Duke of Dunford said, "I seem to have some unexpected business to take care of." With that, the duke motioned for Lord Percival to follow him. Ross, by that time, was already halfway to the door.

When the three men reached the library, the duke's tightly leashed temper exploded. "What in the bloody hell do you mean by barging in on me like that? Have you forgotten every trace of the manners we've tried to teach you?"

"If you want to talk about manners, where were yours when you sprang this latest surprise on me? If I'm going to be dressed for sacrifice, at least I deserve to be told about it. And another thing, *if* I don't follow all those *dictates of decorum* you've been teaching me, maybe it's because you don't follow them either."

That seemed to cool the duke down a bit. "All right, it seems we've come head on at each other from opposite directions and butted—neither of us emerging the victor. Do you want to tell me what you find so objectionable about your ancestral dress?"

"The fact that it's basically a dress—regardless of what you call it. And you never did tell me what's under it."

"The same thing that's under those buckskin pants of yours," Percy said, "so it shouldn't be all that foreign to you."

"The hell it isn't! I don't go around with my backside bared to the four winds." Ross said, then suddenly remembering a time he was on the run and had to ride with his pants slung over his shoulder. "I *know* what it's like to ride a horse bare-assed. I don't intend to do it again." He stalked out of the room.

The Mackinnon looked at Percy. "I'd give half of all I have," he said slowly, "to know the circumstances for that bare-*assed* ride he referred to."

Percy looked at his friend. "So would I. I wager it would be well worth the loss," he said.

"Aye, it would be," said the duke, looking fondly at the door his grandson had just gone through. His deep blue eyes glowed with an inner light. "Ahhhh, to be like that again." He clapped his old friend on the back. "We gave life a good try, didn't we, Percy?"

"Aye, your grace, that we did." Then Percy paused and looked at the duke. "Did you ever . . ." He paused.

"Did I ever what?"

Percy looked a bit red. "Did you ever have a *bare-assed* ride?"

"Aye," the duke said. "More than one." Then he threw back his head and laughed.

Chapter
7

Ross Mackinnon went to the Duke of Dunford's ball.

But he didn't wear the kilt.

Half an hour before he was supposed to be downstairs, Ross was standing in his room thinking this had to be the worst day of his life. He was wishing he could back up and start the day all over when he caught a glimpse of himself in the mirror. It was enough to make his reflection throw up. He couldn't believe the man that looked back was him. He took a step closer. The eyes were his. And the mouth, too. Come to think of it, the hands looked a lot like his. But that was about it.

In Ross's opinion the rest of him was pure-d stranger. Who would've thought it? Here he was, Ross Mackinnon, a man who could outfight, outdrink, outride, and maybe even outwhore half the men in Texas, and what was he doing? Standing here in a black tailcoat, white waistcoat, and small-bowed cravat, looking as if he was trying to be something he was not, and feeling as lost as a short dog in tall grass.

Most of his thoughts were colorful, descriptive words,

words that reflected his uneasiness, words that expressed his irritation over being forced to make a fool of himself by what Percy termed "the enrichment of his social graces."

Damnation. It's one thing to make a fool of myself. Quite another to dress up like one while I'm doing it.

"Just what the well-groomed gentlemen of France are wearing this season," he said aloud, mimicking what that sap Douglas had said earlier. As if Ross gave a hoot about what the well-groomed gentlemen of France were wearing this season—or any other season, for that matter.

He eyed the formal evening attire, knowing clothes like this, on a man like him, stuck out like socks on a rooster. One thing he had always prided himself on—he never tried to be something he wasn't. Wearing all this black and white —well, it looked to him as if he was doing his best to look like a skunk, and it was beyond him why anybody would want to dress up like an animal—any animal. He had to admit he'd seen stranger things. Still, if a body wanted to look like an animal, there were plenty of other animals he would have picked.

He poked a finger between the tight, stiff collar and his neck and gave it a yank. This rigging was uncomfortable as the devil. A man couldn't move properly, all harnessed up like this.

He thought about his brothers and imagined the looks on their faces if they could see him now. The thought brought a stab of homesickness, but he told himself again that he had done the right thing by coming here.

He told himself something else too. *Mackinnon, if you had a lick of sense you'd put your buckskin breeches and cambric shirt back on and go to this fancy shindig that way.*

But he had given his word. And if anything had been

drummed into Ross's head since coming here, it was that a Mackinnon never went back on his word.

He adjusted the coat, thinking at least he had stuck to his guns about wearing the kilt. *Odd name, kilt. Where did the name come from?* He grinned. *Maybe they call it a kilt because a man's liable to get himself kilt by going out in public wearing one.*

All this thinking about the Scots' native dress made him realize one thing. Compared to wearing a kilt, this skunk's-suit attire didn't seem all that bad. Things could have been worse.

"They could be one helluva lot better, too," he mumbled. He wasn't exactly looking forward to going anywhere dressed like this. It made him feel worse than a treed coon. It didn't help any to know everyone would be dressed this way as well. The people downstairs were all used to dressing like this.

Ross was not.

The people downstairs all felt comfortable in these clothes.

Ross did not.

And it wouldn't take any one of them very long to recognize that fact. He was setting himself up for ridicule, and if Ross Mackinnon had one sensitive bone in his body, it was fear of being made fun of.

His reaction might have been a lot less violent perhaps, if a painful reminder from Ross's past hadn't suddenly popped to the surface and burst like a tiny air bubble in the back of his mind. A moment later, the bitter taste of a memory rose like the burn of gall in his throat and he recalled the old pain. The pain of what it was like to be ridiculed.

He had grown up poor. "Poor as piss and potato peelings," as the postmaster in Groesbeck used to say whenever

Ross and his brothers came into town. Being poor meant a lot of things, but one thing Ross remembered most of all was it meant wearing the hand-me-downs left over from his two older brothers. By the time anything made its way down to Ross from Nicholas and Tavis it was past worn.

He felt the old familiar tension inch its way up his neck. The memory of the jeering he had taken was something he had never been able to forget—at least not completely. Even now, the way he had been teased by the other kids' making sport of his clothes—it still rankled. Well he could remember the sneers, the jokes, the misery that always came whenever the boys at school gathered to poke fun at him.

Sometimes he wondered why he had taken it all, why he hadn't turned tail and run, or simply given up. But that would have meant quitting school and letting everyone know he had been bested, and there was something about quitting or being beaten at anything that had never sat well with him—or any of the Mackinnon boys, for that matter. And Ross had never been one to ask his brothers to fight his battles for him. Nicholas and Tavis, the two oldest, had their own battles to fight, and this prompted Ross to keep his troubles to himself.

In spite of the years that had passed, he could still recall the metallic flavor of fear, the sick feeling of wanting to hide, to run away—and just how close he had come to doing just that. How different his life might have been if he hadn't learned one hot, Texas afternoon that there was yet another way.

After one particularly painful ribbing from his schoolmates during recess, he left school, heading on down to the river to nurse his wounds. By the time his teacher rang the bell for school to resume, Ross was skipping stones across the river's glassy surface. The next morning he was invited up to the teacher's platform, where Miss Lori Pettigrew asked him to speak to her at the end of the school day. For the rest of the afternoon he stared at the heads of the pupils in front of him; he wasn't even tempted to dip the curl at the end of Pearline Howser's fat braid into the inkwell on his desk.

When school was out, Ross found himself standing before Miss Pettigrew's desk after the other pupils had left for the day. He could still remember the feel of the smooth planks beneath his foot as he raked the floor with the side of his bare foot.

His mind wasn't so much upon the scolding he was going to receive from Miss Pettigrew but on the torment he would get from the boys waiting for him once he left here and headed for home.

"Ross Mackinnon," Miss Pettigrew had said, "I am concerned about you."

Ross swallowed hard. "Yes, ma'am."

"Do you know why I'm concerned?"

Ross had felt a bit sheepish, standing on this foot and that, his hands thrust deep into his pockets. "I . . . I'm not sure," he mumbled, rubbing the other foot across the floor.

"Speak up, Ross. I can't understand you when you don't articulate."

"No, ma'am. I don't know why you're mad at me."

Miss Pettigrew's face softened. "I never said I was mad at you. I said I was concerned. I'm concerned because you aren't doing your schoolwork as well as you used to, because you skipped school yesterday, and you don't seem to be getting along with the other boys."

"Yes, ma'am."

"Don't you have anything to say besides 'yes, ma'am'?"

"No, ma'am, I don't reckon I do."

Miss Pettigrew sighed. "That won't do, Ross. I won't accept insolence from you. I want to know why you are suddenly having so much trouble at school."

"I reckon it's because of my clothes."

Miss Pettigrew looked astounded. "Your clothes? What has that to do with your problems at school?"

Ross remembered how he went on to tell Miss Pettigrew about his ragged clothes and how they caused the other boys to poke fun at him and call him "Raggedy Ross," or "Hand-me-down Mackinnon." He had been ready to receive the business end of Miss Pettigrew's hickory stick for admitting such a thing, when the strangest thing happened.

Instead of giving him a stern lecture, or even a taste of her hickory stick, Miss Pettigrew said, "No wonder you aren't doing well."

And then Miss Pettigrew went on to do something that endeared her to Ross forever. She came around that desk like a cyclone in a hurry, grabbing Ross by the hand and pulling him behind her so fast two tortoise shell pins popped from her bun and one of Ross's suspenders came unhooked.

Ross let the suspender be, but he picked up Miss Pettigrew's pins and handed them to her, watching as she poked them in her pocket, not missing a step as she did. Out of the schoolhouse they went, and out of the schoolyard too, that knot of hair at the back of Miss Pettigrew's head bouncing this way and that, then walking a few more yards into the middle of the road, just beyond the fence that bordered the schoolyard, where she suddenly stopped. Releasing Ross's hand, she turned to him.

"I have something to tell you, Ross Mackinnon, and I want you to pay close attention and remember every word I say, because I'm not going to repeat myself. You understand?"

Ross swallowed, nodding his head slowly.

"Good. Now, I'm not telling you this as your teacher, and I'm not telling you on school property, or school time. That's why I brought you out here, away from the schoolhouse. I'm telling you this as your friend, on my own time—and on a public road." She paused a moment, as if to see how Ross was taking all of this, then she continued. "If you ever so much as *breathe* a word to anyone that I said as much to you, I'll swear you made it up. Do I make myself clear?"

Ross nodded.

She put her hand on his head. "Are you listening to me, Ross? Carefully?"

He nodded twice.

She dipped her head slightly, indicating her apparent satisfaction before she went on to say, "The next time—and I mean the *very* next time one of those boys pokes fun at you, you double up your fist and give him what for. And don't you stop either. Not until you've cleaned his plow. You hear me?"

Ross heard. It was the same sort of thing his older brothers had always said to do if he ever had any problems, but somehow, coming from Miss Pettigrew, it seemed all right. The next day he followed Miss Pettigrew's advice.

And he had never forgotten the moment. Or Miss Pettigrew either. He would go to his grave remembering the way she had looked that day, not more than a hundred pounds of determined red hair and flashing blue eyes, something quite out of character for a schoolteacher—or a nice Baptist lady. He guessed if any woman besides his mother had been responsible for his always having had a

soft spot in his heart for women, it had to be Miss Pettigrew.

And then he remembered how Miss Pettigrew had died
that summer of diphtheria and the joy of the moment faded
away to silence like a buggy crossing over a bridge.

He was a man full grown now, and the memories were
old, yet the residue of sadness left him feeling irritated at
himself for allowing his thoughts to eat at him like this, and
he looked at his reflection in the mirror to get his mind on
something else.

He eyed the chain of the gold pocket watch dangling
from the pocket of his waistcoat, then pulled the watch out
and checked the time. All in all, having to wear clothes like
this was a pretty sad ending for a man of the saddle to come
to. He put the watch back in his pocket. It was the *only*
sensible thing he had been given to wear.

He left the room and made his way along the corridor
and down the huge, double curved staircase of intricately
carved oak. Truly this was a grand stairway, made for even
grander entries, something Ross would have given his best
saddle to avoid. Looking much more composed and elegant
than he was feeling, he felt the heat of every eye upon him.
He couldn't have felt more ridiculous if he'd been standing
there buck naked. Thanks be to God there weren't many
people gathered in the great hall due to the early hour.

As he reached the bottom stair, he saw the inky-haired
goddess he had encountered earlier. She was wearing a
gauzy white dress with a flounced skirt; the reddest flowers
in Scotland were in her hair, across her shoulders, and
draped across her skirt. He watched her close her fan and
tuck it under her arm as she smoothed the white gloves on
her hands.

He'd like to start with those tiny gloves, peeling them

from her slim, white fingers, a glove at a time and dropping them on the floor. Next he'd remove the dress and everything beneath it, leaving her in nothing but her stockings and satin slippers with those blood-red flowers in that black, black hair.

Who was she?

It didn't take him long to locate Percy and ask her name.

"Lady Annabella Stewart."

"She's a beauty."

"She's taken, I'm afraid," Percy said.

"You mean she's married?"

"Not yet, but she will be soon."

Ross grinned. "Then she's not taken."

"Let it alone. She's as close to being married as a woman can be, Ross. It means she is promised, and that, in plain English, means you can't ask for her hand."

Ross laughed. "I never intended to ask for her hand," he said, looking her over with frank interest. "There are several other parts of her that interest me more."

"I said, let it alone, dear boy. The man standing next to her is John Gordon, Earl of Huntly and her future husband. A craftier devil you'll never hope to meet."

"*Future* husband, Percy. That means she's still fair game."

"Not in Scotland . . . or England."

"England?" Ross grinned. "I don't plan on chasing her that far." He leaned closer and whispered, "I won't have to."

Percy didn't doubt that for a moment. The lad had a way about him, as the duke said. "The girl is English," he said, his tone heavy with warning. "And they have a different way of doing things. She's a duke's daughter, lad, and this is the nineteenth century, don't forget. It's been fifty years since the last Highlanders ravaged the countryside, throwing dukes' daughters over their saddles and abducting them."

"I'm not considering abduction . . ." Ross looked at Annabella again. She was smiling. Against all that black hair, her teeth looked as white as her dress. "At least not yet," he amended. Then he added, "I don't care if she's English, Scot, or naked Nubian. She's still a beauty."

Ross found it difficult to speak. Visions of her danced before his eyes. "I'm not interested in her bloodlines or her past," he said at last, "only her future. Besides, if what you say is true, the girl is more Scot than English."

"God's eye teeth! Haven't you understood anything I've said? It makes a big difference, lad. The lass was *raised* English."

"It wouldn't matter to me if she was a water sprite that sprang from a fountain. I told you, she a beauty, and that's all that matters."

"You're wrong. What matters is the fact that she's taken, no matter how badly you want to dally with her."

"I want to do more than dally." Ross laughed at the sick expression on Percy's face. "Ease up, old man. You should know by now that warnings don't do much to discourage me." He slapped Percy on the back and said, "Don't worry. I swear you're getting worse than an old woman. Don't you know all you'll get from all this fretting is more gray hair?" His tone turned suddenly serious. "You won't change my mind, Percy. You might as well stop trying."

Ross turned to leave, but Percy took him by the arm. "Ross, listen to me. This is nothing to tease about. To meddle in this affair could be worse than foolish. It could be fatal. Treachery has been almost nonexistent in Scotland for decades. One of the fastest ways to revive it is to become involved in this Stewart-Gordon thing. Leave it alone. You could only lose. They are both extremely powerful families."

"More powerful than the Mackinnons?" Ross asked, elevating his brows to an exaggerated height.

In spite of the teasing grin, Percy said, "You know as well as I that the Mackinnons lost a great deal to the Macleods years ago. They're a modest clan now, content to live on what land they have left on Mull and Skye, blending Drambuie out of their malt whisky and heather honey. They've suffered too many losses already, lad. Don't make it more just because you've taken a fancy to a certain lass." Percy cast a glance in the girl's direction. "She may be bonny, but Scotland is full of bonny women. Half of them will be here tonight. Choose someone else."

Ross clapped him on the back. "I'm afraid it's too late for that, old man. You know what they say about the ways of the heart and all that."

Percy wasn't softened in the least by Ross's humor. "The girl is considered to be a prize catch. Sons of some of the most powerful families in England have offered for her. Anyone from Clan Mackinnon wouldn't stand a chance, even if she were free."

Ross's eyes brightened. "Ahhh, Percy. You said the wrong thing that time." He glanced back at the beauty. "I think it's high time the Mackinnons regained some of that lost glory you were talking about." Seeing that Percy's concern was indeed genuine, Ross grinned and his voice took on a teasing tone. "Now, Aunt Percy, don't you go a-worrying about me none. I intend to be on my best behavior tonight."

To which Percy said dryly, "Ha! Do you think me daft, lad?" His next words were laced with warning. "Neither your humor nor your coddling will serve you well in this case. You forget that I'm too old a cat to be fooled by a kitten."

Aware that he had tried his friend's patience, Ross said, "Well, then, if it's any comfort, I won't cause a scene."

"I wish to God I could believe that."

"You can." Ross grinned wickedly. "I've got all these wonderful new manners, remember?"

"I remember," Percy said succinctly. "I pray to God *you* remember."

After Percy departed, Ross found himself a drink and wandered around the room. He noted all the changes that had been made in the great baronial hall for this ball, peered out this great window and that, viewed the garden and sweeping lawns, then paused before the formidable portrait of his great-great-grandmother before moving over to study the belligerent portrait of the first Mackinnon chief. The painting seemed to dominate the entire room.

But none of these things really interested him, for they were no more than an opportunity to keep stealing glances at the beauty in the flowing white gown from all angles. She looked delicious from all of them. All in all, he spent quite some time with the beauty in his line of vision, yet he still hadn't seen enough of her by the time the butler announced the arrival of the duke and added that the receiving line would soon be forming. Ross greeted his grandfather before he was formally introduced to the Earl of Huntly.

Dislike was instant. From both quarters.

Before Ross could acknowledge the introduction, Huntly drew the battle lines. "You seem to have quite an eye for the lassies," he said.

"Do I?" Ross drawled. "And here I've always thought it was the other way around."

The corners of Huntly's mouth turned white, but he was

prevented from saying anything when the Mackinnon spoke. "Aye, the lad has an eye for the lassies, sure enough, but then, no bonny lassie should ever have to put in an appearance at a ball where there wasn't at least one laddie willing to boost her vanity."

After Huntly and his grandfather left, Ross went back to having an eye for the lassies—one lassie in particular. Locking his gaze on Annabella, Ross watched her brother approach her. Even from where he stood, he could see the depth of feeling that flowed between them.

"Bella, you look like an angel in that dress," Gavin said, putting his arm around her slim waist and squeezing it tightly.

"Of all the bounders!" their mother said and promptly slapped her son's arm with her fan. "Gavin, do mind what you're about. You're hopelessly crushing the roses on Bella's dress."

"Oh, sorry, Bella. Dash it all, that was a rotten thing for me to do." Gavin gave his brow a playful smack. "I fear I have trod upon the lilies."

"Or at least smashed my roses," Bella said, giving him a loving hug as she laughed and looked down at her dress. She gave the roses a few minor adjustments. "There," she said, "good as new. No harm done." Annabella regarded her brother through eyes as openly admiring as her mother's were critical.

"Don't let him off so easily," the duchess said, "or he will never be inspired to behave more like a titled Englishman instead of an affectionate puppy with big feet and a little brain."

Annabella smiled fondly at Gavin as he said, "But everyone *loves* an affectionate puppy."

"True, but they don't marry them to their daughters, and

I might remind you that this is a prime opportunity for you to look over the cream of Scotland's crop." Closing her fan, his mother whacked him on the arm. "Now, mind your manners, you pestiferous young pup, and leave off with that bothersome teasing before you catch your father's eye."

"As long as it's his eye and not his tongue, I shouldn't mind," said Gavin.

"The two are a matched set," Annabella said. "You can't have one without the other. *First* you get the eye, then you get the tongue-lashing."

The duchess's disapproving look brought a teasing smile to Gavin's face, but Annabella knew she had reached the limit of her mother's patience. With Gavin, her parents were more charitable; they indulged his escapades and jovial teasing with restrained acceptance. That was due, she supposed, to one of two things: because he was a boy, or because he was the *only* boy. No matter the reason, she knew they would brook no such behavior from any of their six daughters. The flames of humor extinguished, Annabella regained her proper composure and watched Gavin kiss their mother's hand with a comical display of theatrical zeal, then make his way toward their father.

Dearest Gavin. She adored him. Perhaps it was because he was her only brother. Perhaps it was because he was closest to her in age. Perhaps it was because he enjoyed the freedom and gaiety she often felt cheated of in her own life. But the real reason, she suspected, was because Gavin was so lovable—that his unflappable nature, his obvious fond attachment for her, and the way he had always taken it upon himself to be her champion and defender—even against their parents when he felt they were being overly strict—all endeared him to her.

Annabella loved everything about Gavin, from the easy

way he had of wearing his elegant clothes to the smooth way he had of charming everyone around him in a perfectly natural way. She watched Gavin step away, bringing the duke's grandson, who was being introduced to the other members of her family, into view.

Looking away, she occupied herself with deciding which of the lovely young women who had their eye on Gavin would be the one to catch his, when she felt someone's eyes upon her. Turning slightly, she locked eyes with the duke's grandson. She caught the slow, amused smile, and the way he tilted his head toward her in the slightest suggestion of mocking acknowledgment. Before turning her head away, she gave him a direct look, and her eyes glittered with warning.

Immediately, Annabella snapped her fan open to cool her face and flicked her wrist with such force the fan flew from her fingers, striking the Marquess of Pentland, who had the misfortune to be passing by at that moment, in a most embarrassing place. For a moment she was caught in the most humiliating quandary. What to do?

Apologize, of course.

And she would have. Immediately.

That is, if doing so hadn't meant acknowledging her awareness of just *where* her fan had stuck the marquess. It was shameful, she knew, to ignore her behavior—her mother would call it scandalous. It was also quite unlike her to overlook her manners. She knew it was of the poorest taste, but in this case it was something she deemed necessary. In the end, scandalous behavior won out. She ignored the incident.

The Duke of Dunford's rogue of a grandson wasn't so noble. Of all the awkward moments. Caught unawares, she simply stared at him with a drowsy sort of fascination as he looked at her, a curious smile tugging at the corners of his lips. Still as a marble statue, she waited for him to finish his examination, but when he continued to ravish her at his leisure, his gaze sparing no part of her person, it was too much to ignore. In spite of the fact that she felt limp-kneed and weak, she did not allow herself the pleasure of turning away from his rude stare.

She couldn't remember if it was Paul or Peter who said, *Resist the devil and he will flee from you*—but in spite of her forgetfulness, that was precisely what she did—she returned his mocking gaze with a straightforward glare of her own.

As far as deterrents went, that one was pretty ineffective.

Unable to stare him down, she turned away and searched the room for Gavin, anxious to call him to her side. She found him, and felt like stamping her foot in vexation. His back was to her, so there was no way to get his attention. She would have to cross the room now to get to him, and that would throw her uncomfortably close to the one person she had no wish to be close to. Carefully avoiding the duke's grandson, she made her way across the room.

Why is it, she wondered, *that the person I try hardest to avoid is always the one I am constantly stumbling over?* And if not stumbling, at least being caught in his path, which, she noted with dismay, was happening to her right now.

Seeing the Duke of Dunford making his way toward her, his grandson in tow, Annabella smiled grimly and prepared herself.

"I'd like you to meet Lady Annabella Stewart," the duke said. "This is my grandson, Lord Leslie Ross Mackinnon."

Annabella felt the heat rise to her face. She wouldn't put it past this callous ruffian to mention the incident with the fan, or their meeting and the unfortunate accident involving the stray croquet ball.

Bracing herself, she was surprised when Ross took her hand and kissed it as perfectly as any English nobleman. His eyes were on her as she said, "I understand you are as new to Scotland, as I am." She withdrew her hand.

Knowing full well that the lovely Annabella was prepared for him to mention her hilarious incident with the fan, Ross decided to ignore it, but in doing so, he did something he had never done around a woman before. He was caught off guard and left without anything to say. When the words did come, they weren't exactly the ones he would have chosen for this occasion. "As new as you perhaps, but not nearly as lovely."

The minute the words left his mouth, he could have throttled himself. *Not nearly as lovely?* Heaven help him. What kind of idiot had they turned him into?

Annabella could not contain her humor, but she did manage to stifle the laugh that threatened and give him a demure smile. She looked at the duke. "I believe there is a compliment hidden in there somewhere," she said.

"Aye," the duke said, giving Ross a quizzical look, "but you'd be hard pressed to find it."

Ross told himself to keep his big mouth shut. But when did he ever listen to advice? That was probably why he said, "What I meant to say, was . . ."

Annabella looked at Ross, her green eyes narrowed, yet still possessing a hint of humor. "I know what you meant to say, and I thank you for the thought." Then she turned away and said something to Lord Percival.

Ross thanked God the butler appeared and told them where everyone should stand, which blessedly took attention away from the way he had been babbling like an idiot a moment ago.

The Duke of Dunford would be first in the receiving line with Ross standing next to him. After Ross came the Duke of Grenville, and next to him, his wife, the duchess, then their son Gavin, the Marquess of Larrimore, and then Lady Annabella, standing between her brother and her betrothed, the Earl of Huntly.

A receiving line, Ross decided, was a civilized term for torture. Never had he greeted so many people, or seen so many angelic bosoms quivering beneath eyes that looked at him as if they were hoping he was the most impulsive romantic. And never had he met so many starry-eyed, giggling young women tripping all over themselves. Annabella, on the other hand, was the perfect picture of elegance and poise—in fact, she looked at him as if she could see right through him. When she wasn't sending him looks buried beneath a layer of frost.

Some time later, once the receiving line had broken up and Ross had more time to think about it, he was amazed that the lovely Annabella had managed to stay in the front of his mind as much as she had. It was impossible for him to recall any of the names of the other young women he had met.

For a man who changed women as often as he changed shirts, this was a startling discovery. Never could he remember his thoughts being occupied with one woman for long, and never had he met a woman who made him lose his awareness of other women completely.

The orchestra finished a lively, wild tune that was much like the country dances of old, before they began tuning up for a slower waltz. About that time, Percy looked around for

Ross and found him standing at one side of the ballroom. Leaning against the wall, Ross was swirling a goblet of brandy in his hand and gazing at Annabella. Turning to the duke, Percy said, "By the cross of Saint George, Lachlan, that grandson of yours is asking for trouble."

The Mackinnon looked at Percy, but he didn't sound concerned. "What is the lad up to?"

"Trouble. That's what he's up to. He seems to be doing his bloody best to provoke Huntly. Apparently he sees nothing amiss with that. You saw the way the two of them squared off when you introduced them. Huntly's no fool and he has more eyes than the average man—if you consider those slimy-looking fellows lurking in the shadows. It's one thing for Ross to pursue the lass like a starving wolf following a trail of blood, but quite another to let everyone in the room know about it. He isn't making even the slightest overtures toward common sense or discretion. If I didn't know better, I'd swear he was going out of his way to make his interest known."

"You think he's after the lass?"

"He's definitely interested in her," Percy said dryly, "and he bloody well doesn't give a damn if everyone here knows it."

"Is it that obvious?"

"It's so bloody obvious even a babe would notice it."

"There's nae a bairn in the room," the Mackinnon said.

"There's not much sense either. Why are you protecting him?"

"They would make a bonny couple."

"Surely you know she's no match for him," Percy said. "She's been a heavily protected lass and she's too young and inexperienced to handle a man like him."

"And you think it wiser to throw her to the wolves by giving her to Huntly?"

"She would never fall in love with a man like Huntly."

"Aye," the Mackinnon said, "and that would protect her."

"It would as long as she remained obedient and submissive. Huntly has no use for a girl with spirit."

"And you think the Stewart lass has none?"

"I didn't say that. I don't know her well enough to judge."

"You dinna have to know a lass to recognize spirit. It's something that forms a kinship with your own." The Mackinnon regarded Annabella for a time. Then he said thoughtfully, "The lass has spirit. She just desna ken it yet."

Percy looked amazed. "God's teeth! You're far too canny for your own good. How can you know so much about the girl?"

"Human nature is the same everywhere. It's only practice and custom that sets us apart. The lass can't help being a lass any more than the blind man can help being blind. If she had been born a lad, she would have discovered her spirit long before now."

"That doesn't make her a match for Ross."

"The lass is more match than even she knows," the Mackinnon said. "Aye, she's deprived, but she'll come into her own soon enough." His face turned soft and pensive. "She reminds me of my lass, of Catriona when we first met . . . docile as a lamb at first, but soon she was cuffing my ears and leading me on a merry dance."

"Times were different then, and Catriona wasn't betrothed to someone else."

"It wouldna mattered if she were."

Percy looked astounded. "You can't mean you think he

has a right to any woman in Scotland who happens to catch his eye!"

"I'll wager no other lass will come close to snapping the lad's attention."

"I should have known that for all my blustering, nothing would change." Percy paused, looking around the room for Annabella. Once he found her, he studied her, his brows furrowed in thought. In a pensive voice, he said at last, "She seems awfully straitlaced to me—the complete opposite of your outlaw grandson."

"They're both outlaws," the Mackinnon said with a laugh. "She's like dry kindling, ready to burst into flame with just a spark."

Percy was looking very British and very doubtful at this point. "If it's a spark she needs," he said, "she won't have any trouble. Ross is fairly glowing with smoldering passion right now."

"Aye," the Mackinnon said, giving his grandson a fond look. "'Tis a pity the lad wasna born a hundred years ago. He's like the Highlanders of old—unconcerned with propriety. Back then he would have taken the lass if he took a fancy to her." He smiled at Percy's look of dismay and slapped him on the back. "It looks to be an entertaining year. I only hope he keeps a sober head and keeps his wits about him. Grenville is an honorable man." He looked at Annabella, then at his grandson. "I canna say I blame the lad for taking a fancy to the lass, bonny as she is."

"To hell with being bonny. She's a betrothed woman, and Ross looks at her as if he were considering her for purchase. Even the girl is aware of it. She's been sending him the most discouraging looks. Ross is a fool to keep this up after Huntly's remark."

"I imagine he can hold his own with Huntly, or the lass too, for that matter."

"I still say it bodes ill. The kind of looks he's giving her could start a civil war," Percy said.

"Now that would liven things up a bit," the Mackinnon said, turning away from his friend and making his way toward his grandson.

Caught in a moment of reflection, Ross didn't hear his grandfather approach. Unaware that the duke was standing beside him, Ross watched Annabella spin around the dance floor with Huntly—he refused to think of that man as her betrothed. *Annabella,* he said softly to himself. *Sweet, shy, Annabella. You are as lovely as your name,* he thought. When Huntly drew her closer and whispered something in her ear, Ross murmured, "You can do better than that. Much better."

"You wouldna be thinking of yourself as that something better, would you?"

Ross chuckled and looked at the Mackinnon. "Aye, I was thinking just that," he said, imitating the old man's brogue. Then he gave him a direct look. "Will that cause some difficulty for you?"

The duke's eyes twinkled. "It willna. But I dinna ken it will be the same for you." His eyes moved around the dance floor, following Annabella. "You fancy the lass, then?"

"I fancy her," Ross said, thinking fancy too weak a word for what he felt. He could never remember wanting to be alone with a woman as much as he wanted to be alone with Annabella. And the things he wanted did not stop there. Annabella. Even the sound of her name was as soft as a woman's hand.

The Mackinnon sighed, his brow furrowed. "Percy willna see things your way. I'll see what I can do."

Ross turned toward his grandfather, his face frozen in surprise. "You aren't going to order me to stay away, or advise me to leave her alone?"

"Would it do any good?"

"No," Ross said, "it wouldn't."

"Then I willna," the Mackinnon said. "But I ken Percy will."

"Percy doesn't have to know."

"Percy doesna miss anything."

"Talk to him then."

"It willna do any more good than telling you to stay away from the lass."

"Then wish me luck."

"The devil's bairns have the devil's luck."

Ross raised a quizzical brow. "Are you a devil, then?"

"Aye," the Mackinnon said, "I was in my time."

Ross laughed, returning his gaze to the dance floor, and the bright, eager eyes of several young ladies.

Noticing this, the Mackinnon said, "Are you so certain this lass is the one? Do you ken there are many lassies here tonight that seem to have an eye for you?"

Ross glanced quickly about the room, noticing the bright smiles, the flirting eyes directed at him by many young women. They were in such contrast with the scowls Annabella had been sending him all evening that it was almost funny. And then it struck him that that was why none of them interested him. They were too poised, too practiced, and too obvious, while Annabella was the only woman who had ever cracked his head with a wooden ball, or ignored him completely.

Without taking his eyes off Annabella, he watched her

whirl about the room in another man's arms. She glanced at him once, a reproachful look. Ross laughed, and after a moment of reflection, he turned to his grandfather. "If she scowls at me again, she's mine."

Chapter
8

Stiff and uncomfortable in Huntly's arms, Annabella watched the chandeliers blur overhead, hearing the strains of the orchestra grow louder as they swept past the raised dais, only to grow softer as they danced past. Across the dance floor, her mother smiled and nodded her approval. Annabella returned the smile tentatively, then looked away. With her nerves jarred, she drew herself up, catching sight of Ross Mackinnon as they passed.

They were no more than a few feet from Ross now, and the light from the candles brought out the savage darkness and the hard, chiseled lines of his face, yet at the same time seeming to give both light and life to his fine blue eyes. The play of light upon that face seemed to emphasize different parts—now the lips, now the eyes, and at last moving to the straight lines of his nose—as if he were a man of many different faces, all of them excellent in a very masculine way. It was the face of a man who knew how to lay claim to a woman, and the reality of this echoed hollow inside her heart and vibrated through her and filled her with panic.

This had to stop. Immediately.

Her discomfort and confusion was heightened by the feminine, if somewhat naïve, error of thinking she could, with one look, turn the tide of interested pursuit. She frowned. In fact, Annabella not only scowled at him with glittering green eyes, she sent him the most contemptuous rebuff she had ever bestowed upon anyone.

Catching the look, Ross grinned and raised his brows in question at his grandfather, who was making quite an effort to look perfectly composed. "It would seem," Ross said, "that I have found me a lass."

"Aye, and a passel of trouble to go along with her. I hope you ken what this means?"

"I know."

"It wilna be easy for you, lad. You know her father's plans for her, and mine for you as well. I am an old man, and the Mackinnon. I must place the clan above everything, even my grandson's happiness, if it comes to that."

"You are against it, then?"

"I ken there are times you must think my heart is carved from the blackest Cuillin stone, but I am capable of feeling. If I had the power, I'd use it to keep a lass like that out of the clutches of a man like Huntly, whether you were interested in her or not. It doesna take a fool to see the lass isna happy with this match, or that her parents are fond of her. Perhaps she will use their affection to her gain and put an end to this match on her own."

"If she doesn't, I will."

"Think of the consequences, lad. What if you do as you say and put an end to this betrothal only to find the lass doesna care as much for you as you hoped?"

"She will."

"But if she doesna?"

"Then she will still be better off without the likes of Huntly."

"Aye," the Mackinnon said, his white shaggy brows drawn together, "anything is better than that."

The Mackinnon's words were said with such a glum tone that Ross, unmindful that every head in the room turned to stare, threw back his head and laughed.

The room grew immediately quiet, then, as the guests began to talk, it verily hummed with whispers. Having a good inkling as to what the Duke of Dunford's grandson was laughing at, and being highly irked that he had chosen to laugh in spite of the look she had sent him, Annabella wished she could dance out the doors that lined the back of the ballroom and keep on dancing until she reached England.

The earl spun Annabella around the room and away from Ross, his hand at her waist, his eyes pale and gazing over her head. He was as smooth and polished as amber, Annabella thought, yet something about him bothered her.

She felt as if he handled her in much the same manner as she handled her thoroughbred mare—with the slightest pressure—mindful that she was not only well bred, but properly trained as well. He was an enigmatic man who spoke to her very little, and tried, quite unsuccessfully, to maintain a smiling countenance upon a face dominated by a thin, tightly held mouth. She did not know why she persisted in the cowardly hope that he would be overly pleasant to her when he had a perfect right to be sullen. She had displayed little respect or admiration for him beyond the token obedience and recognition required of her as his betrothed. She tried to dispel such morbid thoughts, but the thought of being forever shackled to this man would not leave her.

Suddenly she was thirteen again, standing before a window in a cold library, watching her parents drive away, ill prepared for the harsh life awaiting her at the hands of Mrs. Hipplewhite, the headmistress of a boarding school in Berkshire. Six months wasn't a very long time to suffer before her mother learned of the conditions and came quickly to whisk Annabella away, but it was long enough for her to feel abandoned and all alone in a world that was as cold and empty as a house where no one comes to visit.

She blamed Ross for the sadness she was feeling. It was his fault that she was constantly comparing him to Huntly, although she knew in her heart that she wouldn't have been happy with Huntly even if she had never laid eyes upon this Lord Ross Mackinnon. Still, she couldn't help asking herself why it was that that rakehell Ross Mackinnon wasn't pestering one of the other young women in the room and making *her* life miserable—a woman who was available. The reminder that she was no longer among the ranks of the available settled over her like a gloomy cloud.

"Is something wrong?" asked Huntly.

She was silent, regarding him quietly. Then she said, "No. Nothing is wrong. Why do you ask?"

"You haven't had much to say all evening, and now even that trifling amount seems to have stopped. We will never come to know each other better this way."

Annabella had a feeling Huntly never wanted to know anyone better. He seemed only to want to know worse. Before she could say anything, he went on. "I am not a fool, Annabella, and even if I were, it wouldn't take a fool to see you aren't too happy with the prospect of marriage to me."

Annabella drew a deep breath, but she didn't say anything.

"I am not reproaching you, Annabella. I am merely stating a fact . . . an observation, if you will. However, we are betrothed, and you would do well to be more accepting of the situation. There is, in case you have not been so informed by your family, an obligation imposed upon a young woman who has just become betrothed. She acts happy. Forced, or otherwise. She also acts—even if she has to pretend—as if she enjoys the presence of her betrothed."

A dark shadow plunged into the depths of her heart. Fast-rising panic surged through her. This man, more than anyone she had ever known, filled her with terror. It wasn't that she did not like him, but more that he reminded her of the trappings of a nightmare. And that was how she felt, as if she was trapped in a horrible nightmare and wanted desperately to scream but was unable to utter a sound.

She saw the glint of his eyes and despaired that she would have to spend the rest of her life looking at that face. All she could do was whimper.

His hands gripped her arms painfully and he smiled, dipping his head low, as if whispering some endearment to her. "Behave yourself, my lovely bride-to-be. It won't do to have your father think you aren't having a good time. You can't afford to humiliate him like that, can you?"

Annabella pulled back in a little stiff jerk that gained her nothing. His hands tightened, then he abruptly released her. "Go ahead," he said in the softest tones. "Run off the dance floor. Run into your papa's arms and see how comforting they are. You have no idea how much it would please me to have someone else suffer the same humiliation I have suffered this evening. Don't look so surprised, you idiotic bit of trembling knees and watery eyes. I've seen how the duke's grandson has been sniffing after you all evening."

"I haven't said more than five words to him," she said in her defense.

He laughed. "You didn't have to. Your eyes gave you away, and your actions said more than any trifling words. You can't seem to let him out of your sight, can you?" He made a sound of disgust. "His aunt killed herself over me. She was expecting my child. Did anyone tell you that?"

A wave of trembling weakness settled over her and she felt faint. "No," she said, unable to say more.

Thankfully, the dance ended, and when it did, Huntly excused himself. "I am going grouse hunting in the morning," he said. "I had planned to be gone only two days, but now I see no reason to rush back here to finish out the week. I will be away for the duration of your stay here. One week, Annabella. That should give your father ample time to put things in order and put a stop to that whelp's sniffing about—without my having to be humiliated further. When I return, Annabella—and I *will* return—I expect you to act the part of a dutifully betrothed woman."

"Why are you doing this? I've done nothing for you to be angry about."

Huntly's breath was warm and rasping across the side of her face as he exhaled. He raised his hand to caress her cheek, and he turned her face toward him, ignoring the way she flinched. As quickly as it had come, the fiery anger in his eyes seemed to have banked and gone out. Had she not thought him incapable of it, she would have called the faint glimmer there a hint of compassion.

"Why do you think I wanted to marry you when I could have had countless others? I found that besides being quite bonny, you were fresh and innocent and quite sheltered. It was your lack of tarnish, your freshness that first attracted and held me. Much as I understand your yearning for a younger man, I can't bring myself to give you up. I don't know if you will believe me when I say this, but it isn't my desire to make you unhappy or cause you hurt. What I want is to find some way to make you happy about our approaching marriage. Your father is an honorable man. I am sure he can persuade you to see the way of it, as well as to putting an end to that young pup's infatuation. Unfortunately, I find I am very short of patience when it comes to seeing another man stalking you." He dropped his hand.

"But . . ."

"One week," he said, cutting her off. "I will return in one week to accompany you and your family on their tour of Scotland. I expect to see your thoughts and your loyalties in order at that time."

One moment he was standing there telling her what he expected. The next moment he was gone.

Immediately the room seemed to take on the luster of a fat teardrop; all Annabella wanted to do was to go off by herself and cry. All of a sudden the voluminous weight of the clothing she had on was too much: the layers of petticoats, the heavy silk flounces of her gown, the tightly laced corset with its whalebone stays that gouged into her flesh. Even the flowers in her hair seemed weighted with lead, their burden causing her head to throb impatiently.

She saw her mother across the way and headed in her direction, then checked herself, deciding against it. Her mother was no fool. She would see her eyes as too bright, her face as too pale. Accepting a glass of punch from a passing servant, she joined a group of young girls her age whom she had met earlier. She stood on the fringe and feigned interest in their conversation. Now and then she interjected a thought, her mind, in reality, miles and miles away.

Her breeding told her to enjoy the evening and not let anything Huntly had said spoil it, but another part of her wanted nothing more than to get away. How she yearned to go to her room and slip between the cool, comforting layers of her sheets and lose herself in the unburdened escape of sleep.

She finished the glass, discovering too late that it was champagne, not punch, that she had taken from the passing servant. Perhaps that was for the best. Feeling a bit light-headed, she thought about what could happen if Huntly spoke to her father. *My father might move the date of the wedding forward. He might send me to a convent to spend the coming months in seclusion. He might disown me. He might give me a stern lecture, telling me I have one more chance and I had better not spoil it.* She knew that above all her father loved her, but that only served to add to the already unbearable weight of her feelings of ingratitude that hung heavy upon her shoulders like a necklace of guilt.

While Annabella was feeling at her lowest, Ross was finishing a dance with a fresh-faced young girl named Maeve, who was as light on her feet as she was with her chatter. Walking Maeve back to her friends, he caught sight of Annabella across the room. It struck him that she appeared to have stepped inside herself and gone into a world of her own, so removed did she seem from everything that went on about her. He considered going to her and making some light conversation with her, but something held him back. Lifting a drink off a passing tray held aloft by a confident servant who moved briskly through the crowd, he found a quiet place near the corner where he could do what had interested him all evening: watch Annabella.

She was far too young to bury herself beneath the weight of misery, for it must be misery or some similar affliction that had robbed her lovely face of its rose petal color. He searched the room but didn't see Huntly, although he had seen him leave her after their last dance. Was it her fear or dread of her betrothed, of her impending marriage, that brought such sadness to her face? His brief conversation with Huntly had made him more than aware of the kind of future that awaited her with a man of his caliber, and he could imagine how a young woman with her whole future before her could feel her world coming to an end with the prospect of marriage to a man old enough to be her father. It was the lingering hint of sadness that drew him, that called him to her as no promise of a night of loving between a pair of warm and willing thighs had ever done. It was as if he had taken a drink from a glass that was drugged, and he fought the urge to go to her and take her in his arms.

He watched her leave the ballroom. It was the thought of taking her in his arms and offering her comfort, and nothing more, that drove him from the room, seeking her—not the thought of what he might do once he found her.

Annabella had as her final destination her bedchamber, but she didn't want to attract a lot of attention in getting there. Her head pained her, she felt old, worn and completely exhausted, and one more crumb added to that cake was the fact that all of Huntly's talk about her father had frightened her.

She didn't want to be a burden to her father, or a source of humiliation for him. How she wished she could simply lose her mind, and her obligations along with it. Hurrying down what seemed the longest of corridors, she was anxious to reach the great staircase and make her way to her room unseen. Her head down, her feet skimmed along the stone floor. Suddenly a door creaked open and she thumped against the Earl of Huntly's chest. Two men and two King Charles spaniels followed, the dogs yelping at his heels.

"Oh," she said, working herself out of the grip that clamped like fangs into her arms.

"If I didn't know better, I would think you weren't having a good time," Huntly said. "Don't stand there wringing your hands and looking guilty, you silly chit. Tell me where you were going in such a hurry."

"Nowhere . . . to my room."

"Well, which is it? Nowhere? Or your room?"

The men laughed and that sent the dogs into another yelping frenzy. Huntly put his palm to her forehead. She glanced at the two men, then at the earl. She knew he was testing her. This time she knew better than to pull away.

He smiled. "Pleading a headache, are you?"

One of the men laughed. "That usually comes *after* the bedding, doesn't it Huntly?"

"Shut up, you fool."

The two men laughed and the dogs began running in circles, yapping and barking. Annabella felt sick.

"I don't think your headache will fare any better in your room than it does down here," Huntly went on. "Go into the drawing room and wait for me. I'll have someone bring you some herb tea."

"I have some powders in my room. They work much faster than herb tea. I'll just run up there and . . ." She started around him when Huntly's hand clamped around her arm. "I wouldn't hear of it, sweeting—your going up there to suffer all alone."

The two men snickered and Huntly shot them a silencing glare.

"If you insist on the powders, I'll go to your room and get them from your maid. Betty, isn't it?"

She nodded.

"You wait for me in the drawing room."

Annabella knew when she had been dismissed, and the joy of getting away from him had her galloping heart pumping so much blood into her body she was feeling dizzy from the effect. Anxious to get away from him, something fortifying shooting into her system, Annabella moved faster than she thought possible. She scampered into the drawing room, whipping the door shut behind her. Leaning back against the door, she almost swooned with relief as she closed her eyes and waited for her heart to cease its frantic beating. She cursed herself for being such a coward and so hen-hearted. She hadn't felt this dizzy since the day she ate too many raisins plumped in a sea of warm clover honey and French brandy. The sound of Huntly's laughter reached her ears. Mentally, she placed him on the same list with lizards, snails, spidery things, and sheep's offal—only lower. She wished she had the courage to march back out there in a spirit of high scorn and trumpet her loathing of him, demanding his apology, and when he gave it, announce her refusal to marry him. She didn't, of course. *I'll give you something to laugh about, you . . . you dog lover.*

Dog lover?

Desperation filled her. *Dog lover.* Here she was, unable to call him something scathing, even in her mind. Wishing she had more backbone and knowing wishing didn't make it so, Annabella went to the tapestry-covered sofa and sat down to wait for Huntly. The more she thought about it, the more she decided it wasn't that she didn't have backbone, she was simply too shy to use it. How she wished she could simply get up and leave.

Why can't you?

Huntly will be furious.

So? Let him be furious.

Overcoming her well-indoctrinated reluctance toward

disobedience, she shot to her feet and looked around the room. There was no way she could go to her room now, for Huntly would be there. Likewise, he would come into the ballroom if she went there. There was no other place to go. She would have to wait here. Perhaps she could lock the door and claim it was an accident that occurred before she fell asleep waiting for him on the sofa.

Her weak knees trembled as she moved to the door. She pressed her ear against the wood and listened. The men were still talking.

"You better be going after your lady's powders, Huntly, or you'll have a war on your hands."

"War?" He chuckled. "I doubt it. The chit doesn't have enough spirit to fire a well-aimed shot. As for the headache . . . she doesn't have one any more than I do."

"What are you going to do? Make her wait? We have a game of cards to finish, don't forget."

"I haven't forgotten. She can wait. It will do her good," Huntly said.

Annabella stepped away from the door, feeling completely discomfited. She knew now that Huntly was both a scoundrel and a tyrant. Let her wait, indeed. She moved up to the door once more and heard Huntly continue.

"When she's had time to reflect," he was saying, "and is feeling sufficiently humbled, I'll go accept her apology."

Apology? Annabella almost choked.

For a moment she was thrown off balance, trapped between her yearning to show Huntly just how much spirit she could muster and her desire to keep her father uninformed about what was happening, maintaining her ardent position as the resolute daughter of an English duke. But then Huntly's words came back to prod her.

Apology?

That did it. She was going back to the ballroom, and she intended to have a wonderful time. She opened the door a bit to take a peek. Huntly was still there, and so were the dogs. The moment she opened the door, they both bounded toward her. She closed it quickly, hearing the howls and barks of the dogs on the other side. Now they were scratching on the door.

She knelt and whispered into the keyhole, "Shoo! Go away!"

"Looks like your lady is going to be leading a dog's life," one of the men said, breaking into laughter.

"Not until we're married," Huntly said.

Without another thought, Annabella scrambled to her feet and darted across the room. She slipped through another door, one that opened onto a sweeping slope of lawn dotted with lanterns. She saw only a few strolling guests who escaped the warm activity of the ballroom. She lingered for a moment in the shadows along the perimeter of the castle. The discordant notes of instruments being tuned in readiness for the next set drifted out the open doors, mingling with sounds of laughter and the clink of glasses.

Annabella picked up her skirts and hurried down a winding path, its stones worn smooth with use. The path divided the garden where clematis and roses mingled with foxglove, irises, and meadow rue. Going down three steps, she ducked beneath an arch where roses drooped in rosy foam. In her white dress she would be highly visible, unless she went toward the loch, beyond the wide circle of dim yellow light made by the lanterns. Her heart pounded. What if someone saw her and told her father?

Or worse, what if they told Huntly?

Alone and on the shores of the loch was the last place she

wanted to encounter the likes of Huntly. And yet . . . if she were careful, she wouldn't have to see him at all.

The mist covering the island was growing thicker, the jagged, dark image of the Black Cuillins barely visible in the distance, against the deep blue-black of the evening sky. Ahead of her, Annabella could hear the soft lapping of water against rock.

Night sounds were all around her.

If I never hear the name the Earl of Huntly again, it'll be too soon. How could she hate someone this much—someone she barely knew? She reached the edge of the loch, putting Huntly out of her mind with thoughts of the beauty of the moon shining like Gypsy spangles upon the water. A moment later she stumbled against the overturned hull of a small rowboat. The wood was rotten, but the planks held. A moment later the hull provided her with a seat and she took it, after giving it a proper cleaning with her handkerchief.

Ross wasn't the kind of man to go lurking after a woman. In fact, he had never done anything like this before. In Annabella's case, he broke one of his own rules. He followed her. Stepping into the hallway, he saw her talking to Huntly. Suddenly Annabella stepped back and turned away from him. Ross couldn't hear what Huntly had said to her, but she didn't look too happy. He watched her walk to the drawing room, as elegant and refined as the most genteel lady, but her face was red as a beet and her brow was furrowed, and she walked fast, as if she was in a big hurry to get there—or away from Huntly. Probably the latter.

He watched her until she reached the drawing room and went inside. Ross glanced back at Huntly. He and the two men remained where they were, still talking. Apparently the oak brain didn't have a grain of sense. He wasn't going to follow her.

Ross wasn't so noble.

He went back into the ballroom and walked through it to a door leading outside. The evening air was cool. It felt good after the stuffy heat of the ballroom. He looked out upon a black and white world watched over by a silvery moon, so round and bright it reminded him of the pocket watch his grandfather had given him. Never before had he thought about the color white having such variety, but the world lay before him, in varying shades from the silvery cast of the moon upon the grass to the fleeting shadows of the softest white that danced in and out of the heavy mist, fading to gray. The sky was black, but the earth was blacker. And everywhere the mist lay, looking black as a witch's hat one minute and white as starshine the next. It was a night for secrets, for mystery and intrigue, where the heavens seemed to give their blessing by lowering a misty cloak of concealment.

He went to the drawing room, finding the outside door flung open. He went inside. The room was empty. He barely cracked the door that led into the hallway and saw Huntly and his two friends still there. Huntly's dogs headed for the door and Ross quickly closed it. Retracing his steps, he went back outside.

Where had she gone? He followed the scattered stones of the walk that gently sloped down to the loch, then, looking out over the shadows made by antique statuary and climbing roses, he suddenly saw her sitting like a pearl inside an oyster, all iridescent white trapped in a moonbeam. He headed in her direction and stopped a short distance from her. Annabella was apparently preoccupied and did not see him.

Of course, she had seen the handsome American more than once over the course of the evening—twice by accident, the other thirty or so times by calculated intent. In her mind she wasn't doing anything wrong in looking at him. He was a barbarian, and it was all right, in her book, to look at a barbarian—even a handsome one—as long as look was all one did.

So, she looked. Much the same way she looked when the royal family was visited by that envoy from India last year— the one that brought two Bengal tigers as a gift for Queen Victoria. Time after time Annabella had found herself slipping away from the exposition to approach the animals' cage, just to stand a few feet away and look at the strange, magnificent beasts. She wouldn't have dared to touch them, of course, but there was something exciting about being that close to danger, yet remaining within the perimeter of safety. That was exactly how she felt when she looked at the duke's grandson—excited, because she knew she was courting danger, yet safe, because of her betrothal, unpleasant as it might be.

Her primary reason for leaving the Duke of Dunford's ball had been to gain control of herself and restore her composure, which should have put her in a better frame of mind to enjoy—no, to *endure*—the attentions of her betrothed. If she hadn't encountered the handsome American barbarian by accident. She sighed wistfully and kicked at a stone with her slipper. The stone rolled over a few other stones and stopped. She would have to admit she was rather happy things worked out as they did. It was infinitely nicer down here than it had been back in the ballroom. She didn't want the attentions of her betrothed, and she certainly had no desire to enjoy them—ever.

What she wanted, and needed, was time to think about

what she was going to do. Right now the options didn't hold much appeal: She could drown herself. Or she could give herself to the church.

So much for options.

Another mournful sigh and she looked up through the mist at the hazy ring of light that surrounded the moon. Annabella was thinking that God was up there somewhere in the heavens, beyond the mist and farther away than the moon, probably much too busy with serious matters to pay her small problems any mind.

Annabella had been raised according to the dictates of the time, which included a liberal dose of decorum. Her strict religious upbringing involved a grim daily ritual in which her father led his household—both family and servants—in morning prayer. This daily drudgery was something some people seemed to think was necessary. Annabella had never really understood her parents' fondness for rigorous morning prayer, for if the truth were known, she found the whole thing excruciatingly boring.

Prayer was something she was accustomed to, but in this particular case, it was a little late for prayer—since the betrothal was already official—but it never hurt to try. After all, Daniel *was* in that den with the lions, and look what happened to him.

And what about Jonah? At least she wasn't in a whale's belly. The worst thing that could happen was that God would listen and then leave things as they were. There was one good point about being at the lowest rung on the ladder of despair: One couldn't go any lower.

In Annabella's mind, it was now or never.

Despite her formal religious upbringing, Annabella, when she prayed in private, had a tendency to depart from the traditional Anglican rigidity. Her prayers were more along the line of a running discourse with the Almighty than any form of fervent entreaty, since she, herself, had no particular obsession for ponderous supplication.

"Are you sure," she said matter-of-factly, her serious gaze directed at the moon, "that you have this alliance with the earl and myself thought through? I'm sure you know what you're doing and all, but I see no harm in making sure you hadn't aligned me with a man I find so unattractive, just because we both happened to be available, and in the same general vicinity."

She sighed, wondering if God was making any more sense out of all this than she was. "I suppose I ought to feel a little ashamed of myself," she went on to say, "for bothering you at a time like this, when you have so many other concerns to worry about—things that are more important than a whining girl and her troubles, but I think you should know it isn't devilish easy being betrothed to a man you don't particularly like."

She gazed into the misty glow of moonshine, imagining that to be the Almighty's mantle of flowing white hair. "But, you see, my problems are very important to *me." Now I've done it. Now the bolt of lightning will come.* When it didn't, she breathed a sigh of relief and decided to press on, hoping God took this dramatic bit of prayer as earnest. "Please don't misunderstand. I'm not being ungrateful, and I'm not asking you to go to a lot of trouble to change any of your preset plans for congenial circumstances around the world. But if you just happen to have another Scot lying about— one you need to marry off in a hurry, I wouldn't mind at all if you wanted to reconsider and gave me a different one."

She took a fortifying gulp of air and waited in suspense for a moment, then, as an afterthought, she added, "And if he happened to look like the Duke of Dunford's grandson, I wouldn't mind that in the least."

On this night filled with music and soft, gentle breezes, this young girl could not easily attune her mind to thoughts of a man she wasn't the least attracted to, or to one twenty years older than herself. Thoughts of Huntly soon left her mind, and Annabella, with her elbows resting on her knees, her chin propped on her hands, her eyes on the changing shapes of mist swirling about her, soon occupied herself with delicious thoughts where a certain duke's grandson was greatly admiring her quietness, manners, and dignity.

Annabella knew it was unlikely that the duke's grandson was encapsulated in a world that revolved around a beautiful but hopelessly inexperienced girl—regardless of her quietness, manners, and dignity.

But Annabella liked to daydream. *You just never know when a miracle might occur,* she often told herself.

She always held to a few rose-tinted ideas about what might happen to her if a miracle did indeed occur; and at the present time, she was right in the middle of a most romantic set of circumstances with a frightfully handsome man.

Just exactly what frightfully handsome man it was and what the most romantic set of circumstances were was hidden in a unrecognizable haze, so Annabella saw no harm in giving the man in her vision the face of Lord Ross Mackinnon and putting the two of them together in a heavily scented rose arbor where Ross was busily employed with the kissing of her hand—between spurts of verbosity in which he declared his undying love. Suddenly all of the hand kissing and spurts of verbosity were shattered by a most terrifying noise.

Stopping within earshot of her, Ross was amused at the

way the gracefully poised young woman he had seen earlier had vanished, right before his very eyes, to be replaced by a loose-limbed hoyden draped over a boat hull. He grinned, both charmed and intrigued with what he had heard, and stepped closer, the better to hear her next round of dialogue with the Almighty. Just at that moment a cat ran across his path and he stumbled over it.

As abrupt as a clap of thunder in the still of night came the piercing squeal of the cat as the animal bolted, passing close to Annabella and disappearing into the darkness. She sprang to her feet and turned, feeling the numbness of terrifying fear grip her and turn her muscles to water. The silken cord holding the small ivory fan to her wrist broke. The fan fell to the ground. With a helpless sense of dread, Annabella lifted her eyes and saw in the dimness a few feet away the duke's grandson. He looked as fierce and daring and forbidding as a pirate in his black clothes.

Her heart pounded painfully in her chest until she feared it capable of flying right out of her body. She had never felt more fragile or more terrified.

Across the rocky distance that separated them, Annabella's eyes looked large and luminous and shyly timid. Ross looked at her standing there like a small statue that watches over a garden. "Well, bless my bones," he said in grandfatherly tones. "Have I stumbled upon a beached mermaid?"

Chapter
9

"Indeed you have not, sir, but you most assuredly have scared me out of my wits."

He didn't appear to be listening. "Amazing," he said. "Even from here, your face is as white as your dress. Did the cat frighten you?"

"No, you did . . . I mean you do . . . that is, you are a bit frightening." *Oh, do be quiet, Annabella. Your foot is wedged as far into your mouth as it will go.*

She lifted a trembling hand to her forehead and wondered how she had come to leave the house to escape one man's attentions, only to deliver herself into a worse set of circumstances. This man disturbed her in a far different way than Huntly did. The duke's grandson had a way of looking at her that was . . . well, scorching was the only word that came to mind.

The soft, muted silence of the night was unbroken. Even the water normally lapping at the edge of the loch seemed strangely silent. All about them the mist swirled, like thick ribbons of steam from a bubbling cauldron. Time seemed suspended, as if by magic they had managed to step into a part of the world that lay separate, timeless, and without beginning or end.

Her awareness of this left her trembling with uncertainty. She was ashamed of her cowardice, her trembling, quavering voice, the fear she knew he could see in her face. Any woman of spunk and spirit would have handled the situation with more fortitude, or at least an authoritative manner, and sent the rogue packing with a piece of her mind. All she seemed capable of doing was to stand here, quaking like chicken jelly in her white satin slippers.

With an ease so confident she wanted to shove him into the loch, Ross picked up the ivory fan and handed it to her. "I suppose I should be happy you didn't hit me as you did that poor fool inside. Do you always have this much excitement about when you carry this fan?"

She couldn't help smiling as she reached out to take the fan. His hand closed around hers. This adventure of hers was fast becoming a misadventure—one with a logical conclusion. She felt panic beat at her throat as he made no move to release her hand.

His hand was much warmer than hers, and it was drier. She tried to ignore what was happening and gently extract her hand, but she couldn't move.

Ross was beyond noticing. The moment their hands made contact, he had been stilled by a sharp kick of feeling that left him stunned. There was such perfection in her lovely features that he could think of little else. He knew he couldn't stand here all night, holding her hand and gawking like a schoolboy, but he was powerless to do more.

Immediately he released her hand and took a step back.

She looked at him, feeling giddy with excitement. *Be on your toes, Bella. Be wary. Watch him,* she told herself. *I am watching him. Unfortunately, I'm not a wary person.* "Did my mother send you out to look for me?" she asked.

"No."

"My father?"

"No," Ross said, inwardly laughing at her naïveté. The Duke of Grenville wasn't fool enough to send a man like him out to look for his daughter. No man was that big a fool.

"Then who?" she asked. "Who sent you?"

He stroked the curve of her cheek with the backs of his fingers. She took a step back. "What makes you think someone sent me to find you?" he asked.

Slowly realizing what he was about, she considered herself too smart to answer that. *I recognize a well-laid trap when I see one.* She said nothing.

He chuckled. "Actually, the earl sent me out here with a message for you."

"He couldn't have. He doesn't even know I'm here. That's why I came—to get away from . . ."

"Him," he supplied. "How come you're so clever?"

"Don't be so cocky. We all make mistakes."

"Some of us more than others." His voice was soft now.

When she gathered her skirts in her hand, ready to go, he said, "I may be forced to take your hand again. If you try to leave."

She looked back toward Dunford Castle. "I must go back now. They're expecting me. If I don't return soon, someone will come looking. I can't be found out here like this."

"I want to talk to you," he said. "In private."

She drew a deep breath. "Please. I can't. You don't understand."

She was right about that. At this point he was incapable of understanding anything. He was fascinated, pure and simple.

Every breathy little word she uttered, every one of her adorable antics, each delectable inch of her—she was perfection. What else could he say? She attracted him. She intrigued him. Hell! Just watching her entertained him. One thing he hadn't expected, though: she surprised him. He would have pegged her for one to take off like a scalded cat, or swoon, or giggle like a fool, or do any of a hundred silly things women were prone to do when a man cornered them. Yet she had done none of these things. He didn't think she would even leave if he didn't dismiss her. He wondered what kind of upbringing she had. "Talk," he said, "or hold hands. It matters little to me."

"You mustn't touch me," she said.

"I'm touching you now," he said, his hand coming out to stroke her cheek again. "Would you rather talk, or hold hands?" he asked again.

He looked serious enough to do what he said, so she sighed and dropped her hands to her sides. Then she glanced back toward Dunford. "Truly, I can stay only a moment."

"I understand."

He waited a spell, giving her time to warm up to the idea of talking to him, but he could tell she was only becoming more agitated. He was amused to see the way she was leaving no stone unturned when it came to studying him. She looked down at his legs, then at his feet, and finally at his face. Now, she saw immediately that he had been watching her study him. "Want me to wrap it up?" he asked. In the dim light he couldn't see the color that shot to her face, but he sure as hell could feel the heat.

"I beg your pardon?" she said.

"You were eyeing me like you were considering making a

purchase, so I wondered if you wanted me to wrap it up? Or do they use another phrase for it in England?"

"Another phrase for what?" she asked, feeling gooseflesh popping out all over. "Perhaps I misunderstood."

"Perhaps you did." He studied her. "You're either as innocent as they come or slicker than owl's grease."

Her face went blank. "I beg your pardon?" She seemed to be saying that a lot around him. "What did you say?"

"I said, you're either as innocent . . ."

"No, no, not that. The other," she said, impatiently waving her hand.

"What? Slicker than owl's grease?"

She felt dazed, as if someone had knocked the wind out of her. *Slicker than owl's grease?* Her stomach rolled in revolt at the thought. *Owl's grease?* She put her hand to her head. *Owl's grease? I'm going to be sick.*

"Are you all right?"

"Of course. I'm fine. Really. Why wouldn't I be? We English ladies are quite accustomed to being called such revolting things as . . . as . . . *oiled birds*," she said.

He laughed at her strange way of putting things. He didn't say anything, but his look brought color to her cheeks with scorching intensity. He didn't touch her.

He didn't have to. His gaze caressed her as no hands could. Her mouth felt dry, her throat swollen. She parted her lips slightly, to draw in more air.

He took a step toward her, holding his hand out to weave his fingers into one of the long, glossy curls that lay across her breast. His gaze never wavered. He curled his fingers beneath her chin, lifting her face into the full light of the moon. Now, his hands were at her waist.

How many hands does he have?

With the slightest tug he drew her toward him, and

something about it made her close her eyes. She felt the delicious pressure of his lips upon hers. The suddenness of the kiss prompted an unintentional response within her and she shivered. It was the oddest sensation—embarrassing because it shouldn't be happening, frustrating because she knew she wanted more.

He pulled back, ever so slightly, and said, "My God, you're sweet enough to eat."

"Then, you'd better hurry," she said without thinking. "Because I'm melting awfully fast."

He chuckled and touched his lips to hers once more. Then, holding one hand at the back of her head, he kissed her with more intensity, more feeling. It was a gentle kiss that teased and intrigued, one that drew her curiosity to the forefront. His hands went around her, pressing her against him, fitting her body to his.

Everywhere he touched her she burned. She opened her mouth again to draw in a deep breath.

He covered her mouth with his, his tongue gently probing and exploring. He nuzzled her throat, whispering, "I could get used to this."

His face was cool against the heated skin of her throat. His mouth made a slow ascent, learning her face, kissing her cheek, her nose, her eyelids. His lips were warm and steady as they brushed her forehead. His hand was higher now, caressing the back of her neck, then her bare shoulder. Something about the feel of his flesh against hers set her trembling and her heart beat painfully. She felt as over-plumped as brandy-soaked raisins, swelling and ripe, oozing with the sweetness of warm honey. For one glorious moment Annabella kissed him back, before reality began to creep into her drugged mind. She planted one small hand on his chest and shoved.

He expected her to be coy, to call him a bounder for pressing his attentions on one as innocent as she, or at the least he expected her to box his ears in a violent display of her anger. But she did none of these things. She simply stared at him. It was a look that surprised him, primarily because it wasn't one he had ever encountered before, at least not after kissing a woman. The only way he could describe her face was *free*. There was no anger, no embarrassment, no condemnation, no coyness. She stood there looking at him, as tiny and perfect as a sweetheart rose. He lowered his head to kiss her again, but she pushed him away, this time stepping back to put some distance between them.

"You're awfully prim and unyielding. You were much warmer and more gracious inside when I danced with you."

"I never danced with you."

"Ahhh, but you did, sweetheart. Every time you danced with Huntly, my eyes never left you. It wasn't him spinning you around that room, it was me. Don't deny it. You felt it as much as I did. And I repeat, *you were much warmer.*"

"There were other people inside. Here we're . . ."

"Alone," he supplied. "Does it make you nervous to be alone with a man, or just one you aren't acquainted with?"

He watched the play of emotion across her face and wondered which one was the real Annabella—the enchanting, angry, yet beguiling one who whacked him over the head, the poised, articulate one he was presented to inside, or the nervous, uncertain one he was now conversing with. Not that it mattered. He was bewitched by them all.

"I'm not sure," she said.

"What would it take to make you sure?" he asked, lifting one hand and sliding his fingers through her hair, cupping the back of her head and drawing her closer. He lowered his face to meet hers. "If there's anything I hate to see, it's a woman who has difficulty making up her mind, or a man who won't help her try." He brushed his lips across hers.

"I don't need any help," she said, trying unsuccessfully to pull away. "I can make up my own mind."

"I've seen little proof of that," he said with a soft chuckle.

"Y-you," she stammered. "*You* make me nervous."

Smiling, he touched his lips to hers a second time. "I think that's just about the most encouraging thing you could have said to me, Lady Annabella."

"I'm not trying to encourage you," she said. "What I'm trying to do is *discourage* you."

"You're not doing a very good job," he said, tightening his fingers against her head and forcing it up to hold her where he wanted her. His other hand slipped around her waist as she tried to twist herself and pull away. She made a strangled sound that he didn't consider to be much of a protest when he kissed her again, his mouth moving urgently against hers. When he finally dragged his mouth from hers, Ross continued to hold her in place.

Warnings were going off in her head, but all she managed to do was give a ragged sigh and say, "You take unfair advantage."

"Annabella," he said in a husky whisper, "I will take whatever steps necessary, for I intend to have you. You know that, don't you?"

"Have . . ." she said weakly, then a little stronger, "*have* me?"

Strangely, it was that one surprised remark, coupled with the confused look on her face that made him realize he was moving a bit too fast for her. She was gently reared. He would have to learn to be gentle as well. He looked at her face. For her, he could do that. For her, he would learn to be gentle.

Moonlight worshiped her face. He decided then and there that he had never seen skin like hers, a perfect harmony of the palest ivory and merriest rose, luminous with life. Her eyes were as soft and green as a meadow's bounty, her mouth—he'd never seen lips on a woman that were almost childlike, yet so damnably kissable he was hard pressed not to do just that.

She was looking at him now with eyes that were sensual and innocent and wary all at the same time. *Take me, don't take me; come here, go away,* they seemed to say. Then he looked at her mouth. *Kiss me and never stop* was what it said, and he wanted to. But something stopped him.

Immediately he had a flash of the free way he and his brothers had always interacted with the girls back home. It was hard to believe this girl, no matter how young she was, had never been alone with a man.

Annabella had never thought herself backward or shy, but she felt both as she stood there looking back at him. She glanced toward Dunford. "I really must get back. I've stayed far too long."

"Oh, no you don't," he said, taking her arm. "We aren't through talking." Sensing her discomfort, though he did not understand it, he wanted to put her at ease. "Why don't you take off your slippers and stockings and we'll walk along the water's edge? I would think the water would feel good on your feet after all that dancing."

That brought her up short. "T-take off my shoes? You mean go barefoot?"

He nodded.

"Barefoot," squeaked Annabella. "Out here?"

Her voice held such a tone of awe that he laughed and

looked at her. "That's exactly what I mean. Haven't you ever gone barefoot?"

"Only in my bath . . . or when I'm sleeping."

Ross laughed, enjoying her sense of humor. Only when he looked at her, he saw immediately she hadn't been joking. His mind went back once more to the Mackinnon place on the edge of Tehuacana Creek, remembering how he and his brothers spent almost the entire summer in their bare feet. And across the creek the neighbor girls had shed their shoes a great deal of the time—perhaps not as much as Ross and his brothers, but often enough that he assumed it was commonplace. He could almost see Katherine Simon running across the softly plowed earth, her shoes tied together and thrown over her shoulder, her skirts hiked up and her bloomers showing as she raced his brothers, Alex and Adrian.

Curious now, Ross went on. "Well, wouldn't you like to try?"

She hesitated a moment, but decided she couldn't trust a man like this. She had to get back before her father and the earl came looking for her. Not even her mother or Gavin could hold them off if they caught her out here like this.

"Come on," he said with slow, drawling patience. "What's a little mud on your feet? You can tuck your skirts up so they won't get dirty." He smiled and held out his hand. "Although I think you would look rather cute with a smudge or two." He considered her for a moment. "Have you ever gotten *dirty*, Lady Annabella? Real dirty?" He reached for her hand and she drew back.

"Dirty? No . . . well, perhaps a little when I'm gardening."

"Then you should try it, *Lady* Annabella. There's nothing like it. I'll take my shoes off and walk with you."

She had a fine picture of that. She had an even finer picture of her father coming out here catching the two of them stomping around in their bare feet. Propriety swelled like indignation within her. "I don't know about a backward place like Texas, but in England a gentlewoman does not go walking in the water or anywhere else with a man alone, nor does she remove her shoes in a public place."

"Says who? And anyway we aren't in Texas or England. We're in Scotland, and as far as I can tell, there aren't any rules against a lassie taking off her shoes. You can't imagine what it feels like to feel the earth beneath your feet and cool mud squishing between your toes."

For a moment she looked as though she might toss back her lovely head and laugh heartily, but she seemed to think better of it. Holding her arm, Ross led her back to the rowboat. He took a seat and pulled her down to sit beside him. "I wonder," he said, looking at the face that was all passive innocence, "what else have you missed out on?"

"I haven't missed anything. I have been very well educated . . . for a lady, you might say."

"You have?"

"Yes, I have. I draw and I paint, and I'll have you know I've been thoroughly drilled in the deportment that becomes a gentlewoman."

"Oh, I'm sure you've been thoroughly drilled. It's obvious with every rigid little step you take. Don't you ever loosen up?" As an effort to make her laugh, he said, "Why, I bet you walked around in your schoolroom with books on your head."

But the laugh faded when she said in such a serious way, "Indeed I did, and spent many an hour with a board strapped to my back as well, and even more hours sitting in a backless chair to work on my posture—which Miss Aimsley said was dreadful, *simply dreadful!*"

He turned to look at her. "You aren't joking, are you?"

She frowned. "Joking? Indeed I'm not. Why would I be joking? The *Young Ladies' Book* says, *'Dignity of manner is next to modesty.' That* should be the greatest endeavor of the female. It does not mention joking anywhere. Therefore, one must assume it is undesirable in a woman."

"What was your life like as a child? What were you allowed to do for entertainment?" Remembering the way the Mackinnons had all played out of doors in the warm months, coming inside for taffy pulls, parlor games, and sing-alongs when the weather was bad, Ross assumed the life of a young English girl would have some similarities. Once again he was surprised.

"We were permitted to play spillikins . . ."

"Now, *that* sounds like a lot of fun," he said, wondering if *spillikins* was as much fun as it sounded. "What else?"

"We embroidered stove aprons, and one of us was always making flowers of silk or wax. My sisters and I played the piano, and there was always gardening and stitchery."

"Stitchery?" he asked, remembering the lovely needlework his mother had done: embroidered pillowcases, kitchen towels, cloths for the table.

"Cross-stitch and tent stitch," she went on to say. "We copied verses from Psalms with black silk thread on the coarsest old tammy cloth."

He lifted a curl, feeling its cool, silky touch. "What were you like as a little girl?" he asked.

"Skinny and terribly quiet. I was afraid of my father when I was quite small. His voice was so gruff."

"And now? Are you still afraid?"

"I respect him very much, but I'm no longer afraid of

him." She laughed. "Of course, I learned at a very early age what I had to do to please my father, so he wouldn't shout and upset Mama or call down the governess. I practiced very hard at becoming the best, most obedient daughter that I could possibly be, so Papa would be pleased with me."

"What were you afraid of if you didn't please him? That he'd send you back?" He gave her a lazy smile and stretched his legs out.

She had a sudden vision of that and in spite of herself, she laughed. "No, of course not. It's just that when I was very young, I was always daydreaming. It used to infuriate my father, and he would scream at the governess that she wasn't giving me enough to occupy my mind. Then the governess would cry and threaten to quit, then Mama would start to cry and tell Papa how difficult it was to find a good governess, and my sisters would all cry and say everything was all my fault because I was so spoiled and selfish."

"So you learned to be very, very good and to please everyone?"

"Of course I did." She scowled at him. "Lord Ross, I may be a trifle too good-natured and a wee bit naïve, but I'm far from stupid." Her frown deepened as she seemed to hear a voice inside her head say, *Oh? Don't you think it's pretty stupid to stay out here talking to a man like this when you are betrothed to another?* She ignored the voice. "I learned at a very early age just what I had to do to keep the peace and maintain my family's goodwill."

"And that was to please everyone."

"Yes, although you make it sound like something horrible, when it wasn't. I'm far from miserable or mistreated, and I would suspect that there are a lot of people like me out there."

"If there are, I've never met any of them," he said softly. "But your way may be right. I wasn't born into the same kind of family you were. We were farmers . . . honest, hardworking, God-fearing farmers—dirt poor, but happy. My parents both died when I was just a lad, but I remember them both, and I remember there never was a time that I was afraid of either one of them. I've never worried about pleasing anyone, save myself. But then, Texas is a far cry from England, isn't it?"

"Oh, very different indeed, if all the things I hear are true, that is."

He laughed. "Oh, they're probably true," he said.

"I would like to visit this Texas of yours," she said, her mind filled with imaginings of what it would be like there. A well-tutored and well-read young woman, she recalled many of the things she'd been taught about that fascinating, yet frightening place called America. Nervous with anxiety, she studied him, imagining him thundering across the vast prairie, pursued by a marauding horde of murderous Indians, or facing some nameless gunslinger on a dusty, deserted street, his gun belt low, his fingers itching just above the trigger. But the image that distressed her most was the one of him standing in a pub—or whatever its Texas counterpart was called—his arm around the waist of a woman wearing a lot of spangles and feathers and little else.

"I should like to take you to Texas with me," he said at last, his eyes never leaving her face.

"I shouldn't like to go with you," she said.

"Why not?"

His gaze wandered over her face, the wintergreen eyes, the mouth. "Lady Annabella," he said at last, taking her face in both of his hands, "You aren't going to make this easy for me, are you?"

She turned her head away, not knowing what to say. Before she had any inkling of what he was about, he put his hands on her shoulders and turned her toward him, one hand tilting her face upward to meet his kiss, his arms going around her, enclosing her in a warmth and comfort she had never known existed. For a moment she was too shocked to do more than submit, then, against every reason of sanity and honor, her arms went around him to hold him in much the same manner as he was holding her.

When he broke the kiss and lifted his head, he looked down at her, not letting her go completely, but loosening his hold upon her. She felt uncomfortable beneath his scrutinizing gaze and wondered about the odd expression upon his face.

"Are you sure you're betrothed?" he said with a degree of humor that she found quite irksome lacing his voice.

"I'd never joke about *that*," she said sharply, feeling the edge of her anger disappearing. Annabella wasn't certain as to why, but somehow she could not resist that smile of his. Unable to help herself, she smiled back, feeling the stiffness ease out of her body. "I've never met anyone like you before," she said.

"Somehow, that doesn't surprise me," he said.

"You're very brazen, and quite the most forward man."

"Only when I want something."

"And do you? Want something, that is?"

"You aren't *that* backward," he said with a laugh.

She was of half a mind to tell him to mind his own business when he looked at her, and here it came again, that smile of his, curling comfortably and without effort. That was all it took—just one soft look, one melting smile, and her heart raced. She wondered if she would ever again see anything as warm and inviting as that smile. It was a pity he couldn't bottle it as the Mackinnon clan did their Drambuie. A smile like that—it was worth a king's ransom.

Her thoughts were so centered upon smiles and bottles and ransoms that his next question caught her a bit off guard, especially when she felt his fingers softly stroke the tender skin just below her ear.

"Do you kiss every man the way you just kissed me?"

She knew as certain as there were hedgehogs in England that that was a loaded question, but she was just a little too curious and a little too vexed to let it ride. "Why?"

He shrugged and looked back toward the castle as if he were growing bored. "I was just wondering."

His casual gesture was simply too much. Really piqued now, she clenched her hands at her sides. "Were you thinking there was something wrong with it, then?"

"No, I just had to keep reminding myself I was kissing a woman and not a marble statue. Who taught you to kiss?"

She knew it was a dangerous game she was playing with this man. She was woefully inept and he had probably kissed enough women to be awarded a medal for it. It was more than obvious that this man had not been in England or Scotland long enough to become civilized, for his behavior was more in line with what she had heard about the scandalous times of Lord Byron, when the *ton*, and indeed the whole of England, seemed bent upon outraging society —a time when morals and manners were at their lowest ebb.

If she hadn't known better, she would have sworn this man was a holdover from those times. But he wasn't an Englishman, or even a true Scot, since he had been born in America, and that probably explained it. She was inclined to agree with what she had been told about Americans—that they were an ill-bred lot, for in truth, this oversized brute with his smoldering eyes and heart-thundering grin had displayed nothing but unconventional ways and the roughest of manners since the moment she met him. Truly, he must have a bit of the barbarian in him. Yet, in spite of all this insight, regardless of all the danger signs, her anger had been sparked, and for a brief moment she wavered.

But Annabella had been painstakingly reared by conscience-minded parents who taught her to behave at all times with the innocence of a babe and the purity of a bride's blush. From an early age, she had been taught that passion and sensuality had no place in a young woman's life. Wild as a Gypsy heathen as a young child, Annabella had had to spend many long hours sitting rigidly upon a hard stool and even more hungry nights after being sent to bed with no supper before her rebellious nature had been curbed.

But once it was curbed, it had stayed curbed. Ever mindful of her manners and her breeding, she took a firm hold of herself and gave Ross a look that said she was more than insulted. Then she tried to look away. But he took her chin in his hand and forced her to look at him. "You shame me with such talk," she said. "I told you I am unaccustomed to being alone with a man. I have never even kissed my betrothed."

Although the thought of that pleased him, Ross could only stare at her for a moment. Stone-cold innocent? He looked her over slowly. Her hair was damp from the mist and her skin looked as pure as fresh cream. Impossible. How could any woman with the body of a dance-hall queen and the face of a goddess be wrapped in chaste purity and remain untouched? Impossible. With a tone of obvious skepticism that he made no attempt to hide, he said, "Are you telling me the truth? Ever?"

"Of course—not that it's any of your business."

She started around him, but his hand detained her. "How old are you?"

"Old enough to know better than to allow you to kiss me. I'm sorry I did."

"Yes, well, I hadn't meant to kiss you, if it's any consolation, but a man who does everything with planning and forethought has very few memories worth keeping."

Looking at him, she wondered if he could hear how her heart throbbed thunderously, making each breath she drew an act of labor. She knew it, she knew it—just how wrong and improper it was to be out here with him, alone and unchaperoned. She had been raised like a flower, planted and nurtured in a walled garden, while he had always been as free from worry and restraint as the wind, and truly, that was what they were: the wind and the flower. And saints above, it was a warm, tempting wind blowing through her petals tonight.

She looked into his lazy eyes and thought, *This is how women get a bad reputation.* She wondered what he would do if he knew what she was thinking, if he had any inkling of just how curious she was about the mysteries he obviously knew so much about. She lifted her hand and touched her lips, remembering the dampness from his kiss that had lingered there only moments ago. *Too much,* she thought. *Too much and too soon.* And then she remembered Huntly, and knew it wasn't only too soon, it was too late.

He was so close—too close—and the warm play of his breath upon her cheek too disturbing. His voice was low and throbbing, his words throwing back the lid to Pandora's box. How could she resist?

"Why don't you leave me alone?" she asked. "Why must you persist? You're only making it more difficult for me."

"I know," he said, reaching for her hand. "You're shaking. Are you cold?"

"What I am is uncomfortable, and it's your fault I feel that way."

"I'm sorry about that. I could make you feel better," he said. "If you'd let me."

She stared at him blankly.

"Sweet Annabella, surely you know what happens between a man and a woman," he said with a hint of humor. "I couldn't possibly do that out here. We'd get sand in our drawers."

"Of all the despicable . . ." She jerked away from him, but he held her fast.

"Why are you so angry? You know why I followed you."

"Don't think for one minute you can seduce me."

"Then why are you so disturbed by the possibility?"

"I'm not in the least," she said reproachfully.

"Good. Everyone," he said softly, "has to start sometime, somewhere. I always feel there is no time like the present, don't you?"

"I—I—I'm not sure," was all she could manage, for by this time she was so rattled she wasn't sure of anything save her own name.

"Aren't you just a little curious?"

"Curious?"

"About the things that go on between a man and a woman?"

"No!" she said with such fervor he laughed.

"Are you afraid?"

She nodded her head violently in agreement. She was more than afraid. She was terrified. Terrified of what he might do. Even more terrified that she might like it.

"Are you afraid of your parents knowing," he asked softly, "or of me being the one to show you?"

This conversation was going nowhere fast, for she had no inkling of the things he hinted at. Truly, whatever she knew about those things was innocent enough to be discussed in church—and the things that weren't so innocent were wee enough to be inscribed in flowing script upon the head of a pin.

Cleverness and mother wit having deserted her, she said nothing, but merely looked away, her mind filled with thought. True, she was wrong to be out here. True, if she were caught with him like this the things her father said about "those kinds of women" would be whispered about her as well. At any other time in her life, Annabella would never have allowed such things to happen. But her life was suddenly different from what it had been. A deep sadness filled her.

She couldn't seem to shake the feeling that with the announcement of her betrothal she had been sentenced to death. It wasn't that dying was so very, very bad, but just the timing of it. She regretted the thought of dying before she had really had a chance to live. And she wanted so desperately to live—if only for a season—like a butterfly. Without thinking, she stared at him again. Whatever the reason, she couldn't stop.

Everything about him fascinated her. *What's it like, to live?* she wondered. *To really and truly live?* This man had lived. Signs of it oozed from his pores and gleamed like the bluest fire deep within his eyes. And the moment she thought it, she knew it was the truth. There was something wild and free about him, something that made his clothes carry the fresh scent of the outdoors, that made his hair look windblown, even when it was not. Awareness slowly creeping upon her, she saw his amused look. She knew she must be looking at him in such an enraptured way he was sure to laugh. She could not bear to have him mock her, or to hear him suggest that she "run along like a good little girl."

It was fear of humiliation that prompted her to jerk away from him and run up the hill, stepping out of her right slipper as she ran. Ross watched her go. He wanted to go after her but was uncertain as to why he didn't.

When the whiteness of her dress was no more than the luminous flutter of a moth in the mist, he started up the sloping hillside toward Dunford Castle, walking slowly, his mind on Annabella, who by now, had completely disappeared from sight. He had walked only a few yards when he came upon her slipper, a tiny white satin thing lying on its side in the damp grass that edged the stone path.

He picked the slipper up. It wasn't much bigger than his hand. He looked at it, turning it over and over in his hand, tracing with his thumb the line of dampness that had turned the color dark. He looked back toward the castle; though he saw no trace of her, he had never felt another person's presence so strongly. What was wrong with him? Was he going mad? Is this how it was done, just a few strange feelings that distorted truth and gradually consumed until there was naught left of reality?

He had no answer for that, just as he had no answer for his strong attraction to this slip of a lass. He wasn't the most patient man, but perhaps—perhaps in time he would understand. Percy had taught him that patience often surpassed learning, but Ross wasn't sure this was true in his case. Perhaps his mother had known him better than anyone else, even though she had died when he was just a lad. More than once, when his father said, "Ross, you dinna climb a ladder by beginning at the top," she would soothe

the frown of impatience on Ross's brow. Even now, he remembered what she had said: "Ross, my wee laddie, your father dinna ken patience is a flower that grows not in everyone's garden."

The night closed around him, misty, dark, and full of mystery. He stood there for a moment in the gathering gloom, content to stare at the last place he had seen Annabella running up the path that wound and coiled like a snake across the grass toward the castle. For quite some time he remained there, her slipper in his hand, his mind reliving everything that had happened only moments before. He thought about this woman whose destiny he knew lay intertwined with his own. He lifted his eyes to the haunted mountains that lay just beyond a stand of pines and wondered how many of those who had come before him had stood at this very spot . . . names that were lost and no song or legend remembered them.

He felt the past reach out and call to him, and the thick cloak of mist was rolled back, and he beheld a soft gray light. From out of the light he thought he heard a voice, but knew he couldn't have. The light faded and the evening deepened to darkness once more. *I can't be hearing voices. Unless I'm going mad,* he thought and turned away.

As he looked about him, he saw only a fleeting shadow pass over the waters. The waves softly lapping the shore seemed to sigh and fall silent.

Ross dropped the small slipper into his pocket and began walking up the path. The lights from the castle were barely visible now, but he knew he could have found his way back blindfolded. He felt—no, he knew—something stronger than himself guided his steps now. He thought about Annabella, knowing the lass was part of all this; he was eager to know how it would all come about. The future stretched before him, hidden and gray and still, but the lass was his. He knew that now. And the joy of it flooded his heart like a burst of sunshine. It wouldn't be easy. It wouldn't come quickly or without its price. The way would be wild, and dark, and full of mystery. But it would come, at its appointed hour. And when it was over, it would, he knew, be well worth the price.

He reflected upon that. He thought about Annabella. And then Ross Mackinnon whistled a few bars, feeling his soul flood with laughter.

If he had been a coyote he would have thrown back his head and howled.

Chapter
10

Annabella fell into a deep sleep.

She was on the moor. From out of the darkness came three horsemen of apocalyptic revelation. The first appeared on a black horse, the second on a red horse, the third on a white horse. When they had thundered past, she saw in the distance a fourth horse, pale as the mist, and riderless, following truly and steadily as if trying to overtake the other three.

The rider of the black horse was a sinister, evil shape robed in black; his face was hidden behind a black helmet and plume. He carried a two-edged sword and slashed both right and left with it, leaving a trail of treachery, destruction, and death in his wake. Behind him came the second horse, red as molten lava, the color of war. This rider she recognized from her previous dream, and as before, his face was hidden in a swirling mist, only this mist was red—blood red. His body was covered with yards of plaid. As he thundered past, the sound of bagpipes saturated the air. And then came the third horse, its rider beautiful and clothed in blinding light. Suddenly a blackness came, flowing like thick smoke away from the black horse and cloaking the world in eerie silence as quiet as the coming of fog—a brooding darkness that surrounded like a sleepless night. Back, back it came, a great black mist, swirling and silent as smoke from a fire, surrounding first the red horse and then the white, and the world stood still. A horrible, evil laugh rang out like the clang of a battle ax, and the pounding of her own heart grew still. A scream lodged in her throat as the pale horse approached; its hooves were shod with fire, and it sped into the blackness, and she knew this pale, riderless horse was death. With a cry of grief, she watched the pale horse emerge from the blackness like a cold, penetrating wind, a figure, pale and shrouded in mist upon its back. And then the blackness began to fade, and when it had cleared, only the riderless white horse remained.

Annabella looked at the horse with horror, and it came to her slowly, as a cloud moves across the sun. She knew now. Someone's death was foretold. But whose? Before her very eyes, the white horse began to shrink and shrivel until, like a sigh it dissolved into nothing.

She awoke the next morning, exhausted, her heart heavy and like lead within her. Glimpses of the vision still swirled in her head. The vision she had seen last night had been a warning. She was sure of it. Someone, someone she knew was going to die and she had been warned of it. She shivered, feeling cold and alone. She looked about her. What had looked so comfortable was nothing more than a cold room with walls of gray stone. She felt no sense of peace, and yet no turmoil either. What she felt was nothing—a vast emptiness as if something alive and precious had slipped out of her during the night. There was no warmth in her life now, no warmth in the wake of her dream. Yet she could feel it—the faintest glow of heat radiating from somewhere nearby.

She sighed and closed her eyes, feeling the touch of Ross Mackinnon's lips as they had felt last evening when he kissed her. That was no dream, but reality; no cold emptiness, but a saturation of warmth. She fell back upon the bed, feeling the heat of him as it bore her back, the intensity of his warmth every place he touched her. She could feel his rough, warm, calloused hands as they caressed her. His touch had been surprisingly gentle. The feel of him was so real, she dared not open her eyes for fear of losing the warm comfort of it. For a long time she lay there hoping to hold on to a memory. Then, at long last, she released it and let it go.

She sat up abruptly. She wasn't ready to let some unknown person die without at least trying to help. She had to find someone to talk to, someone she could trust, someone who would see she had some value other than her worth as a bartered bride. She could not speak of such things to her father, or her mother, either, for that matter. She thought of Ross and dismissed him at once. With a great heaving sigh, she felt dejected. There was no one she could talk to, no one with whom she felt at ease.

No one except the old duke, the Mackinnon.

With renewed vigor, Annabella leaped from the bed intending to pull the bell rope to summon her maid, then thought better of it and decided to dress herself. Betty could be such a bother at times, always asking questions when Annabella wanted to think, or being sullen and closemouthed when she wanted to chat. At other times she was worse than Annabella's mother—always fussing over this or that, bossing and telling her what to wear and how to wear it—exactly like her mother.

Throwing open the doors of her wardrobe, Bella eyed the

dresses inside. She selected one that was more simple than the others, a red-and-green plaid taffeta. She braided her hair in a long single plait, then looped it back and tied it with a big green bow. Without a moment to waste, she hurried from the room.

It was still early, and if she were in luck, she could find the old duke—for he was an early riser—before her mother awoke.

She found Robert in the parlor, dusting. "Top of the morning to you, Robert," she said. "Have you seen His Grace—the Mackinnon?" she added, not wanting him to think she was looking for her father.

"He's taking an agreeable stroll, my lady."

"An agreeable stroll?"

"A stroll that puts him in an agreeable mood."

"Oh," she said, and laughed. "Well, where would one go to take an agreeable stroll?"

"His Grace usually frequents the path that runs up the hill to the glen."

"Thank you, Robert."

"You are most welcome," Robert replied, but Annabella had already departed in a swish of plaid taffeta.

The heat was strong when she set out. Spring breezes carried warmth that caressed the mossy hillside like a persuasive lover, melting snow that ran in gurgling trickles over stony havens and formed a deep tarn before spilling down a waterfall into a churning beck, only to be lured away to the duny shores of the sea, past mudflats and lobster traps and old wooden boats lying derelict when the tide was out.

Above her the sky was intensely blue, the clouds white and bunched together like fleecy sheep. Overhead an eagle soared, but she did not pause to watch—she was too absorbed in making her way along the ancient peat path that climbed and wound its way upward, to where the air was thin and blue patches of snow still resisted the coaxing warmth of spring. She passed barns with thatched roofs and old abandoned crofters' huts and a few milestones, and went on and on—hopping, stepping, and jumping now and then, and always huffing and puffing, because the moors were very rough, full of man-traps, jags, and holes.

She interrupted the hillside drink of an enormous red stag, who cautiously lifted his head as she approached, then swiftly turned and disappeared down another path. The stag was magnificent but awesome and frightening with its thorny display of antlers. She was sorry to have disturbed his drink, but happy that he decided to let her be and turn away.

By the time she spotted the Mackinnon just ahead, her heart was thumping against her breast like a mill clapper.

"Hullo!" she called. "Hullo, Your Grace!"

The Mackinnon was sitting on a jutting boulder that afforded him a nice view of the Highland glens and the tiny loch below. He was a bit shocked to see the lass up this far, because it was a considerable walk even for him, and he'd been taking this same hike for more than forty years.

Watching her hurry toward him, he wondered if he should scold her for being out like this all alone, but then he figured the little lass had had more than her share of scolding. Besides, it was hard to scold a lass as bonny as this one. And she was bonny. Not an ounce of Viking blood flowed in her Celtic veins, he vowed, for she was as small and dark haired as the ancient Gaelic-speaking *Scots* who had first come to the Hebrides from Ireland so long ago.

He lifted his brows in amusement when she came to a narrow beck not more than three feet wide. She stopped on the opposite side and looked at him in silent entreaty. He remained expressionless, wanting to see what the lass would do, knowing if he had to help her, he could do it just as well in a minute or two as he could now. She hesitated another moment before making her decision to proceed on her own and skipped lightly over lichen-covered stones half submerged in frigid water to reach the other side.

His eyes were bright with approval. He wondered if the lass would have tried half as much in England.

A few dozen steps up the winding path brought her to the Mackinnon's side. "I'm glad I found you, Your Grace," she said, between gasps for breath.

"Weel, sit yourself down and catch your breath before you swoon," he said, not failing to notice the tense rigidity and expectation in her expression.

The duke was spared having to say anything else, for as she drew even with him, she dropped down beside him and said, "I'm ever so glad I found you, Your Grace. Oh—I've said that already, haven't I?" She clasped her hands over her knees and looked longingly over desolate mountain passes before turning back to look at him. "You see, I've been walking for quite some time, and had almost given up finding you. I had all sorts of visions of having to walk all that way back all alone and without having found you. Of course, if I hadn't found you, I would have just turned around and walked right back the way I came." She stopped talking, partly because she had finished what she had to say and partly because she had used the last bit of breath in her small body.

"Why did you come?" he asked.

"I wanted to talk to you, you see. I've had the strangest dream and I don't know to whom I can talk about it, besides you, of course."

He looked surprised. "I dinna ken why you want to ask me. Why not your mother or your father?"

"Well, it may not seem obvious to you," she said, "but I cannot speak of things of *this* nature to either of my parents."

The Mackinnon looked at her. "So, you had a dream," he said. "Do you have the Sight?"

She thought about that for a moment. "I don't think so," she said, remembering her mother telling her once that her grandmother had had the Sight. "This has never happened to me before." She went on to tell him about the dream, about the three horsemen and the lone, pale horse that stalked the other three like Death.

"Aye, I ken it to be Death the same as you."

"What should I do?"

"There is naught you can do, lass, except let it go. Nothing will be served if you hold on to it and make yourself sick. The death belongs to another. You canna change that."

"But . . ."

"Ease up, child. You've been given the gift of seeing something that will happen, not the ability to change it." The Mackinnon looked about him. "It's getting cold and the mist is closing in. We'd best be going back down."

Annabella wasn't the only one who had dreamed the night before. Not long after the duke and Annabella returned, Ross found his grandfather in his study. "*Audentes fortuna juvat,*" he said to the Mackinnon. "What does it mean?"

"*Audentes fortuna juvat,*" the Mackinnon slowly repeated, taken unawares by Ross's question. "Who told you about that?"

"No one told me. I heard it."

"Where?"

"I'll tell you in a minute. What does it mean?"

"It's the Mackinnon motto. *Fortune assists the daring.*"

Ross watched his grandfather go to a huge oak cabinet and open the heavy carved doors. The duke removed a small box inlaid with ivory and mother-of-pearl, which he opened with a key he kept in his desk. He took something out and crossed the thick Persian carpet, handing a small box to Ross. "I had planned on giving this to you later, but since what I was saving it for willna happen, I might as well give it to you now," he said. Then, seeing Ross's puzzled expression, he added, "Go on, open it."

Ross removed the lid and saw a silver clan badge that displayed a boar's head crest. Encircling the boar's head was a belt-and-buckle surround where the words AUDENTES FORTUNA JUVAT were engraved. "It's a bonnet badge common to the Mackinnon clan," the Mackinnon said.

"What occasion were you saving it for—the one that *willna happen?*" Ross asked, his affection for the old man evident in his voice.

"The occasion of your wearing a kilt for the first time."

"You're right," Ross said with a scowl. "It willna happen."

It was a surprise to Ross that his grandfather didn't start an argument, as he usually did whenever Ross's wearing a kilt was mentioned, but this morning the Mackinnon was more interested in something else.

"I told Percy to tell you nothing about the Mackinnon clan badge or crest until I gave this to you," he said. "I ken he didna listen too keenly."

"Perhaps he did," Ross replied. "Percy didn't tell me."

"Who did?"

"I wish the hell I knew," said Ross. "I told you, no one told me. I heard it."

"Where?"

"I heard it last night, in a dream." Ross watched his grandfather's face turn pale and noticed how his hands trembled as he placed the inlaid box upon his desk.

Ross paused, running his hand through his hair and looking at the wall over his grandfather's shoulder as if he expected some sort of help to materialize there. "I know this sounds like I've been dipping into the Mackinnon reserves of Drambuie, but I swear to heaven I was as sober as a stone when this voice seemed to come right out of a cloud-colored light." He paused and looked in a puzzled way at his grandfather. "You think I'm a blithering idiot, don't you? That I'm a few pickles shy of a full barrel?"

The duke leveled his penetrating blue eyes at him, and Ross wasn't sure he wanted to hear what his grandfather was about to say.

"No, I dinna think that, lad. But I do think you're the first Mackinnon to hear those words—in that particular manner —in over a hundred years. It's happened before in the Mackinnon clan—three or four times. I didna ken it would happen again, at least not in my lifetime."

Ross was thinking, *Just what I need—nighttime visitors appearing like magic from the past. Visitors that have my life all mapped out for me.*

"Is it a good omen?" he asked, hoping he hadn't been set aside for affliction and torture so the Mackinnons could have another martyr. A great sufferer he wasn't, and sacrificing his life for some high-minded principle or being tortured to death to achieve martyrdom was definitely not his brand of whisky. He liked living, and he intended to live just as long as he possibly could. If he were to pick a motto, it would be: *Better to be a live coward than a dead hero.* Any fool knew a live coward would live to fight another day, but a dead hero? All he would get was a marble slab. Ross wasn't too fond of marble, anyway.

"Perhaps it isn't a good omen now, but eventually . . ." The Mackinnon's voice trailed off in a foreboding way.

"What do you mean, eventually?" Ross asked, his voice high-pitched and cracking.

"You willna have an easy time of it, lad."

"Listen, God may have written out a plan for my future, but He didn't sign it."

His grandfather didn't look too convinced, and that made Ross sigh wearily. "Whatever it is," he said, "I won't do it."

"It willna do any good to resist. Those who hear the voice must go through a severe trial before achieving their end."

"Will you please not refer to it as an end?" Ross said.

"All right. You will swim some rough waters before you reach the far shore."

"More wonderful news. Tell me, has anyone *not* reached that far shore? Alive?"

"I dinna ken that anyone has died from the swim, if that's what you mean."

"I suppose I should be thankful for that."

"Aye, you should."

"When was the last time a Mackinnon heard those words?"

"Before the battle of Culloden."

"Well, that's wonderful. This conversation is getting more and more cheerful by the minute," Ross said, giving his grandfather the eye. Seeing the far-off look on his face, he wondered if the old duke was listening.

The Mackinnon was listening, but he was seventy-two years old, and his mind didn't always follow the lines of convention. Take right now, for instance. While he was finding more pleasure in this grandson of his by the minute, he couldn't help thinking about how close he had come to never seeing the lad. He had spent every night for the past ten years on his bony knees, praying in earnest that he would live long enough to see the whelp of his son John. And now that prayer had been answered. It was enough to make an old man cry.

Ross was still eyeing the old man and thinking how like an eagle he looked, with his white hair down past his shoulders, his sharp blue eyes, his overall gamecock appearance. "I don't suppose it's possible to undo what's been done . . . you know, sort of reverse things . . . maybe tell them to go try the voice on someone else?"

The Mackinnon looked for a moment as if he was on the verge of laughing, but he gave his attention to the way Ross was pacing the floor with an overabundance of nervous energy. "I dinna ken that is possible now, lad. You dinna have a choice. You were chosen and the fat is in the fire. The matter is out of your hands now."

"I just wish I knew *whose* hands things were in." Without saying another word, Ross turned and strode briskly out of the room.

The Mackinnon watched him go, feeling his mind slip a little. It was like that sometimes. One minute he felt sharp as a tack, the next minute his mind was as dull as a crofter's hoe. At this moment Ross reminded him of someone, and lost somewhere in that maze of his mind was the name he couldn't quite grasp. It might have been one of his brothers; but just now he couldn't remember his brothers—in fact, he didn't even remember how many brothers he had. His mind was a lot like his old legs—they felt as spry as a lad's one minute, then grew cold and numb the next.

Only this morning he had watched the parlormaid shine the huge silver tray that sat on the sideboard, and he remembered how he used to take that tray and slide down the stairs, sitting on it, racing one of his brothers—who preferred to slide down the banister—to the bottom of the staircase. It had been great fun then, and this morning he had been tempted to give it another try. How sad it was to know that in a day or two, he would look at that tray like he had never seen it before, and ask the maid if it was new.

"I dinna mind growing old," the Mackinnon mumbled to himself, "but I canna bear to watch everything slowly wear out."

But then he thought of his grandson, as fine a strapping lad as he'd ever seen. The lad brought the promise of new life into the cold stone walls of Dunford, and a liveliness into his creaky old limbs that had not been there since Kate died. He shook his head. His grandson was a rounder and a hellraiser and he balked at everything new.

The Mackinnon smiled and leaned back in his soft leather chair. He wouldn't have it any other way.

A minute later he was fast asleep.

It was an hour later when Ross stood at the window of the great library, twirling the globe of the world and absently watching Annabella make her dainty way down the stone walkway to the coach that was waiting to bear her and several other ladies to town for shopping.

The coachman's son, a small lad of five or six, came running up to her carrying a peacock feather, which he proudly presented to her. Annabella leaned over and whispered something to the lad, then gave him a hug. Ross wondered what she would have done if he had been the one who presented her with that feather. Already he was feeling his customary impatience to be on with things gnawing at him. He wanted Annabella, and knew with every breath he drew that she had been promised to him—after a trial, as his grandfather put it. One part of him said a woman like Annabella would be worth any trial, yet another part of him couldn't help wondering just how severe this trial would be.

He wanted Annabella, and he wanted her badly, but not badly enough to die from it. No woman was worth that. Looking at her, he reminded himself that the Mackinnon said no one had as yet died from his trial. He prayed in earnest that his grandfather was right, or at least that he wouldn't be the first.

Out of breath and feeling as if she had thrown her clothes into the air and run under them, Annabella wondered why she had agreed last night to accompany some of the duke's female guests to town when her mother had enough sense to agree to a game of whist in the parlor. She didn't need to shop, and now that Huntly had left, she didn't need to get away from him. Another hour's sleep would have served her better, or a game of whist. But then she remembered the duke's grandson, and found yet another reason for accompanying the ladies to town. Suddenly eager to shop, she glanced up to see Maura standing beside the carriage.

"Have you seen Caitlin and Kate MacDonald?" Maura asked.

"No," said Annabella. "They weren't in the hallway or near the front stairs. Do you know if anyone else is coming to town with us?"

"It'll just be the four of us as far as I know, unless someone else has decided to come at the last minute."

Hearing voices behind them, Annabella and Maura turned to see Lady MacDonald and her two daughters, Kate and Caitlin, hurrying toward them.

"Looks as if Lady MacDonald has decided to go," Annabella said, watching the woman hastily pull on her gloves. Her overplump bosom heaved with each breath she drew.

The five women settled themselves in the coach for the ride into Broadford. The coachman cracked the whip and the coach lurched forward just as Annabella looked out and saw Ross Mackinnon standing at the window of his grandfather's library. As their eyes met, he dipped his head in recognition. Annabella quickly turned her head away and began rubbing at a speck on one of her kid gloves.

Lady MacDonald complained heavily all the way to Broadford. The coach was too crowded, she claimed. Annabella thought there was ample room, considering they had crammed five women inside and *one* of them took up enough space for two. But Lady MacDonald wasn't to be appeased, not even when Annabella pointed out that the squabs were deep and very comfortable and exclaimed that she had "never ridden in a more well-sprung coach."

About the only thing they did agree on was the state of the road into Broadford—if indeed, one could call it a road. A well-rutted trail was a more apt description. But the way into town was a lovely one, and Annabella thought no painting could have done justice to it; indeed, no words she could think of did either. Words like *magnificent* and *breathtaking* seemed too commonplace and mellow to describe mountains that seemed to rise right out of the sea and shoot straight up into the sky. The somber grayness of yesterday had given way to a sunny brilliance of such a pristine character that the whole world seemed fresh and whole and newly created.

The coach gave a lurch and sent everyone leaning far to the right as it rounded a curve and passed over a deep gully, then bumped down a little narrow, twisting road that wound down the side of a hill and passed through a thin slice of woods where the sunlight came down in thick, brilliant shafts that looked substantial enough to slide down.

Once they had to pause for at least twenty minutes while a sheep dog moved his herd of black-faced sheep across the road. "Sheep are such humble little creatures," said Annabella. "They're always shy and huddled together in little bunches, as if they're afraid to face the world on their own."

"They're filthy beasts that make the most dreadful noise," said Lady MacDonald. "I can't stand the sight of them."

"But you love your haggis and your warm wool shawls," said Kate.

"Humph!" said Lady MacDonald.

For the rest of the journey, Annabella settled herself back in the seat between Maura and Kate and listened to Lady MacDonald wheeze and complain about the dust while trying to learn something of the countryside, which was so very different from England. Here there were no odd-shaped pastures, no hedgerow trees. Everything was well plotted and laid out, the quickset hedges narrow and clipped low, like a garden. There were no may or black-thorn blossoms, no rambling roses, and not a sign of violets or primrose growing in the shade. But the skies were clear and the Black Cuillins were hazy in the distance, and everywhere she looked the Isle of Skye was pleasant and tranquil and abundantly green.

Caitlin fell asleep and began to snore lightly. Lady Mac-Donald was wheezing so loudly she apparently couldn't hear, but Maura and Kate did and they began to giggle. Annabella couldn't very well ignore two giggling women she was sitting between, and the sight of Caitlin's head rolling all over the back of the seat and the sound of her snoring were funny—and on top of that, *anything* seemed funny when one was sitting between two people who were laughing. It was difficult to keep a straight face, but Annabella managed.

The drowsy little village of Broadford lay scattered around its wide bay, while *Beinn na Caillich* and the Red Hills seemed to stand guard in the distance. They passed a few lobster creels stacked along a fence not far from the Broadford River. Two young boys stood on its bank fishing for trout and salmon, casting curious looks at the coach, but turning away when the girls waved. Moments later the coach pulled to a stop in front of the Broadford Hotel.

After shopping for two hours, buying bonnets, wool paisley shawls, and an ivory fan or two, the women met back at the hotel for tea before starting back to Dunford. On the return trip, Annabella sat next to the window and listened to Caitlin, Maura, and Kate recount stories of their childhood, stories of little girls who were given a great deal more freedom than she or her sisters were ever allowed to have.

Annabella closed her eyes, giving way to the rhythmic sway of the coach, the soft caress of warm, penetrating sun upon her face, and slept. Some time later she was awakened when the coach jerked to an abrupt halt, throwing her and her two companions on the seat with her, forward. "What happened?" Lady MacDonald asked with a groan, shoving Kate off of her and back into her seat.

The coachman leaned his head down and said something about a broken wheel.

"Fiddle," said Lady MacDonald. "Whoever suggested this shopping trip ought to be shot. Now what shall we do? Sit here like a gaggle of geese waiting for some nodcock to come along and offer us a ride back to Dunford?"

"Aye," the coachman said, coming around to open the door, "this is a busy road. I ken another coach will be along soon." He announced with his next breath that he was setting out for Dunford and would send another coach back for them.

Half an hour later, Annabella sat in an empty coach, watching her companions crowd themselves into a rickety farm cart. Even if there had been room for one more, she would have been skeptical of that contrivance. It didn't look strong enough to hold itself together, let alone carry a load.

With promises to send someone for her as soon as they arrived at Dunford, and Lady MacDonald's stringent remarks on the reliability of coaches being built nowadays, her companions waved and were off, one wheel of the tiny cart wobbling under its newly acquired weight, the other creaking ominously. Soon it crested a hill and rolled out of sight.

Annabella sat back in the coach and waited, but after what she surmised to be over two hours had passed she was uncomfortable, stiff, and blessedly tired of sitting inside a coach that wasn't going anywhere. She found the strain of sitting in the coach any longer far worse than the thought of walking. Without further thought, she climbed out of the coach and started up the road.

It was a warm day with no wind and blessed with a cloudless blue sky. Puddles left from an overnight shower collected along the side of the road, but the road itself was dry. As she passed beneath trees, golden spikes of sunlight left blotches on the road, and she considered for a moment stopping there to wait beneath the great sweeping boughs of a tree she could only identify as one that did not grow in England. But she was as tired of waiting as she was of sitting, so she continued on her way.

The scent of heather filled her senses and she removed her bonnet and retied the wide satin ribbon, hanging the hat from her arm. Before long she began gathering wild flowers that grew along the road, and for lack of a better place to put them, used her bonnet, which soon looked like a basket overrun with color.

All this walking made her warm and her feet hot. She remembered that Ross had invited her to remove her shoes that night on the shores of the loch, and she toyed with that idea briefly, but that was about as far as the thought went. She might be walking down the road, common as a peasant, but she wasn't going to go barefoot like one.

She came to a place where a smaller road forked off to the left. Certain that this fork was one that led to Dunford, she turned down it. An hour or so down the road, it became narrower and cluttered with stones and bore the marks of a road little used. About the time she was wondering if she should turn back, the road ended at the edge of a small beck that gurgled and gushed with frigid water, thawed from melting snow. A few rotted timbers lying alongside told her there had been a bridge of sorts here at one time, but that was long ago. At its narrowest point, the beck wasn't more than six or eight feet wide. The stones that lay scattered in the water were small and covered with lichen. She couldn't step on them, even with care. Even to try, she feared, would leave her with more than her slippers wet.

At this unpropitious moment she heard the unmistakable sound of a horse approaching and turned to see Ross Mackinnon ride up, looking bigger than Edinburgh and twice as splendid.

"You gave up on waiting in the coach, I see?" he said, swinging down from his horse.

She ignored that. "Did you see Lady MacDonald and the others?"

"I did. They are all safely tucked between the stone walls of Dunford by now, where you would be, if you had remained in the coach. Do you have any idea how long I've been looking for you?"

"I thought I'd meet whoever came for me a bit sooner if I walked."

"And you would have . . . *if* you had stayed on the main road. Why did you leave it for this cow trail?"

"I thought it was the turn-off to Dunford."

"This road doesn't go anywhere. The one you're thinking of is another mile or two away," he said.

She looked away. "I suppose my mother is quite distraught."

He grinned. "She was. She ordered me to wait for her to change into her riding habit so she could accompany me."

"How did you persuade her not to come?"

Ross laughed. "I didn't. I left before she could change."

"You didn't," she said, in horrified tones.

"I did, and I wouldn't hesitate to do it again."

Annabella felt the bubbling of a laugh and clamped her hands over her mouth.

Across from her and watching, Ross had drawn a shaky breath that seemed out of step with his others. The humor left his eyes, a lingering smile hovering about his mouth. With no real idea of what he was thinking, Annabella plucked a wilted yellow flower from her bonnet and offered it to him as she said, "Perhaps you can appease her by bringing her flowers."

"That flower," he said, not taking his eyes from her face, "would get me in considerably hotter water. It's wilted beyond recognition. You'd best throw it and the others away."

She looked at the wilted flower. "I think I'll keep it," she said, thrusting it back into her bonnet with the others.

He looked her over appreciatively, from her exquisite face down to the tips of toes that seemed too shy to leave the security of her long, flowing skirt. He noted the fashionable bonnet dangling from her arm, stuffed with meadow flowers and a peacock feather dropped by one of the Duke of Dunford's peacocks angling out to one side.

"I suppose," he said coming closer, "that it's time to hoist you on the back of my horse and get you back to Dunford, before my grandfather and your mother have every chambermaid in the area armed with feather dusters and storming the countryside looking for you."

She knew he was joking, but his words rang true. Her thoughts angled in the direction of concern for her mother, but she looked at him and lost her train of thought. There was something disconcerting about a man who looked at a woman that way. "Yes," she said in a quite distracted way, "I suppose she might."

Unwilling to accept the fact that she was betrothed to another man, he studied her smooth, young face. The full afternoon sun graced her porcelain cheeks and dusted them with amber powder, and he thought he had never seen skin as smooth or as finely textured, at least not on anyone above five years old. And once again, he had never seen a face or eyes—save the expressive face of a child,—display more feeling and more emotion. She had the body of a seductress, the face of an angel, and the openness and lack of awareness of a child. Never had he seen her use her uncommonly good looks to her advantage, and for a woman who looked as she did, that was remarkable.

With one swift movement, he plucked her from her feet and swung her up into his arms. Before she could register surprise, he stepped into the water, splashing across the beck with her.

Being in a man's arms was awkward for her, and the moment they reached the other side, she asked him to put her down. "Please," she said, looking into his eyes with such pleading that he was helpless to do anything less than she asked.

He lowered her to her feet, but he didn't release her. Instead he pulled her closer, losing himself in the slow penetrating sensation of just how good she felt. But she was shy and inexperienced and stiff as a board, and he knew he had to get her back. "I'd better get you back," he said. "Can you ride?"

"I prefer to walk."

Tucking the reins into the back of his waistband, he walked along beside her. The road was rougher now, more like a winding path than a road. Rain had collected in potholes and the ground in between was soggy heath, making walking slow and difficult.

"You're getting your slippers muddy—and your skirts as well."

"They're ruined anyway. What's a little mud after so much walking?"

"Just the same, I think you should ride. Come on, I'll give you a boost up."

"I told you, I'd rather walk. Why can't you leave me alone? Don't you have anyone else you can bother?"

He looked thoughtful for a minute. "Nope. You're the only one I can think of," he said. "A gentleman wouldn't let a lady walk while he rode."

"And how would you be knowing anything about a gentleman?" she asked. "I'm surprised the word is even in your vocabulary."

"Oh, I know about gentlemen, all right—not that I ever rightly remember seeing one, but I've heard of them." He laughed. "Ease up a bit and give me a fighting chance. No man likes to see a lass walking—not even a muddy one."

He stuck his thumbs in his leather belt and continued walking comfortably beside her. She saw such amusement in the depths of his vivid eyes that her acute irritation gave way to immediate embarrassment, which she was sure sent flames of color to her cheeks. To get her mind on something else, she took a swipe at a smear of mud on her sleeve. "I must look as if I've been wallowing in pig swill."

"Someday I shall show you how to get really muddy and enjoy it," he said casually.

"You aren't going to teach me anything, because I shall go to great extremes to see that you and I never cross paths again."

"Why are you being so stubborn?"

"I'm not stubborn. I'm simply not interested in having anything to do with you. There is, you know, a vast difference between the two."

"There's a vast difference between the two of us, but that doesn't mean we can't ever come together. In fact, that's just what I would love to do. Come together."

"You speak of it in rather epic terms, as if you're describing what happens when two stars crash into each other—or two goats."

He laughed. "In some ways it is a lot like that, for fragmented is how I think I could describe myself afterward."

"Afterward?" She turned her head toward him, and he noticed she had the most adorable frown between her eyes when she was vexed. "Are we talking about the same thing?" she asked.

"Probably not," he said, laughing. "If we were, I have a hunch you'd be slapping my face about now."

Intuitively, she shivered, feeling a sense of dread and a need to cower away from him. This man was too much for her: too overpowering, too raw, too unrefined. There was an audacious luster to this man that was both fresh and flagrant and much too forbidding. She really did not know the man at all and had no idea what he might do now that she was out here in the middle of nowhere with him. Never had a man seemed so tall, so menacing, so capable of confusing her with nothing more than his presence.

Wariness and confusion were evident in her eyes, which were as green as a Highland glen—eyes that narrowed in a way he found irresistible.

"I think . . ." she began.

Suddenly he stopped her by pressing his hand lightly over her mouth. "You talk too much," he said. His thumb traced the fullness of her lower lip. "Such a waste for a mouth that could be put to much better use."

Her intuition told her she was treading on thin ice. She tried to pull away but found herself hauled up against him, his body much more serious than the teasing play of light so evident in his eyes.

He looked down into that lovely heart-shaped face, seeing the grassy greenness of her eyes, so open and trusting. "Don't look at me like that," he said softly. "You don't know what it does to a man to have a woman look at him like that."

He had fully intended to press his suit a bit, to see just how far he could get with her, but there was something about her that brought out the good in him, all the things he had thought nonexistent, lost, or buried too deep ever to surface. She reminded him too much of the things that were good in the world, and that made him feel as if he were staring down the barrel of a Hawken rifle with something helpless, like a spotted fawn in his sight. He couldn't pull the trigger. No matter how hungry he was.

"You probably don't," he said softly, "I can see that you

prefer to remain ignorant—but in any case, you shouldn't be afraid of me. I'd be the last person on earth to ever do you harm—even if it meant my life."

He stared at her and something about the way he did brought a dizzy rush of weakness to her knees. The spell was broken, but not before the effect of that warm, intense look in his eyes made her feel suddenly more alive than she had ever felt.

It was difficult to imagine, standing out here on a tranquil moor with him that there was such a thing in the world as pain and misery and suffering. At this moment, the world seemed fresh and newly created, and oh, so full of promise, with all that she desired no more than a heartbeat away. All she had to do was reach out and take it.

Chapter
11

There were times Annabella remembered she was betrothed. There were other times when she did not.

Sitting at her dressing table, with Betty brushing her hair, she was lost in thought. It was past time for her to put in her appearance at breakfast, but she was unable to do any more than she was doing about it. Annabella was lost in a brown study, wondering just why it was that the things most remembered were the things best forgot. Memory, it seemed, had a life of its own, and a stubborn will as well. How she wanted to forget. Forgetting had a way of making her mild mannered and sweet tempered, but whenever she remembered she was cross as crabs. It boded ill for the daughter of the Duke of Grenville to be cross as anything, for tolerance, it seemed, was something her father preached, but had little of.

About that time Betty tangled the brush in something determined to stay where it was and gave Bella's head a powerful yank.

"Ouch!" Bella said, coming out of her chair and giving

Betty a cross look. Judging from the foul expression on Betty's face, she didn't seem to be faring any better than she was.

"What's wrong with you this morning?" she asked Betty.

"Nothing, ma'am."

Annabella sighed, lowering herself back down into her chair. "Fudge and stuff, Betty. Your face is as dark as Egypt. I've never seen you in such a pucker. Something is definitely wrong."

"I dropped a tray in the hallway this morning and Her Grace saw it."

"Is that all?"

"I broke *all* the dishes," Betty wailed. "The teapot, the creamer, the cup and saucer—even the sugar bowl."

"Did Mother say anything to you?"

"Yes, ma'am," Betty said between sniffles. "She said to His Grace, 'I'll settle Betty when I come back up.'"

"Oh, posh. You know as well as I that a *settling* from my mother isn't any worse than a couple of swipes with a feather duster. Here, give me the brush. You go to the basin and wash your face. There are worse things that could happen to you, you know. You've faced my mother before and lived to tell about it. What if you had to face the Earl of Huntly every day for the rest of your life?"

Betty burst into tears, and that set Annabella's mood back one hour. Once again she was remembering the details of that which she wished most to avoid altogether.

When she went down to breakfast, she was what her mother referred to as "cross as crabs."

She arrived too late for breakfast, the serving board having been cleared of the morning's fare, so she settled for a cup of tea and a scone with her mother. The duchess spent the next half hour trying to interest her in the latest bridal fashions from Paris. Glancing out the window at the endless miles of purple heath stretching as far as the eye could see, beneath an aquamarine sky veiled with wisps of white, Annabella thought, *How lovely and like a bride the world is.*

As usual, anything that reminded her of weddings made her want to change the subject to one that centered on more pleasant thoughts.

Her father and brother had returned, their stories about their hunt for grouse keeping Annabella and her mother up half the night. She wondered what it would be like to go hunting, then decided it wouldn't be something she liked. Directing her thoughts to something more to her liking, she wondered what it would be like to shoot Huntly. Now *that* was something to think about. Drumming her fingers on the table, she asked her mother just how much longer they would be staying here at Dunford.

The duchess, who was spreading marmalade thickly over the top half of her scone, paused and looked at Annabella strangely. "A week, Bella. Our original plan was to stay one week. I've told you that at least ten times."

"I know, but I kept hoping you and Papa would change your minds. I wish we were leaving sooner."

"Bella, for heaven's sake. We can't go dashing about the Scottish countryside the way we do the streets of London. Travel here takes time, and that means we must linger for at least a little while at each destination before we take off again. One does not tour Scotland in the same manner one looks over the latest fabrics at Madame Toussard's Dress Shop."

Annabella's expression turned even more woeful. "Just the same, I wish we were leaving. I find this place excruciatingly boring."

The duchess patted her hand. "I would imagine you are

bored because you sit around moping most of the time. Why don't you go for a walk? It's lovely outside this time of the morning."

"A walk," repeated Bella. "You think a walk will cure anything." Bella rose to her feet. "Fudge and stuff. I wouldn't be surprised if you recommended a walk to a dying man." She looked at her mother with pleading eyes and a lip that seemed bent upon trembling. With a voice heavy with dramatic overtones, she said, "There are some things that a walk cannot cure, and a broken heart is one of them."

With that, she ran from the room.

Gavin, who was just entering, found himself flattened against the wall. He watched Annabella until she disappeared, then exchanged glances with his mother.

"If you've come in here to visit, sit down," the duchess said, spreading one last lump of marmalade. "If you came in here to ask me what's wrong with your sister . . . don't. I gave up trying to figure out a young woman's mind after the second girl."

"Today is Thursday," Gavin said, giving his mother a sly grin. "I think Thursday is Bella's day to be cross."

"Every day is her day to be cross of late. I don't understand how I could have nurtured that child all these years only to discover I don't know her," the duchess said, her curled hair bobbing backwards and forwards. "Where did she learn such disobedience?" she asked. Then, with a sigh of resignation, she answered, "From my side of the family."

"It isn't just disobedience. She doesn't want to marry Huntly, Mama. Surely you know that?"

Tears sprang to his mother's eyes as she began fishing beneath her sleeve for her handkerchief. "Of course I know it," she wailed. "I just don't know what to do about it. I've tried everything I can think of to get her excited about the wedding, but nothing I do seems to interest her. I never thought she would persist this long. If she doesn't come around soon, I don't know what I'll do."

Lady Anne went on to impress upon Gavin the strain she was under, always trying to appear cheerful and happy when her heart was breaking over the sadness of her daughter. "It isn't easy being a mother, you know." She was sobbing now. "I don't know how God could have been so careful to put mothers in charge of everyone else's happiness, only to forget to put any one in charge of theirs."

"Have you talked to Father?"

"Your father is a dear man," she wailed, sobbing harder. "But sometimes he can be a complete unfeeling man."

While Gavin listened to the duchess, Annabella went outside for that walk her mother was so fond of suggesting. After an hour, she could hardly say her spirits were elevated, but her mood had mellowed somewhat.

She sat for a moment upon a garden bench, thinking of her home in England, of cowslips and gillyflowers, feeling she had picked a bouquet of them, and now they would never grow again. She walked for a while along the winding path bordered with rue and thistle but caught a scent of bay rum as it drifted over the hedge. She heard the crunch of gravel and started to peek through an opening in the shrub, but decided not to. She knew who walked on the other side. She knew the two paths came together just ahead, so she turned away, not wanting Ross to see her.

She stopped by the stables and looked through the fence, watching Lord Percival and the duke fussing over a new spindly legged colt trying to stand, but even there she felt left out.

Turning away from the paddock, a field of haystacks and fat curly sheep caught her eye and she headed in their direction. The sheep eyed her with curious interest as she approached, but soon they lost interest and went back to grazing. She stepped over a ramble of stones where the fence was falling down trying to decide if she was going to risk sitting on the tumbledown fence and ruining her skirts, or continue to stand. Lost in thought, she did not hear the cadence of approaching footsteps, but she caught again the scent of bay rum.

"If it's lost sheep you're looking for, I'm afraid these already belong to someone."

She turned around, her surprised look settling on him. Ross stopped beside her, bracing one leg on the low fence, resting his arms on his knees. He was standing close—too close—and she wondered if he could hear the frantic beat of a heart that felt too wild to be contained inside her chest. She wanted to say something, anything, to break the tension of silence that stretched to the point of snapping. She wanted to turn and run. She would have left then, if he had not turned to look at her, stopping her with a gaze so intent it held her immobile and just a little frightened.

He lifted his hand, touching her cheek with one finger. "I've never known anyone with just one dimple."

A cold shiver fluttered the length of her body. She wasn't certain if it was because of his touch or the lazy way his eyes seemed to glide over her face. "You still don't. It isn't a dimple."

"No?"

"It's a scar."

He cupped her cheek and lifted her head into the light to study the line of her jaw. A faint white scar ran along her jawbone from her ear almost to her mouth, where it curved upward, ending in a dimple. He looked at the other cheek, studying its perfect symmetry, its perfection, unmarred like its counterpart. "A scar," he said at last, still somewhat amazed that he hadn't noticed it before, "but an old one."

"Yes. Quite old."

"How old were you?"

"Barely five."

"You were hit?"

"No."

"A riding accident?"

She nodded.

"Were you going over jumps?"

She laughed. "Nothing so glamorous as that. It was my sister's pony—a fat, tame little thing with an unruly mane and a fondness for apples."

He smiled. "No cart?"

"No." Even short, simple words were difficult, the moisture sucking at her throat, the words seeming to drain her of precious breath.

"Were you thrown?"

She laughed again. "You seem to be persistent in wanting this to be something it is not. There was nothing so noble about it. I wasn't thrown. I fell off. My sister was leading me around the stable yard at our country house in Maidstone when a dog frightened the pony and he ran away with me. I lost my balance and fell. I hit the side of my head on a plow. One of the chisels went through my cheek."

She understood then that she ought to have left when she had the chance. Somehow he had chased away the doldrums and made her forget her shyness around men. Perhaps she should go now, but she told herself it was too late to turn and run. Indecision made her lower her head. He slipped his forefinger beneath her chin and lifted her face into the sunlight.

He looked at her face again, seeing the smooth skin, the

faintly visible scar. There were none of the telltale signs of such a nasty wound as she described: no gouged skin, no proud flesh, no puckered scar, nothing but a lovely dimple he wanted to kiss. "It healed remarkably well. You must've had one helluva surgeon."

She laughed, and he noticed how the dimple went deeper. "I did. My grandmother."

"Your grandmother? She sewed your face?"

"Yes. She said she wasn't going to wait for that old drunk in town to butcher my face. Later my mother told me that my grandmother knew it would have been too swollen by the time the doctor arrived, and my grandmother was an excellent seamstress. I've been told I had the most beautifully crosshatched jawbone in all of England."

"And now," he said, "you have simply the most beautiful one."

She turned her head away. "I wish you wouldn't talk to me like that."

"All women like to be talked to that way."

She lifted her chin, determined that he was not going to work his way into her affections any more than he already had. "All other women perhaps, but *I* don't like it."

"At least you came to *that* conclusion on your own."

A breeze seemed to come out of nowhere, whisking across the hayfield and swirling bits of chaff and straw, then, losing some of its bluster, left as silently as it had come. Over the fence, two ewes seemed to be having a disagreement, and down by the barn a cat howled as if someone had stepped on its tail. Her senses seemed more acute now—for awareness was all around her.

"You aren't a lass who can think for herself. That must make your life seem awfully dull."

"The only thing I find dull is standing here talking to you."

Suddenly he was close enough to put his hands on her shoulders. He was right. She couldn't think. With him standing as close as he was, with his big hands upon her, she found she couldn't breathe either. As she had always done, she tried to reason her way out of an uncomfortable situation. *There is no reason for a grown woman like you to tremble like a frightened child, simply because a man has his hands on your shoulders.* As far as relief went, that didn't do much good. She knew she must look like a thickwit standing here blushing and tripping over her words.

All her turmoil was on the inside; outwardly she stood quiet and still under the weight of his hands, knowing deep within her that she should be putting up some sort of resistance, even if it were a token one. He was so different, so much more straightforward than anyone she had ever known. He had a way of slicing right through the codes of polite conduct to where the barest of facts lay. She had never known anyone who talked as he did—the way one thought. Thoughts were private things, things to be tempered by convention and etiquette and rearranged into carefully chosen speech. This man was raw. And basic. And very disturbing. She wondered if he could read her thoughts.

She could not keep from looking at him, at the well-tanned face, the teasing light in his eyes, the mouth that smiled at the slightest urging. He had said she did not think for herself, and she wondered how he had noticed her lack of courage so quickly. She felt ashamed that her lack of backbone was so obvious.

"There's no need for you to be brooding over what I said. It's easy enough to learn to think for yourself. It's like anything else. You have to want it bad enough to reach out and take it. No one will hand it to you."

"I'm not brooding," she said shortly.

"You're brooding, all right. I've seen that look enough. Most of the somber, bitter women in the world start out just like you. You're getting that pinched look on your face already. Give you a few years and your nose will be touching your chin."

Stunned, she simply stood there, unable to speak. He had caught her off guard. She had assumed that because of the trouble he had gone to be with her, he would not sink so low as to speak as he had. It was one thing to be cut to the quick, and quite another to be caught unprepared. Because of the unexpectedness of it, the wound seemed to bleed more profusely.

Perhaps what really hurt was her deep sorrow at knowing her future even before hearing his cruel prophecy. Since the announcement of her betrothal her life had looked as barren and unpromising as a peat bog. And now his crude and callous reminder of her bleak future, her spinelessness, only served to suggest to her that she had been a fool to enjoy his attention, and to pretend for a moment of insanity that her life was any different from what it was, or to think foolishly that she was the same happy girl she had been a few months ago. It all served to tell her that she had absolutely no business standing here with this man. No business at all.

"Don't cloud up and rain on me now," he said. "Are you so accustomed to being coddled and protected that you dissolve into tears the moment someone is honest with you?"

"I am not crying."

"Maybe not, but you will be soon enough, I'll wager."

"You might wait until one is guilty of the crime before you heap on your accusations."

"I only said that to warm you up a little bit, to see if you had any spirit left in you at all. It's hard to tell—you're wearing such a cross look."

"I am not cross!" she said, surprising herself by showing more spirit than even she knew she possessed. "And I don't cry when someone is being honest. I admire honesty. What I don't admire is cheeky rudeness. The way you talk, anyone would think I didn't have a brain—or a backbone—which is not the case. I am smart enough not to allow such blatant disregard for a person's feelings to pass for polite behavior. If I seem strange, perhaps there's another reason. You shocked me, that's all."

He didn't look like he believed that for a minute.

"I'll do more than shock you before it's all over," he said, with a look that seemed to strip away the layers of pretense and denial and go right to the core, which was, as they both knew, the simple fact of his being a man and her being a woman and both of them having more than a passing interest in each other. She would rather have been anyplace else at this moment, other than the place she was. Mortification set in. How could she bear to look at herself in the mirror ever again? Her cheeks, she knew, were blazing. Her heart pounded oddly, against the confines of her head. She felt herself fighting for breath.

"There's no need to stand there panting like a lizard on a hot rock," he said. "It won't change anything, and it will only serve to ruin the rest of your day."

His words shot along her backbone and made her shoulders pinch. "Does everyone in Texas talk the way you do?"

"I don't know. How do I talk?"

"Well your speech—besides being odd, is . . . What I'm trying to say is you don't make any sense."

He looked at her for a moment as if he was considering something; then he laughed.

"It's a good thing I'm betrothed. We would never suit."

If he was surprised, he didn't let on. "Why not?"

"We're just too different."

"In what way?" He grinned and looked her over good and proper. "I mean, besides in the obvious ways a man is different from a woman."

"I know what you meant. You don't have to carve it in stone. I'm not *that* thick-witted. Perhaps an analogy would be more appropriate. You *do* understand gardening, don't you?"

He was really grinning now. "You mean planting all those little seeds that turn into squash, turnips, and pumpkins?" he said with flaming exaggeration.

"The plague take you," she said, her nose going up a notch. "I was thinking more in terms of *horticulture*."

"Go on. I'll do my best to follow."

"I come from a world quite different from yours. I'm like a plant that is part of an enormous concept; one that is planted at the proper time, in the proper place; one that will make up a small part of a very orderly and well-maintained garden. I've been watched over, fertilized, watered, and given the exact amounts of sunshine and pruning, always nurtured and protected from the elements. I grow and mature and blossom, but always within the confines of my garden. But you—you're like a weed whose seed is dropped along the wayside and begins to sprout on its own, growing in a crack in a crumbling wall. When you bloom, your seedpods are scattered by the wind. You have no home, just as you have no purpose."

"Perhaps you're right, Lady Annabella, but I do have something you don't have. I have a taste of reality, of what life and the world is all about, while you haven't really lived at all."

"That isn't true."

"Isn't it?"

The tension between them stretched dangerously. "No, of course it isn't." *Don't look at me like that. You don't know what it does to me.*

But I do know. It's the same thing your look does to me. "I think it is true, and I'll prove it to you."

This had to stop. Things could not go on like this. Somewhat stunned and motionless, Annabella stared at him as he closed his eyes and inhaled deeply. When he opened them, he looked at her. "Look around you. Take as long as you wish, then tell me what you see."

She looked at him in a puzzled way, her head tilted to one side. She cast a quick look around their surroundings, coming swiftly back to him. "I see the countryside."

"Worse than I thought," he said. "Lass, you need help." He stepped closer. "Turn around. Go on. I won't hurt you."

"That's what our cook says everytime she hides the meat cleaver behind her back and goes after a chicken."

He laughed, and she cast a speculative look at him and then turned around, feeling his hands slip over her eyes. "Now, tell me what you just saw."

I saw you. Only you. "I told you. I saw the countryside."

"Could you be more descriptive?"

"Could you be more vague?"

He laughed. "I'm not being vague. I asked for a description. Tell me what you saw. What *kind* of countryside."

"I saw the *Scottish* countryside. *In bloody daylight.*"

"Pretend I've never been to Scotland and you're describing it to me. You can't say it looks like *the Scottish country-side*, since I don't know what the Scottish countryside looks like. Describe it to me."

"It looks just like any other countryside. The earth is brown and green, the sky is blue and white. There are trees and water. What are you doing? This is silly. Take your hands away."

He dropped them. "You still won't see anything."

"You don't make any sense at all. I don't know why I'm wasting my time talking to you."

"Because you like me better than you let on. Because you like all this attention I'm giving you. Because you know you don't want to marry Huntly. Because you *do* want to stand here with me. But enough of that for now," he said. "How would you like it, Annabella, if someone asked me what you looked like and my answer was, *She looks like any other woman. She has long hair and two eyes and two arms and the same number of legs.* Would that be an adequate description of you, do you think?"

His words had a sobering effect upon her, but she forced herself to laugh. "I would hope I make more of an impression than that."

"Yet that's just what you've done. One day you're going to see the earth isn't green and brown at all, and the sky isn't blue and white, and that there is more around you than trees and water. You can't see it now, because you've been taught to see the world through someone else's eyes, but one day . . . One day you'll know, and when you do, your life won't ever be the same."

She started to say something, but he silenced her with his finger across her lips. "Don't say anything. Not now. It's too soon, I think—too soon for you to really understand. You've a way to go, lass. You must learn to walk before you can expect to run." He chuckled and rubbed his thumb over the creasing frown between her eyes. "Don't fash yourself over all this newfound knowledge. We've time. There'll be no hurrying for us. Not with anything."

He waited, feeling the tension of indecision in her small body. Would she trust him enough to let go and ease up a little, or would she panic and sashay away? He leaned closer and whispered, "I know what you're thinking: Trust everybody, but lock your door. Is that right?"

He felt the way her laugh made her relax. "You're close," she said, allowing the tightly held muscles to relax. "You did this on purpose, didn't you?"

"Did what on purpose?" he asked innocently. "Offered you a little friendly conversation?"

"Words like scruples or honor aren't even in your vocabulary. You came over here like a biscuit buttered on both sides, and don't you try to deny it. You know I'm betrothed, yet you intentionally set out to be forward with me." *Please stop this.*

I can't.

I'm promised to another.

I don't care. You don't love him.

I don't love you either.

No, but you damn well could.

Stay away from me, do you hear. Stay far away.

"Now would I do such an unchivalrous thing as slinking around like a biscuit buttered on both sides?"

"Yes. You would . . . you did."

"When a man's caught, he's caught." He held up his arms in surrender. "I plead guilty as charged," he said, leaning over to whisper the words in her ear. He didn't stop there— but kissed the curve of her cheek, more quickly than the flutter of her pulse.

"Stop that!" she said, pushing him away. "I wasn't raised to display my affections publicly."

"That's fine with me, sweetheart. I'd rather do it in private anyway."

There was no way to win against this man. It was useless to try. She didn't say anything else.

He didn't want to spoil the sense of tranquillity that existed between them, so he was content to take her arm and lead her along the narrow path that followed the stone fence. He wondered if she felt it too, this easy, relaxed state they seemed to have settled into.

He needn't have wondered. She had noticed it, and that prompted her to put an end to it by asking, "Where are we going?"

"Where would you like to go?"

"Back to England," she said quickly.

"On foot?"

With sublime effort, Annabella tried not to laugh, but it was hopeless. "I would ride on a broom if it would get me there," she said.

He laughed. "It seems I'm always having to ask you for a second choice. England is out, I'm afraid. Would you settle for a short stroll around the grounds of Dunford in its stead?"

That drew her up short. Indecision settled like a mask over her face.

"I don't suppose your nanny or governess ever instructed you on the proper behavior in a situation such as this, did she?"

As he said this, he leaned low, his words carried on the current of his warm breath that teased her senses. The gall of the man was unbelievable. Now his bloody chin was resting on her shoulder. What familiarity. What impertinence.

What uncouth ruffians these Texans must be. But in spite of his tacky, flashy ways and crude behavior, his disturbing nearness seemed to wipe all thought of propriety and convention from her mind, while at the same time robbing her of her natural rhythm of breathing.

Nothing, absolutely nothing had prepared her for the utter and complete chaos that was going on inside her. Nothing was functioning properly and nothing was in its proper place. Her heart seemed to be everywhere it wasn't, for why else could she feel it pounding in her temples and throbbing in her throat? And what were these flutters that felt as if she'd swallowed a flotilla of agitated butterflies?

There was certainly no sound reason for what was happening here. Why would a respectable woman feel such fluttering and timorous excitement over the simple matter of taking a stroll in broad daylight? She was behaving like a true cabbagehead, all stammering confusion at the mere closeness of a member of the opposite gender. She had been schooled in the many manifestations of polite conversation, including those with members of the opposite *s-e-x.* So why was she at such a loss of dignity and self-possession?

Although he was no longer whispering to her, his face was dangerously close to her ear, doing she knew not what, but whatever it was he was about, *he* knew what he was doing, for she was certain it was no accident that he could do such remarkable-feeling things with nothing but his nose.

Stupid as it might sound, and indeed it did sound stupid, the man *was* using his nose. Right this minute he was nuzzling her with it. And what was worse, she liked it. God's eyelashes! Was she daft? Here she was, walking quietly along, enduring his touch, knowing as she did that she should protest the familiar way he was putting his hand (or nose, as the case may be) against her person with such disregard for propriety and for her position as a betrothed woman. She was doing her best to compile a mental list of reasons why she should not be strolling about the grounds of Dunford Castle with this man, but by the time she got to number four, he nuzzled her again, and she forgot points one, two, and three.

It was no use.

At last she decided to make the most of it, unaware that Ross knew the exact moment she gave in. His pleasure in being with her no matter how unpleasant she tried to be was slowly transformed into a sense of complete and utter peace. They walked along like this for some time, neither of them speaking, both of them feeling they had so much to say.

At last he said in a soft, subdued tone, "One of these days we'll tell our grandchildren about this day and then we'll look back upon it and laugh."

Annabella almost fell over her own feet. *God's breath! I just met the man and now he has us with grandchildren. I really must avoid this man. He's not just dangerous, he's a bloody idiot!* "Were you dropped on your head a lot when you were a child?"

"I don't think so."

"How about trees? Did you fall out of many?"

"Not that I recollect."

She stopped and looked at him, square and straight in the face. "Then you really are crazy, aren't you?"

He tapped her on the nose. "Over you, lass. I thought you knew that."

She was prepared for almost anything but that confession and the look he gave her. His face was relaxed, his mouth slightly uplifted, his eyes as calm and blue as a Highland loch, and she felt the strength of his words penetrate her heart and she knew she would have to take extra precautions never to be alone with this man again.

His arm was draped lightly across her back, his hand relaxed against her hip. Her mother had warned her against men like him, and she wasn't foolish enough to allow him such privilege. She reached down to pick up his hand and transfer it elsewhere, only she wasn't sure just where to put it, for every place he touched her wreaked havoc.

You can't leave his hand there, she reminded herself. Taking his hand in hers, she paused a moment, reflective. She had never held hands with a man before, never had an opportunity to judge the weight and texture of a masculine hand. What was it about *this* hand that made her shiver at its touch? What secrets did this hand hold? What delights was it capable of?

Pulling her thoughts back to what she was about, she dropped his hand away from her body, increasing the tempo of her step, hoping to pull away from him.

A moment later his hand was back on her hip.

She pushed it away.

He put it back.

This time she left it there.

He began to rub her just above the waist with the back of his thumb. She ignored it. He became a little more daring, moving his hand up over her ribs as if they were stairsteps. Now it was dangerously close to her breast. She ignored that as well.

"Why don't you put up more of a fight?" he asked after a period of extended silence. "Has that family of yours destroyed your sense of value completely? You know I came to you *well buttered* and on purpose, yet you put up no more than a token display of annoyance. Why aren't you curious?

Why aren't you asking me what I hope to gain by picking at you and putting my hands on you? Why haven't you slapped my face or shoved me over this stone fence? Where are the words of displeasure, even hate, that you should be hitting me with? What would I have to do, I wonder, before you reacted and stood up for yourself?"

She had never felt so close to crying. She had never been more determined not to. She might not be up to shoving him over the fence, but she wouldn't let him see how hurt she was.

"I don't know how anyone can stand to be around you," she said. "Did they run you out of Texas? Is that why you came to Scotland?"

"Not too bad," he said, "for a beginner, but you lack conviction. Is that the best you can do?"

"You are an insufferable swine, sir!"

"Better, but you had to go and ruin it. You were doing pretty good before you softened it with the 'sir.' You don't curse a man with kindness, lass. You should box my ears, or at least give me your coldest stare. Another one to try would be gritting your teeth, or throwing something. That way I'd know without a doubt just how much you really do loathe me," he said.

"I don't grit my teeth, and I'd be afraid to throw something for fear it would be something I liked. Then where would I be? You would still be as obnoxious as ever and I would only be angrier because I had broken something valuable. I'm afraid I'm destined to be a milksop," she said.

He laughed. "I don't suppose that is all bad. You're too warmhearted to give anyone a cold stare. You have the damndest eyes, you know that?"

She did not respond.

Ross sighed and leaned closer. "Annabella?" he whispered, his breath coming warm and soft across her skin.

Annabella parted her lips in breathy surprise. She didn't speak. She didn't move. A strand of damp hair fell in her face and she pushed it away. When at last she spoke, she chose her words carefully. "If you would kindly leave me alone, I should like to walk the rest of the way by myself. That *is* why I came out here."

They stood there for a moment in complete and utter silence. Nothing stirred: Even the sheep in the pasture seemed to know what was expected of them, and the trees around them seemed as stiff and expectant as the mist that began to creep slowly across the heath. The air seemed heavy and chill, hanging motionless all about them. The silence was foreboding and she felt a sense of dread as if she had been given a chance for a reprieve and she had failed to take it—a stupid idea really, since there was nothing even this man could do to save her.

How odd that she wanted to tell him about the strange, unexplainable sentiments she was feeling, wanted desperately to talk to someone who would understand the sadness she felt over meeting a man like him when it was too late.

They came around a turn in the path and saw Gavin coming toward them.

"The devil take you," he said. "I've been looking all over for you."

Annabella didn't say a word.

"It'll take her a minute to warm up to conversation," Ross said. "She's too busy enjoying her suffering at the moment."

"Don't be deceived by him," Annabella said. "He is not as funny as he thinks."

Gavin grinned at Ross. "I'm sorry to see you've been

strolling with such an ungrateful member of the Stewart family. It isn't like Bella to be so cross."

"It's my fault," Ross said. "I'm afraid I teased her a bit too much. She'll take a few days to get over the soreness of it. It'll be a while before I hear any thanks from her."

"A cold day in Hades is what it will be," Annabella said, walking away.

Gavin glanced at his sister just as she went through the door and closed it. "Is that what's really wrong with her?"

"I'm afraid so. I rubbed her fur the wrong way and set her teeth on edge."

"Well, she'll come around soon enough. Annabella is a forgiving sort."

"Too forgiving," Ross said, and started walking toward the house. Gavin followed. "How long has your sister been betrothed to Huntly?"

"Not long enough for him to gain her sympathies. She doesn't care for the man."

Ross gave him a steady look, then opened the door. "And you blame her?"

"Hardly. Oh, I suppose he's all right in his proper place."

"And what place is that?"

"Here in Scotland, with me in England. And not betrothed to my sister."

"Your parents seem in favor of the match. Why didn't they settle on an Englishman for her?"

"Annabella has to marry a Scot. It was in the betrothal contract of my parents—something about the youngest daughter having to be pledged to a Scot."

"Even so, it seems Huntly couldn't have been the best of the lot. He's old enough to be her father."

"He's a very well-respected man."

"In English circles, perhaps. Here in Scotland, a man's

family name will carry him just so far and then it's up to him."

Gavin looked thoughtful. "You seem to be displaying more than a passing interest in all of this. Why?"

"I plan to marry the lass," Ross said.

For some reason, Gavin didn't look surprised. "A betrothal is binding and cannot be broken, except in rare instances when both parties give consent. How do you plan on overcoming that?"

They were in the kitchen now, which was deserted at this time of day. Ross sat down at the table and stretched out his legs. "I'd be a fool to tell you that, now wouldn't I?"

Gavin grinned. "Oh, I don't know. Persuaded, I could be a strong ally."

"Angered, you could be a formidable foe," Ross stated flatly.

"True, but there are times that I think I'd sooner see Annabella a spinster than to see her wed to Huntly."

"It's a hellish choice no lass should be forced to make."

"Well," Gavin said with a laugh, "perhaps you'll succeed and then she won't have to."

"Perhaps I will," said Ross. "I certainly intend to try."

Gavin sat down across the table from Ross, arms braced as he leaned forward and whispered, "Do you think we stand a chance of stopping this betrothal?"

Surprised, Ross looked intently at the man he had heretofore considered his foe. "We?" he asked. "I don't remember cutting you in."

The smiling countenance that stared back at him was all friend. "I'm in," Gavin said. "Do we?"

"Aye," Ross said. "As long as I'm breathing, we stand a chance."

"As long as we're both breathing," Gavin corrected. "You're going to need me on your side, you know."

"I won't turn down the offer," Ross said.

"Good. As my father says, *the tongue of a wise man lies behind his heart.*"

Ross shrugged. "Who knows? They say the heart is half prophet."

Chapter

12

"Where is everybody?" asked Annabella.

It was half-past eight the next morning when Annabella paused at the door of the dining room and saw her mother sitting alone at the long, mahogany table. The duchess glanced up as Annabella entered the cheerful room.

Actually, *cheerful* wasn't really Annabella's choice of a word to describe the dining room, but her mother's. Annabella's choice was *optimistic*. Now, some people might think a room could not be perceived as being optimistic, but that didn't bother Annabella, for there were times when she was blissfully unconscious of convention—at least *mental* convention.

It was a way she had of escaping the rigid expectations she had lived with all her life, a way to elude for a time the dictates of such matters as decorum, propriety, and etiquette. Her life might be crammed with restrictions, but there were no such restrictions in her head. There, she was blessedly free to think at will. And one of the results of all this freethinking was her tendency to characterize rooms—

and the Dunford dining room, with its half-circle bay and floor-to-ceiling sash windows was, in her opinion, optimistic. Perhaps that was due in part to the brocade drapes of the brightest shade of deep gold, which were always tied back in the morning to let in the most mellow shafts of amber sunlight.

Annabella's gaze lingered on the lovely room as her shoes tapped out a solitary message across the glossy wooden floors, the staccato tones disappearing the moment she reached the Persian rug. "This place is as deserted as a tomb. I never knew a house could be so quiet."

"And much more pleasant because of it," said her mother.

The dining room was a collage of distractions that Annabella would have delighted in at any time less fraught with destiny. But this morning she paused at the sideboard and gave the hand-painted Chinese paper—*bird and flower pattern*—a glance. The glance was a hasty one, but long enough to form an opinion. The birds, she decided she did not like, and without further thought on the subject, she removed the lid of the first silver serving dish, stepping back when a column of cloying steam rose from the traditional Scottish dish of herring in oatmeal.

She stared at the herring, deciding it didn't look any better than it smelled, and clapped down the lid. Remembering the words of Samuel Johnson, *"Oats and grain, which in England is generally given to horses . . . in Scotland supports the people,"* she found yet another English way she preferred to that of the Scots. She wasn't sure she would ever become accustomed to some of these favored Scottish dishes.

With much less enthusiasm, she removed the next lid and found Aberdeen butteries, which faintly resembled her own

English scones but were not as tasty by half. But she was hungry, so she took one.

"Your father and Gavin have gone to Edinburgh."

She dropped the butterie and turned to stare at her mother. "To Edinburgh? I thought we were *all* going to Edinburgh."

"Your father decided the trip would be too rushed and too hectic for us, and they could make better time going on horseback instead of in the carriage. I suspect he knew we would be more comfortable here."

Annabella picked up the butterie, placing it on her plate, and removed the next lid, finding Scotch woodcock, a seasoned scrambled egg placed on buttered toast and topped with an anchovy and two capers.

"But I'm not comfortable here," she said, taking a serving of the woodcock, then replacing the lid. "I'm ready to leave."

The duchess looked a trifle disturbed. "Annabella, I am sorely vexed to see your mind so ruffled and discomposed. I had hoped that you would warm to the idea of marriage, ere now."

"Well, I haven't, but that isn't the reason I'm so uncomfortable here—at least now that Lord Huntly is gone." She carried her plate to the table and took a seat across from her mother. "When are we leaving here? I want to go home— back to England."

The duchess sighed and stirred her tea, placing the spoon in the delicate saucer with a *clink.* "I know you do, Bella, but your father feels it would be best for you to remain in Scotland."

"For how long?"

"Until the wedding, I'm afraid."

The first wave of agonizing homesickness hit her and she

gave her mother a dismal look. "And you? How do you feel, Mother?" She asked the question, but she knew the answer. Overwhelmed with despair, she was feeling she had been deserted by everyone, even her mother.

"You know I want you to come back home, but I must agree with your father's decision."

If possible, Annabella felt more depressed than before. "But why? Why must I stay here until the wedding? What could it possibly hurt for me to go home one last time?"

"Because Scotland will be your home—*is* your home now. Returning to England would only make it more difficult to leave a second time."

Annabella felt tears burn the back of her eyes and knew a flood of tears would have come if she hadn't been in the presence of her mother. *Never return home? Never see England again?* "You mean I am to be married *here?*"

"Your father deems it best." Seeing her daughter on the verge of tears, the duchess said, "Try to look on the bright side, Bella. There are so many lovely places to be married here in Scotland. Why, you could be married in the same kirk your father and I married in, if you like. All of our family and friends from England would attend. It isn't as if you would be surrounded by strangers."

But that was exactly how Annabella felt: surrounded by strangers. Even her own parents seemed strangers to her now. And how else could she feel, for it seemed even they had turned against her. Grief welled inside her. For all her life she had done her dutiful best to be a loving, obedient daughter, never giving her parents a moment of grief, always striving to be what they expected and wanted her to be, even above what she, herself, wanted. *Why must it always be this way? Why must I always sacrifice what I feel, what I want, in order to comply with what my parents want?*

Annabella was hurt and confused. She knew her parents loved her dearly—there was no doubt of that—but they always wanted her to live up to their expectations. Why was having her parents' approval so important to her? Why did she always have to give up part of herself to please others? Perhaps it was too late to ask this question now. She had been this way, had been this other person for so long, she wasn't sure the real Annabella existed anymore. She felt she had lost everything: Her parents. Her home. Even herself.

For a moment Annabella didn't say anything. She had an odd, newly awakened consciousness of a wrongness in her life. Her heart began pounding as the scene of a few days ago flashed back into her mind as vividly as if it were just happening. She had been talking to Ross, down by the loch, the night of the ball. He had asked her:

"What else have you missed out on?"

"I haven't missed anything. I have been very well educated, for a lady, you might say. I draw and paint, and I'll have you know I've been thoroughly drilled in the deportment that becomes a gentlewoman."

"Oh, I'm sure you have been thoroughly drilled. It's obvious with every rigid little step you take. Don't you ever loosen up?"

Suddenly Annabella felt the most scalding anger she had ever known surge into her heart. Her parents had betrayed her, thrown her to the wolves. "You must hate me very much to do this to me," she said, trying her best to speak slowly and calmly.

The duchess wasn't at all prepared for the severity of this mental jolt, and it showed in her expression. "Why, Annabella, how can you say such a thing? You know your father and I care as much for you as for your sisters."

"But you let them marry Englishmen."

"We've been through all of this before, Bella."

"I know, and it's never been resolved. I can't marry Lord Huntly, Mother. Please don't make me. I won't ever give you a moment of trouble. I'll never ask to marry anyone. I'll be a spinster. I'll stay in my room for the rest of my life. I'll do anything." She paused for a breath. "I'll go to America."

"You needn't wring your hands and beg, Bella. You will marry Lord Huntly," said the duchess angrily. "It's already been decided. I, like you, have no say in the matter. Your father has arranged for you to marry Huntly, and *that's* what you will do."

Annabella realized the futility of pleading further with her mother. The duchess wouldn't be swayed any more than her father. Annabella's anxiety, her misery, welled up within her, and with a helpless shriek she leaped up from the table and fled the room, running up the stairs.

Lord Percival had just returned from a ride with Ross. He had planned on leaving in a few days to return to his home in England, but at the old duke's urging, he decided to stay on a bit longer. He had reached that decision only this morning and was on his way to inform His Grace when he happened to see Annabella dash up the stairs.

Poking his head into the dining room to see what all the ruckus was about, Lord Percival was almost run down by the duchess, who was hot on her daughter's trail.

"Honestly," she said, "I don't know what has come over that child of late. It's a blessing in her favor that her father isn't here to witness this, but I'm of half a mind to tell him everything that's happened here this morning. Indeed I am." Without further ado, she rushed up the stairs, moving as if someone had set her skirts afire. A moment later Annabella's door was slammed.

Lord Percival shook his head. *Women,* he said to himself. *Who can understand them?*

Upstairs, the duchess was pondering just what she ought to do about the scene that had just transpired. With great severity, she said, "By the wife of Job, I don't know what ails you, Bella. Now you come back downstairs and eat your breakfast and stop all this wailing before you make yourself sick."

Bella raised her tear-stained face and looked at her mother. "I shall never eat again. My heart is too full of sorrow."

The duchess felt her face twitch. She forced back a smile. "Well, you needn't bother your heart. The food goes in your stomach. Now, do come back."

"I can't. Besides, it isn't even a decent English breakfast."

"But I thought you liked woodcock."

"I suppose I do, at times—but today isn't one of them. I couldn't possibly eat it now, not when I'm suffering from an affliction."

"An affliction?" Lady Anne repeated, feeling some of the steam go out of her.

"Yes," Bella said. "The most woeful kind."

Her lips twitching, Lady Anne said, "And what kind is that?"

"Being handed over to the enemy by my parents. When I've met someone else I like ever so much better."

That simply floored the duchess. "Annabella, what on earth are you talking about? Whom could you have possibly met that . . ." Sudden understanding dawned. "Oh, dear," she said, shaking her head. "Quite the most horrid . . . Oh, I do wish your father were here."

Annabella raised her head. "Well, I, for one, am glad he's not."

But her mother wasn't listening. Moving to the side of the bed, she patted Annabella's head. "I must do some thinking on this," she said. "You try and get some rest. We'll talk again later."

Annabella lay there for what seemed an eternity after her mother left, but it was useless. She couldn't sleep. She didn't want to eat. All she could do was lie there and think about Lord Huntly and how much he resembled his King Charles spaniels. It couldn't have been worse if she'd been forced to marry one of them.

Needing some time alone and out of doors, she left her room and went downstairs to take one of her mother's fortifying walks. Seeking solace in the garden, she sat upon a cold, hard bench carved from stone, which was surrounded by catmint, lady's mantle, and clematis. She had been sitting there for over an hour when her mother joined her.

"I know it's hard," Lady Anne said, taking Annabella's hand in her own, "and difficult to understand our ways and our reasons for doing the things we do, but please believe me when I say, we do love you, Bella. Dearly. Your father means well—as do I. I know our ways aren't always right, Bella, and all I can say in our defense is, all our mistakes are well thought out." Seeing the incredulous look upon Annabella's young, tear-streaked face, Lady Anne said, "You probably won't understand this until you have children of your own."

"I won't ever have children of my own, for I shan't ever marry."

"You will."

"I shan't. I'll be dead of a broken heart, ere long. I know I will."

The duchess put her arms around her daughter, stroking her dark glossy head. "You've always been such a delightful child, Bella, so considerate, so mindful, always trying so hard to please. I never thought you might be unhappy."

"Well, I am. I feel so miserable. And I hate it. I hate feeling this way. I hate growing up. I hate the thought of leaving home, yet I don't want to stay there for the rest of my life, either." She doubled up her fists and pounded her lap in frustration. "Oh, I don't know what I want," she said, looking at her mother. "But I do know what I *don't* want."

"What is that, dear?"

"I don't want to marry anybody—*ever*. And I *especially* don't want to live in Scotland."

"I know. I felt the same way when I was your age and had to leave Scotland and live in a horrid place like England." Anne smiled at the stricken face looking so earnestly at her. "It's true," she said, wiping the tears from Bella's cheeks with her handkerchief. "I told my father I would rather become a nun than marry an Englishman and live in England."

"What did he say?"

"He said I was being ridiculous, that I of all people should know good Presbyterians did not become nuns."

"So you became a martyr instead."

The duchess laughed. "Hardly that. I grew to love your father and that wretched place he called home, just as you will. Time, Bella. All it takes is time."

Something I don't have, Annabella thought. *Not with that pestiferous grandson of the duke's accosting me at every turn. And making me wish he would catch me,* her tormented mind reminded her. Pulling her thoughts away from Ross Mackinnon, Annabella said, "Has a date for the wedding been set?"

"No. Your father feels you should remain in Scotland for at least a year before the wedding. That will give you time to know Lord Huntly a little better, to understand Scotland and the Scottish ways, and become more settled with the idea of living here."

"But where will we live for a whole year?" Annabella asked, noticing the way her mother looked suddenly tense and a bit anxious.

"Mother, you aren't going to leave me *here*, are you? Alone?"

The duchess looked a bit guilty. "We can't stay here for much longer. Your father must get back to England, so he was thinking of taking your uncle Colin up on his invitation to have you stay with them."

"I see," Annabella said, suddenly feeling too distraught even to cry. Her whole world had shattered right before her eyes and lay glittering and fragmented at her feet. Her sense of betrayal was great. She felt she didn't have a friend in the world.

Understanding her despair, the duchess looked thoughtful for a moment, then her face brightened. "Of course! You would like that ever so much better." Clasping her hands together, she said, "How would you like to stay with your aunt Mackenzie?"

Oh, joy. More strangers. Just what I need. "Aunt Mackenzie? I barely remember her." And that much was true, for Una Mackenzie had visited her sister Anne in England once a few years back, since it was easier for Anne to make occasional treks to Scotland to see her family than it was for half of the McCulloch clan to come to England.

"You will like staying with Barra and Una," she went on. "Your cousin Ailie is just about your age—perhaps a year or two younger. And Allan isn't much older. They live in

Wester Ross—not too far from Loch Maree. Bella, it's a beautiful place. I know you would simply love it there."

I would love living on the moon if I didn't have to marry that spaniel-faced Huntly. By this point in time, Annabella didn't care where she went, as long as it was far, far away from Ross Mackinnon *and* Lord Huntly—and she threw her father in with the other two, for good measure.

Men were the source of all the trouble in her life. She didn't care if she never saw another one. And she didn't care if she never saw Scotland again either.

Scotland, her Scots kin, the man she was to marry—they were all strangers to her. She sighed. Little difference it made where she weathered the storm. *Oh, to be in England again, to return home, to see the bleaching green where I used to lie in the grass and make daisy chains and necklaces of dandelion stalks.* But those things were as lost to her as the young girl she had once been. Annabella was too sad to cry, too sad to feel anything save an acute sense of defeat. Aunt Una or Uncle Colin. It didn't matter. All was lost. "Whatever you think, Mother."

The duchess was on her feet now, a spark of excitement in her eyes. "I'll speak to your father when he returns from Edinburgh. Perhaps your uncle Barra Mackenzie could come for you, or Gavin could escort you and then meet us in Edinburgh on our way back to England."

"Gavin," Annabella said slowly. "I hadn't thought about his leaving too."

"Of course he must, dear. He is, after all, our only son and your father's heir. There is much waiting for him back in England, you know—although I fear he will go to wild oats as too many light brains given to newfangledness do." Seeing she was getting a bit off the track, she corrected herself. "But don't you fret so. You know no one could keep the two of you apart for long. I've always said you and Gavin were closer than twins. Now, cheer up. Gavin will be back in plenty of time for the wedding—before the rest of us, unless I miss my guess."

The duchess looked utterly satisfied with herself. "I'll go this minute and write Una straightaway. She will be so happy to have you. All of her children are married and gone, save Ailie and her brother Allan. The last time she wrote, she lamented the loss of her big family and told me how empty and lonely the house had become."

Giving her daughter one last look, the duchess said, "Well, I must be off. I've a fortnight's work to do in a few days. I'll post the letter to Una, then we'll see about having a seamstress in. You'll need some additions to your wardrobe."

Why? Prisoners don't need wardrobes.

After her mother charged from the garden like a saint with a mission, Annabella took a lengthy walk around the garden, stopping by an old fountain made of lichen-encrusted gray stone. She stood beside the fountain, listening to its happy song and trailing her fingers through the water as she wondered about that place called Wester Ross.

"You're a hard lass to find," a voice behind her said. Annabella turned to see Ross Mackinnon strolling toward her, that same irksome grin on his face she remembered from the last time she had seen him. "If you're going to throw yourself into that birdbath, tell me now and I'll disappear."

"It would almost be worth the effort," she said, "if it meant I didn't have to talk to you."

"Ah," he said, his eyes telling her how much he enjoyed this. "But we both know the duke's obedient daughter would never do such a thing as that."

"I might surprise you," she said with the greatest dignity.

He studied her critically. "You might—one of these days, at any rate. But it'll take some coaxing on my part, I fear. You aren't a lass to throw caution to the wind and act on impulse."

The scattered fragments of her composure began to collect themselves and muster together into one flagrant display of something she could only call idiocy. "That's something you should be thankful for, since it would be pure impulse to slap your cocky face."

Coming to a stop in front of her, he reached out and touched the side of her face, using one finger to trace a slow path across her pale, flawless skin, then dropping lower to circle her throat. She slapped his hand away.

"It's different, isn't it?"

"I don't know what you mean. What is different?"

"My touching you," he said blandly. "It isn't the same, is it?"

She scowled at him. "Must you always speak in riddles? 'It isn't the same' as what?"

"As when Huntly touches you."

"You are . . ." She searched her mind. "Worse than vile." It wasn't too good a word for a severe dressing down, she had to admit, but it was all she could come up with at the moment.

He was laughing now. "Worse than vile?" he repeated. "Is there anything worse than vile?"

Annabella felt the fire upon her cheeks. She took a step back. "I have already answered that question," she said with the greatest dignity.

He took another step toward her and she took a counterstep back. "I'd be careful if I were you. You're close to being in the compost, although I don't know but what it might be worth letting you fall, just to see it: Lady Annabella sitting on her tuffet covered with light loam, leaf mold, river sand, and well-rotted dung."

"Stop it, do you hear? I think you are the most despicably odious man," she said, the rest of her words choking her into silence.

"No, you don't, much the worse for you."

He saw the way her eyes grew huge and round with apprehension. "Relax, Miss Predictable. I'm not going to pounce on you here amongst the flowers, although I can hear it now, you running inside to shout that I have trod upon the lilies."

His smile was lazy and confident, and he looked her over with slow, approving appraisal. "That particular shade of blue becomes you. You know, I think this is the first time I've seen your bosom heave with irritation in a low-cut gown." He ignored her gasp of outrage. "But in all honesty, I must admit I like the effect in this one better." He laughed at her sudden attempt to cover herself. "Crossing your arms over your . . . front . . . does not achieve the results you are looking for. All you've succeeded in doing is pushing everything up a bit higher."

"Ohhhhh!" she screeched. "Will you ever cease? What must one do to make you stop?" She gathered her skirts in one hand and started around him.

"I know one surefire way," he said, putting his hand out to stop her. "A kissed mouth is a silent mouth."

"I'll take your verbosity, thank you—crude as it may be." She eyed him with all the resentment she could muster, looking down at her arm, which was gripped in his hand, and then back up at his smiling face. "Your mind must dwell at the very bottom of the pit of lewdness, for I have never met anyone like you—or anyone who went out of his way to provoke me as you do."

He released her arm. "It could be partly your fault, you know. Take away fuel, take away flame." He laughed at her blank look and caressed her cheek as he said, "You would do well to remember you don't put out a fire, lass, by pouring oil on the flame."

Annabella did not know why, but for some reason, she found this man quite the most likable and irresistible person she had ever encountered—and at the moment she wanted to dislike him the most. *This must be how it is done*, she thought. *This is how one goes crazy.*

She looked up at the face that was smiling down at her, and knowing she was a fool for doing so, she returned his smile, feeling her frustration melt faster than a tallow candle.

It was the second time that day she sighed in defeat. "You are past hope, you know that?"

"That's what they say."

"Why did you carry me across the stream that day, when I could have ridden your horse?"

"I preferred to carry you."

"Why?"

"Let's just say it was because I saw a woman worth wading for," he said, looking down at her. In the sunlight her skin had the rich color of fully opened pink roses and the freshness of a late June morning. He inhaled her fragrance through every pore. She smelled like strawberries. He thought about the way she had looked when he walked into the garden and found her hidden in a shrine of climbing white roses, tiny and still, like a small statue that watches over a garden. God, he wanted this woman, wanted her with every fiber of his being.

She saw the way he was looking at her. "It can never be,"

she said, her voice turning suddenly soft. "You are wasting your time and risking much—for both of us."

"Then we'll just have to take our chances."

"I'm afraid that option is out as well," she said, remembering her discussion with her mother only moments ago.

"Do I dare hope that hint of sadness in your comment means you are lamenting the possibility that things might not work out between us?" He pulled her tight against his chest, his lips pressing against the top of her head.

"I wish nothing more than to be *assured* of the fact that things don't."

"You don't wish that, lovely Annabella," he said, laughing softly. "You don't wish that at all." He released her, but continued holding her by the shoulders as he looked down into her upturned face. "Forget all this nonsense about marrying that dog lover and come away with me."

"Are you insane?"

He laughed. "Probably."

She pushed away from him.

"Okay," he said jovially. "Forget I said that. I'm not going to toss you over my shoulder and haul you away, pirate fashion." His vivid blue eyes were suddenly as soft as a spring breeze. He gave her a lazy look. "I'm a patient man. I can wait."

"Till doomsday, for all I care."

"You're shaking. And your voice is unsteady. Are you cold?"

"No, I'm not cold. I simply find you irritating. I always feel this way when I'm around you."

"I could stop that . . . if you'd let me."

"No, you'd only make it worse—I mean—why don't you just leave me alone?"

"Can't," he said, taking her in his arms and drawing her back against his chest.

"You might as well give up," she said, her voice breathy and unsteady. "I'm a lot smarter than you think. I know what you're about. You can't seduce me."

"Then you've nothing to worry about, have you?" His lips were in her hair, kissing the soft fringe that edged her face, his breath stirring more than the curls that nestled there. "You are immune to this sort of thing, aren't you? So strong. So capable. So determined to resist. Nothing I do has any effect on you, does it?" His breath was even and warm, the touch of his lips gentle as they moved in a slow, circular pattern aross the smoothness of her troubled brow, down the straight, dainty line of her nose, to brush faintly across her surprised mouth. "This," he said in a whisper, "is something you hardly notice."

His hands firm around her waist, he drew Annabella completely against him before she had a chance to steady the breathing that threatened to become a pant. Everything inside her was where it shouldn't be, doing something it had never done before. She was a mass of confusion; body parts were suddenly too large for her chest, and those that weren't threatened to spin off into oblivion. So many questions she had about the male anatomy were suddenly, and shockingly, answered. Shot full of holes was her theory that she was a strong woman and could resist anything. This man made her body quiver and her determination dissolve.

She knew nothing about intimacy, but she was gathering some mighty strong clues from the places where her blood ran thick and warm. She was hot. She was cold. She wanted to say *yes*. She was thinking *no*. She must stop this. Now. Weakly she said, "Stop it, some more," and heard his soft chuckle.

"Are you sure you want me to?" he whispered, nuzzling her. Then his mouth closed over hers, and he showed her yet another way to kiss. Her eyes were closed, but everything behind her lids exploded with color. She felt weightless and tingling, as if she were drifting above herself, out of the world she knew into that black void above, where she hovered, close enough to reach out and touch a star.

He was barely conscious of her small hands pushing against his chest. "What's the matter?"

There was a modest pause. "I lied."

The sound of his laughter rolled in elated tones across the garden wall, over the simple rose-covered arch that divided the garden and the lawn, to sweep across the lavender hues of heather-covered hills beyond. He clasped her face in his hands, moving his mouth back and forth across hers, absorbing her sharp gasp. He kissed her softly, gently, and for quite a long time, before he broke it by whispering her name over and over.

"You take unfair advantage," she whispered.

"Yes, and it's going to get worse," he said, just before he released her.

A moment later she was still in the garden. But she was standing there alone.

The next morning Ross was in the library with Percy when his grandfather came in, his white, wiry brows lifted in delight. "By the by, I do believe it's time for you to take the lad to Edinburgh, Percy."

"Do you think it's time?" Ross asked. His mind on Annabella, he knew it was too soon. He needed more time with her.

"I take it you have decided not to accompany us?" Percy said.

The old duke dropped into a friendly leather chair that beckoned. "I'm too absentminded to sit on a horse. I'd forget where I was and topple off."

Percy said, "What about the carriage?"

"My blasted leg is too stiff to sit in a carriage for any length of time," he said, giving his leg a slap. "Damn me if it isn't getting numb as well."

"You put up a good struggle," Percy said, "but I doubt that is the real reason."

The Mackinnon laughed. "You're right. It isn't. I simply don't want to go to Edinburgh. Truth is, I am exasperated with Unitarians, Whigs, Americans, brokers, bankers, solicitors, and the Quaker aristocracy. I'm an old man, and expect to spend the rest of my days right here, being coddled by you, Percy, and buoyed by the ministrations of my grandson —which is a long-winded way of saying: I quit."

Ross threw back his head with a shout of laughter as Percy said, "So, you're ready to turn the helm over to Ross."

"I am—lock, stock, and barrel. But I suspect he needs to see a bit o' Scotland first, and have his last fling, and there's no better place to start than Edinburgh."

"I could take him to England," said Percy.

"What for?" the duke said with a snort. "The English are a sober lot. If the lad is going to learn to drink and drink deep, he'll do it here, at home, on good Scottish soil—with good Scots whisky."

At the mention of home, Ross realized he hadn't really thought of this old gray fortress as home, but in reality, that was exactly what it had become. There was a rightness to it, a feeling of belonging he had never felt back in Texas. Maybe that was why he was the one out of all the Mackinnon boys who rolled around like a loose stone, never finding a place to lay his head for long.

"When do we leave?" asked Percy.

"Within the week," was the Mackinnon's staunch reply. "And now we'll wash our words down with a glass of good whisky."

Ross joined his grandfather and Percy for a drink, his eyes resting for a moment on the lingering gray light outside the window, the soft greenness of the hills reminding him of Annabella's eyes.

Annabella. Her name ripped through his mind like a gunshot. He was just beginning to bring his lass around. He wasn't ready to leave her yet. Ross tried to probe for a logical reason to stall the trip to Edinburgh and came up with nothing. He wished he had more time to be with her, more time to teach her to trust him, more time to put her in touch with herself. Instead he continued to stare at the grayness out the window, listening to his grandfather and Percy plan away with his life.

Chapter

13

The Duchess of Grenville looked out the window into the garden below and wished she hadn't.

"What the devil is going on out there?" she said in a worried way as she drew back her hand, allowing the heavily tasseled silk drapery to fall back into place. She turned away from the window, an anxious look on her face. She began pacing the floor, then paused to look at the window. "Oh, Bella, Bella, Bella. What are you doing, child?" She began pacing again. "What shall I do? I do wish Alisdair were here," she said to no one. She began to pace in earnest now, back and forth across the floor of the bedroom she had occupied at Dunford Castle since the ball, her silk skirts swishing, her hoop thumping against the furniture, her mind reeling with the scene she had observed a moment ago in the flower garden when she happened to look out her window.

Annabella's mother was a very decent sort of woman, one who desired only the happiest and best things for her children, but she was not one to tolerate flagrant disregard of propriety. What she had just witnessed was, in her book, most assuredly flagrant disregard—for there was no doubt in her mind that Annabella knew what was expected of her as a betrothed woman *and* a Stewart. Neither of which should be groping with a rogue as handsome as Lachlan's grandson. She thought about Alisdair, trying to decide what he would do.

She knew Alisdair would tolerate no such behavior from his daughter when he returned—and he would give Bella a scolding to end all scoldings, whether his wife reminded him of Shakespeare's words—*"Trust not your daughters' minds / By what you see them act"*—or not. She threw up her hands. It was times such as this—well, today was one of those days she felt as if her wits were wilting. She simply didn't know what to do. Try as she might, the duchess couldn't decide what she should do in such a case. Indeed, these were trying times. Her wife's heart told her to march with authority to Annabella's room and confront her with her discovery, then confine her to her room until her father came home and let him deal with the matter.

Yet her mother's heart told her to cushion the blow to her child as much as she could. Of course she would have to tell Alisdair, but perhaps it would be better to have Annabella safely ensconced at her sister's home before she did, and that way she could report the matter to Alisdair and at the same time inform him that she had taken care of the situation.

But it was her woman's heart that was so sympathetic to her young daughter's affections. Well she could remember what it was like to be young and if not in love, at least infatuated. And well she could remember what a handsome devil of a grandson the old Mackinnon had. If ever she had seen a man who looked as if he could seduce a woman and have her thinking it was all her idea, it was Ross Mackinnon. No, her woman's heart could not fault her daughter in the least. And so it was a troubled Duchess of Grenville who sat upon her bed and gave much thought to what she was about. After all, the peace and tranquillity of her family was at stake here, as well as her daughter's future and happiness.

An hour later she hadn't resolved much, but she had learned one thing: the heart of the woman and mother were far ahead of the heart of the wife. At last, with a prayer for guidance, she decided what she must do.

The duchess prayed all the way to Annabella's room, reminding God as she went that it would have been much simpler for all concerned if he had nipped this thing in the bud before it had a chance to blossom. But even as she thought it, she knew that when a young woman was bent upon falling in love with a hero, one would, without fail, stumble into her lap—or the other way around.

It was amazing to the duchess that all Annabella did when she marched with authority into her room and confronted her with the goings-on in the flower garden was to stare. Actually, staring was a pretty good response, for that stare said far more than words ever could. Annabella stared as if she had personally been violated, as if someone had come into her room and yanked down her drawers.

And that was precisely how Annabella felt. Violated. She looked up at her mother, who looked as if she had just been heavily starched and ironed. Annabella wasn't in the mood to be favored with one of her mother's sermonettes at the moment.

"You needn't look at me as if I have been sneaking peeks at your journal," the duchess said. "Friend or foe, I'm here to help you. You're in a passel of trouble, young lady, and something will have to be done about it. Gavin and your father will return shortly, and I deem it best to have this thing settled and done with before they arrive."

"What are you going to do? Boil me in oil? I haven't exactly been soliciting the attentions of the duke's grandson, you know." Annabella just wasn't thinking all of this was as bad as her mother was making it out to be.

But the duchess was bent upon a lecture, and a lecture it was—on why a young lady, and most certainly a betrothed one, did not go scampering about a rose garden with a man, allowing him to take *certain* liberties.

"He did not take liberties—at least, not in the way you think."

"Annabella, my mind might not be functioning, but my eyesight is perfect." Her mother threw up her hands again. "Oh, stuff and bother. None of this will make any difference to your father. You know how he has that dreadful tendency to punish first and ask questions later." She gave Annabella a look that was overburdened with significance and went to the armoire, removing her daughter's valise.

"What are you doing?"

"I'm saving your life, or at least your pride. I'm taking you to your aunt Una," the duchess said, her voice emitting a certain tone of utter satisfaction as she added, "all by myself. I feel it will go ever so much better for you if you are tucked away and out of mischief's reach by the time your father returns."

Annabella watched her mother stare down at her valise as if she were committing it to memory and never expected to see that particular valise again. "When are we leaving?" she asked.

"At first light," the duchess replied. "I've already taken the liberty of speaking with His Grace, and he has kindly offered us the use of his coach, which will take us to Broadford. We'll take the ferry over to Kyle of Lochalsh. His Grace has another coach there that he has put at our disposal."

But Annabella wasn't listening. Her mind had been trapped in horror a few words back. Her mother had spoken with His Grace about all of this? The same *His Grace* who was Ross Mackinnon's grandfather? Annabella was horrified at the thought. "Mother, you didn't tell the Mackinnon . . ."

"No, I didn't. What do you take me for? A cabbagehead? Although, I must say, I had every right, mind you, to tell him all the goings-on of the past few days. Really, Annabella. I'm beginning to feel like a sheep with all my bleating over the bubble you have gotten yourself into. How I wish old age would start creeping up on me so I could quietly slip into a blissful state of mental infirmity where the most taxing thing I had to do was listen to the prattle of my grandchildren."

The duchess's words were said in a befuddled, rather disordered voice that made Annabella wonder if her mother hadn't gotten her wish and slipped peacefully into that blissful state already. But she knew that wasn't so. Since she was old enough to remember, her mother had been saying such things to her. And since she was old enough to remember, Annabella had always listened quietly, offering no comment, asking no questions. But this time she asked, "Why? *I'm* the one that's being shipped off to Western Roses."

"Wester Ross," her mother corrected. "By the by, I don't fathom why you are looking as terrified as a sheep at a shearing. I daresay a visit to your aunt isn't the same thing as being locked in the Tower of London. You should thank your lucky stars, my dear girl, that I have decided to play the part of the sacrificial lamb and confront your father all alone in this. Would that I could, *I'd* go and stay indefinitely in Wester Ross myself. Don't you think for a moment that if you remained here there aren't are worse things that could happen to you at the hands of that . . . that . . . that grandson of the duke."

Annabella, of all people, knew that, for foremost in her mind was Ross, blue-eyed and loose limbed, grinning his way into her heart in a way that was more endearing than an overzealous lick from an affectionate puppy. She watched her mother slap the valise on the bed and fidget with the straps to open it. "What worse things, Mother?" A month ago Annabella would not have had a question like that enter her modest little mind, much less find the fortitude to ask it.

As it happened, her mother didn't have much more intestinal fortitude than Annabella. In answer, she went back to the armoire and began removing clothes, packing them in the valise, as if by doing so she could quickly and efficiently roll up Annabella's questions with them and tuck them away, out of sight. The duchess began to wring her hands and look miserably about the room, as if she was searching for the nearest way to exit. "A man like that is very experienced at *those* sorts of things . . . with young, susceptible women, I might add."

"*What* sorts of things?"

"The *usual* sorts of things, Bella. I have seen many men like Lord Mackinnon in London—the kind who will pursue pleasure until they overtake it."

"Overtake what? Why can't you be a little more exact? I think myself capable of understanding the rules of courtship."

"You've been taught them, yes, but it is unfortunate that

the young and inexperienced have a tendency to seek refuge with a wolf when fleeing a fox." She peered at Bella for a moment to see if any of this was making any sense to her. Judging from the blank expression on her daughter's young face, Lady Anne knew this latest attempt at explanation had gone completely over Annabella's bonnet. "Dear child, I am not a veritable walking storehouse of knowledge, but I do know a woman has a tendency to swallow anything, as long as it has been spiced with flattery. I can only say that some men have a way about them—a certain familiarity that breeds attempt."

Seeing her mother's pinking face, Annabella wondered why it was that questions never seemed to be as embarrassing as the answers. It also occurred to her, because of the way her mother stuttered and stammered, all the while wringing her hands, that her mother didn't know much more about this sort of thing than she did.

Her mother went on to say, "I am only telling you these things, you understand, because you are to be married soon. It is important for you to remember that your betrothal has already bound you to your future husband in many ways, Bella. And once you are married, your body will be his to dispose of as he sees fit."

"Dispose of?" asked Annabella in a horrified tone.

The duchess quelled that look with one of her own. "I am not speaking of murder, child. I am simply trying to point out how our lovely Queen Victoria and her handsome Albert have given us such a splendid union to follow. Once you are married, you will understand. There is nothing more sublime than to be taken to the heart of your beloved husband, to share his counsel, to be the chosen companion of his joy and suffering." With her hand clapped across her breast, an expression of sublime awe upon her face, the duchess said, "It is no wonder a woman has such a time deciding whether modesty or gratitude should preponderate."

"Well, I for one shan't have any difficulty deciding," Bella said. "I want nothing to do with either." *No wonder, indeed.* Annabella wanted to throw up. In no form or fashion could she imagine herself being the companion of Lord Huntly's joy—in truth, she doubted he had any. As far as modesty or gratitude went, she would have no trouble being modest around him. The more clothes the better. Layers of them. With lots of buttons.

Her mother held up a pair of cotton drawers and gave them a vigorous shake before folding them in a neat square. "All in all, Bella, it would serve you better if you spent more of your time bent over your embroidery frame and less time languishing over Lord Mackinnon." The duchess cast a quick eye in Annabella's direction. "I don't think Lord Huntly is such a bad-looking chap, do you?"

"No, he is really very much a handsome man."

"Yes, I suppose he is," said her mother thoughtfully. "If only he could be persuaded not to wear that ghastly coat of goose-turd green. Really. A nice bottle green would suit him much better, or even one in that popinjay blue all the London dandies seem to favor." Her look turning wistful for a moment, she added, "Perhaps he will, once you've married, for then you will be his chief ornament."

Annabella felt new resentment flare. She didn't want to be Lord Huntly's chief ornament. She didn't want to be anyone's chief ornament. If a woman had to be an ornament, why not be the only one? Chief ornament. Was that what drove women to while away their hours gluing bugle beads to mirror frames?

About this point in time, Annabella decided it might be

best to do as she frequently did after a question-and-answer session with her mother, and simply stop trying to puzzle out the duchess's train of thought.

For the next hour, while her mother busied herself with packing and admonishing, Annabella looked longingly out the window, past the pines that lined the narrow lane just before it dipped down into an open glen where an old stone bridge, overgrown with lichen and moss, spanned a narrow brook. Only yesterday she had stood on that bridge, gazing down at the water that vanished beneath her, as if some giant mouth had opened and swallowed it.

In some ways her life was a lot like that little stream—running down a predestined path and vanishing before her eyes into a yawning mouth where, when she looked, there was only darkness beyond it. Her mind spun backward to her childhood, a time when her life was her own, a time when she was indulged and had a will of her own. Surely this was why they called it the springtime of youth, for as she grew older, the seasons of her life had changed to fall and now to threatening winter. She shivered, feeling herself being hurled forward into a cold and bleak time. And like winter, something cold and hard settled within her, something she could not force away, something brittle and unfruitful as a seedpod encased in a layer of cold, unforgiving ice.

The next morning the world was covered in mist, the dampness cold and wet enough to be called rain—or so Annabella thought.

Feeling as miserable as the weather, Bella climbed into the coach behind her mother. The Mackinnon was there to say good-bye, and Percy, too, but the one person she hoped to see most was strangely absent. Feeling as low as the coach wheels that dug into the wet road, she settled back into the coach and prepared for a long, long ride.

The coach jostled its way north, following the muddy Kishorn road that did not by any stretch of the imagination resemble a road—not even faintly. Trees grew in abundance —aspen, rowan, wych elm, bird cherry, goat willow—all interspersed with wild roses, a scene Annabella would have enjoyed more if the sun had been shining. The wheels slid and squished their way across high corries, through Bealach na Ba, the pass of the cattle, toward Applecross. It was a mountain of such grandeur that it made Annabella feel a small, insignificant part of creation.

"Upon my word," said the duchess, her knuckles white from gripping the upholstery to keep from sliding, "I don't remember telling this coachman I wanted to soar with eagles." She poked her head through the window for a hasty look and gasped, then promptly drew it back. "I have never been up this high in my life."

Annabella, who had promised herself to remain close-mouthed for the entire journey, would have found the horrified look on her mother's face worthy of a laugh—if she had been in the mood for laughing, which she was not. She did decide to speak, however, after flipping over several pages of the book in her hand until she located the place she was looking for. "It says in my travel journal that we are crossing the nesting territory of the *ptarmigan*—commonly called white winged grouse."

The duchess said, "Crossing their nesting territory, you say? Hmmmm . . ." Then, with a knowing look directed at Bella, she added, "I seem to be doing a lot of that lately." She rested her head against the back of the seat with a sigh.

"I do hope the way down isn't as bad as the way up. All of these sharp turns are unsettling to my constitution."

They forgot to notice whether the way down was as bad as the way up, for the breathtaking views of Skye on their precipitous descent showed them everything from the stony sandstone uplands to the coastal woods of Applecross—a view too magnificent and wild for them to think of anything else. Once the driver stopped and Annabella poked her head out in time to see three red deer spring down the side of the mountain.

"How lovely they are," she called up to the driver.

"That they are, lass, but you'll never see a sight anywhere like the wildcat that lives in these parts. They're as haughty and elusive as a pretty woman, with the greenest eyes this side of heaven. Eyes much the same color as yours."

"Oh, I'd love to see one. Do you think we shall?"

"I doubt that, miss. Shy creatures, they be."

Annabella pulled her head back inside the coach as it lurched forward. "What else does that travel journal of yours say?" the duchess asked.

"About which area?"

"Wester Ross," the duchess said with a tone of exasperation, "since that's where we're headed and what primarily concerns us."

Annabella had been staring at the lovely green satin bow on her mother's bonnet, but pulled her attention away to search for her wicker basket, where she had tucked the slender volume entitled *A Ladies' Guide to the Scottish Countryside.*

Opening the book, Annabella looked at her mother. "You know, it surprises me that you, being a native Scot, don't already know everything that's written in this book."

"You will remember that I was a very young bride and

have not lived in Scotland since. Besides, my home was near Loch Awe. No one but the men in my family ever ventured up here. Until my first visit, I always thought of Wester Ross as an austere place of brooding landscapes— not much of a place a lady would choose to visit."

"I'm glad your visit changed your mind."

"It didn't. It's still an austere place, but bonny just the same."

Annabella opened the journal and began to read to her mother about the sights it recommended for a lady to see. The duchess made it a point to tell her that she had no intention of stopping anywhere along the way and thus prolonging the journey. "Although I do find it pleasant to hear about such things," she said.

Annabella answered her mother's latest sally with a nod and closed her eyes. She was thinking what a strange turn her life had taken over the past few months. Here she was betrothed to a man almost as old as her father, forced to live in a strange country, and now, the piece of fruit that toppled the fruit bowl: she was being carted—like so much baggage being dumped—to the home of her aunt and uncle, who were virtual strangers. Strange thing, life. One day it was roses; the next day, horse droppings.

They arrived at the inn at Applecross an hour later and were off again early the next morning. It was still raining as they embarked, making the travel slow and miserable, but the duchess was determined that they were going to reach the home of the Mackenzie before night. Each time the driver suggested they stop and rest, she rammed her parasol against the roof of the coach and said, "Onward, my dear man. Onward." Then to Annabella, she said, "We are going to reach your aunt Una's if we have to hitch ourselves to the wagon to do it."

It was times like this that Bella believed her mother to be Scot to the core. The duchess was good company, Bella decided, for her mother's vivid descriptions and burning Scots determination did prove humorous at times. Evidently it paid off, for it was still light when they began to descend a deep narrow glen through which ran a brattling little stream, the first one Annabella noticed that was running toward the Atlantic. On either side of them the hills rose to a great height—bare, rocky, and stripped of almost all vegetation save a few determined tufts of heather. It was a rather destitute place, mottled by huge stones and boulders and unfit for sheep or goats—one even the birds seemed to avoid. Already twilight was entering the glen, and Annabella looked up, missing the light from the peat fires of the shepherds flaming the hills above that she had grown so accustomed to since coming to Scotland. Indeed it was a dismal place—the valley of the shadow of death.

And then paradise lay before her: a place of smooth, mirrored water and soft green islands. Behind the lake, slopes of a mysterious mountain rose to cast a gloomy shadow across the loch, and Bella opened her journal to learn the mountain's name: Ben Slioch. "It sounds like a name from the Bible," she said. "Ben Slioch."

"Slioch," her mother repeated. "I can't remember what that means in Gaelic. Arrows, I think."

"Spear," Bella corrected. "My journal says it's partly sandstone."

"With a name as gritty," said the duchess.

"Loch Maree," Bella whispered as the road opened to a moory plain bordered with hills. On either side of them, sparse patches of corn and potatoes seemed in keeping with the half dozen or so pathetic cottages that dotted the brown heath.

"There's a boat full of people just ahead," Bella said. Her mother looked out and ordered the driver to pull up.

"It's a wedding party," the duchess said, her words almost drowned out by a piper in full Scots dress, the wild notes of his bagpipe strangely melancholy for such a festive occasion.

The driver came around to tell them they would have to go by boat across the loch, there being no road the coach could follow. "I've made arrangements for another conveyance on the other side," he said.

As their things were being loaded on the boat, Bella listened a moment to what the boatman in the other boat was telling the wedding guests. She didn't understand it, of course, since it was Gaelic, but she listened, liking the sound. "I wish I remembered more of my Gaelic," her mother said, coming to join her. "He is telling them stories of the loch. It's legend haunted, you know. There are ruins of an old monastery on one of the islands, and a Norse prince and princess whose lives ended in tragedy are buried there. See that little island over there?" She pointed and Bella nodded. "He is saying, 'The burliest Scot I know would think twice before going there after dark.' It's supposed to be haunted by fairies and wraiths and every land and water sprite known to man." The duchess fell silent, listening with her brow knitted in remembrance of the words Bella found so strange. "He's saying something about that island—that there's a tiny lake in the middle of the island and another tiny island in the middle of that lake. In the center is a tree where the queen of fairies holds court." She listened some more, the knitted brow giving way to a full frown. Then with a helpless shrug she shook her head. "I give up. He's talking too fast for me to keep up and my Gaelic is too rusty." She kept her head upright and closed her eyes. "It makes me remember just how much I've forgotten." When her mother opened her eyes again, Bella saw a new light gleaming there, a light of determination. "I'm going to find me some books in Gaelic to take back to England," the duchess said. "I should be horsewhipped for allowing so many things to slip from my mind." She smiled wanly and patted Bella's hand. "Try to rest a bit. We should be at your aunt Una's in less than two hours."

Bella did as her mother asked, her thoughts turning to Ross Mackinnon the moment her eyes closed. She wondered what he was doing now, and if he had even noticed that she was gone.

Ross noticed, and he wasn't too happy when he found Annabella gone.

"Gone!" Ross shouted. "What do you mean, gone? Gone where? With whom?"

Lord Percival blinked with each overemphasized word Ross shouted. "Please . . . spare me. You are nigh to rupturing my ears."

"I'll damn well rupture something worse than that if you don't tell me what's going on here."

"I just told you. Her Grace and Lady Annabella left early this morning while you were riding. They had stayed here much longer than they originally intended and decided it was time to get back on their schedule."

Ross glared at his grandfather. "Did you have anything to do with this?"

"Nothing more than to loan them a coach." With elevated

brows, the Mackinnon asked, "Would you rather I had them walk?"

Ross relaxed a little. "Something here isn't up to snuff and I intend to find out what it is."

"What do you mean, not up to snuff?" Percy asked.

"I mean, I think you two know more than you're telling me."

"We only know that the duchess asked His Grace for the use of a coach. She deemed it fitting to keep their destination a secret. A Scot likes his privacy and respects that right in others, Ross. In truth, it was none of our business *where* they were going."

Ross eyed his grandfather. "I dinna ken you'll get any answers by frowning, lad," the Mackinnon said.

Without giving Ross the opportunity to respond, Percy went on to say, "The ladies' untimely departure is only a few days ahead of ours. Even if they had remained here, you would be leaving in a few days, and that's the way of it."

"They could've given me a chance to say good-bye."

"Maybe they would have if you had been inclined to look at the lass with more of an eye of the philosopher . . . or a Methodist," the Mackinnon said, slapping Ross on the back as he and Percy doubled over with laughter.

That only made Ross angrier. Seeing this, his grandfather said, "There isna a thing to be done about it now, lad. You've got your future to see to, and you canna be chasin' the lassies about while you're doing it. Sometimes it's a hard lesson to learn."

"What is?" Ross said, his anger subsiding a bit.

"First things first. A man can't stand up and sit down at the same time," the Mackinnon said.

"Why the hell not?" Ross said.

Percy spoke this time. "As Blake said, '*If you trap the*

*moment before it's ripe, tears of repentance you will surely
wipe.'*"

"I believe the rest of that quote says, *'But if you let the
ripe moment go, you can never wipe away the tears of
woe.'*"

Percy lifted his brows and looked at the Mackinnon. "The
lad has a good memory," he said.

"Only when it suits him," said the Mackinnon.

Chapter
14

Seaforth.

Rising out of the night like a black-fingered beacon pointing the way. Seaforth. A mansion that looked to be a first cousin to a stately castle, so grand it was, even when cloaked in the chilled swirling mists of darkness.

And it was dark when they arrived, darker than dark when the coach passed through the last eerie shadows of trees and burst upon a clean stretch of road over a windswept moor. Seaforth. It lay grand and sprawling before them, for the mist was lighter here and Bella could see how the land lay about them—the way the road came winding down to meet them like some grand carpet rolled out for their arrival. She felt her heart throb with anticipation, yet the signs and sounds of weariness were everywhere: the arched and sweating necks of the coach horses, their breaths coming fast and steam-filled like so many boiling teakettles; the clink of metal bits; the weary stretch of worn leather; and Annabella's own exhausted groan as she alighted from the coach, her legs almost giving way beneath her from being too long in one position.

Standing before the immense proportions of the grand house that rose majestically before her, Annabella took no note of her weariness. Indeed, she was feeling nothing more than a twinge of disappointment that it wasn't a sunny afternoon instead of the dead of night when they arrived, for she would have loved seeing such a grand and noble house on their approach. As it was, all she could see was the towering black silhouette rising out of the earth, its spires and gables sharp in contrast against the midnight blue of the surrounding sky.

A moment later she followed her mother to the door. Taking the great knocker—a heavy brass ring in a lion's mouth—the duchess gave three smart raps that echoed throughout the great house and came bouncing back at them. Lights behind the many mullioned windows began to appear all over the house. Moments later the massive door swung open with a threatening groan, but whoever—or whatever—opened it could not be seen.

Bella shivered and peered into the great hall. It was lighted by a twelve-branch candelabra sitting on a round marble table in the center of the room. Eerie shadows played tricks with the light as it danced off the panes of deeply set windows that lined the great hall on either side, just beyond rows of tall marble pillars that supported the roof. Monoliths of gleaming black granite rose to the ceiling, fluted and carved with crests, standards, and ensigns, strange beasts and birds, and even coronets of rank. Bella recognized immediately the pattern for an earl—eight balls on tall spikes alternating with eight strawberry leaves.

Suddenly a head was thrust around the door and Bella's curiosity was quenched.

"Is this the home of the Earl of Seaforth?" asked the duchess.

"Don-faighneachd ort!" the woman said. "A plague on thine asking!"

The door slammed, almost taking the tip of the duchess's nose with it.

The duchess, who was getting more put out by the minute, rapped on the door again, using the handle of her parasol.

The door swung open once more, and the same grizzled head poked around it. "And a plague on you for your rudeness," the duchess responded quickly, before the woman had a chance to slam it a second time. Bella did take note of the fact that her mother did not endanger her nose a second time.

Bella, who by this time had already stepped back behind her mother, was peeping around her to see what she supposed was the housekeeper, a stout, ruddy-faced woman with long silver braids and light blue eyes that looked as if they would, under circumstances other than these, be merry. But there was nothing merry about the woman dressed in a gray wrapper with a nightcap askew on her head, wiry strands of silvery-gray hair poking out here and there. Holding a lamp aloft, the better to see the visitors, she greeted them cordially. "What do you want?"

"I would like to see the Earl of Seaforth and the countess."

"Weel now, you would, would you? And might there be a particular reason for coming here this time o' night askin' such?"

"Yes, there might," the duchess snapped. "But it is none of *your* business. Now, stop standing there as if you're carved from Grampian stone and go inform his lordship that his sister-in-law, the Duchess of Grenville, is standing on his front stoop freezing to death and sure to catch a chill in the night air, while his surly housekeeper interrogates her."

The woman's eyes surveyed the duchess from head to foot and back up again. "His sister-in-law, you say?"

"My good woman," Her Grace said, giving the woman a poke with her parasol, "I am Lady Seaforth's sister, and I am fast losing my patience. Kindly do as you are bid and fetch the earl and my sister or I will go in search of them myself—dragging them out of bed if need be." Without another word, the duchess turned to Annabella. "Come, Bella." Taking Bella by the hand, she pushed her way past the housekeeper. "God's teeth! A more difficult time I've never encountered. Where are your manners, my good woman?"

"Dinna be expecting me to toss my bonnet over the windmill at the sight o' two misplaced visitors in the dead of night. I dinna ken if ye be Gypsies or thieves."

"Indeed?" said the duchess. "And do you often encounter Gypsies and thieves that go about dressed as we are?"

"Och! I canna say if I have or not. But it's possible," the housekeeper said, giving the duchess a sweeping look from head to toe. "*If* they be good at beggin' and thievin', that is, Yer Grace."

By this time the duchess had had just about all she was going to take. She rounded on the woman, giving her a few more pokes with her parasol—this time with each word she emphasized. "Listen, my *dearie.* You march your reluctant little legs up the stairs and tell my *sister* that I want to see her. *Now,* if you please."

Not daunted in the least by the duchess's stand, the woman said, "Are you expected?"

In Annabella's mind, the wiry woman was either the

bravest or the stupidest woman she had ever encountered. But the look the duchess gave her apparently did the trick, for the woman left, mumbling to herself as she went. A few months ago this type of behavior would have been something Bella would have taken more notice of, but since coming to Scotland and learning more about the people, she was coming to understand that this woman wasn't being rude, she was simply being a Scot.

A few minutes later, Una Mackenzie came shrieking into the room and embraced her sister; her husband, a redheaded, chaffy-cheeked fellow of great size, came thundering after her, his eyes skimming over the duchess and her sister locked in a tearful embrace to light upon Annabella standing to one side. He held the lamp in his hand aloft.

Annabella blinked in the bright light as everything about her went out of focus—everything, that is, except her uncle's face. It was quite a face, actually, one to inspire poets or lay a challenge to a painter, a face legends are made of— or nightmares. Her immediate reaction was to run. Too terrified to do that, she gave him a weak smile and took a step back. He grunted and turned toward the sisters, who had separated and were talking with animated gestures.

"Banshees and relatives are the only things that would be rousin' a man from his sleep in the dead of night," he said as his sister-in-law embraced him with what Annabella recognized as fondness.

"Och!" said the duchess, "and dinna teel me ye aren't a wee bit pleased I'm nae a banshee."

Openmouthed, Annabella stared at her mother. She had never, in all her years, heard her mother speak like this. In Bella's opinion, her mother had nothing to worry about. She hadn't lost any of her Scots brogue.

"I dinna ken if you be a banshee or nae. 'Tis a fact that hasn't been proven," the earl replied.

"Now, Barra, aren't you pleased to see me?" asked the duchess.

"I'll answer that when you tell me why you're here."

"I've brought Annabella for a visit."

"Who?"

"My daughter, Annabella."

"The shy-faced innocent with the big eyes?"

"If you're speaking of the young woman standing behind you, yes," the duchess said, giving Annabella a thoughtful look. "Although I never thought of her as shy-faced."

"The lass is timid as a field mouse," he said, turning to cup Annabella's chin in his huge hand and tilt her face up toward the light. "Not an ounce of spunk. English to the core."

Annabella's mother was still looking thoughtfully at her. "Well, I never thought about it, but perhaps you're right— although I have had, on more than one occasion, the opportunity to suspect spunk or something of that ilk was lurking there . . . especially of late," she said, letting her voice trail off to nothing as she became absorbed in thought.

Bella felt her uncle's eyes probe relentlessly for some time before he released her chin.

"Perhaps," was all Barra Mackenzie had to say on the subject.

It was then that Bella realized what was meant by the term *Scots brevity*.

An hour later Bella, who was already undressed and in bed, watched her mother do the same. "What a disparaging fellow," Bella said. "I do believe I've never encountered anyone so prone to hairsplitting. Verily, I felt taken apart, limb by limb, and inspected like a piece of overpriced mutton."

Her mother laughed. "Oh, Barra has intimidating ways about him, but a finer man you'll never find. He's of the tarry-at-home school of farmers, a good father and provider, loving to his family, prudent, and honest as the day is long."

"A farmer? This hardly looks like the abode of a simple farmer."

"I never said *simple farmer*. Farming, if done with the right amount of wit and devotion, can be quite prosperous. Don't be forgetting our own prince consort is a farmer."

"Oh, you mean a gentleman farmer?"

"Yes, and quite wealthy by Scottish standards."

Annabella frowned. "I still think he'd make a marvelous henchman."

The duchess laughed. "Goodness, Bella. What a morbid thought."

"All my thoughts have been morbid of late."

Her mother climbed into her bed. "Well, try to think of something pleasant, dear, and let's enjoy our time together. Tomorrow Una will have our things unpacked and mine moved into another room. We may not have this much time to ourselves after that."

The next morning, Annabella was having a bad time of it, for she overslept and when she entered the dining room, she found she was too late for breakfast. "Go to the kitchen and tell Cook to give you something. There's always a nice cauldron of oatmeal gruel simmering on the peat. It would be good with some salt herring," her aunt Una said.

Annabella went, not for the oatmeal gruel and herring, but on the hope of getting a piece of dry toast and a cup of tea. Cook, who was a robust woman with a neat brown braid crisscrossed over her head, was thankfully an understanding soul, for she didn't mention the oatmeal and herring to Bella more than once.

"If you don't mind, a cup of tea and a piece of dry toast is all I want."

Annabella had no more than sat down to her toast and tea when the kitchen door flew back and the great, hulking form of her uncle filled the doorway. "You mean you dare to eat?" he asked in tones that were mildly tender. "I'd be careful if I were you. Persephone nibbled only a few pomegranate seeds and sealed her fate."

If he was trying to intimidate her, that about did the trick, for Bella choked on the dry toast, gasping and wheezing until Cook took pity and whacked her between the shoulder blades and sent the toast crumbs on their merry way, a few dislodged spinal bones along with them. While Bella gasped for air, the earl shook his head and pushed the door shut with one foot. He went straight to the teapot and poured himself a cup, his eyes on Bella the entire time.

The toast she was able to finish off in three swallows; the tea she gulped down in two. Her mouth was scalded by the hot tea. As Uncle Barra approached the table, she sprang to her feet.

"You dinna have to take flight like a frightened field mouse," he said. "I never gobble the heads off of anyone over the age of fifteen."

Cook giggled and the Earl of Seaforth went on to say, "Bless me, but you're a spindly little thing. Don't you ever eat?"

Her jellied bones were suddenly infused with a shot of stiff dignity. She lifted her head and said, "Of course I eat."

Barra laughed. "You need a little meat on you, lass. Maybe then you wouldn't be so shy-faced. Gain a few stones and you might gain some backbone along with it."

Cook laughed and mumbled something in Gaelic. "*Cha deanar seabhag de'n chalamhan.*"

Barra eyed Annabella for a moment, then threw back his head and laughed. "Bless me, but you may be right."

"What did she say?" asked Bella.

"She said, 'You canna make hawks out of kites.' "

Bella wanted to say she had always had a special fondness for folksy platitudes, but she didn't—not because she was afraid, she reminded herself, it was just that she had been taught to be respectful to her elders. Yes, that was it—respect for her elders.

Cook said something else in Gaelic and Bella forgot her fear and manners. "It isn't polite to speak unfamiliar languages in front of those who don't understand," she said.

The earl's black shining eyes opened just a bit wider as a slow grin spread across his face. "Weel now, the lass does have a wee bit o' backbone buried beneath all those layers of English pudding."

"It doesn't take backbone to understand when someone is being intentionally rude."

"Be quiet, lass, or I'll gag you."

Annabella fled the room with the sound of her uncle Barra's laughter piercing her soul. Turning down a long hallway, she uttered a small prayer for more intestinal fortitude than the good Lord had seen fit to give her thus far. A spine with all the hardness of a boiled egg might be sufficient for a gentlewoman in England, but in Scotland it simply wasn't enough.

The rest of the afternoon Bella spent alone, touring the house and keeping out of the way of her uncle. The mist had lifted and sunlight poured through the many windows, lifting her spirits and bathing each room in warmth and brightness. Everywhere she looked she saw magnificent tapestries and paintings by what had to be masters. French and English furniture as fine as any to be found in England filled each room of the T-shaped home. As she wandered into the two-story baronial hall with its paneled walls and four fireplaces, she couldn't help thinking it was the finest country house she had ever seen.

While Annabella wandered about, taking note of the many paneled rooms and ornamental plaster ceilings, her mother was on her way to the library. By the time Bella went outside to meander along paths bordered by herbaceous shrubs and peeked at flower beds in old walled gardens, the duchess was deep in conversation with her brother-in-law.

The Earl of Seaforth scowled at his sister-in-law. "What do you mean, she's betrothed to the Earl of Huntly?" he asked, not minding in the least that his words were harsh and blunt. "Were you that anxious to get rid of the lass, or did you set out to marry her to the biggest fool in the Highlands?"

"We weren't anxious to be rid of Bella. Why would we be? She has always been such a delight—a perfect lady. As for the other, how were we to know he was a fool? Alisdair was more interested in making a good match for Annabella to ever consider that a man with such credentials might also be a fool," replied the indignant mother.

Barra wasn't the sort of man to be easily put off. "And what about you? You were always a good judge of character, Anne. If my memory serves me."

"I'm sure your memory serves you very well."

His eyes lit up, a slow-spreading grin on his face. "Well enough to be remembering that you were not too discreet about your feelings and your objections to me as Una's husband."

"That was in the beginning," Anne said, "and you will remember I did come around . . . eventually."

"Aye," Barra said. "Eventually."

She gave him a swift, probing glance and smiled. "I suspect you like me all the better for it, Barra. You aren't one to be impressed with a woman too easily influenced, or one who doesn't speak her mind. Now, back to Huntly. I never pegged him for a fool because I never met the man until the arrangements were made."

"So, you betrothed the lass and brought her to Scotland to meet the fool you'd picked. When are you taking her back home?"

"We aren't. Alisdair thinks it best for her to remain in Scotland. He thinks she will adjust better if she doesn't return to England."

Barra's brows drew together thickly and he stared at the toes of his boots. "Hmmm. Perhaps he's right." He looked intently at his sister-in-law. "And this visit to Seaforth was to introduce her to her long-lost kin?"

"No." She went on to explain that Alisdair and Gavin were in Edinburgh and she had seen what transpired between Bella and Ross Mackinnon from her bedroom window. "So I thought it best to get her away from Dunford— with all due haste."

"Away from Dunford," he repeated, "and the duke's grandson. But not particularly in that order."

"Well, yes," said the duchess. "Can you blame me?"

"I dinna know if I blame you or not. I haven't seen the lad you whisked her away from. Perhaps the lass has more spine than she shows—betrothed to one man, pining for another, and secreted away to the castle of an evil relative. Sounds like something right out of a Greek tragedy." He shook his head. "So the lad is the Mackinnon's grandson.

Well, well, well. Tell me, how does the old man feel about this attraction between his grandson and the lass?"

"Who knows?" Anne threw up her hands and began to pace back and forth. "I don't know. He is fond of Bella—and his grandson as well. I suppose he would see it favorably, if Bella weren't betrothed." She stopped pacing. "Do you know the old duke?"

"Aye, I know him. He saved my life once—a long time ago—and I've never repaid the debt."

"It's a difficult debt to repay. One's life does not come cheaply."

"No," Barra said. "It does not." He glanced out the window in time to see Annabella walk into the old pinetum filled with conifers and Douglas fir that lay behind his library. For a moment his dark eyes, with their quickly veiled interest, regarded the glossy black head that gleamed brightly in the full afternoon sun. Every debt-owing impulse beckoned him to orchestrate a few moves in the old duke's favor, while familial ties said to leave it alone. Family ties won by a hair's breadth. When at last he spoke, it was of a different vein than his thoughts. "I can scarce blame Huntly for wanting this match. She's a comely lass. But much too refined and beautiful for the likes of him."

"Last night you were saying she was shy-faced and spineless. Today you say she's a comely lass. Have you changed your mind about her?"

"No. She's still too easily intimidated to make much of a go at it here in the Highlands."

"You don't care for her, then?"

"To the contrary. I like the lass. As a lad, I always had a tenderhearted fondness for stray kittens. I brought more than my share of them home and hid them under my bed."

"Now, *that* doesn't sound like you, Barra."

"Och! Stabbed in the heart with a dirk," Barra said and laughed.

"What did you do with them? Toss them in the loch with stones tied around their necks?"

"Hardly that. I fattened them up and set them free when they were able to take care of themselves."

"Well, I can hardly do that with Bella."

"No, but I can."

"She's a little old for tutoring, and it's a little late to try making a Highland lass out of her now. She's spent too many years being refined."

"Oh, I don't know about that," Barra said. "Scots blood always rises to the top—like cream. It might be just what the lass needs."

A moment later he opened the doors that led into the garden. Bella glanced up and saw her mother and her uncle walk out to join her. A curse formed vividly in her mind. She didn't want to be with anyone right now. She wanted time to be alone. Didn't this brute have any manners? Didn't he respect such things as privacy and solitude? Her uncle, she noticed, was frowning. She scowled and lifted her chin, determined not to be outdone by this callous, ill-mannered relative of hers, this blackest of sheep in the family. A moment later his laughter came like a crack of thunder. Startling. Unexpected. Clamorous. And brief.

She clenched her skirts, determined to make a rapid exit, when his voice stopped her. "What say you, lass? Don't you find the idea of marriage to the Earl of Huntly a wee bit frightening?"

She paused, giving him a severe look. "I find the story I've heard about Seaforth a bit frightening, Uncle. I've been told there is a lady ghost that wanders around here at night, dressed in pink and carrying her head. Is it true? Have you seen this lady?"

Barra threw back his head and laughed heartily. "If you've nothing to say on the matter, I'll not ask again. I only sought to know if this be a pleasing match to you, but I can see the answer to that well enough in those wildcat eyes."

Her mother looked at Annabella. "Well, bless my soul," she said. "You know, Barra, I think you may be right. She *does* have the eyes of a wildcat, doesn't she?"

"Aye," Barra said. "It's a good sign."

Annabella, remembering the favorable comments the coachman made about the elusive wildcat, took that as a compliment. She didn't smile at her uncle, but it was the first time she didn't frown.

Mrs. Barrie, the housekeeper, came to the door to summon the duchess to tea with her sister.

As Anne stepped through the doorway, Barra said, "I've never seen a lass with eyes as green as a mist-shrouded field of heather."

"They're green as glass, and they don't miss much," was the duchess's reply. This drew another laugh from the earl as she disappeared from sight.

Annabella decided she liked this man. Today, standing here in the loveliest of pinetums, the dazzling rays of sunlight setting the red of his head aflame, he wasn't as frightening as before, not by half. Suddenly she felt herself enjoying the way he didn't seem any more enamored of Huntly than she was.

"I take it you don't much care for my betrothed," she said.

"Dinna be mouthin' words for me, lass. I've no desire to see one of my own daughters married to that devil, but that's none of your affair." He shrugged. "Dinna worry your head with it."

"But I do worry," she said rather helplessly. "I don't care to wed Lord Huntly, but no one asked me about it."

"Your father isn't any more prone to be consulting a lass about his business than I am."

"Since the day my betrothal was announced, I haven't been able to find anyone who will speak to me of this matter. I see I misjudged you for a man of honest answers."

When he laughed, the very earth about them seemed to tremble. "And I misjudged you for a lass with no spunk."

"I'm afraid you were right, Uncle, in your original judgment. My spunk is fleeting at best. I've more jelly in my spine than bone, I'm afraid."

"Well, if it ever gets to going too poorly for you, you send word to your uncle Barra and I'll make a fast raid on Huntly and bring you back to Seaforth."

"Don't fill her head with stories, Barra. You know there hasn't been a raid in Scotland in fifty years—although I expect it chafes you to admit such."

They both looked up and saw Una standing in the doorway.

Barra grinned at his wife and Annabella felt a stab of longing. A man like Huntly would never look at her like that.

"Aye," Barra said, "but I hear often enough that history repeats itself."

It was a lighthearted comment at best, and Bella took it for what it was, an attempt to lighten her mood, but she could not help finding a quiet sort of comfort in feeling her uncle Barra would do exactly as he said, if she ever sent the word. It was a comfortable thought, and an endearing one.

"Where is Anne?" Una asked.

"Looking for you, more than likely. Mrs. Barrie called her to tea."

Una left and Annabella said, "Are all your problems solved so easily as your offer to raid?"

"From time to time."

"Do you see any solution to my dilemma?" she asked.

"A solution?"

"Simple or otherwise," she said, "as long as it's a solution."

"I wouldn't be a good Presbyterian if I said *no*, would I. There is always prayer."

"I know that. What I'm asking is if *you* see any way out for me?" she persisted.

The humor left his eyes. "No."

"So I should lose all hope and be led into this marriage as meekly as a lamb to slaughter?"

He remained silent for a moment, then said, "I imagine you will do what you see fit, regardless of what I think."

It wasn't the answer she sought, but it was an honest one, and one, she felt, that hit close to her own true feelings. For some time now she had been experiencing the strangest feelings she could only call rebellious, for they were in direct conflict with her father's wishes. She wondered if she should pursue this vein with this strange relative of hers. She did not yet understand her strange feelings of kinship with this man who was hardly more than a stranger to her.

"Have you ever known anyone to avoid marriage once the betrothal was contracted?" she asked.

"Aye, but putting your hand into a basket of adders seems a bit severe."

She watched Mrs. Barrie stride through the door, heading toward her. Looking back at her uncle, she said, "I suppose I am doomed to this marriage, then."

Barra met her eyes and smiled briefly. "I trust you will set your mind to working out a solution," he said. "I am not overly fond of having Huntly as kin. As for any help from me, I don't mind giving it, as long as it doesn't set me against the Duke of Grenville."

She knew at that moment that he understood her feelings and that he not only understood but felt that way himself. It gave her an odd sort of comfort and an even odder sense of closeness with this perceptive uncle of hers.

"Your mother would like you to join them for tea," said Mrs. Barrie.

"You'd best be going, then, lass. Your mother is a more formidable soul to be reckoned with than the likes of me."

Apparently Mrs. Barrie did not trust Bella to come by herself, for she directed her most dour expression at her and said, "If you will come with me, I'll take you there."

Tea lasted over an hour, and Bella spent most of the time listening to her mother and aunt talk. Now they were discussing Barra and Una's five older sons, who were all married. Annabella remembered there were two younger cousins about her age still at home. The duchess apparently thought of them about the same time.

"Where are Ailie and Allan?" she asked.

"They've spent the past fortnight at Barra's sister's. Lorna just had herself a fine baby boy, and her husband Willie is down with a back injury. I sent Ailie and Allan over to help with things. They're due back today or tomorrow."

After drinking her tea, Annabella excused herself and left her mother and aunt still deep in conversation.

Bella was tired, having spent the afternoon at such an unexciting pursuit as taking a ride in a gig, which promptly broke down, forcing her to walk the six miles back to Seaforth in her most delicate slippers. By nightfall Bella's feet were hurting, and once she kicked off her slippers in her room, she saw the reason why. Her feet were warty with blisters. She had just started soaking her feet in a soothing pan of warm herbal water brought by an unsmiling Mrs. Barrie when she heard some intermittent tapping against her window. She wished it away, but after a few minutes, she gave up and hobbled across the floor, threw back the bolt, and opened the window. Picking up the bedside lamp, she held it aloft and poked her head out.

Her irritated gaze was greeted by a deeply scowling face peering at her from the tree three or four feet from her window. Startled, she saw a copper-haired girl about her age dangling, rather precariously, from one of the limbs.

"Whatever are you doing in that tree at this time of night?" Bella asked.

"Coming to see you, although I must admit you are far too dense for me to have bothered. Will you please stop staring at me with that stupid-sheep expression and offer me a hand?"

"Who are you?"

"I am your cousin Ailie, you nitwit. Now give me your hand before I fall." She wiggled herself around to anchor her body with one arm as she extended the other for Bella to take hold of. Without giving it any more thought, Bella reached for her hand. A moment later her cousin braced her foot against the ledge beneath the window and pushed away from the tree. She came through the window with such force that they both went sprawling.

A moment later Ailie was on her feet, glaring down at Bella. "Are you going to lie there gaping like a frightened mutton, or are you going to get up?"

Accepting her offered hand, Bella slowly came to her feet, her mind too occupied with taking in the sight that declared herself to be her cousin. "*You* are my cousin Ailie?"

"I've already told you that, haven't I?"

Bella nodded, thinking her cousin was not the refined, neat person Aunt Una was. Ailie was the spitting image of her father, Barra. The girl was pretty in a wild sort of way—pretty and unkempt—there was nothing of the daughter of a titled man about her. Her dress, although new and of lovely design, was rumpled and torn in a place or two. Her face, although quite lovely with a slender nose and blue eyes, was a bit darker than fashion dictated. Her cousin did not cover her face and arms with long sleeves and bonnets, apparently, for there was a healthy sprinkling of freckles across her nose.

Ailie went about the room inspecting Bella's things, opening her jewel chest, glancing over a note Bella was writing that lay on the desk. "Who is Gwen?"

Bella snatched the paper and turned it face down. "A friend. Do you mind?"

"Of course not. Why would I care if you have a friend—although I am a wee bit surprised. You aren't very friendly, you know."

"And I suppose you are. What are you doing here?"

"I came to meet you."

"Couldn't you use the door?"

"Not at this hour. I suppose this is a bit unconventional, but if Father caught me sneaking in here, he would have me in thumbscrews by morning." She picked up Bella's silver-backed looking glass and peered at herself. "There's an old pit prison here in the original keep. Did you know that?"

"No."

"Well, there is, and we have a well hewn out of rock."

"How nice."

Ailie spied a bowl of cherries on the dressing table and put two in her mouth, pulling out the stems and tossing them out the window with the pits. "I hope those grow. I think it's such a shame to waste perfectly good pits, don't you?"

"Oh, yes," Bella said lightly. "I always spit mine out the window."

"You are very strange, do you know that?"

"Then we should do well together, for I find you strange as well."

"Oh, I do hope we get on." Ailie moved to Annabella's open trunk. "What are you doing?" she asked. "Unpacking? Oh, do let me help you." With charitable zeal, Ailie began pulling first one thing and another out of the trunk. "If the circumstances were any different, I might not have come to see you, but you see, there is only my brother Allan and myself here, and the nearest girl my age is more than twenty-five miles away. Of course, my mother and the household staff are females, but I'm not allowed to fraternize with the help, and although my mother is the dearest thing in the world, it's a trifle hard to make one's mother into a best friend. I mean, you can't exactly tell your mother all your secrets without fearing she might tell your father. You understand that, don't you?"

Bella nodded in confusion, for in truth, she hadn't understood a word her cousin said.

Chapter
15

Shortly after the Duchess of Grenville came, she went. Back to England that is, for a fortnight after their arrival at Seaforth, Bella's father and brother arrived from Edinburgh in the middle of the night. Shortly after their arrival, the roof fell in on Annabella's hopes.

The whole thing started innocently enough the evening before their arrival, when Ailie's beautiful, golden, puffball of a cat, MacBeth, did something no self-respecting tomcat would ever do. He had kittens.

Annabella and Ailie had, for two whole days, devoted their attention to the utilization of a basket of seashells Ailie had collected the summer before. Since the rage of ornamentation for the home at present was the use of seashells to decorate toilette boxes, pincushions, trinket boxes, and the like, the cousins had precisely grouped their shells—according to shape and color—in piles scattered about the floor.

Annabella, having entered the room ahead of Ailie, immediately set to work applying glue to what was to be a shell-encrusted flower pot. With a handful of shells in her hand, she had just begun to press the shells into the glue to form an interesting border when the door opened and Ailie burst in and cried, "The *dreadfulest* thing has happened, Bella. Come quick! MacBeth has had kittens!"

Annabella jumped up quickly, leaving her glue-smeared pot, and hurried with Ailie to the barn, where MacBeth lay in the hay behind the rick where the dairy cows were milked. Annabella picked up one of the blind, mewling kittens as Ailie exclaimed, "I thought he was just getting fat."

"He was," a voice said, "only it wasn't from eating."

Annabella looked around to see a young man not much older than herself step out of a nearby stall, leading a sleek gray.

"Oh, Allan, is that your new gelding? Are you going for a ride?" asked Ailie, going around the horse and giving him a good looking over.

"Yes, he's a beauty, isn't he?" He looked at Annabella. "Don't you think you should introduce me to our cousin? You are Annabella, aren't you?"

"Yes," she said, thinking Allan reminded her so much of Gavin, for they were about the same size and age.

"Do you ride?" Allan asked.

"Frequently, although I haven't had much opportunity since coming to Scotland."

"Then I'll take you riding with me soon," he said, swinging up onto the gray's bare back.

The two girls watched Allan ride out of the barn before their attention went back to the kittens.

"I still don't know how MacBeth had kittens," Ailie said, still somewhat dumbfounded.

"I think you'll have to change his name to Lady MacBeth now," Annabella said.

They stayed with the kittens for a while before Ailie said, "Well, I'm going to the kitchen to tell Cook the news. Do you want to come?" she asked.

"No, I'll stay here for a while and then I'll go work on my shells," said Annabella.

After personally inspecting all seven kittens, Annabella carefully placed the last one next to its mother and prepared to leave when a dark, looming shadow stretched across the floor of the barn. Annabella looked up and saw the frightening form of her uncle standing in the open doorway. She had grown quite fond of this uncle of hers, but he was still capable of striking terror within her with just one look. Surprise written all over her face, she gasped and said, "Oh, it's you."

She felt as awkward as her words sounded. Her uncle Barra stepped into the barn and fixed her with a stare that made her squirm. "You dinna think you had been cornered by a *ferlie*, did you, lass?"

Bright splotches of rosy color spread across her cheeks as she said, "You surprised me, that's all."

"A lass surprised is half beaten," he said. "Come into my study, fondling, I want to talk to you."

Annabella's knees quivered. An official summons from Barra Mackenzie ranked right up there with cataclysmic happenings and divine revelations. "But . . . but . . ."

"Don't stand there sputtering. If I wanted to do you bodily harm, I would have ordered you to the pit prison in the keep, before breakfast. Come along with you now."

"You mean you want me to come now?" she stammered.

"I dinna ask you now hoping you will come tomorrow. And I'm not in the habit of answering a legion of questions whenever I summon someone. I've stated my reason for

seeking you out," he said. "If you choose to come, I'll be
waiting for you."

The Earl of Seaforth left as impressively as he had entered. *I'll be waiting* . . . It wasn't exactly the wording to
make one break any records to get there. Pessimistic, she
remembered that according to Ailie, Allan had once said of
his father, "It's a good thing you aren't one to talk back, or
he'd cut your tongue out," Annabella fought the urge to
hide in the barn with the kittens for the rest of the day.

By the time she reached his study, Annabella was a
mental wreck and frightened out of her wits. As cautious as
a whore in a confessional, she opened the door and crept in.
With her hands folded piously in prayerful entreaty in front
of her, she entered the room, wondering at her sanity for
doing such a thing, although it was a little too late for such
thoughts now. Judging by the dark scowl upon his face, she
had failed, and failed miserably, in her attempt to placate
her uncle with humor. She stared at the large knife in his
hand, the blade of which was as long as her forearm.

Without a word, he let fly with the knife and it whizzed
across the room and buried itself up to the hilt in the heart
of a straw-filled form of a human shape. With her heart in
her throat, she gazed at Barra Mackenzie.

"There is nothing I find less palatable than a boiled egg
with a hard shell and a mushy middle," he said. "Before you
were a twinkle in your papa's eye, quakling, I had more
scars on my conscience than there are hairs on your head.
While I rather admired your paltry display of pluck, it was a
rather naïve thing to do. Bear in mind it would please me
greatly to see you stiffen your backbone, but remember as
well that I am not in the habit of occupying myself with the
snotty-nosed impudence of a nursling. Sit down."

In the flash of a second she was in the chair across the

desk from him, her mind frantic with wondering. *What have I done? To whom have I done it? What will he do to me for doing what I don't know that I've done?* Taking a deep, fortifying breath, she asked, "I might know better how to act, if I knew the reason I am here."

"You think you have that right, do you?"

"If I'm to suffer the consequences of it," she said.

"Much better," he said. "One should learn to be direct or say nothing. Common sense plus a dash of daring is a good thing to have. You're learning to overcome your cowardly habit of indecision."

"You might be cowardly too, if you were my size—*and* a woman."

"Whining in anyone is ineffective, and it's a puny tool at best. Any fool can pluck hairs from the nose of a dead lion. Wisdom is a woman's tool, and a man's strength is not its match. Keep your head, lass, and your self-respect along with it." He leaned back in his chair. "Don't look so forlorn. It's not as difficult as it sounds. We Scots have a saying, '*Set a stout heart to a steep hillside.*'"

A little relieved, she asked, "You didn't call me here because of something I've done?"

His brows lifted. "Why? Have you done something?"

"Nothing to merit a tongue lashing."

"Then we'll proceed. Your father is on his way here with the intention of hauling you back to England and putting you in the tower under guard."

"We don't have a tower."

"Don't get technical," he said. "I was merely letting you know it's a serious matter that brings him."

"Anything that brings my father is serious. If it brings him in a hurry it's *more* than a serious matter, but I'm happy with the news he's taking me home."

"I intend to talk him out of it."

"You mean you want to keep me here? In Scotland?"

"Yes."

Annabella felt her heart constrict. Her eyes burned. Fighting back tears, she asked, "Would I be considered impudent and snotty-nosed if I asked why?"

He laughed at that. "Because I aim to help you, quakling, and I can do it best if you remain here."

"If my father has made up his mind, he won't be swayed, Uncle. I can vouch for that."

"He will when I tell him of my discovery of your plans to secretly marry . . ."

Annabella sprang from her chair. "What?"

". . . one who has, I believe, made some three offers for you already—the Marquess of Tukesbury."

"I wouldn't marry him for the world. I don't even like him."

"You know that, but does your father?"

"He will if I tell him."

"Sit down, lass, before I throttle you."

Annabella shot into the chair.

"Now," Barra went on, "you can deny it, but you realize, of course, that knowing your distaste for marriage to Huntly, your father would be a fool not to believe that you would jump into marriage with any young, handsome Englishman who came along, rather than take the path chosen for you."

"Except for the fact that I don't *like* the marquess."

"Inconsequential," he said.

"My father knows me better than you think. He won't believe it," she said. "He knows I'm too much of a coward to defy him."

"I wonder," Barra Mackenzie said, and smiled. "Run

along now. Your first lesson is still as warm as fresh milk. Give it a chance to cool."

When Annabella was summoned to her uncle's library the following day to discover that her beloved brother and her more than irate father were waiting for her—along with her mother, her aunt, and her uncle—her first and by far most daring thought of her entire life was to bolt for the nearest door and keep running until she dropped from exhaustion or fell into the sea, whichever came first.

That thought was followed by a feeling that since she could think of nothing to say in her defense, her best defense was to say nothing at all.

During the time the duchess was explaining what she had seen going on in the garden beneath her window at Dunford Castle, Annabella busied herself with imagining what actions her father could and would make—none of which were very appealing to her.

"And so I thought the best thing to do, in your absence, was to separate the two of them before any damage could be done," the duchess said.

Bella's father answered, his voice trembling with anger, "You did the best thing that could be done under the circumstances, my love. I won't be so lax in my duty with Bella again. Every precaution will be taken to see that she is kept out of harm's way until the wedding. Bella, stop looking as though I've just ordered you to be boiled in oil. I have decided you will remain sequestered, here at Seaforth, until the day of your wedding."

Her stricken gaze flew to her uncle Barra, who was occupied with something outside the window. Forcing herself to look at her father again, Annabella gave a startled cry, "But . . ."

"Save yourself the wasted effort of pleading. My mind is

made up. Your mother, Gavin, and I leave for Saltwood in the morning. Your uncle has graciously offered to keep you under his thumb. Try to conduct yourself in a dignified manner until we return."

"When will that be?"

"A week or so before the wedding."

"Couldn't Gavin . . ."

"Your brother is needed at home, Bella. He doesn't have time to play nursemaid to you. You should know that."

"But, Papa . . ."

The Duke of Grenville looked at his daughter—the one daughter who had never given him an ounce of trouble. That is, until recently. Still, the memory of his youngest was fresh upon his mind. He sighed. "You need a tighter rein on you, Annabella, but I don't mean it to sound cruel, or like punishment. You know your place, as well as you know I want only what is best for you. I wouldn't have considered pushing you into a marriage like this if it hadn't been for that grandfather of yours."

Later, after she left the library, Annabella went to the barn and sat on an overturned bucket. One of MacBeth's kittens was on her lap. She was about to put the kitten back by its mother when Gavin found her. He gave her a warm smile and told her not to worry.

Annabella gave him a look of disfavor. "I doubt you would be sounding so cheerful if it were you being left behind."

Gavin laughed and mussed her hair, then called her an infant. "You wouldn't say that if you knew the things that await me in England. My days as a rakehell are over, I'm afraid. Sometimes I wonder if it's worth all the things I have to do, just to inherit a title. In some ways, Bella, my life is more out of my control than yours."

Annabella knew this, and she knew in his heart that Gavin really had no desire to become a duke. He wasn't against it, but he wasn't obsessed with the idea either. It made her feel worse to know that in spite of the turmoil in his own life, he would do his best to be smiling and teasing whenever he was around her and always try to keep her in a good humor.

"I don't know when I'll see you again," she said, her voice quivering. "It's such a long time until the wedding. A whole year."

Gavin's brows lifted. "Are you wanting to rush it, then?"

"No, but I might consider it, if it meant I would see you sooner."

"I'll be back before the wedding," Gavin said. "Father promised me I could come back."

While Annabella couldn't go so far as to say her spirits were lifted, she did admit that having Gavin's return to look forward to did improve her mood somewhat.

Early the next morning Annabella stood beside one of two massive stone lions that flanked the front door and took one last, long look at her family. Her eyes were bright and angry with determination not to cry. All her life she had struggled to be the daughter her father would love and be proud of, and what had it brought her? Punishment. Banishment. A forced marriage. She tried to look back over her life to see where she had gone wrong, but like looking back for her tracks after walking through water, everything seemed to have vanished—just as her life in England had vanished.

For the loss of her home, she tried to grieve, willing tears of sorrow and loss to come forward, but none came. She tried to call up beloved, happy times, fond memories of her childhood, but like the summoned tears, none came forth.

Annabella had no fond, cherished memories of her childhood. It wasn't that she felt abused, or even unloved, for she
knew her parents loved her, in their fashion. She simply did
not feel beloved, and that was what she wanted above all
else, to be beloved and cherished, to feel she had some
value. She was like one of the toys in the nursery—one of so
many lovely things one hardly took notice of her, and so she
spent her childhood years standing on a shelf, being taken
down occasionally and shown to friends and relatives, or
scolded for the dust collecting on her dress, then, finding
her hair brushed and her arms stuffed into a new dress, she
would be placed back on the shelf.

And now after so many years she was being tossed out of
the nursery, callously sold to the peddler willing to pay the
highest price. For Gavin, it had been different. He was the
long-awaited—and only—son, while Bella was nothing
more than the last in a long succession of daughters.

During all this time Barra Mackenzie studied his niece,
remembering how he had said, "The lass seems biddable in
temperament."

Alisdair promptly said, "She is biddable in temperament
only because she has been trained, like a vine, to grow that
way, not because it is her natural wont."

"And what do you think is her natural *wont*?"

"To run wild as a heathen without discipline or self-con-
trol. I tell you, Barra, a more difficult time I've never had of
it. Bella has required more of a strong arm than all the other
children put together. By the time she was two years old, I
knew I had a little hellcat on my hands. She was as willful
and headstrong as they came. A firm hand is what turned
the tide on all that. Believe me, it wasn't easy, guiding her
in other directions, although I can't say I'm exactly pleased
with the outcome. She's a bit bookish and far too intelligent

and educated—more than is necessary for a woman, I think. All in all, she's been a trying child to rear. If she is malleable at all, it has come through force."

Just like her marriage, thought Barra.

As the Mackenzies stood with Annabella, watching the elegant ebony traveling coach of the duke and duchess make its way down the winding road in a cloak of dust, Barra put his arm around Una's shoulders and let out a long sigh. His dejected niece disappeared into the house.

"Having the lass here will be good for Ailie. She'll be a mite more pleasurable to have tea with and to make a fuss over the latest fashion books than Allan," he said.

Lady Seaforth cast a skeptical glance at her husband. "You are oddly congenial about all of this. By the by, I would have sworn you were in a suffering state over having the lass thrust in your care."

"Hmmmm," was all Barra said, for he was smiling at the remembrance of a bit of whimsical idiocy that had occurred the past morning between this poor, lost lass and his daughter.

Ailie had invited herself to spend the night in Bella's room and had just removed her clothes and was sitting on the bed with her cousin, watching her write in her journal, when they were summoned across the hall into the room occupied by Annabella's parents.

Sitting *en chemise* when they were first summoned, the girls jumped up and made for their clothes at the same time. In the confusion, the *pot de chambre* was knocked over and before they could summon help, the entire contents had meandered out their door and across the hall and beneath the door directly across the way. When His Grace the Duke of Grenville opened the door to inquire as to the delay of his daughter and niece, he promptly stepped in the reason.

Chuckling to himself, Barra shook his head. He could have expressed his opposition and had the lass carted off with the rest of her family, but he was not a man who always took the easy way out. As it was, he surprised his wife and agreed to quarter his niece until the week of her wedding—after first having a man-to-man talk with Alisdair.

After so many scars, what was one more to his conscience?

A month after their arrival in Edinburgh, Ross and Lord Percival departed, their destination Dunford but not by the most direct route. Ross, still nursing his wounds over the hasty departure of Annabella and her mother, wasn't yet ready to return to Dunford and his grandfather. He was steadfast in his belief that the old man had something to do with the duchess's abrupt decision to take her daughter away. Time, he told himself, was what he needed. More time away from Dunford and his grandfather.

He was a bit put out with the old man, but he knew his grandfather wasn't going to be around forever. He didn't want his anger to be what pushed him into an earlier death. He would simply do as he had done for the past several years. He would wander from place to place, drinking and whoring until he purged that ivory-skinned beauty from his mind and loins. To Percy, he simply said he wanted to see more of Scotland. And in a way that was true.

From Edinburgh they made their way to Aberdeen, then Inverness, going across the Highlands to Ullapool, where Ross decided he had seen enough of Scotland. "A man can do just so much drinking and whoring, Percy."

To this, Percy merely lifted a dubious eyebrow.

Ross laughed. "I know what you're thinking, man, but it's true. I'm plumb tuckered out, as the old man said."

"Are you sure you're ready to go back, or do you simply need a good night's rest?"

"No, I'm ready. Even drinking and whoring taken too far begin to . . ." He paused and looked at Percy. "What's the word I'm looking for here?"

"Cloy."

"Right. Even whoring and drinking taken too far begin to cloy."

"And as Blake so eloquently put it, *'The road of excess leads to the palace of wisdom.'"*

"Lead on," Ross said, slapping him on the back. "The only excess I want now is an excess of sleep. God's bones! I've never been so tired. It's hard work keeping so many women happy."

Percy didn't say anything. He couldn't. He was laughing too hard to speak.

Four days later Barra Mackenzie sat in his study reading a letter from his cousin, Robbie Fraser, who lived in Ullapool.

I have taken the liberty of suggesting that my old friend, Lord Percival, and his charge stop off at Seaforth on their journey south. You will remember Percy as the man I became friends with when we both worked so hard to have the Corn Laws repealed. I know you will like him. Although he is not a farmer, he is much like you, a good man who holds his own plow.

They should arrive on Tuesday, the fourth. I know you will extend to them every courtesy that you have shown me on my numerous visits to Seaforth. Oh, just the mem-

*ory of eggs, cold veal pie, tongue, and hot, hot salmon
under a ray of sun in those pastoral fields of yours, all
polished off with a good shot of whisky.*

*In my exuberance, I almost forgot to tell you the name
of his charge—a young man, American by birth, but Scot,
I believe to the core. He is a grandson to the old duke at
Skye and goes by the name Ross Mackinnon.*

Ross Mackinnon. Och! and double och! Barra had heard
that name often enough to cause him immediate worry. And
then it hit him. *The fourth.* Today was the fourth. Without a
moment to waste, he sent for Una, and in the same breath
he dispatched a bevy of cleaning women to the fishing cottage that was less than a mile from the main house.

"Send them to the fishing cottage?" Una asked, giving
Barra a strange look. "Are you daft, man? I doubt Annabella
has ever been fishing in her life, and we both know Ailie
holds no fondness for it."

"I'm not sending them there to fish, love. We are expecting guests and I am simply removing the bait."

Barra recognized the angry thrust of his wife's chin and
gave her a hug of conciliation. "I know this doesn't make
any sense to you, but time is of prime importance here. I
don't have time for explanations, other than to say one Ross
Mackinnon is on his way here and the lass needs to be away
—at least for a while until I've had time to form an opinion
of the lad. There isn't time to plan anything else. You will
have to find a way to explain to them."

"But what will I tell them? They aren't children. And you
know what a mess I make of lying."

Barra kissed the top of her head. "Yes, love, I know, but
there's no help for it now." He gave her a pat on her back-

side. "Now off with you. There's work to be done. We've guests for dinner."

Una hurried toward the door, then paused. "You do like Bella, don't you?"

"Aye, I like the lass," Barra said. "Why else would I be going to so much trouble to skirt her away until I see if this Mackinnon is any better for her than that fool, Huntly?"

Una sighed in agreement. "Even after all these years, I still love you, Barra Mackenzie," she said.

"Aye," Barra said. "I always knew you for a wise lass."

Barra Mackenzie watched his wife of thirty years walk away. *Even after all these years?* He shook his head, a slow grin forming. He didn't completely understand his lass.

Even after all these years.

A short while later Una entered the fishing cottage, which was nothing more than an old black house that had been used by crofters years ago and then abandoned. Barra, not wanting to see anything go to waste, had made it into his fishing cottage. Una, getting into the spirit of things, had taken it upon herself to soften the bare bones of it and add a few homey touches of her own. When she finished, she declared it to be "the doll house I never owned."

Barra had grumbled a bit and said something to the effect that "any man who lets his wife decorate his fishing cottage ought to swear off whisky."

But when it was all said and done, he did have to admit Una had outdone herself on this one, for the little black cottage was as cozy and comfortable as a pair of old slippers that were run down at the heels.

Groaning under the weight of the heavy wicker basket she carried, Una flung back the heavy oaken door and found herself in the glow and warmth of the firelit kitchen. With a grunt of exertion she heaved the basket up on a long trestle table made from plain, unfinished boards. "There," she said, giving Ailie and Annabella a glance.

"Is all of that for us?" asked Ailie.

"Aye. This should be enough food to last you a week."

"Or a year," said Ailie, "unless you don't expect us to do anything but eat."

Una looked around the quaint little kitchen with its well-worn plank floor, and took a seat at one of the benches that flanked it. "Just as I thought," she said. "You'll get on nicely here. This place is warm as toast. Not a suspicion of a draft."

The kitchen occupied one end of the larger of the two rooms of the cottage—the smaller of the two being the bedroom. Perhaps that was where it got its charm, for there was something cozy and inviting about having a house that combined the kitchen and parlor—although parlor was a wee bit ambitious a word for this room. Near the fireplace were two large armchairs with fabric covering worn and shiny from wear. It was in these chairs that Bella and Ailie sat—waiting, Una assumed, for her to leave. But she wasn't in any hurry. It had been a while since she had ventured this way, and the cozy little cottage seemed to put its arms around her and invite her to stay. She had forgotten just how charming a little cottage could be, with its rows of mismatched plates gleaming from the cupboard, and the exposed rafters, smoky and hung with dried bunches of herbs, heather, and wild sea grasses, and over on the shelf a tiny plover nest with its two cracked, speckled shells.

It was the kind of place a man could be happy in, a place free of care and worry, a place made for feasting and song, and later on talking in low tones with a glass of whisky and a smoke—for everything here was cheerful and merry, from the pieces of furniture that seemed to greet one another from opposite sides of the room to the flicker of firelight that played over all, making no favorites.

Una let out a satisfied sigh. "I rather fancy this place. Want me to stay here with you?"

"No, we do not," Ailie said, leaving her chair and standing beside her mother. "And besides, you know Papa wouldn't hear of it." Taking her mother by the hand, she said, "Here, let me help you up."

Una seemed in no hurry to move. Ailie threw a pleading glance toward Bella.

"Aunt Una, aren't you needed back at the house to help hold those two *ogres* at bay?" Bella asked.

Una's hands flew to her face. "Oh, my, yes! I almost forgot. Here I am looking a sight, when I'll be having guests for dinner." She hurried toward the door, then turned back. "This is a wonderful place. Enjoy it, won't you?"

"We will, Mama."

The door closed and Ailie looked at her cousin. "Did you believe that story Mama told us?"

"Which story?"

"About the *ogres*—those demented despoilers of virgins."

"Of course. Why shouldn't I?"

"Oh, I don't know. I suppose it isn't that I don't believe her as much as that I . . . Well, bless my soul! I've never seen a *driven, demented, despoiler of young virgins* before, and I would so like to know what one looks like, wouldn't you?"

Annabella shook her head violently. "No. I wouldn't."

Later that night, at least an hour after they had eaten their supper of cold mutton and potatoes, Ailie and Annabella lay in bed, trying to go to sleep, neither of them having much luck. At last Ailie sighed. "I wonder if they're young lords? And of course they have to be handsome."

"Who?"

"The despoilers of virgins, of course. Who else?"

"You certainly spend a lot of time thinking about those two," Bella said. Then, reflecting upon what Ailie said, she asked, "Why would they have to be handsome?"

"Because no virgin in her right mind is going to let herself be despoiled by an ugly man."

"Oh, right," said Bella, her voice trailing off as she pondered Ailie's wisdom.

Judging from the noise coming from the vicinity of Ailie's bed, Bella decided she must be having a difficult time going to sleep. About that time the bed groaned and Ailie muttered something in frustration. A moment later Ailie said, "Are you *sure* you don't want to go have just one look?" Her voice, sadly wistful, was laced with a hint of hopefulness. "One tiny peek? We could sneak up to the window and . . ."

"How utterly wicked. Do you realize it would be the most appalling scandal if we got caught? Now, do hush up and go to sleep, Ailie. You are sporting mischief and you know it."

"Where's the harm in that? You sound too much like an old woman. We're young. That's the time for being as free as sunshine—that's what my papa says. Actually, what he says is, 'Ailie, my wild Scottish rose, you're only young once, so make the most of it. Happiness when you're young is as free as sunshine.' He and Mama are always talking about the mischief they did when they were young. Mischief when you're young is perfectly all right." Ailie went on talking, but Bella wasn't listening.

You sound too much like an old woman.

The sad thing about those words was that they were painfully close to the truth. Bella didn't know if she sounded like an old woman or not. But she felt like one. That gave her a start and she began to think more upon it. It was true. She did feel old. Ancient, in fact. And oddly enough, it wasn't Ailie who had fired those feelings, she realized, for they had been festering within her like a deeply driven splinter. And the person who had driven that first splinter of doubt beneath her skin was Ross Mackinnon. It had been Ross who planted those tiny seeds of awareness, who made her yearn, just a little, to speak words of her choosing—to see life through her own eyes and not those of someone else. She felt as though she should hate him for that, for making her desire something just beyond her reach. But she couldn't.

"Why are you so stern, so hard with yourself?" Ailie asked after a moment of silence. "You've never been allowed to be really and truly free, have you?" She asked those words as a question, yet Bella knew she did not expect an answer, for it was obvious that she already knew. Something about the way she said the word *free* made Bella envious, for she mouthed the word as if it were the closest friend she had—something she could pull up by the roots and take with her.

It all began innocently enough, just that same gradual warming sensation in her stomach, the fluttering of her heart, the perspiring palms—the same symptoms Bella always had whenever she contemplated something forbidden. "The devil's own brand of temptation" was her mother's way of putting it. Bella sighed and, as she always did, willed the yearning away.

But something strange happened. The more she willed it away, the more it came back, stronger and more resolute. She began to question herself. Who was this person inside her, this grave and voiceless critic that plagued her? Who was this tormentor that urged and prodded her on toward an attitude of fruitless servitude, only to judge her more stringently for the mistakes she was driven by this same voiceless critic to make? She glanced at her cousin. Ailie looked so fresh and free sitting there on the edge of the bed, life and vitality sparkling in the depths of her eyes, long coils of rich chestnut hair curling over her shoulder.

She was thinking Ailie looked so happy sitting there, the amber light from the lamp picking out the red-and-gold highlights in her hair as if it wanted to stroke them. Her skin looked warm and glowing, her face almost celestial, and Annabella thought she looked as one blessed, for there was no mark or blemish upon her life because she was as pure and clean and honest as one who had never had to practice restraint, or been forced to curb her instincts and her words, one who had never felt the agony of self-betrayal or the abject misery that came from abstaining from life. *She has never had to live by the code of temperance and moderation, and so she has never learned to doubt her own feelings; she always does what she desires, always expresses the emotions she is feeling, not those others might find more pleasing.* And as she thought these things, Bella couldn't help wondering, *How does a person get to be as free as that?*

Ailie was still talking, saying "As soon as we get up to the house . . ." And she filled the rest of the sentence with pictures of such varied and vivid descriptions of what they would do that Bella could not see how one little night could contain it all.

Bella was never sure exactly whether it was her own yearning or simply her weary surrender to Ailie's endless chatter that made her roll over at last and say, "Ailie, do let's sneak up to the house and see what these despoilers look like." As an afterthought she added, "But we must take care to see we don't get too close."

"You're right. You can't very well go to the altar if you aren't a vestal virgin," Ailie said as the two girls dressed.

If Bella had been allotted more time, the wheels in her head might have begun to turn, but Ailie was not known for her patience. She had already taken two black cloaks from the peg by the door and was handing one to Bella.

No English spy could have cloaked himself any better or moved with any greater stealth than Ailie and Annabella as they pulled the hoods over their heads and slipped out the cottage door. Cooler weather was definitely on its way, for the night had turned cold, cold enough to put frost on the ground by morning.

The cousins made their way toward the great house, inching their way through the darkness. "Do hurry up, Bella. Even if they are young, they'll be creeping with age by the time we get there."

Bella pulled her cloak closer around her, keeping her eyes on the lights of Seaforth in the distance and the dark shadow of Ailie's form just ahead. "Do you have any wildcats about?"

"Sometimes, but mostly they stay higher up—except on rare occasions."

Bella was just hoping tonight wasn't one of those rare occasions when they drew close to the stables and carriage house. "Let's go through here," Ailie said, opening the door to the stables. "It's closer . . . and warmer." They passed several stalls where curious horses came forward to stretch their necks over the doors to see who was about. Suddenly Ailie stopped. "Look!" she said, pointing at a great black horse.

Annabella looked closely at the animal. "He's very pretty."

"Yes," said Ailie, "but he isn't one of ours." Before Bella

could respond, she added, "And neither is this one." Bella
followed the direction of Ailie's point to see a beautiful bay
with a delicate Arab head.

"They must belong to the despoilers," she whispered to
Ailie.

Ailie patted the bay's nose. "Just think. Here we are,
petting the noses of the horses of the most despicable rakes
in Scotland."

Bella, who was trying to understand just what was so
glamorous about that, said, "Where did you hear that they
were the most despicable rakes in Scotland?"

"I forget where," said Ailie, "but I'm sure I heard it."

"Or made it up," said Bella. "Come on." A moment later
Bella was in the lead.

When they arrived at the house, the lights were on in
several rooms. "Let's try the dining parlor," Bella said.
"They might still be eating." But a look through the dining
parlor windows showed only old Dugal, the butler, and
Sibeal, the cook, clearing the table.

"The music room," offered Ailie. But the windows there
were dark.

"Your papa's study," Bella said. "The lights are on."

They arrived at the window, but it was too tall by half for
the cousins to see through. "Back to the stables," Bella said.
"We can get one of the saddle racks to stand on."

A few minutes later the saddle was unceremoniously
dumped in the floor and the cousins tugged and pulled the
saddle rack to the study window. "I'm taller," Ailie said.
"I'll go first and help you up."

Once she was up, she held out her hand. Bella had just
pulled herself up when Ailie put her face to the window,
apparently seeing something she liked—for a moment later
she wiggled closer and pressed her nose flat against the cold

pane. "That," she said with openmouthed satisfaction, "is what I call a man."

With gluttonous haste, Bella put her face to the window and came to the same conclusion. Her astonished gasp was both immediate and short. Not believing what she had just seen, she did as Ailie had done and wiggled closer, pressing her nose against the pane.

It wasn't so much the pressing of her nose that made her lose her balance but simply the sight of Ross Mackinnon tossing down a glass of whisky.

The sight of a man of such fine form made the two of them forget for a moment where they were and what they were standing on. Leaning as they were against the window caused their feet to push against the saddle rack beneath their feet. The rack teetered precariously on two legs for a brief moment before tipping over, sending the cousins to the ground in a tangled heap of legs and petticoats.

Ross heard the commotion outside the window. Perhaps it was because he was standing nearest the window, but more than likely it had to do with his past, for a man who had spent a good many years jumping in and out of beds learns to keep one ear tuned to what was going on around him. This had saved him more than once from being caught red-handed in bed with some man's daughter, or another man's wife. A quick glance at Barra told him that he hadn't heard anything, or if he had, he wasn't letting on.

It's probably a sheep dog prowling about, he told himself as he stepped to the window. Lifting his glass to his mouth, Ross took another drink, seeing a cloaked figure run across the yard and disappear into the darkness of the stable. He could tell it was a woman by the way she ran. His curiosity piqued, he tossed down the rest of his drink and yawned.

Barra smiled and made his apologies for keeping Ross and Lord Percival up.

Percy, as it turned out, wasn't quite ready to retire, so Ross went to his room alone. A moment later he was through the window and crossing the yard, headed for the stables. Seeing the door at the opposite end was open, he wasted no time searching the stable but made straight for the door, reaching it just in time to see a cloaked figure running along a grassy path that went between the hedges. Keeping to the shadow of trees, for the moon was high, he made his way along the narrow path, soon losing sight of his quarry. A moment later he came upon a small cottage sitting at the end of the path. The lights were on, and a lazy curl of smoke came from the chimney.

His first impulse was to return to the house. In fact, he started to do just that, taking a few steps and then stopping. Turning back to look at the cottage, he considered it for a moment, then shook his head and started away once more. He stopped a second time, a bit baffled as to why he felt as though something beckoned him to the cottage. At last, giving in to the urge, Ross turned toward the cottage, going not to the door but to a lighted window beside it. He was still baffled by the strange pull this cottage had for him. Perhaps it was the humble abode of a whore who made her living from the men who worked the Mackenzie's vast estate. Ross had always had a knack for ferreting out women. Perhaps a whore was what he needed now—one to help him get that black-haired beauty out of his mind. Yes, what he needed was a whore.

What he saw was no whore. But it was what he needed. Annabella.

He blinked, but when he opened his eyes, she was still there. Annabella, a lamblike creature who stood chastely in her laced and beribboned underthings talking to another girl who was pulling a nightgown over her head.

The other girl said something to Annabella, then left the room. Ross kept his eyes on Annabella. Annabella with the haunting eyes as green as Scotland's fells; Annabella with the rosebud perfection and all the self-assurance of a beetle swimming circles in an inkwell. He smiled in remembrance.

The last time he had seen her was in the flower garden back at Dunford. He had left her standing, as fragile as a butterfly, in the sun's warmth, a blushing rose that would tell her grandchildren years from now that someone had loved her at seventeen.

He had expected to see her again, of course, looking much as she had that day at Dunford. He never expected to find her standing beside a bed removing her clothes. And then it occurred to him: why the hell was she removing her clothes here, instead of in the big house?

Suddenly a slow smile of understanding stretched itself across the handsome planes of his face. Whatever Barra Mackenzie's relationship with Annabella was, he was obviously aware of what had been happening between them. Was that the reason she was whisked away from Dunford? He didn't know, but he would find out the answers before long. One thing he did know: likable though he might be, Barra Mackenzie was a crafty bastard.

The moment the other girl left the room, Annabella began unfastening her chemise. A moment later she was naked to the waist. Ross felt like the worst pervert in the world. Even with his decadent past, he had never had to resort to peeking in windows at half-naked women. But there was no way in hell he could have pulled himself away from that window. As the chemise came off, black coils of hair curled like a scythe over her shoulders and breasts.

Entwined with jet curls, her full, lovely breasts were blushed with colors that would rival the palest pink rose. He watched her pick up her gown and frown down at the row of buttons before sitting down on the bed to undo each one of them with the devotion of a child dressing her doll. *But this was no child.* And the thoughts he was having weren't those a man would have for a child either.

Buttons undone, Annabella pulled the gown over her head, then wiggled out of her drawers. A moment later the other girl returned with two glasses of milk. The two of them sat on the bed, their heads close together as they talked. He studied the other girl for a moment. She was about the same age as Annabella—taller, with lighter hair— but the way the two of them were together, he doubted the other girl was a servant.

Tomorrow, he thought. Tomorrow he would find out about the other girl. More important, he would find a way to be alone with Annabella. She would be surprised to see him, no doubt. As would Barra Mackenzie if he found out. But it would be worth it, no matter how angry Barra became. The lass was destined to be his. And he had a feeling she knew it as well as he. Nothing else mattered.

Tomorrow.

The delicious thought of it warmed him. Tomorrow he would see her. Tomorrow she would be equally happy to see him.

His mind filled with all the possibilities—ways she would show him how much she had missed him. He closed his eyes, hearing the slow, sultry tones of her voice as it called him closer . . . closer. He knew his lass. She would throw herself into his arms the minute she saw him.

Chapter

16

She broke a water jug over his head.

Only minutes before, Annabella made her way down to the well, carrying an empty clay jug that Ailie had thrust into her hands and instructed her to fill with water.

The well at Seaforth had its own little house, a miniature cottage built over the well site. But inside it was nothing like a cottage. Cold, dark, and dank, it was a creepy place at best. Stepping into the shadowy interior, she was greeted by the musty odor of age and damp wood. Cobwebs stretched across the rafters, and she was certain there were bats there as well. Finding the place creeping with things that crawled, she filled the jug quickly, anxious to be on her way.

She was uneasy about being this far away from the main house. Only that morning Ailie had called her a "superstitious goosecap" for being in such a worry about the ghost stories she had insisted upon hearing until the dawn had cast its first light.

Ross, having seen her go in, decided to wait for her on a

bench beneath a tree adjacent to the path she had just used. In a hurry to return to the cottage, she was looking at the pathway. She didn't notice there was anyone sitting beside it—the bench was partially concealed by dense shrubbery. As she passed, Ross, thinking she had seen him and was simply ignoring him, said, "Take one more step and I'll take more than some of your time."

About the same time Ross spoke, Annabella noticed a great hulking mass rising from the shadows of a nearby bush. She let out a shriek of surprise and turned. Terrified, and not recognizing his voice, she brought the clay jug down over his head just as he was rising to his feet.

With rivulets of water running down the creases of surprise that lined his face, Ross couldn't think of anything to say except "If this is the way you greet an old friend, I feel sorry for your enemies."

"Oh!" cried Bella, recognizing the cherished, watery features of the man she had just done her best to render unconscious. "The devil take you, Ross Mackinnon! I didn't know it was you."

"I don't know if I should be happy or just plain relieved. Does that mean you're glad to see me?"

She ignored that. "What are you doing here?"

"I came to see you."

"I'm not sure if I understand all of this. My mother brought me here to get me away from you, and now you have come. My uncle hides me away and now you are here." Still confused, she looked at him and said, "Why are you really here? How did you find me? Were you looking for me? Just me? Truly? I don't believe you."

She had such a wonderful way of speaking that seemed to be exactly the way he imagined her thought processes to work—something he found as utterly charming as he found her. He must tell her that one day.

However, he had more important things to say to her just now. When he looked down at the lithe, dark-haired lass in the shimmering gray gown that seemed to have been spun from moonbeams, he lost his train of thought and stared intently at the rapt expression, the beautifully shining eyes that gazed at him with such trust. Ross felt both his anger and irritation vanish like air bubbles rising to the top of water . . . *pop* . . . *pop* . . . *pop*.

"Never mind why I'm here," he said at last. "I need to dry my head a bit before my hair freezes to my head. Strange summer weather they have here. I don't suppose you have something inside your cozy little abode that I could use, do you?"

She couldn't help feeling a little suspicious about now. "I might."

He was taken aback by her quick retort, but instead of a spark of anger, he felt a grin tugging at his mouth. She was getting to be a saucy little thing. He wondered just how saucy she could be.

"Let me tell you something, beauty. You just did your dead-level best to bash my brains out, along with dumping a gallon of ice-cold water over me. Now, my clothes are wet and freezing and sticking to my hide. My head is so cold it's slowing down all rational thought—which, it may interest you to know, is precisely where the last thread of reluctance to throttling you is located. In other words, if you don't make a little bit of an effort to right the wrong you've done, I may forget I'm a gentleman and you're a lady and do something that would make more than your eyelashes flutter. Do I make myself clear?"

Apparently he made himself a little too clear. It had been

his intention only to test her a little, to see just how much spunk she could show, but he saw immediately he had over-played his hand a bit. Although she seemed to be trying mightily to show her disregard and, yes, even defiance, she wasn't holding up too well, for her lips were pale and drawn, the lower one quivering as if the herald of tears.

But Annabella was as proud as she was easily intimidated, and she wasn't going to cry if she had to bite holes in her lip to keep from doing it.

Hoping to ease her fears and get her in his arms as soon as possible, Ross felt he could show her his feelings much more easily than he could tell her, so he smiled as he reached for her, wet and freezing though he was. But the smile was too weak and came too quickly on the heels of his harshly spoken words. She gave him a glance stuffed full of sharp little daggers, then shoved him away, stepped lightly around him, and dashed for the cottage.

She slammed the heavy oaken door but didn't push the bolt hard enough to secure it. Ross, only seconds behind her, broke through the door just as she reached the fire-place. Turning to face him, she did her best not to cower as he looked at her and asked lazily, "Searching for more water?"

Annabella thought she detected a trace of humor in his voice, although the dark-haired giant didn't offer her any encouragement with that stare of his. He took a step closer. "Let's back up a bit here and see if we can't sort all of this out," he said. "I am up for an early morning ride when I see the cause of too many sleepless nights running through the woods as if the devil was after her. I dismount and ap-proach, seeing she is occupied. Being the gentleman I am, I patiently wait for her, but she ignores me when she comes out. I speak to her at last. The next thing I know a pot comes smashing down over my head and gives me a baptism with water as frigid as the look in your beautiful eyes."

He looked down at her, at her face, her throat, her breasts. "What are you doing here, lovely Annabella—and more important, what are you doing sequestered here in this cottage instead of the big house?"

She glanced at the glowing coals in the fire and turned away to add another log as she said, ever so casually, "It amazes me how some people can show such a blatant disregard for another's privacy. It should be obvious I came here to be alone."

"Look at me when you talk," he said and was rewarded with a scornful glance. "Only you weren't alone. Who was the other girl?"

Annabella paled, but she had already decided it was best to tell him the truth about everything. She was confident that he would find it out for himself by hook or by crook. "Ailie," she said.

"And who is Ailie?" he asked. "A maid? A newfound friend? Or a long-lost sister?"

"Cousin," she replied. "One of recent acquaintance."

"Barra Mackenzie's get?"

She nodded. "His youngest daughter."

"Who, or what is Barra Mackenzie to you? And if you say your uncle, so help me I *will* throttle you . . . or stuff your mouth with sugar plums."

"But he is my uncle—by marriage. He's married to my mother's sister, Una."

"My, my, there's no end to the surprises." Then as abruptly as he had steered the conversation in this direction, he shifted it. "Why did you leave that day without so much as a good-bye?"

Once again, the truth seemed the best approach, for it

occurred to her that the truth was probably always the first
and only choice around such a man. Annabella stiffened her
backbone and tilted her chin up, forcing herself to establish
eye contact with him. His words, she saw immediately,
were far harsher and more demanding than the gentleness,
the near-caress she saw in the bottomless blue depth of his
eyes. There was a fine-edged anger that lingered in him
today, something she had not seen since that day when he
came storming into the room to confront his grandfather
about the kilt. But no matter how she saw him—good-hu-
mored, angry, preoccupied—there was always a whisper of
gentleness about him, a feeling that no matter how much
she challenged him, no matter how angry he became, he
would never be completely out of control.

She knew also that she would suffer no bruising consequences at this man's hands, that no matter where things
ended up, he would always hold a certain amount of respect
for her, if only for the fact that she was a woman and something he obviously had been taught, or learned on his own,
to respect. It was one more round of confidence to the shy
budding of courage in a heart that she had always thought
chicken to the core. The sweet stinging awareness of it cut
like salt in an open wound.

"My mother saw us in the garden. She felt it best to bring
me here to stay with my aunt and uncle until my father
returned from Edinburgh and decided what should be done
with me."

"And has he returned?"

"Yes. Come and gone."

"Without you, I see."

"Without me."

"Why? What would make him leave you here?"

She went on to explain her father's decision to leave her

here until the wedding. She did not mention her conversation with her uncle Barra.

"Bastard," he said. "It's inhuman enough to betroth his own daughter to a man like Huntly without treating her with such disregard." His look was hard. "For the love of God. He may be your father, but the man is a bastard, through and through."

"My father is no bastard. He's a just and upright man who thought he was doing what was best for me. He had no way of knowing I would . . ." She faltered, but composed herself quickly. "That I would find the Earl of Huntly so displeasing." She tried to sound cheerful. "I daresay I'm not the first woman to find herself in such a predicament, nor the last, I'll wager."

With a man like this—well, she would always know where she stood. She felt her determination to resist him melting away. She had neither the desire nor the motivation to send him on his way, for her betrothal to the Earl of Huntly was motivation enough to throw herself into this man's arms and let him have his way with her—whatever way that was.

Only last night she had lain in this man's arms—at least she had done so in her dreams—and within the empty chambers of her unfulfilled heart, deep within the hollow void in her spirit, she had opened and welcomed him, praying that this interest he had shown in her might flourish and grow as perfectly planted seeds into something as strong and sure and fine as the heather that grew upon the moors. But with the dawn had come the first rays of reality and the cold truth of how her life wasn't her own to live as she desired but was merely an extension of her father's fancy. And so, with the fleeing darkness, all thoughts and hopes that had lingered in fairy-tale proportions vanished with the last fleeting shadows. She awoke knowing she would see Ross Mackinnon today.

Fate had been kind to her—or was it unkind? She had difficulty in understanding which. Kind, she supposed, in bringing his path to cross with hers once more, but most unkind if it had plans to divide them again and send them off to go their separate ways. She was not so naïve to think he had come after her, for there was little doubt now that he was one of the men who had stopped by for a few days' visit, one of the "despoilers of virgins" her aunt Una had spoken so laboriously about—and more than likely it was a well-deserved description.

She almost smiled remembering how Ailie had said the *despoilers* had to be handsome, for no virgin would want to have her virtue taken by an ugly man. And how true that was. Bella could think of no handsomer man, no finer specimen of manhood to do the honor of deflowering her, than this beautiful man. She shuddered in memory of how that honor had been given to Huntly the moment he signed the betrothal contracts.

Yet she told herself, *It's your virginity. Give the honor to whom you please.*

Bella fully expected to be struck blind for such blasphemous, disrespectful thoughts she was certain bordered on sacrilege. But instead of being struck blind, it was as if her eyes were opened. Suddenly she remembered something Ailie had said, *You can't very well go to the altar if you aren't a vestal virgin.*

And that was that.

This handsome young devil who stood before her had shown a definite interest in her, and she was going to do everything in her power to whet that interest. She reminded herself that she was set to marry that hellhound

Huntly. That was the worst thing that could possibly happen to her. So what did it hurt, what harm could come from having a go at turning things around? The worst that could happen if she failed would be marriage to Huntly, and that was already certain. Once you hit rock bottom, you couldn't sink any lower. *If* she gave herself to this man and let Huntly discover that fact, she might find herself with a null and void betrothal contract.

You might also find yourself a humiliated spinster for the rest of your life.

All right. What was worse? A humiliated wife? Or a humiliated spinster? She thought about the way Huntly fawned over his King Charles spaniels, feeding them chocolates and kissing them on the mouth. For a brief, blurred moment she saw him feeding chocolates to one of those dogs, the face misting and changing shape until it wasn't the spaniel he fed at all, but herself. It was enough to make a body sick. At least a humiliated spinster would be free.

She thought about the possibility that this man standing here engaged in such thoughtful scrutiny of her might—just might—fall in love with her, and that would solve all her problems. But when she studied him, she decided that whatever gentleness she felt in him, whatever kindness or interest he had shown toward her, those were far removed from something as noble as love; in truth, she had not even witnessed anything thus far that suffered to be as ignoble as lust.

What she did see was interest. Waves of dejection washed over her. He had sought her out today simply because she was here and convenient. Nothing noble in that. In the mysterious depths of his eyes, along the smiling lines of his lips, there hovered no inkling that it might be difficult for him to turn his back upon her and walk as simply from

her life as he had entered it—nothing that spoke of changing the teasing, playful rogue into a devoted lover and help-
meet. No, this man did not hover on her every word, or
tremble at the mere mention of her name, nor was he likely
to throw himself prostrate at her feet and beg her to go to
the far corners of the earth with him. A man like this one
would toy with a woman as a full cat would tease a mouse—
not hungry enough to eat, but content to while away the
hours at play for as long as she interested him.

She looked up at him, her face open and honest. "Are you
here to seduce me?"

Ross felt as if he had been kicked nine ways from Sunday.
For once in his life he was completely flabbergasted. "I had
thought to take you fishing. I can see now that that would
be a great disappointment—or at least a poor second to
what you had in mind. While the idea does have merit,
you're safe enough—for today."

A deathly paleness settled over Annabella, driving away
everything but her humiliating shame. She lifted her small
face and stiffened everything from her resolve to her spine.
She had bungled this in the worst way.

Fishing? Dear God in heaven, it was too humiliating for
words.

Ross watched her warring with herself, fighting for control and winning the fight. She stood before him now, looking every inch the regal yet sad lady that she was, gowned
most appropriately in the softest shades of mourning gray.

"I beg your forgiveness for such a coarse and vulgar outburst. I know it must have left you quite speechless," she
said.

"You can say that again. I can say one thing for you,
you're as changeable as the wind."

"If you don't mind, I would like to be alone."

"Like hell."

Annabella lifted her chin higher along with her mounting resolve. She had left herself open for this kind of shameful abuse by lowering herself to speak as she had. She had been foolish to think him gentleman enough not to take advantage of it and treat her with contempt. She had been wrong. "Please leave."

"Not on your sweet life."

"You shouldn't be here. I will be in the hottest water imaginable if my uncle learns of this," she said.

He succeeded in looking quite innocent. "I'm doing no harm."

"There's harm enough in just your presence. You are here, uninvited."

"So, invite me. Then we can be as happy as two hogs with their heads in a slop bucket."

Her green eyes opened wide. "Two hogs . . . what?" She felt disoriented—something she felt a lot around him. She dismissed the whole thing with a wave of her hand. "Oh, never mind. You talk more strangely than you look." She pressed her hands to her temples. "Nothing has been as it should since I left England. Everything is so confusing. I'm not certain of anything anymore."

"That makes two of us."

"You never did tell me why you're here."

"I did. I came to take you fishing."

"I don't want to go fishing."

"Why not?"

"I hate fishing."

"Annabella, have you ever been fishing?"

She looked around as if checking to see if there was anyone else in the room with them who might hear her answer. "No."

"Then how do you know you hate it?"

"I just know."

He didn't answer, but rested his back against the wall and regarded her impassively. He wore no hat, and his clothes were those same strange things he must have had a particular fondness for—buckskin trousers and a blue shirt, rough, scuffed boots, a wide belt with a gun hanging from it in that odd fashion he seemed to favor. At last he spoke. "You're sure you don't want to go fishing?"

"Positive. Without a doubt. Absolutely certain."

"That sure, huh? Well, that's probably quite wise of you," he said, grinning as he pushed away from the wall and came to stand in front of her. "I'm not the world's best fisherman, anyway."

He cupped her face in one hand. She felt the heat from his palm as he lifted her head until her eyes locked with his.

"Seduce you . . . hell. Annabella, what in God's name prompted you to ask me something like that? What made you think I was here to seduce you? Surely you don't think that's all the value you have—that the pleasure you can give a man in bed is your sole worth?" He shook his head. "Have I done or said something to make you think I had less than honorable intentions toward you?"

She didn't answer.

"Well? Have I? Answer me, damn you. I want to know what's going on behind those tempt-me-with-the-devil eyes of yours. No, don't turn away. I want some answers, and I want them *now*. Tell me why?"

"Because I wanted you to take my virginity," she burst out.

"What?"

"Oh, never mind," she said. "It doesn't matter now, anyway. I knew the minute I said it, you wouldn't do it. Especially now that you've seen what a helpless, hopeless nitwit I am."

He threw back his magnificent head and laughed heartily, then drew her against him and rested his chin on her head when the humor laughed itself out. "Little beauty, haven't you guessed by now that it's at times like these, when you're so refreshingly honest and at your nitwit best, that I realize I will never be able to live without you?"

If it was possible, her eyes grew bigger and rounder. "Does that mean you've decided to take my virginity?"

"Is it still up for grabs?"

She winced at his choice of words. "A simple yes or no will suffice," she said stiffly. "There's no need for rhetorical questions."

He stared down at the proud, almost pathetic young woman before him. He knew what she was asking, that she sought one of two things—perhaps both. Either she had resigned herself to the idea that she was going to marry Huntly, and had some inkling of what it would be like to be his wife—treated like a possession instead of a woman—and that had prompted her to come to the decision to give herself to him to see, for one glorious night, what it could be like between the two of them; or she was taking a desperate gamble, hoping to lure him into deflowering her so she could break the news to Huntly and thus bring things between them to an end.

Neither reason held any appeal for him.

"No," he said softly, his hand caressing the softest skin this side of heaven that lay at the base of her neck. "If it makes you feel any better, I don't think you meant a word of what you said. I think you're upset—you're disappointed, wounded, hurt. You're like a drowning man who grabs at straws."

He was right, and the thought of humiliating herself without thinking as she had done was more than she could take. Two enormous tears welled within her eyes and trembled like dewdrops on her lashes for a moment before spilling over and splashing down her cheeks.

"You see," he went on to say, wiping the tears away with his thumb, "I know you better than you think. You're too fine, too honorable a woman to stoop to those tricks. And you aren't naïve enough to offer yourself like that without thinking of the risks, the consequences to yourself and those you love."

Down the tears traveled until, one by one, they dropped in dark gray splotches upon the bodice of her gown. She tried to wrench herself away, but he held her fast. "Easy now, there's no need to bolt for the door. They say the truth hurts, and I guess it does, although it seems a downright shame that a woman's head can be turned by flattery, while all the truth gathers is pain or anger."

"I'm not angry," she said, taking a swipe at her tears with her sleeve. "If you must know, I am filled with shame."

"Why? Because of what you asked me?"

"No, because you were right. I'm not that kind of woman. I do think of consequences. I don't want to bring shame down upon myself and my family—and now I've done both by humiliating myself this way."

The way her lip quivered was adorable and he had never wanted to kiss a woman more than he wanted to kiss her right this minute. But now *he* was thinking of the consequences.

"I'll never be able to look you in the face again," she wailed and buried her face against his chest.

"Why? Am I that ugly?" he asked.

She pulled back, her face wet with tears, her voice punc-

tuated by sobs. "Don't . . . th . . . think y . . . you
. . . can . . . m . . . make me . . . laugh."

"I would never stoop so low," he said, fighting to hold
back his laughter. "May they cut out my tongue . . . boil
me in oil . . . chop up my liver and feed it to the . . ."

"Vultures," she supplied, just before she socked him
lightly on the arm.

"Blow," he said, holding out his handkerchief.

She blew her nose. "Are you never serious?"

Melancholy, it seemed, had robbed her of her humor and
a certain amount of her resilience, and he was reminded of
the days when he had first met her, when she had seemed
every inch the regal princess who had no pain, felt no
shame. Even then, he had felt this strong attraction for her,
this feeling that whatever happened between himself and
this woman, he would never meet another who touched him
quite the way she did. He didn't understand it. He didn't
know why. But someone had made the rules for her to follow, rules that would only benefit those who made them,
not her. Why did she have to suffer to please her family?
Why did she have to lose in order to win? He thought of her
life and how she had no control over the events in it, how
she had been restrained, then shaped and formed like bread
dough to fulfill a chosen destiny—as a calf is fattened for
slaughter—to marry a man befitting her family.

Meeting that family had given him a pretty fair picture of
what her life must have been like before he stumbled into
it. Her family loved her, that much was evident, but he had
seen families like that before, families that lost track of
themselves and allowed too many other things to crowd out
the space that had been given for feelings. His heart went
out to her, for she still had enough fire left in her that she
didn't want to go down without fighting, but she was floun-

dering now in waters that were as unknown to her as they were deep.

A haunted quality lingered about her like a great, heaving sadness that reached out to him. He discovered her emotions, her feelings affected him even more powerfully than her beauty or her desirability. She shuddered and he looked down into eyes that were a clear, clear green, dusted with gold. Her face was pale with a spot of color high upon her cheeks. Her lips were red and soft, ripe for kissing, but as she looked at him, a glimmer of distress lingered there.

"Don't be sad, lass. You'll forget it in time."

She shook her head.

"It won't seem so bad by tomorrow. You'll see."

"No," she said wearily, "this time I think my thoughtlessness has gone too far."

He looked pleasantly surprised. "Is your character so weak that it won't bear such a small burden as this?"

"Perhaps it isn't my character that plagues me."

He wasn't smiling now. "What is it? What bothers you and turns you sad?"

How could she answer him? What should she say? That his presence filled her with so much hope? That reality stole it away? That the time she was with him passed so quickly, and the times they were together were all too few? No, she could not say these things to him, so she said nothing.

They looked at each other and all consciousness of anything else seemed to slip slowly away. There were no barriers between them now, no cruel reality, no strange twists of fate. They were only a man and a woman, brought together and pulled apart, without really knowing why.

As if sensing her discomfort, her misery, he touched the

side of her face. "Don't lose hope," he said. "We'll find a way."

His hand was warm and solid and she turned her face into it and kissed his palm, hearing the air rush from his lungs as she did.

"I have lost hope," she said. "My cause was lost before it ever had a chance to get started."

"Don't be so quick to predict the worst. Have you no faith?"

"No," she said. "Not anymore." A second later she said, "Why do you persist when you know as well as I that all of this is pointless? Why me and not some other?"

"Are you fishing for compliments?" he asked. "Not that it matters, I suppose, because there is nothing here that I am trying to hide. I like the heart of you, Annabella, and I like your brand of freshness. I've a feeling there's a reason for all of this and I'm determined to stay on the back of this bronc and ride it to the end. Not much has come to me in my life, and maybe that's because there never was much I wanted—until now. I have an easy enough way about me, but I can be as fierce and determined as the rest of them when I have a cause. Something has drawn us together and I won't see it pushed away. I wouldn't turn back now if a hundred Huntlys stood in my way."

She looked into his face, her throat growing dry and tight. Her pulse pounded like surf against her ears. She couldn't bear for him to look at her as he did. His ridicule or even his anger she could have taken, and yes, even fed upon. His indifference she could have lived with. Or was it pity? Yes, she could have fought even the ravages of that.

But this? This understanding. This warmth. This feeling of kinship she felt with him. It was too much, and too powerful, and it reminded her of what she wanted and could never have.

Misery welled up inside her. She could not bear to look at him like this, the way he stood before her with the casual, comfortable ease that one would find in a favorite stuffed chair. His upraised arm was braced against a support beam, his other hand with the thumb hooked in his belt loop, his fingers splayed as if pointing to that part of him that lay beneath the stressed buttons of his well-fitting pants. And everywhere, lamplight seemed to worship him, touching him with adoration. So lost in thought was she that the sound of his voice penetrating the silence startled her.

"Angel heart, don't grieve so. What you suggested in all your humiliation will take place. Have no doubt on that score. But when it does, it won't be because you sought the answers to some questions, or because you offered yourself in shameful exchange for a way out of a detestable marriage. You aren't a sacrifice, and when you and I make love I won't be taking—and you sure as hell won't be giving, because, lady, I can promise you that I give as good as I get. When you and I come together, it won't be like two trains going toward each other on the same track, and it won't be like some pale and fragile rose I've decided to pluck and enjoy for a moment and toss away. God knows I've had enough of those to know what I'm talking about."

She felt his arms come around her tightly, holding her so close that she not only heard his words but sensed they were humming through flesh and bone to touch flesh and bone.

"True love is a slow grower, lass; it won't thrive unless grafted upon a vine of equal merit. Once it has taken root, it will flourish and be like evergreen, lasting forever." He tipped her head back, his eyes warm and liquid as he lowered his head. "Fate may have given you parents, but take heart, sweet Annabella. Choice will give you a mate."

If ever a heart took wing, hers did. But she had no more time to think about what Ross had said, or the sudden flight of her heart, for when his mouth closed over hers, the world tipped crazily and stood still. How long had she thought about this moment, how had she imagined what it would feel like if she could kiss him with all thought of Huntly and all the niggling feelings of guilt banished from her mind? If she could kiss him as she was kissing him now?

Light-headed from the swell of emotion and her efforts to tone down her own exuberance, Annabella swayed against him. That was all the encouragement Ross needed. "Such a sad little lass," he said. "Such a beautiful, sad lass." He moved his hands up and down her back. She was so slender he could feel each tiny bone of her body. "You aren't much bigger than a sparrow," he said.

"Thank you," she said, pulling away to look at him. "I think." She looked up at him and he laughed, pulling her back into his arms.

"You're very beautiful, do you know that?" He laughed again. "Of course you do. I'm sure every fool in London was besotted with you. You probably had them raising more hell than an alligator in a dry lake, just to get one dance with you."

An alligator in a dry lake? Are these words of comfort where he comes from?

His arms tightened around her, cradling her against him. There had never been any real physical affection between Annabella and her father, and Gavin, although he loved her dearly, was too young and in too much of a hurry to take much notice of such a thing as hugging his little sister on occasion. Her mother and her sisters had been affectionate with her, of course, but that wasn't the same.

Being held in a man's arms was entirely different. A man —whether it was father, brother, or lover—gave a woman something in a hug, a gentle caress of comfort and confidence that no woman could. The feelings Bella was experiencing now were different from any she had felt before. And it wasn't a matter of passion, since passion was a relatively new emotion to her, something still in its fledgling stages. What she felt now went beyond passion to comfort. There was something sure and honest and strong about being held in this man's powerful embrace. Something that made her want to stay there. Forever.

If only she could.

He pulled back a bit and looked down at her. "Heaven help me, you're softer than a moth's nose and you've got me all stirred up inside. I feel as if I swallowed a hornet's nest."

Softer than a moth's nose? Where does he get these comparisons? Has he ever felt a moth's nose? Has he seen one? Do moths even have noses?

"Annabella, are you going to keep on giving me trouble or are you going to give in to your own free nature and see where it leads? In other words, are you going to cooperate?"

"Cooperate? About what?"

"Letting me court you in the way you were meant to be courted?"

"No," she said, and laughed. "It's a little late for that, I'm afraid. You don't court a betrothed woman. *Especially* when she's betrothed to someone else."

"Don't keep bringing that up around me," he said seriously. "It makes me mad enough to stomp some rocks every time I hear it, and I don't want to be angry now—especially when I'm here like this with you."

"I must say, this is most unusual," she said. "Strange, even."

"How so?"

She threw up her hands. "The way everything is happening here. You seem to be interested in me . . ."

"*Seem to be?* Listen, beauty, I don't *seem* to be anything. I'm interested, all right. When a man closes in on a woman faster than greased lightning, you *know* he's serious. If you didn't know it already, *serious* is more than interested."

"Don't try to confuse me. You say you're interested and I offer myself to you—but you refuse. In the next breath you say any reference to my betrothal is most upsetting to you. *You* don't make any sense at all."

"It damn well is upsetting."

"There you go again. If you don't want me, then why should it matter who has me?"

"Don't want you? Listen to me. *Don't want you?* Where did you get a damn-fool idea like that? Good God. Don't you know I'd marry you right this minute if I could?"

"Marry me? How can you say something as ridiculous as that? You don't love me. You hardly know me."

He saw her scoffing look and heard the harsh words. He gripped her arms and looked seriously into her face. "Our love is just beginning, sweetheart. Time will see it to its proper depth. You can't rush love any more than you can quench it."

"But . . ."

"Annabella, will you shut up?"

"Why?"

"So you can kiss me," he said.

"Hmmm. I don't know," she said. "Men like demure,

chaste women—my mother told me that much. A woman brazen enough to kiss a man outright—I . . ."

He didn't wait for her to finish but began placing little nibbling kisses all up and down her neck. Bella sighed and moved her position to give him better access. "That," he said softly, "is what a man likes. A lass who's full of cooperation."

"Cooperation? Isn't that where this conversation started? I think we're going in circles."

"Isn't that what love is? A never-ending circle?"

This man, she thought as his mouth covered hers, *could talk a leopard out of his spots.*

Before either of them could say anything else, the door opened and Ailie stepped inside. Bella let out an inelegant yelp and jumped back. Before she had a chance to collect her scattered thoughts and introduce her cousin to Ross, Ailie crossed the room and stopped in front of him, saying, "I know you. You're one of the decadent despoilers of virgins, aren't you?"

"Don't tell me you're here to volunteer," Ross said. "Two offers in one day. That must be some kind of record."

Ailie seemed to be somewhat intrigued by that. "Two offers?" she asked, turning her head to stare at Bella. "Who was the first one?"

"Blast and double blast," Annabella said. "Can't anyone be trusted to keep his mouth shut anymore?"

Ailie looked aghast. "You mean it's true? *You* offered yourself to him?"

"It *wasn't* like that," Bella cried.

Ailie didn't pay any attention to Bella, however. She was too busy looking Ross up and down. "I can't believe you offered yourself to him . . . not that I blame you any," she said. She glanced at Bella. "It doesn't seem like you."

"It *isn't* like me." Annabella said hotly. "After all, it was *your* idea."

"*My* idea?" Ailie said as if dumbfounded as to how on earth Annabella could have thought something like that was her idea—although it wasn't such a bad idea at that. Slowly, understanding began to creep in. "Oh, that."

Ross watched Ailie's face pass through three shades of red before sticking on scarlet. She squirmed a bit before saying, "I suppose I just came barging in here . . . interrupting something."

Annabella sighed. "You didn't interrupt *anything*."

Ailie had the audacity to look crestfallen. "I didn't?"

"He turned me down," Bella said. "Flat."

Ailie's surprised expression was directed at Ross. "You did?" She shook her head in disappointment. "You can't be a decadent despoiler, then."

"I'm not a decadent . . . Shit! It wasn't like that. And I didn't turn her down—not down flat, anyway." He turned to Bella. "It was always my intention to take you up on it, just not right now—a counterfoil, so to speak."

Ailie puzzled over everything Ross said for a minute, but Annabella's understanding was right on target. "A *counterfoil!*" she shrieked. "As in a receipt?" She was closing in on him now. She could never remember being so angry in her life. How dared he insult her like this—and in front of her cousin. Her anger gave way to rage.

"Do you really think my offer was to be taken at *your* whim, like some . . . some *raffle ticket?* Even this ridiculous discussion is *my* business, not yours." She poked him in the chest. "And it's *my* decision to be taken *whenever and if ever I choose*." She poked him again. "Just *whose* virginity are we discussing here?"

"It sure as hell isn't mine."

"Don't try being clever. You aren't."

"No, maybe I'm not, but I sure am lucky."

"We'll see about that," she said. "We'll just see about that."

And Ross and Ailie saw something they had never seen before. They saw a woman transformed right before their very eyes—into a shrew.

The cozy little kitchen in this cottage was well stocked, and more importantly, everything was housekeeper handy—something Annabella found to her liking at this particular moment. Furious at what was happening and the way things were going, Annabella was ready to draw the line on all the pushing around she had had in her short life. She picked up the first thing she saw, which happened to be a pair of sugar-nippers and threw them at Ross. He laughed and ducked.

Annabella saw red. Vivid red. Blood red.

The next things she grabbed were the brass stacking weights off the balance. Then the tinplate grater, a vegetable chopper, a wooden potato masher, an oak thible, a long handled ladle, an English trivet, a sugar tin—the lid came off and sugar went everywhere.

By now Ross had stopped laughing. He had decided she might be serious, since he was ducking things on a fairly regular basis.

Ailie was dusting sugar off herself, but she too was laughing—she had found refuge in the doorway that led to the bedroom. Out of the range of fire.

"Out! Out! Out!" Annabella shrieked.

"What's got your dander up?" Ross asked while dodging again. "What did I do?"

"Get out of here and don't ever come back!" Annabella screamed, picking up the dasher head from the churn and hurling it like a discus. The churn would have followed if it hadn't been full of milk. She had no inkling of what she threw after that, but Ailie was keeping a pretty good account.

"One butter print," Ailie said, "five clothes pins, two spoons with resin-filled handles, three bundles of hemp sulphur matches . . . no, make that four." When Bella went for the cast-iron fish kettle, Ailie stopped counting and Ross shot through the door.

Luckily for Ross, the fish kettle was too heavy for her to throw.

"I'll be back," he called out.

"I'll be waiting," she yelled out the door as she let fly with the oatmeal roller. It struck him between the shoulder blades.

"Damnation," he said, heading for the trees. "That woman could teach an arrow how to fly." *She'll be sorry. As soon as she's had time to cool down and think of what she's done, she'll be sorry*, he thought and dived through the shrubbery.

Chapter

17

Annabella had never felt so exhilarated. She had never felt so pleased with herself. She had thrown a fit. She had expressed her anger. She had broken free.

Yesterday she had taken a giant leap and jumped free of the restrictions in her life. Today she was still traveling on the momentum of that leap. She was something she could never remember being before. She was wonderfully and thoroughly happy with herself. And that, she discovered, was a far cry from being happy with one's surroundings or one's set of circumstances.

Nothing had ever fortified her like the knowledge that she had honestly faced a situation and taken a risk to be herself without pretending to be something she was not. Living within that tight little perimeter of existence permitted to her was not really living. She could see that now. Life was either giving up false beliefs and taking a chance to free yourself or a self-inflicted prison.

The desire to jump free had always been there, but Annabella had been taught always to look before she leaped, to think things through. And yet whenever she thought things through, weighed the good against the bad, and recognized the dangers, she always retreated into the security of what was familiar to her: the security of obedience. For once in her life, she had taken over, pushing everything else aside. For once she had reacted, not according to the codes of the times, not according to the teachings of the church, and not according to the instruction and expectations of her parents. She had been herself and done something *she* wanted to do.

And that felt good.

There seemed to be no reason for Annabella and Ailie to continue their stay in the fishing cottage once Ross had discovered they were there, other than the fact that the girls had grown quite fond of the quaint little cottage and heaped all the blame for their having to leave upon Ross Mackinnon's back.

For the next two or three days, things settled in quite nicely, with the sound of Barra Mackenzie's baritone laughter flooding the castle at periodic intervals. Barra, it seemed to everyone, had formed a fast friendship with Ross and Percy, and the three men along with Allan were together constantly, whether they were hunting, fishing, golfing, or sitting around the fire with a glass of whisky or Drambuie telling stories.

Soon the few days Ross and Percy had originally decided to stay turned into a week.

"Your uncle has invited them to stay on for a while," Una said to Annabella one afternoon.

Una was sitting before a large weaving loom. Annabella, sitting beside her, watched her aunt's nimble fingers roll thread around the warp beam and secure it with a weight. Bella helped stretch the warp to the cloth beam, silently wondering just what her uncle was up to by this latest move of his.

She had been spending an hour or so each day with her aunt here, in the weaving room, learning the loom and readying herself to try her hand at weaving soon. Una pressed the pedals and the heddle raised and lowered the alternating threads. As the weft was guided through the gaps, Annabella let her mind go back to what her aunt had just said about Ross and Percy's extending their visit.

"Uncle must be enjoying their company," she said. "Is that why he's invited them to stay?"

"That and a few other reasons, I suppose. You know how men love to talk. They spent the entire morning in Barra's study going over farm journals and discussing farm animals, of all things. Now I ask you, how could anyone talk about cows and pigs for four hours? We've always run a fine herd of Ayrshire cows, but now Barra is talking of buying Jersey and Guernsey cows. "I said, 'Our Ayrshire cows give us enough rich milk. Why do we need different ones?' But I doubt my opinion will stop progress. I have a feeling that come next spring, we'll be seeing a few of those Jersey and Guernsey cows dotting the pastures, up to their udders in buttercups."

A strong slice of rich afternoon sun cut across the loom and flooded Bella's face. Una laughed. "By fall that shaft of sunlight wilna be hitting you in the face, lass. When the sun drops lower in the sky, it'll be giving me an eyeful." She paused a moment and looked outside. "The fog has lifted and it's turned out to be a fine, fine day. Why don't you find Ailie and the two of you go outside to get some sunshine? You're much too pale, Bella. The sun will put a little color on your cheeks."

"Mother said a lady should never get sun on her face."

"Oh, pooh! A little sunshine never hurt anyone." Una looked thoughtful. "I wonder where your mother got all those ideas she's filled your head with? She surely didn't have them as a child. Why, there wasn't a more tangle-haired, mud-splattered lass in the Highlands." She sighed. "Well, never mind all that. You run along now and get your hour in the sun." She turned toward Annabella, taking her hand in hers. "You're young for such a short while, Bella. Make the most of it. Don't waste your youth trying to be old. You'll be there soon enough. Live each day as if it were your last. Make no excuses for yesterday, no promises for tomorrow. Tomorrow belongs to God. As they say in Turkey, today's egg is better than tomorrow's hen."

Annabella laughed and hugged her aunt. "Have you ever been to Turkey?"

"No, but I've been in love. I ken what you're going through, lass."

Annabella looked at her aunt, hoping to discover something in her countenance that would clue her to what she was about, but her aunt's features were closed. Una Mackenzie was very much like Bella's mother in looks. Her posture was straight and regal, yet approachable; her eyes were a softer gray than Anne's and full of more understanding. It was as if her mother had been remade into a softer, gentler, more compassionate woman who looked every inch a mother. Annabella guessed that was what it was about her mother that seemed to put distance between them. The duchess did not look like a mother. She looked like a beautiful doll one would display on a bed but was never allowed to play with, while Aunt Una was the doll being pulled down the stairs—*bumpety, bumpety, bump*—by its one good arm, the other having been lost in a tug-of-war. At one time this doll had been as beautiful and finely made as the other, but time and use had given it a patina that comes only from loving hands.

Looking at her aunt, Annabella could see how living life to its fullest had plumped out Una's figure somewhat and put the lines of laughter upon her face. And work such as cheese making and lace tatting and weaving and a hundred other chores Una lovingly performed had coarsened her hands. Bella almost smiled, remembering the first few days she had been here, and how her mother had said, "Una! Faith, I cannot understand why you persist with these menial chores when you have so many servants about. No gentlewoman does her own milking and washes her own linen. Why do you persist?"

"Because I enjoy it. It fulfills me."

"Fulfills you?" the duchess had said. "Dear, dear, Una. There is something dreadfully wrong with a woman who must raise blisters on her hands in order to feel fulfilled."

Una had simply laughed. "What else would I do? I can drink only so much tea."

Annabella was still smiling when Una stretched and kneaded her back, her eyes still on the window. "If I didn't know it was closer to fall, I'd swear it was springtime. Just look at that sun. Why, it's as golden and mellow as a round of cheese. Now, go on with you. You'll have plenty of other opportunities to learn weaving. Next week, I'll show you how to make lace."

As she went downstairs, Bella was thinking of how different her life was now. She would even go so far as to call herself happy, if it weren't for the dark cloud of uncertainty about her future that always hovered over her head. She pushed all unpleasant thoughts away.

"Afternoon, miss."

"Good afternoon to you," she said, waving at the old butler. She was remembering how he used to speak to her only when she spoke to him first. A lot of things had changed since she had first come here. And no one was more astonished than she.

Within days of her coming, the spirit of self-sufficiency she saw in everyone here at Seaforth had spread to Bella.

She had never known so many tasks were required to run a household, or that you had to be fit as a trout to do them. Housekeeping was hard work. Laundry day, for instance. That was something that required strength and stamina.

Before Annabella had been at Seaforth very long, Ailie had coaxed her into the laundry—on a Monday, of course.

"Laundry is *always* done on Monday," Ailie said.

"Why?" asked Bella.

"Mama says it's because we always cook a great joint of venison on Sunday, and there's enough left over for Monday. That way, Cook can spend less time in the kitchen and help with the laundry."

Annabella looked around the great room that was reserved for laundry. Apparently there was a lot of work to do on washday, for there were several women already at work. Wicker baskets of carefully sorted clothes were everywhere. Bride, the laundress, was boiling the dirtier clothes in a copper, while Dorcas, her helper, was washing the finer things in a dolly tub. To Annabella's horror, linen was bleached by the disgusting practice of soaking it in urine, which contained ammonia—or so she was told.

Seeing her horrified look, Ailie said, "It is *human* urine, Bella," as if that made a great difference. "Some people use hog manure. Don't look so ghastly. Everything is washed in clean water afterward. Mama said they do the same thing in England. In fact, the English . . ."

Bella didn't want to hear the rest.

Laundry day was only the beginning. Early the following morning Ailie had her up at daybreak to hurry into the kitchen, which was already bustling with activity—Tuesday officially being baking day. The kitchen hearth was fueled with peat, and already the fire was built, a cauldron suspended on a chain receiving the ingredients for Scotch broth: neck of mutton, barley, turnips, leeks, peas, cabbage, and carrots. Already the kitchen was warm and cozy with the abundant smell of yeast. Round loaves of bread lined the table.

Ailie enlisted Annabella's help to cut crosses on the top of cob bread. "To let the devil out," she said.

Then it was put on the hearth, covered with an inverted pot, and surrounded by burning peat. While that baked, oatmeal was mixed with a thible, shaped on a riddleboard and rolled with a ridged rolling pin before being made into oatcakes and baked on the griddle.

Truly the kitchen was a wonderful place, even when it wasn't baking day. The larder was the storage place for all the staples. What fun it was to open the crocks and see what was inside—flour, peas, dried fruit, sugar, meal, broad beans—which were used to make the most delicious pease pudding back in England.

Annabella made a mental note to inquire as to their use here in Scotland—she rather doubted that it was for pease pudding. The meat safe was suspended from the rafters. Here the meat was hung to ripen. Eggs, cheese, and butter were on the shelves with dry goods.

During the following week Bella had spent most of her time in the kitchen, watching food being salted, dried, and pickled. Each time she went there, she settled down on her own stool near the pastry table, where she learned to grate suet. This was rubbed into flour, then mixed with water and patted into a china pudding basin for grouse-and-steak pudding. This always made her mouth water for the marvelous English suet pudding she had grown up with.

While Cook—whose name was Sibeal—made such dishes as potted hough (hough being a beef shin), Forfar bridies, which was akin to her own Cornish pastry, Scotch collops, or a wonderful crab soup called partan bree, Annabella listened like a child at her knee as Sibeal outlined the value of herbs for cooking and medicinal purposes.

Soon Bella's nose was in the black japanned spice tin, or poking around in the spice chest, as she learned to sort aromatic berries, buds, bark, fruit, roots, or flower stigmas taken from plants that grew in the hot countries her governess had taught her about—countries that were so much more real to her now as the strongly flavored scents drifted around her. "It's a pity they can't flavor the ink with these spices," she said to Cook one afternoon.

Sibeal gave her a strange look. "Now, why would ye be wantin' to flavor yer ink?"

"So you could smell the spices when you read about all those places," Bella said, much to Cook's delight.

A castle like Seaforth was a delightful place for one whose entire life had been so controlled that a young woman's inquisitive nature was limited. Here, in this great aging fortress, no boundaries existed, and every question brought answers. Yet some of the staff, like Dugal and Cook, were watchful of her at first.

She was, after all, English.

But soon even the watchful and the leery began to respond openly to the young English lass with the sad eyes. The staff and visitors to the castle accepted her presence, her inquisitiveness, her questions as commonplace; they accepted as well, her earnest praise, her open admiration, her intelligent input and suggestions. Soon they were listening for the musical tones of her laughter or the lilt of her odd British accent. They laughed at her funny way of saying things and admired her gentleness, her openness, her kind heart, her sense of humor, her ability to laugh at herself.

And when she wasn't present, they whispered and carried tales about the kind of family that would treat the puir lass so, one that would wrap her up in rules and regulations like a mummy and then marry her off to a man old enough to be her father. No wonder the lass had sad eyes.

After leaving her aunt in the weaving room, Annabella found Ailie in the kitchen. "I was just coming to find you. Have you looked outside, Ailie? It's beautiful." she said. "As warm as a fresh-laid egg."

Allan was in the kitchen as well, his head bent over a bowl of cock-a-leekie soup. Allan was in his usual rare form, and in between spoonfuls he was teasing Malai, a pretty blond lass who helped with the baking. "Ahh, Malai, my lass. What do you say to you and I going out to the barn and having a nip o' cheese?"

Malai was holding a sycamore rolling pin, looking as if she couldn't decide whether she wanted to roll out the dough before her or throw it at Allan. "I dinna ken why ye think I'd be goin' to the barn wi' the likes o' ye."

"I know how much you enjoyed the last time we went," he said, winking at Annabella.

Malai must have decided the word was mightier than the rolling pin, for she went back to rolling out the dough as she said, "I be thinking yer memory is shorter than yer privates, if ye think that."

As the kitchen exploded with laughter, Ailie and Annabella decided it was time to depart. "Come on," Ailie said. "I told Cook we'd go down to the well and draw some water."

Remembering the last time she was at the well, Annabella shuddered. "I don't like that place. It's full of spiders."

"That one isn't used very much. We use a different well —one that's much closer," Ailie said.

Once they reached the well, Annabella turned the crank as Ailie guided the wooden barrel, and as she cranked, she wondered what her parents would do if they saw her looking as common as a housemaid, with her white apron and her nose sprinkled with flour and freckles, turning a crank to draw water from a well.

"We'll use the hoops," Ailie said, attaching two buckets to a hoop. "Now, step inside the hoops," she said. "Watch your skirts."

Annabella hitched her skirts and stepped inside the hoop. At this exact moment Ross Mackinnon happened by. Sitting astride his horse, he looked as tasty as freshly baked bread.

With a laugh, he pulled up beside her and said, "Don't drop your skirts on my account."

"How odd," Annabella said. "You look exactly like the kind of man who would encourage a woman to drop her skirts."

"Drop them, raise them, it matters not—as long as the lady in them has limbs as shapely as yours."

Annabella took off so fast she was immediately thankful Ailie had suggested the hoops, for they kept the pails from banging against her legs as she walked. Not once did she look back to see if Ross or Ailie followed. As it turned out, Ailie was right behind her and came into the kitchen a few moments later. "*He* isn't with you, is he?" Annabella asked.

"No," said Ailie, "he looked ready to topple from his horse in a fit of laughter last time I saw him."

"Come on," Bella said. "I want to finish smocking that apron."

"You go on," Ailie said. "Mama wants me to help her pin a pattern."

Annabella collected her smocking on her way to the library, the most wonderful room at Seaforth and her very favorite because it had none of the attributes of a sitting room.

It was filled with novels, plays, and journals for idle time, as well as books for serious study. It was a room one could spend weeks in and still not see everything. Aside from the usual portraits and furniture, this library was richly equipped with games, portfolios of engravings, and scientific toys—the Scots being quite an inventive lot.

The sun was going down, so she moved to the mullioned window and lighted a resplendent Aladdin lamp on a round, skirted table. A marvelous old chair, fat with stuffing, was next to the table. It was Bella's favorite place to sit. With her feet on a footstool, she spread her smocking across her lap and began drawing up the gathers she had taken last evening. She worked at this for over an hour, and during that time the maid came in to light the peat fire, which soon reached out to surround her like a thick woolen blanket.

She began sewing the gathers with a honeycomb stitch, then lowered her hands to rest on her lap. The last shaft of fading sunlight broke over the mountains and flooded her chair in golden warmth and her eyes felt heavy . . . so . . . very . . . very . . . heavy. She nodded off to sleep.

The dream was wonderful, though it didn't start out that way. She was being held prisoner in a drafty stone tower in a black castle. She had been taken from her home, the white castle, and imprisoned in the black castle by an evil prince who always wore black. She pined for her lost love, the red prince, whom she feared she would never see again. But then he appeared, bursting through the doors with a sword in his hand.

The red prince looked a lot like Ross Mackinnon, but that only made him more attractive. He took her in his arms and kissed her. He kept on kissing her until everything began to spin, faster and faster; at last she feared her heart would stop. She gave a start and clasped her hand over the thundering heart within her breast.

She opened her eyes, not knowing for a moment where she was. Staring into the light from the Aladdin lamp, she saw a figure beyond it, fuzzy and in shadow. She blinked again and rubbed her eyes. Slowly the fuzzy figure in the shadows began to clear. Ross Mackinnon sat spread like a Christmas table in the chair across from hers. An open book lay in his lap. His legs, encased in those animal-skin pants he had such a fondness for, were stretched out in front of him, the tips of his boots brushing her skirts.

"The sleep of the innocent," he said, picking up the book, which she could see was entitled, *Valentinian.* "*Care-charming Sleep, thou easer of all woes, / Brother to Death,*" he read, then snapped the book shut. "You were smiling. You must have had quite a dream. Was I in it?"

"Yes," she said, coming full awake. "I dreamt about a barnyard. You were the pig."

He laughed. "You've changed a lot, you know that?"

"I have? In what way?"

"You're prettier now, more relaxed, more human. I like the freckles, by the way."

"Thank you. My mother will have a fainting spell when

she sees them, I'm sure. She'll keep me in lemon plasters for a month. Mothers can be such fusspots, you know."

"Annabella, I'm in love with you."

Annabella looked up and, seeing the blank, suspended look on his face, felt her heart begin to pound. Within her rose a terrible hope and, equally painful, a great fear. She wanted so desperately to go to him, to kneel at his feet and lay her head on his lap, to feel his gentle hands stroke her hair. The desire grew, blossoming more fully with each throb of her heart, until she had no way of knowing if it was born of desperation or physical longing. "You can't be."

"I can. I am. Question is, what are we going to do about it?"

"That discussion would be foolhardy and pointless. I am not free to love, or marry, in any case."

He shot to his feet, swinging away from her with the powerful grace of a war-horse. He doubled his fist and slammed it against the wall, and his curse sliced through the air with the sharpness of a two-edged sword. After a few minutes, he turned toward her, standing still and alone beside the leaping flames, his expression pained and full of hurt. He picked up one of the chess pieces from a nearby table and studied it. "How does it feel to be a pawn?"

She sprang to her feet, her smocking falling to the floor. "You have no right to speak to me like that," she said. "You aren't as pawky as you think. You speak of pawns. You should know about pawns, seeing that you can advance only a square at a time yourself. I doubt you'll ever reach the eighth rank."

She turned on her heel and marched out of the room with all the airs she could put on. Annabella was livid with anger. She took the stairs two at a time and slammed the door to her room the moment she was inside.

He stopped the door with his foot and kicked it open.

She whirled around, her face pale with shock. "Have you lost your wits? What do you think you are doing? This is my bedroom, you dolt. You can't come in here."

"Wrong. I *am* in here, and *here* I'm going to stay until we settle this thing once and for all."

"Are you daft?" Her head tilted to one side. "*What thing?*"

"This." He kicked the door shut and Annabella began backing away. In three strides he crossed the room and yanked her into his arms with such force the collision forced the air from her lungs in one giant *whoosh*. Before she could open her mouth, he opened his and placed it over hers. It wasn't the gentle kiss she remembered.

His desire for her had been riding just below the surface for too long. It took no more than the feel of her soft body against his to send it gushing forth. He twisted his fingers in her hair and the pins flew to the floor so that the long silken skeins fell cool and heavy over his arms. He twisted her, angling her head to cradle it in the crook of his arm and kissed her with branding possession. Like a man with no sight, he moved his hands over her, touching, feeling, learning each part of her, his calloused fingertips rough against rustling taffeta and warm, womanly skin. He touched all the places he had wanted to touch for so long, learned the secrets of her he knew only in his dreams. She was his. Every goddamn inch of her. Every bone. Every breath. Every freckle that adored her nose.

And her mouth. Dear God, that mouth. A man could go insane kissing a woman like her.

Annabella gazed up into the handsome angles and planes of a face that had become so dear to her, and the sadness of it struck her swiftly. His was a face she would never grow tired of seeing, if she were only given the chance. He had said he loved her, and she wished with all her young woman's heart that were so. There was so much to learn about him, so much to love. He was recklessly handsome, with the firm jawline of a man that commanded respect, but when he smiled, all the boyish charm he possessed came out. He had one of those smiles the women in London called devastating.

Devastating.

She liked that in a man, she decided. He was all the things a man should be, all the things she had ever prayed for. He was all the things she could never have.

He must have sensed she was about to push him away, because he brought his mouth down hard, silencing any words she was about to say. Dazed with passion and longing, she knew this could not go on, simply because it could not be. To allow things to go any further would only serve to make her more unhappy and miserable than she was. It wasn't fair to her. It wasn't fair to him. It was the most difficult thing she had ever done, to push away the very thing she wanted most in the world. With every ounce of newly acquired spirit she possessed, she broke from him, using her hand to wipe her mouth. "Get out," she said, panting.

"Are my kisses that bad—that you have to wipe the taste of me away?"

Annabella was stunned to see the white-hot flame of hurt and anger smoldering deep in the blue depths of his eyes. This man had always seemed in such control, always so invulnerable, so full of self-assurance, so ready to bounce back that she never dreamed words flung in desperation would find their mark, let alone sink as deeply as they apparently had.

"What's the matter? Can't you talk? Does it leave you speechless to have a man empty his guts and pour his heart out with declarations of love?" he asked in a jeering, hate-filled voice. "Does it give you a sense of power to know a man yearns for you until his insides are so twisted he can't think straight?" He grabbed her and dug his fingers into her arms. "Tell me," he said, giving her a shake.

She couldn't speak. She tried, but the words were too laden with grief, too heavy with anguish. The only way she could respond was to show him. She put her arms around his neck and went up on her toes to kiss him lightly on the mouth.

He jerked away as if he'd been shot. Before her very eyes, his beloved features hardened into a tortured mask.

"Damn you," he said. "Damn you to hell!" He grasped her arms to disengage them, to put her away from him.

"No!" she cried, clutching him harder. "Ross, hold me. Please . . . please hold me and never let me go." His grip was hurting her as he struggled to push her away. Still she clung to him, tears of desperation falling freely down her face. She twisted her hands in his hair and pulled his head down. She kissed him, uncertain, untutored, but with tenderness and understanding. The moment her tongue touched his lips, he froze. Through layers of his clothing and hers, she could feel every muscle in his body draw up tightly. With a groan he tightened his arms around her, drawing her against him with crushing strength. His mouth closed over hers, his tongue plunging boldly, questioningly into hers, asking, seeking.

Her own tiny moan answered him as she followed the dictates of her own passion and longing. *This* was what a kiss was all about. *This* was what she had known would exist, somehow, sometime, somewhere. He kissed her. She kissed him back. His body was wild for her. Hers was ready for him. He ached to carry her those few short steps to her bed and make love to her until hell froze over.

With tremendous effort he put her away from him. His breathing wasn't the only thing hard.

He wanted her.

But he couldn't have her. Not now. Not here. Not this way. He took her sweet face in his hands and wiped away the last trace of her tears with his thumbs. "How could anyone be so beautiful, so infuriating that a man wants to bite his own arm?" He kissed her lips softly and wrapped his arms around her tenderly, cradling her against him with the lightest touch. "Just let me hold you for a minute," he whispered. "I need to feel you against me before I let you go."

Suddenly someone knocked at her door and Ailie called out, "Bella? Are you in there?"

Frantically, Annabella looked at Ross, not knowing what to do. He was in her room, where he should not be. With a quivering voice, she said, "Yes, I'm here."

"Well, open the door, oakhead!"

With a deep, fortifying breath, Annabella crossed the room and opened the door. She was so prepared for a lecturing outburst that she said, "Before you go jumping to conclusions," she said, "I can explain everything."

Ailie drew up short and stared at her. "What are you talking about? Explain what?" Tilting her head to one side, she said, "Bella, do you want to talk to Mother?"

"No. It's a little late for that," Annabella said, turning around. She was both speechless and stunned to see Ross was not in the room. She wanted to shout with happiness. He must have gone out the window, and bless his dear soul, he even closed the window behind him.

Looking grim, Ailie blurted out, "Have you given Ross your virginity?"

"No," Annabella said, "it's worse than that."

"Worse?" Ailie croaked. "No one ever told me there was anything worse." She grabbed Annabella's arm and tugged her toward the bed, pushing her back to sit upon it. Pulling up a boudoir chair, Ailie dropped into it with all due haste and took Annabella's hands in hers. "All right," she said gravely. "Tell Ailie all about it."

It was said with such a note of seriousness—one that was so unlike Ailie that Annabella couldn't help herself. Seized with uncontrollable giggles, she gave a shriek and fell back across the bed, consumed with laughter.

Chapter

18

Annabella didn't get much sleep that night.

Thoughts of Ross kept her awake long after the household had settled down for the night. The pinkish-gray light of early morning was already streaking the sky when she dozed off at last. She slept for what seemed only minutes before she was rudely awakened by someone shaking her with near violence. "Bella? Och! You sleep like the dead."

"I am as good as dead," Annabella said, pulling the covers over her head. "Go away and let me sleep."

"Sleep? It's half-past ten and we've an important job to do."

Bella opened one eye. "What kind of job? If it's cleaning the pig swill or scrubbing the kitchen floor, I want no part of it."

"Pedair MacBrieve sent word half an hour ago. He needs our help straightaway."

Bella opened the other eye. "I never heard of anyone by that name."

"Of course you have. I just told you."

Bella was about to tell her she meant she had never heard of Pedair MacBrieve before this minute, but Ailie looked primed enough to take on Queen Victoria and the Royal Navy, so she thought better of it. "Who is Pedair MacBrieve?" she said finally.

"A crofter who lives nearby. He sent word that his back door is swarming with bees."

"And he sent for *us?*"

"Of course. You know Mama and I keep bees. We often get sent for like this, whenever someone finds a swarm."

"Oh, how lovely. We've been called out of bed to tackle a raging swarm of bees. I can't tell you what a relief that is. I was beginning to fear we'd been called to gather prawns' eyelashes at high tide." Sitting up in bed, Annabella asked, "What can you do with a swarm of bees? Besides being stung to death. Kill them?"

"A whole swarm? Of course not. They're much too valuable for that. Now, up with you." Dragging Bella from the bed by one arm, Ailie began pulling clothes out of the wardrobe. "We're going to bring them home with us."

Bella dived into the bed and pulled the covers over her head. "You go on," she said through muffled layers. "I'm not feeling well."

Ailie laughed. "I dinna ken I had a coward for a cousin, but that's to be expected of the English."

Up popped Bella's head. "We English aren't cowards. We're sensible. There is a difference, you know."

"All right," Ailie said. "Be sensible, then. Get up. We need to hurry."

An hour later the two girls, wearing long coats, gloves, hats, and veils arrived at Pedair MacBrieve's hut, and just as he had said, a seething bunch of bees as big as a cheese wheel swarmed over his door.

Annabella was terrified of them.

Ailie was not. "Here," Ailie said, picking up the wooden box she had carried from home. "We'll put them in here."

That looked easier said than done. "What are you going to do, tell the bees to jump into the box and clap on the lid?"

"*O ye of little faith.* You hold the lid," Ailie said, handing it to Bella. "I'll get the bees."

That was the most sensible thing she had heard all day. Bella held the lid as Ailie picked up a dead branch and carried it with the box to the swarm. "Come stand beside me and be ready to hand me the lid when I tell you."

Annabella crept slowly forward. "If I get bitten . . . just one tiny bite . . ."

"You won't." Holding the box beneath the swarm, Ailie took the branch and knocked the swarm loose. The bees fell into the box. She threw away the branch. "Hand me the lid." Bella did, happily, and backed away. Ailie clapped the lid down and said, "There. What a nice swarm. Thank you, Mr. MacBrieve."

Turning to Annabella, she said, "Well? What do you have to say for yourself now?"

"*Ancora imparo,*" Annabella replied with a shrug. "I learn," she added, seeing it didn't seem to be in Ailie's repertoire of foreign sayings. "Michelangelo said it."

On the way home Bella asked, "How did you do that without being bitten?"

"Swarming bees are almost always completely harmless," Ailie said. "Most of the time they're so full of honey that they can't do much more than swarm."

When they arrived back at Seaforth, they went straight to the beehives. Annabella, who was getting braver by the minute, even volunteered to place the swarm in the straw skep. She did, without one bite, and felt inordinately satisfied with herself once they had covered the skep with canvas before placing an earthenware pot over the whole thing.

One of the swarming bees must have taken a wrong turn somewhere, for when Annabella began removing her gloves, she felt a stinging bite on her wrist. With a yelp, she jerked off her glove and slapped the bee away.

"That won't do any good now," Allan said, swinging over the fence and coming to join them. "The stinger is already imbedded in your skin. Here"—he took Annabella's hand—"let me see if I can get it out."

By the time he pulled it out, Annabella had a red welt that burned like fire. "Go on up to the kitchen and tell Cook to put something on it," he said.

The girls started off as Allan grabbed Ailie by the collar. "*You*," he said, "are coming with me."

"What for?" asked Ailie. "What did I do?"

"Mrs. McGinnis has three sick children and her husband is down with an injured back. Mama is sending food and milk. She wants you to come with me, to see if we need to send for the doctor."

"But Annabella . . ."

". . . Won't die from a beesting," he finished. "Come on, Miss Busybody. I left the cart in the road, just over the fence."

They started away, then Allan stopped. "Go on to the cart, Ailie. I have to ask Bella something." When Ailie started to speak, he said, "Go on. You can ask me about it later."

As soon as she turned away, Allan came to stand beside Annabella. "Do you know a man named Fionn Alpin?" he asked.

Annabella considered the name. "No, I don't."

"Do you remember ever hearing that name?"

"It isn't familiar, and it isn't a usual name, at least not to me. I'm certain I would remember hearing it if I had."

Allan nodded and started to turn away.

"Why do you ask? Who is Fionn Alpin?"

"I'm not sure. He stopped me on the road today, when I was exercising the gray. He wanted to know if I was from Seaforth. For some reason I told him *no*. He began asking a lot of questions."

"What kind of questions?"

"About you and Mackinnon, mostly."

"Have you told Uncle?"

"No, but I intend to."

She shrugged. "It's probably someone my father hired to keep an eye on me," she said. "He wants to make certain I don't fly away."

Annabella watched him go and saw that Ailie hadn't gone to the cart, but was waiting for him down the way. Allan caught up with her, then the two of them raced to the fence. Ailie was laughing when she got there first. In her haste to climb over it, Ailie snagged her skirts, then dropped on the other side, apparently unharmed. The pony nickered and the cart started off. The creaking of the huge wooden wheels was strangely in harmony with the sounds of Allan and Ailie's chatter. Annabella turned away and started toward Seaforth. She went a few feet and stopped, then turned back toward the fence. She had never climbed a fence before, but Ailie made it look so easy—and daring.

Bella soon discovered that fences weren't as easy to climb as she had assumed. Hitching up her skirts as she had seen Ailie do, Bella eyed the stone wall that was almost as tall as she. The stones were blackish gray and rough, covered with lichen, and had bracken growing in the crevices. Dried leaves crunched beneath her booted feet as she approached the fence. Once there, she braced her foot on one stone, grabbed the top of the fence, and heaved herself up. It took some doing, but she located a resting place for her other foot and pulled herself slowly to the top, scraping her elbow as she did.

Sitting on top of a fence, she learned, gave one the advantage of a rather lofty perch from which to survey the world. The meandering stone fence seemed to follow no distinct plan, but it did appear to mark the boundary between the rolling, heather-splashed heath and the clefts and shelters of the rugged fells beyond, where outcrops of brooding gray rock looked harsh and cold—and so wildly beautiful it excited her heart with wanderlust. From this lofty perch she could see the reedy little loch, the melancholy moor with its almost savage monotony, and in its center the single track of a narrow winding path, where Ailie and Allan's cart was now no more than an insignificant dot upon the face of history.

A brown hare glared at her from the heather; overhead a lone eagle circled the icy-blue backdrop of Highland sky. She looked at the harsh reality of the world around her, aware now of its demanding environment and understanding the reason for the Scots' legendary resilience.

Theirs was a fragile presence in a land filled with crumbling ruins and a faded past filled with glory. Scotland with its thin soil and inhospitable mountains was a place of rich glens and tea-colored rivers; it was a land with a timeless spirit, full of mischief and grit, impervious to the passage of time. She knew the springy feel of its peaty heath beneath her feet, the leaden color of its thrashing sea. It was reality. It was fantasy. It was the place where the footprints of history reached the end of their journey.

Funny how the mind works, she thought. Here she was, sitting on a fence in the wilds of Scotland, and when she should be concerned with just how she was going to get down without breaking her fool neck, she began to think about Scotland—she was responding to it like the lament of the sad skirl of pipes. And it was here on the top of this fence that it struck her just why she was so bewitched by this powerful and complex land. Scotland was both defiant and compassionate, obedient and daring—something she wished herself to be. But its greatest gift to her had been its sharing, both land and landscape, people and pride.

It had also given her a liberal dose of common sense, and that common sense was telling her she wasn't going to think herself down from the top of this fence. From where she sat, it looked a long way to the ground. She glanced over her shoulder at the direction she had just come from. That looked a long way as well.

She was pondering her descent when the yapping of Bennie, the sheep dog, reached her ears and she looked up in time to see him burst through the brush on the other side of the road. Bennie ran to the fence and barked twice, then turned and ran back to the brush he had just bounded through. Bella was wondering what Bennie was about when the undergrowth rustled, then parted, and the object of all his overjoyed behavior stepped out. Ross Mackinnon looked as surprised to see her as she was to see him.

She could tell he had been out hunting, because he had his rifle, and a bag used to hold grouse was thrown over his shoulder. He was dressed in those clothes he preferred, which always gave him an air of casual disregard. He was hatless as usual, and his hair was windblown and partly in his eyes. Neither his casual disarray nor the stark countryside did anything to detract from the general picture of him.

The overall effect was rather like watching a thoroughbred hurl a fence at a steeplechase—for when she looked at him, her heart always lodged in her throat.

He must have seen her the minute he stepped onto the road, for he drew up short and looked her over with calculated ease. After all, he was no fool, and any fool could see he could take all the time he wished and look his fill, since it was quite obvious she wasn't going anywhere fast. He had plenty to look at, too. To the straitlaced, her appearance would have been declared scandalous; by humorous standards she was something to laugh at. She wiggled around, trying to pull her skirts free, at least enough to cover her drawers and petticoats, but all her wiggling only served to expose her limbs, which were already overexposed, a bit more.

"You could stop gawking at me in that nasty fashion and help me down."

"I could," he said, "and I might, but first I want some answers. What are you doing up there?"

"Viewing the countryside."

His lips were curved in either a sneer or a smile. From this distance she could not tell which. A moment later he crossed the road and stood before her. It was a smile, she decided. She looked down on the top of his head as he asked, "Are you alone?"

"Yes, except for you and Bennie."

"Where's your shadow?"

"You mean Ailie?"

He nodded.

"She had to leave . . . with Allan."

"You mean they left you up here?"

"Yes . . . I mean no. I didn't climb up here until after . . ." She tugged at her dress again. "Will you stop staring at me like that?"

"Like what?"

"As if you think I'm a pile of pastry and you're about to put your hands in the dough."

He laughed. "I don't know why, but common sense tells me to let that dog lie."

"I would think if you had any common sense at all, it would tell you to help a lady in distress."

"Are you distressed?"

"Not personally . . . at least not yet, but I soon may be, and my situation, as you can see, is one of distress."

"How'd you get up there?"

"I climbed."

"Then climb down."

"I might fall."

"I doubt it, but the leaves will cushion you if you should." Seeing the look on her face, he laughed. "You'll be glad you did it yourself, once it's over. Go ahead. Try it."

"How?"

"You can't teach a setting hen to cluck," he said. "Some things have to be learned. Go on, you'll do fine."

She wasn't as overflowing with confidence as he was, but she knew him well enough to know he'd be content to stand there leering at her all day if she didn't try getting down without his help. What other choice did she have? The cold from the stones was penetrating her backside through her petticoats, and sitting on the fence wasn't all that comfortable anyway. Besides, it wasn't nearly as much fun as she had thought it would be.

Her first attempt wasn't too successful, and she paused, her feet dangling high above the ground, thrashing the air, as she looked for a foothold. With a cry of exasperation, she pulled herself up with her arms and lay like a dead man tossed over a horse's back.

"Lick your flint and try again," was Ross's sage advice.

"Do what?"

"Start over."

"Why didn't you speak English the first time?"

"I thought I did."

"I mean, *my* kind of English."

By this time her temper was in fine form, but she managed to hold her tongue. She worked her way down, knowing she was as awkwardly ungraceful and unladylike as one could imagine, and that she was giving him the most unobstructed view of her backside.

One did what one had to do.

Once her feet touched the ground, she turned away and started walking down the narrow lane that led back to Seaforth. He fell in step alongside her. She did her best to ignore him, but that wasn't too effective. Pushing back an errant strand of hair, she was startled when she felt his hand take hers. She drew up short, her heart pounding as she looked into his face. His long fingers caressed her hand, his thumb rubbing the red welt on her wrist. "What happened here?" he asked.

"It's a beesting."

"And here?" he asked tracing the long, red scrape on her arm.

"Climbing the fence."

"When you were a little girl, did your mother kiss your hurts and make them go away?"

"No. Why should she? Kissing a hurt doesn't make it feel better."

Some people, she suddenly realized, *fall into holes unsuspecting. Others step into them with both feet.*

He laughed. "Oh, but you're wrong. It does make it better. Much better. Let me show you." He led her off the road, behind the thick fringe of hedges and low trees to a spongy carpet of early summer grasses, and pulled her down to sit beside him. Taking her hands in his, he turned them palm up and kissed them softly.

These kisses were even more devastating than the more conventional kind. Her entire body quivered in response, as if fanned by a hundred butterfly wings. Her constitution was as fortified as a pat of melted butter. For a flickering of time he continued to caress her hands with his, then he carried them upward and placed them around his neck, nudging her backward with the weight of his body as he did. Bathed in the pungent aroma of grasses, she lay stunned and inert beneath him, her heart pounding wildly with anticipation.

He stared down into her lovely features. Even her hair seemed untroubled, lying in tranquil curls over her shoulders and breasts. Her wide eyes, her slightly open lips nearly drove him crazy. He yearned to taste her again, to kiss her and keep on kissing her until she was as wild with desire as he.

He lowered his head and did just that. He kissed her and kept on kissing her, until his hand came up to learn the shape of her breast. Passion ruled her face, but even then he saw the faintest flicker of sadness in her eyes.

He wanted to kiss and drive the sadness from her life with his love, but he knew he couldn't do it, knew that there were things in her life that only she could resolve, knew he could do no more than to reassure her of his love for her. Would it be enough? He hoped to God it would be. It was all he had to offer her.

His hands found their way inside her dress and bared her

lovely breasts. He lowered his head, stroking her with his tongue. She closed her eyes and cradled his head against her. With a wordless groan, Ross kissed her with a sudden, urgent hunger, feeling her response to his passion was as great as his. Not breaking the kiss, he caressed her, touching her breasts and teasing their points with his thumbs, and feeling her immediate response. He followed the trail of his hands with his mouth, kissing her everywhere. She gasped with pleasure and twisted against him, trying to get closer.

"Sweet, sweet . . . you have the sweetest skin. I want to wrap myself in it and never get up. Take me. Wrap me inside you. I love you. I'll always love you," he said, slowly sinking into a world of blindness, where he functioned with only half a mind. Desperate to join his body with hers, he ignored the warning signals that were dully clamoring inside his head. His hand followed the line of her legs, locating the hem of her skirts and lifting them, instinctively touching her thigh, the flat smoothness of her stomach. His hand was beneath all her clothing now, touching. Skin against skin. With no barriers between them. He moved his hand between her legs and she opened to him, warm and sweet and melting. His kisses were more urgent now.

"I ache for you," he said. "You're going to have to stop this, because I can't. Not now. It's gone too far."

A strange excitement curled within her, a sensation of recklessness and pleasure that felt as wild as it felt free. He was here, now, and all hers. She could kiss him, and touch him. There was nothing to prevent it. Nothing to hold her back.

She loved him, she knew that. His love was something she could never have, not completely. But she could have *now*. She could have this moment to remember during all the times to follow when he would be lost to her. Somewhere in the back of her mind she knew and accepted her part in her own fall from grace. She could not blame him. The fault was as much hers as his. Besides, none of this made any difference now, for as he said, it was too late now to stop. "Please, Ross," was her only response. "Please."

She could feel the long, hard line of him pressing hot against her belly. As always, there was no haste in his movements, only the slow, steady assurance that he knew what he was about. He knew her body better than she did, knew where to touch her to make her open like a fern frond, where to stroke her into a liquid heat. His very slowness, the insistence, the devotion, sent her hot blood racing and drove her wild. His finger was inside her now, circling, easing, stretching her to accommodate him. Dear God, did his patience know no end, no limit? A heaviness gripped her, and she felt her body tighten. A moment later he was between her legs, kissing the wild sweetness of her mouth as she lifted her hips. He felt himself slip slowly inside her, then he eased himself slowly and gradually deeper. "Oh, God!" he said. "So this is heaven."

She reacted with a sharp gasp. The pain she had been led to expect was no more than the beesting, the pleasure afterward more than its own reward. She encircled his neck with her arms, feeling the skin was moist and smooth as she strained upward to meet him.

She had no desire to lie back and be taken, but felt the overriding need and joy of wanting to be one with him, to be his partner, his equal in every way. His thrusts were surer now, and quicker, and she accepted the urgency, matching it with her own until a tightness formed like a small kernel of truth deep within her belly, increasing, expanding, growing frantic in its seeking of a way out.

As a jagged flash of lightning rips across a midnight sky, her body jerked uncontrollably with unchecked passion. She knew, she knew, for all time she knew. For all time this moment, this man, this joining would be hers. She could not be sorry, for only joy flooded her soul. God hadn't seen fit to hand her the universe, but he had allowed her to touch a star.

He held her against him for a long time, neither of them speaking, as if by doing so they would shatter the perfect peace that existed between them. "Are you sorry?" he asked at last.

"No. I'm only sorry we didn't do this sooner." She rolled against him and buried her face in his neck. "Oh, Ross, what can we do?"

He held her close and stroked her. "I don't know, but I'll think of something," he said. "You aren't going to marry Huntly. I do know that much."

"How can I not? I can't bring shame upon my family. I can't humiliate them by throwing everything they stand for in their faces."

"I know," he said softly. "This overwhelming sense of fairness, your acceptance of what is right—it's one of the things I love about you. Don't worry. There has to be a way out of this for us, a way for me to take the blame."

She raised her arms and pulled him down to her. A moment later he lifted his head. "It seems fate or circumstance is always working against me." He kissed her again, softly. "You must have a legion of angels watching over you." Her arms were still around his neck and she tugged at him, feeling his resistance. "Would that I could, angel mine, but unless I miss my guess, that creaking I hear in the distance is the herald of your cousin's untimely arrival."

He kissed her again, and she gave herself up to it. He was right, there had to be something they could do. There had to be. Suddenly his words came back to her. *There has to be a way out of this for us, a way for me to take the blame.*

Chapter

19

To lose something before you really had a chance to have it was both cruel and unfair. But when had her life been any other way?

The following morning a letter arrived from Dunford. The Mackinnon wrote that he hadn't been feeling well of late and although he was still in the best of health, thought it was time to get on with the task of preparing Ross to be the duke and laird of Clan Mackinnon. *"I am turning my business affairs over to him now, along with the overseeing of our Drambuie interests. You can tell that long-suffering Englishman, who has been more worrisome than an old mother hen clucking over her chick, trying to perform the formidable task of turning a rounder into a proper Scot, that the time he has been waiting for has come,"* the Mackinnon wrote. *"The papers are being drawn up now, and your presence here is necessary, in order to bring you up-to-date on details and concerns that will require your immediate attention."*

The future Duke of Dunford and the long-suffering Englishman left that afternoon for Dunford. Just before he rode away, Ross found Annabella in a small room off the kitchen she and Ailie had claimed for their projects. On this day they had put harvest time behind them, having packed away their barley heart wreaths and the corn husk dolls made for Plough Sunday, and turned their somewhat sporadic yet enthusiastic attention to the coming Advent season and decorations for Christmas. For over a month the cousins had been gathering baubles and trinkets, nuts, ribbons, feathers, berries, candles, evergreen branches, and bits of colored fabric to use for making decorations for the tree, as well as garlands and wreaths for the house.

Earlier that morning Ailie had gone with Allan to the widow McCracken's to gather peacock feathers from her roost, since there were no peacocks at Seaforth. Annabella had decided at the last minute to stay behind, in order to dye the feathers they had already collected bright shades of red, yellow, and green—and any other colors she could make by mixing those three. This was a rather involved process that required several bowls for mixing, as well as numerous piles of feathers, sorted according to size and shape.

She was bent over this ambitious project with stained fingers and feathers clinging to her clothes and hair when he found her. He stepped into the room, the draft from the opened door sending a swirl of delicate goose down fluttering about. "Close the door, quickly," she said, turning around to see him standing behind her. "Oh, it's you," she said, her eyes big with surprise. "I thought you might be Ailie."

He glanced around the room, then back at her. He reached out to pluck a feather that rested in her hair near her temple and picked another bit of fluff from her long eyelashes. She looked up at him and smiled, and the warmth of it surrounded him. Without saying a word, he took her in his arms, holding her close to him for a moment, not ready to speak, not wanting to tell her he was here to say good-bye.

They stood that way for some time, she with her arms around his waist, her cheek against his chest; he with his chin resting on the top of her head, his hands rubbing her back. At last he released her and stepped back. His eyes were a dark blue and he spoke with great seriousness. "My grandfather has written for me to return. Percy and I are leaving in a few minutes."

He sighed heavily, gazing at her as she stood so small and straight with all her pride evident. He could not help wondering what her thoughts were. Her apron was smeared with bright-colored stains, her hair dusted with feathers, but she had never looked more lovely. There was a fresh eagerness, a peace he had never seen in her before. He reached out to take her hand, carrying it to his lips, smiling at the purplish stains edged in red and green. He kissed her fingers, one by one. "Each kiss is for a hundred reasons why I don't want to leave," he said, taking her in his arms as he drew her against him. His words failed him after that. Her body was too soft and too warm and too close. He wanted her too much. "Annabella," he whispered hoarsely. She looked up at him, her lips parted, and he was lost. Her hands caught in his hair as his head lowered to dot her with hard, persuasive kisses. His hand found her breast and she sighed as her head dropped back. He was kissing her throat now, slipping the buttons of her bodice loose, parting the satiny fabric, sliding his hand inside, drawing a soft, shuddering gasp from her as his fingers spanned the gentle swell of her breast. His head dropped lower, and he touched his mouth to her nipple, pressing light kisses there.

Agonized by the feel of his mouth upon her breast, she drew his head closer to her aching flesh, moaning when his other hand slipped beneath her skirts, caressing the firm warmth of her inner thigh. Whispering his desire, he let his hand slide over the soft fabric of her drawers to find an opening. Touching the wet silk, knowing she wanted him as much as he wanted her, he groaned as his fingers entered her. Desire raced through him like fire-kissed brandy.

He heard her distressed whimper. "What's wrong, love?"

"The door, Ross. There's no lock. Anyone could walk in."

It was enough to cool his senses. He could see that despite the fire of desire in her eyes, she was shy and uncomfortable. He closed his eyes, inhaling deeply, willing the thundering in his heart to go away. She was new to all of this, and was deserving of his self-restraint—something he had precious little of whenever he was with her. He looked into eyes that met his with such love, such trust, and for a moment he panicked, afraid he might not be able to give her what she deserved, that he would be unable to control the fire that still raced through his blood. "Love, forgive me . . . you're so perfect . . . every part of you is so dear."

He dropped his head against hers and closed his eyes. For a few minutes he did not move, holding her against him, his hands where they were, willing some semblance of control to return to him. Then, with a ragged breath, he drew his hands away, lowering her skirt, and closing the buttons on her bodice.

He looked down with love and tenderness into yellow-green eyes, rose-petal skin, and the gentle curve of a smile. Admiration, love, and confusion commingled in him, and he felt the corners of his own lips curve in response. He wanted to say something clever, to tell her all the beautiful things he felt in his heart, but his mind seemed disconnected from the physical part of him, and all he could say was "Of all the things I could have given you, it pleases me most to see you smile. Tell me why you do."

"I was thinking about the feathers," she said.

"Feathers?" he repeated, unable to hide the surprise in his voice. Of all the reasons he expected her to give, supposing they would be somewhat flattering to him, never in his wildest imaginings did he expect her to respond with *feathers*.

Seeing his baffled expression and knowing what he must be thinking, she laughed softly, and coming up on her tiptoes, kissed him. "Feathers," she said, "as in how I can explain to Ailie why they float out of my chemise when we undress tonight."

"Or your drawers," he said with a grin.

It must have been the grin that shattered her, for her expression turned painfully serious. "Oh, Ross," she said, turning her head away, "I wish you didn't have to go. We've just found each other. It isn't fair."

Taking her by the shoulders, he turned her toward him, gazing at her with frustrated longing.

She searched his face, his eyes, knowing that what she was feeling, he felt as well. "You'll be back," she said.

"You can count on that," he said. "The minute I can, I'll take off faster than a scalded cat."

She smiled. "I don't suppose I can ask for anything faster."

"No," he said. "That's about as fast as it gets." He held her against him, speaking over her head. "It's funny how things work out. Becoming a duke means I have to leave you. It's like a wind that blows out a candle and fans a fire to flame." She looked up at him as he said, "I know I have to go, but not now. It's too soon, too soon after . . ." He stopped, kissing her forehead. "I want you to know this is the only thing that could make me go, the only reason I would leave you now. I know what . . ."

She put her fingers over his mouth. "You don't have to worry about that," she said softly. "I don't feel used and abandoned, Ross. I know you better than that. I trust you more, as well."

His arms tightened around her as his mouth closed over hers. "I don't deserve you," he whispered.

She laughed. "Oh, yes, you do."

He pulled back, smiling down at her. "If that's the way you feel, I'm going to see that I get you." He kissed her quickly. "You remember that," he said. "Whatever it takes, whatever I have to do, or sacrifice, I will. Nothing will keep me from having you. Nothing."

Chapter
20

"Your lass has had company while she's been residing at Barra Mackenzie's," Fionn Alpin said.

The Earl of Huntly tossed down the last of his brandy. "I'm paying you, and a healthy sum, I might point out, to bring me information of merit, not tidbits about my betrothed and her tea parties."

"I beg your pardon, your lordship. Here I was erroneously assuming a male suitor was information of merit." Fionn picked up his hat and turned toward the door.

"Just a minute." Huntly fed the spaniel at his side a tidbit from a silver tray and stared into the fire. "Sit down and tell me what you know."

As Fionn talked, Lord Huntly's face grew intense. The intensity soon turned into a white-hot rage. The bitch was making a fool of him and he longed to put his hands around her throat, but he held himself in check and showed no emotion save a look of determination. When Fionn finished, Huntly nodded. "That will be all. I'll handle things from here on out. You may settle up with my secretary on your way out."

Once Fionn had left, Huntly scowled as he pondered just what he should do about this. He felt trapped, in a deadlock. It wasn't a feeling he liked. The Stewart bitch was unimportant, but her fortune was a prime factor here. He couldn't risk his marriage to her by confrontation, and he couldn't lose her fortune by calling the marriage off. The only thing he could do was to notify her father and hope his intervention would be enough—and soon enough.

He wrote the letter that night, dispatched it with his fastest courier, and readied himself to wait.

A week later the Duke of Grenville stood with his back to the fireplace as he studied the face of his son. "I don't know if it would do any good to let you go," he said. "I thought I knew my daughter, but now, I don't know. I can't seem to predict how Annabella will react any more."

"Please, let me go. Bella will listen to me," Gavin said. "I know she will. You know how close we've always been."

"You think you can attend to this matter?" the duke asked flatly.

Gavin grinned. "If I can't, I have no business being your heir."

"You will have to be firm with her, Gavin. I know that may be hard for you. Remember, it's for her own good. Your sister must be brought to heel immediately. Huntly is furious, and well he should be. Whatever it takes, you must see to it that Ross Mackinnon is kept as far from her as possible."

Gavin nodded, looking at the book on Scottish law that lay open on his father's desk.

The duke moved to stand behind the desk. "I will send a

letter to his grandfather, and one to Colin as well. See that you give this one to Barra as soon as you arrive." He handed an envelope to Gavin as he sat down. "One other thing. I've moved the wedding date up. Your mother and I will arrive in Scotland within the month. Tell Annabella the wedding date has been set for December twenty-first."

Gavin had been sitting on the corner of his father's desk, swinging one leg as he toyed with a crested silver letter opener. "That's less than six weeks away," he said, dropping the letter opener.

"I'd have it sooner if that were possible," his father replied. He looked up as the clock on the mantel struck the hour. "If you're going to make that ship, you need to be off. Don't forget to kiss your mother good-bye. She's dripping like a wet winter, worried that something will happen to you. Seems she had another one of those dreams of hers last night."

Gavin laughed. "Mother always worries, and nothing has happened to me so far. But I'll stop off and tell her good-bye."

The Duke of Grenville watched his son stroll from his study, remembering the day he was born. It had been a difficult delivery and the memory of Anne's screams haunted him still. He would never forget how the hours dragged on, as if the clocks had stopped and time existed no more. A cold fear gripped him and he remembered the agony of waiting—waiting for some word and hearing none, growing more fearful with each passing second.

And then Dr. Bradford had led him into her room and placed his son in his arms. Anne had reached for him, twisting her fist into the cloth of his coat, telling him she knew she was going to die.

"Promise me you will watch over him when I'm gone," she said, her eyes glazed and her face glistening with sweat.

"I promise," he had said, calling the doctor aside to talk.

"She's delirious," Dr. Bradford said. "She's had a hard time of it, but she is in no danger of dying. It's probably the drops I gave her for pain that have distorted her senses. Your wife and your son will be fine."

Several days later, when Anne was feeling much better, she had said, "I don't understand it, Alisdair, I know I was dying. I had this terrible feeling of death. I was crying because I'd been told I would be taken from my son."

"Dr. Bradford said it was the drugs he gave you. They distorted your mind. You are fine now, and so is the baby."

The Duke of Grenville leaned back in his chair, pondering just why his thoughts had gone in that direction, when he had so many other things pressing upon his mind. He picked up the silver letter opener Gavin had left on his desk. He stroked the blade between his fingers, then opened the drawer and put it away.

Gavin. He had been so preoccupied with his mission, he had let his son leave without really telling him good-bye. He closed the drawer and left the room.

"My son," he said to the butler as he approached the front door. "Where is he? Has he left yet?"

"I'm sorry, Your Grace. Your son is gone."

Chapter
21

Annabella was sitting in the parlor when Gavin entered. She looked up to see the captivatingly formed features of her beloved brother. She dropped the length of scalloped edging she had been crocheting and rose to her feet, the ornate scissors fell from her hand and dangled from the silk cord around her neck. "Gavin, you're here!" she said, crossing the room and seeing the minute she did that this wasn't a social call. "I didn't know you were coming."

"Bella, what is going on? Father is in a blistering rage. Mother has taken to her bed. And I've been dispatched to Scotland to shake some sense into that lovely but rattled head of yours."

"In regard to what?"

"The time for claiming innocence is past. Huntly has gotten wind of Mackinnon's presence here and he shot a letter off to Father. And Father has shot one off to Uncle Barra. You've stirred up a lot of mischief here. I hope it can be resolved without anyone paying too dear a price. You're sitting in a cauldron that is about to boil over, and it could boil over into all of our faces."

"What does Father expect me to do?"

"For starters, we've got to send Mackinnon packing and he has to promise to stay away from you . . . far away."

"Ross is not here," she said. "He's been back at Dunford for almost a month now."

"At least that's one thing in our favor," he said.

Annabella's face was pale, her lips pinched. "Is Huntly coming here?"

"Not that I know of, but I wouldn't put it past him. He's not known for his easygoing temperament, although I hope he does stay away, for your sake."

"I can't marry him," she said at last.

"You *what?*"

The tone was the same she would imagine him to use if she'd just announced her intention to walk into St. Paul's stark naked.

He looked at the lovely figure in emerald-green velvet with the huge, round eyes and said, "Don't be killing me with one of those looks of yours. It wasn't my idea. I'm here in an official capacity only. As Father's emissary. I talked him into letting me come by convincing him I could talk some sense into you."

"Then I'm sorry you have come all this way for nothing. I said it before and I'll say it again—I'll keep on saying it until someone believes me. I am *not* going to marry Lord Huntly."

"Just what in the bloody hell are you going to do? Have you thought about the scandal?"

"I've thought about it, yes. I've also thought about living my own life for a change."

"A nice idea, but an impractical one. A seventeen-year-old girl . . ."

"I'm eighteen now. I had a birthday last week. We had a lovely party. I wish you had been here, Gavin. It was the first birthday of mine you missed."

"I'm sorry, puss. I would have been here if I could. You know that."

"Yes, I do."

He began pacing back and forth across the room. "Seventeen, or eighteen, it makes little difference. You are bound by a betrothal contract. You know it's a legal document, don't you?"

"I know, but I'm sure if we talked to Huntly, if we explained to him that I'm in love with someone else, that—"

"In love?" he said, cutting her off. He started to say something else, but just then he frowned. "Oh, Bella. You haven't given yourself to Mackinnon, have you?"

"And if I have?"

"Damnation!" Gavin said, slamming his hand against the table next to him. "This is worse than either Father or I thought. Much worse."

She looked skeptical. "I'd like to know how it could possibly be worse, unless of course, I were already married to John. Now, *that* would be worse!"

"Well, you're not married to anyone. But you sure as hell need to be." He shook his head. "This is the worst . . ."

"It is not."

"It is, and I'll tell you how it's worse. You were a virgin when Huntly signed those documents. You aren't one now. That changes things—a lot of things."

"Huntly doesn't know."

"He will soon enough."

"Not if you don't tell him."

Gavin looked at her as if she didn't have her baskets stacked right. "Huntly may be a sap, but he's no idiot. He will know, Bella, on your wedding night. Even a moron would know that."

Her face flamed. She wanted to slap herself in the face. *Idiot! Of course he would know. What was I thinking?*

Gavin paced the floor in silence. After a long while he came to her and put his arm around her, pulling her against him with a comforting hug. "Don't look so hopeless," he said at last. "It isn't the end of the world. Above everything else, I'm your brother, Bella. We may still be able to straighten this mess out . . . or die trying," he said with a laugh.

"Straighten it out? You mean in a way that I'll still have to marry Huntly?"

"That's what I'm counting on. The first thing I've got to do is—"

"Gavin," she said, feeling so frustrated she was about to cry, "I don't want to marry Huntly. I won't marry him."

Gavin began pacing again. "I know you don't want to, Bella. Believe me, if it were in my power to do something, I would. You know that. Believe it or not, I like Mackinnon. I'd rather have him for a brother-in-law than Huntly." He stopped, looking at her. "Above all, I want to see you happy, Bella. I'd give my life for you, you know that."

She burst into tears and Gavin crossed the room and took her in his arms.

"Oh, Gavin, what am I going to do? I'm so miserable. I love Ross. He's everything I ever dreamed of. He's . . ." She buried her face in his jacket, unable to say anything more. What difference did it make anyway?

She had no idea how long she cried, or how long Gavin, with his infinite patience, his loving understanding, stood there holding her, letting her drench his shirtfront and jacket, offering her words of consolation, being her strong arm to lean upon.

At last the strain of seeing her in such misery proved too much for him. "What can I do?" he said at last. "I can't stand to see you like this. I fear what this marriage would do to you more than I fear Father's wrath." He kissed the top of her head and put his handkerchief to her nose, and told her to blow, as he had done so many times before.

Dear, sweet Gavin. He had never failed her. He had always been there for her when she needed him.

"Dry your eyes, Bella," he said, "and try to compose yourself. All isn't lost, at least not yet. I'll go to Huntly and see if I can persuade him to agree to put an end to things between you. If he has any honor at all, he won't want a wife who doesn't want him. No man would."

She threw her arms around his neck. "Thank you, Gavin. I knew you wouldn't let me down. You never have. I'll never stop thanking you for this, for as long as I live."

"You're going to have to stop for a little while, or I'm never going to get out of here," he said, laughing and kissing her cheek as he pulled her hands from around his neck. Giving her hands a squeeze, he released them, saying, "I'd best be off. Thank me when I get back."

"Are you leaving now?"

He nodded. "As soon as I talk to Uncle."

"But it's dark, and Uncle isn't here. He's in Ullapool with Allan."

Gavin nodded and said, "Then I'm off without talking to Uncle. If he returns before I do, tell him there's a letter on his desk from Father. But tell him not to do anything until I get back." Then he disappeared around the door. She watched him go.

"What would I do without you?" she whispered, dropping wearily into the chair. "What would I do?"

Two days later Gavin was at the Earl of Huntly's home, Mercat Castle. He was standing near the fireplace. Huntly sat nearby in a leather chair.

Huntly called his dogs to his side and listened to what Gavin had to say. When Gavin finished, Huntly looked at him sharply. "How charming. You seem overly eager to serve the cause. Pity you came all this way on a fool's errand. I have an agreement with your father." The earl's tone was not smooth enough to hide the ugliness that lay just beneath the surface. "I'll discuss matters with him, not his whelp." He picked up a letter on his desk. "You know, I do wonder why you are really here. I received this letter from your father only today. It's quite enlightening. It is also of a completely different nature from the speech you have just delivered. Who sent you, I wonder?"

"I was sent by my father and I act for him," Gavin said. "Shall I take your silence for agreement?"

"The only agreement you have is the official one. The terms of the contract will remain as written. I do not choose to withdraw. The marriage will take place as planned. Hearing of Annabella's obvious passion for the Mackinnon's grandson is most unsettling to me. The Mackinnon and I have long been at odds with each other, and his grandson's interference in my affairs only brings back old and bitter memories that would be better left dead—at least for them."

"I have nothing to do with your old feuds, or the principals involved. My concern and my only concern is for my sister."

"Come, Larrimore, are you more fool than I believed?"

"As I said, my concern is for Annabella."

"Then let me give you some advice. Perhaps you should have a dram of concern for yourself."

A cold wave of air swept down the chimney and the flames dimmed, then burst to life. "Why should I be concerned for myself? I am a mediator, nothing more."

"You are involving yourself in more than you know."

"I don't know what you are talking about."

"I am not talking about your sister, although the lass does play an important role. But that is none of your concern."

Huntly rose from his chair when Gavin said, "I would think you would have more honor than to want this marriage. It can't be a noble cause that forces a man to marry a woman who doesn't want to marry him."

Huntly smiled. "You won't succeed in provoking me to relinquish what is mine. I'm old enough to recognize such an obvious ploy. You are free to think what you will. You'll not change my mind. It's useless to try. You may take that message back to your sister, or that bastard Mackinnon— whichever you serve—and tell them that I, unlike them, am a man of my word."

"I'll relay the message, although I don't think that will be the end of it."

"While you are relaying messages, you might relay this one as well. Tell your sister that if she persists in acting like a bitch in heat, I may be forced to treat her as one."

For a moment Gavin simply stood there looking at him. At last, when he spoke, he chose his words carefully and spoke them articulately. "You have my word that I will do everything in my power to persuade my father to break this contract with you. If that isn't legally possible, then I can promise you that after he hears of this, he will severely reduce her dowry. You may get my sister, but you won't get the fortune that would have come with her."

"Get out!" Huntly said, the veins on his neck straining to carry the rush of blood that turned his face blood red. "Get out!" he said again. This time his words were a high shriek.

Gavin left, and Lord Huntly stood frozen in place until Fionn Alpin entered.

"You look like you could use a good stiff brandy," he said after taking one look at Huntly. "What did Larrimore want?"

"Trouble. Mackinnon, it seems, has beaten me to the kill. My angelic bride-to-be isn't as innocent as one would think."

"He came to tell you that?"

"He didn't have to tell me. I could see it in his eyes."

"The Mackinnons again. It seems you have made a complete circle," Fionn said. "First the aunt, and now the nephew."

"You can leave Flora out of this."

"Why? You've carried a grudge against the old duke for years, although I don't know why."

"Then let me tell you why. You know I was in love with his daughter—with Flora."

"Aye, and I know Flora hung herself and that you hate her father. But I don't know the connection between the two."

Huntly poured himself a brandy. "I loved Flora, but I couldn't marry her. I had to marry someone with a dowry. After the wedding I went to her—on my goddamn wedding night, to explain to her that it would change nothing between us. I told her I loved her, that she would want for nothing. She went crazy, calling me names, hitting me, breaking things. I tried to calm her down, to make her see reason, but she still fought me, wilder than before. I tried to make love to her. She fought me, and I persisted . . ."

"It was you?" Fionn said. "It was you who raped her?"

"I didn't think . . . I didn't know what I was doing . . . what I had done. Something went wrong. My mind snapped. I didn't realize what I had done until I saw all the blood. I thought she was dead, so I ran."

"And she killed herself rather than tell who raped her."

"She killed herself because her father found out she was with child. My child. I didn't know that she carried my child, or that her father found out about it until later—until the bastard told me. He blamed himself for her death. He had threatened her, threatened to keep her baby and send her away where she would never see it or me again if she had any more to do with me. It was that threat that made her fight me that night. That threat that made her push me away."

"And so she killed herself to put an end to it."

"Aye, and I'll not lose another lass to a Mackinnon. Ever."

After another glass of French brandy to calm his nerves, he called for his horse to be saddled.

"Where are you going at this time of night?" asked Fionn.

"I have pressing business in Edinburgh," Huntly said, then lowering his voice, he added, "After I kill the Marquess of Larrimore."

Chapter
22

Twilight was all about him as Ross made his way across the windswept heath, the trees behind him now, their shadows long and thin, stretching out before him as if trying to pull him back.

The smell of salt was in the air. An army of flies buzzed around him. His legs ached. A deadening sleep seemed to creep upward from his feet. His horse snorted and the bit rang hollow against his teeth. Strange noises seemed all about him and he had the feeling he was awake and in a strange ominous dream from which there would be no awakening. Suddenly a great shadow passed over him, a shadow shaped like giant, outstretched wings, and darkness seemed upon him all at once.

Cold stars glinted faintly through the gathering mist, and dampness seemed to penetrate to the marrow of his bones. And then he saw it, the towers and gables of Seaforth, rising stiff and dark and silent into the shadows of night like sentinels calling him forth.

His burden lay heavy across his legs. The numbness was

in his bones now, but he knew he was close. He guided his horse up the steep, narrow road that led to Seaforth. When he reached the front door, he slid off his horse. The reins fell to the ground unheeded as he pulled the body off and into his arms.

When he reached the door, Ross kicked it with his foot. Once. Twice. On the third kick, it opened. A long yellow beam of light flowed outward from the open door.

The streets of heaven are paved with gold.

He stumbled inside.

Upstairs, Annabella was in her dressing gown, brushing her hair, when she heard a commotion downstairs. Someone screamed. She dropped the brush and was halfway down the stairs when she saw Ross standing in the great hall, her brother's body draped like a bloody battle flag in his arms.

No, her mind screamed. *Not Gavin . . . please, not Gavin.* But it was Gavin, and no amount of denial would change that. Her terror-filled eyes could not move from the sight of her brother's blood smeared like a great stain of guilt across the front of Ross's shirt and down the front of his pants.

She had loved this man—loved him and he had killed her brother. *No, not Ross. Ross couldn't. Ross wouldn't.* She looked at Gavin's body. *He's dead. Dead . . . dead . . . dead.* Even then, she refused to believe Ross would do such a thing.

Not Ross, with the smiling eyes and the gentle hands. Not the man who had loved her so gently and so well. *No*, her mind screamed. *No. Please, no.* But as the words of denial faded, the last words she had heard Ross speak rose like great black wings of promise in the shadowy recesses of her mind.

Whatever it takes, whatever I have to do, or sacrifice, I will. Nothing will keep me from having you. Nothing.

Not murder, she wanted to shout. *Oh, dearest God. Not this. Not the murder of my brother.* But the words would not come. Something within her shattered and she felt overpowered, as if some thing, some groping, terrible thing, had seized her. She heard the sound of hooves thundering as something dark passed over her mind—a great, black shadow that grew darker as the sound of hooves grew louder. The thunder of hooves stopped, and the shadow began to swirl, faster and faster until it died away, leaving nothing behind but silence and a riderless white horse.

A long wail pierced the air, moaning like the wind—the cry of a lonely, anguished creature. It grew louder and louder, then ended with a shrill, piercing scream that left a chill in the blood. And then there was nothing.

It was then that Annabella realized the scream had been torn from her own throat. "Oh, my God!" she shrieked, hurrying down the stairs. "He's hurt." She ran to them, seeing Gavin's blood was everywhere. "Is it bad?" she asked. "Is he hurt badly?"

"He's dead," Ross said. "Stabbed in the back."

Her face was blank, her eyes vacant. "No," she said, pushing Gavin's hair back from his cold, pale face. "He isn't dead. Bring him upstairs. I will tend his wound. He'll be fine. You'll see."

Barra gripped her arms and shook her. "Gavin is dead, Annabella. Don't be denying the truth of what you see, lass. Admit what you see."

Una placed her hand on Barra's arm. "Don't, love. Don't make . . ."

"She has to realize the truth. Her mind won't be right

until she does." He shook Annabella again. "Say it, lass. Tell me Gavin is dead."

"No!" she screamed, breaking away from Barra's hold. Wavering on the brink of hysteria, she wrapped her hands around her waist, rocking back and forth as she began to chant. "He can't be dead. He can't be dead." Her voice faded slowly to a hoarse whisper.

Una came to her, but she pushed her away. "He's my brother. He isn't dead. He can't be." Slowly sinking to the floor, Annabella felt the world spinning around her as her words came back to her like a shattering echo, and a great force sucked her into a black void.

"Bring the lad in here," Barra said. "Allan, you go for the doctor and the officials. And send word to your uncle Alisdair in London."

"The doctor?" Ailie looked up, her face streaked with tears. "If Gavin is dead, why do you need the doctor?"

"Gavin has been murdered. An official will need to see the body. Now, help your mother get Annabella upstairs.

Barra turned to Ross. "How did this happen? Where did you find the lad?"

"On the road not far from here," Ross said.

"Was he dead when you found him?"

"Yes, but not for too long. His body was still warm." Ross shook his head, looking at Barra in a helpless way. "Why would anyone want him dead? It wasn't robbery. He has plenty of money on him."

Barra shook his head, then rubbed his eyes. "I don't know why anyone would want Gavin dead. He's barely known in these parts."

"Well, someone knew him well enough to want him dead."

"Aye," Barra said. "Someone did."

Annabella lay on her bed. Her hands were like ice. Her brow was damp. A great sucking breath seemed to be drawing the life from her. The dream kept coming to her, again and again, until all she could remember were the four horses—black, red, white, and pale—and the agonizing reminder that her brother was dead and that Ross had Gavin's blood on his hands.

She lay there for a long, long time, fully awake, her eyes vacant and staring at nothing. Her whole body ached with cold, but she didn't care. Her head, where it had struck the floor, throbbed painfully. She was glad for the pain and wished for more—enough to wipe out the pain of Gavin's death, the pain of knowing Ross had killed him, the pain of knowing it had all happened because of her.

Gavin.

Gavin had always been there. He was something she took for granted. And now he was gone. It was the only time he had ever let her down. Her brother. Her beloved brother. And now he was gone. Dead. Her life was over. She could see that much clearly. The vision of the four horses came to her often now, but it no longer caused anguish in her. She had separated herself from pain now. Pain. It could not touch her. She could not see what happened around her, only that which lay in her past. She saw Gavin as a child, pushing her in the swing in the oak tree behind Saltwood Castle, sending her higher and higher, the sound of his laughter drifting back over her like the tickling flutter of snowflakes. She could see her father giving Gavin his first pony when he was seven and how Gavin took her for the first ride.

Father. He will hate me now. As I hate myself.

She saw her mother, who could never hate her, although she would never be able to forgive her for what she had done. And her sisters? Would they hate her as her father would, or would they simply turn their backs when she entered the room?

Una came into her bedroom with a cup of hot broth for her. Annabella turned her face to the wall. Her aunt smoothed the hair back from her face and pulled the cover up beneath her chin, then turned away, closing the door softly behind her. Thoughts of Gavin crept forward. Bella tried to push them away. She did not want to think of Gavin. It hurt too much. Thoughts of Gavin would drive her mad.

The pain of knowing he lay somewhere in stone cold silence was more than she could bear. Gavin was cold. He lay upon something hard and cold. His coldness called out to her. She had to help him. She couldn't leave him cold. She pulled herself from the bed and the world spun around her. Her eyes closed and she dropped to the floor, lying upon the cold stones, too wounded to cry, begging God to let her die.

When Una came with her breakfast the next morning, she found her on the floor and said, "Oh, child, child, you mustn't take on so."

On the third day she drank a glass of milk and ate three mouthfuls of soup, only because Una reasoned she needed something in her stomach if she was going to the funeral.

Una bathed her face and laid out her black silk dress. Ailie came in to help her mother fasten the row of buttons down the back. They led her to the mirror and began brushing her hair. Annabella looked at her reflection and saw a pale face with huge eyes and witch's hair. "Bitch," she screamed and threw a perfume bottle at the mirror. It shattered, bits of glass digging into her hands, but she did not care. She welcomed pain now. It was her only companion.

When Ailie or Una tried to speak to her, she turned her face away.

She went downstairs and sat in the library with her brother's body from eight o'clock the morning of the funeral until half-past three when they came to take him away. She rode in the carriage behind him, never taking her eyes from his coffin. She was so weak she had to be helped from the carriage.

After the funeral, she was put to bed with a sedative to help her sleep. During the next few days, she existed in her own world. Not even Ross could get through to her. Anytime he tried, she made no response, not one flicker of emotion that even showed she had heard him.

She understood everything he said, but her heart was twisted with grief and guilt. Annabella could not help thinking it had been her fault, the price that had been extracted to pay for her disobedience. If only she had listened to him that day. If she had agreed with the things he had said.

But she hadn't. And now he was dead. Death was so final. As final as the ending of the love she had shared with Ross. It wasn't that she no longer loved him; nothing could put an end to that, not even knowing he had killed her brother. She hated him. She wanted him dead. But none of those things could make her stop loving him.

Tears scalded her eyes and she turned her head away. She didn't know what she was going to do. The wedding, of course, would be off—wouldn't it? Dear God, she could not go through with it now. Her mind raced ahead to the time when her parents would arrive.

Three days after the funeral, Ross found Barra in his study. His worry and concern for Bella was driving him to desperation.

"I know you don't want to leave her at a time like this,"

Barra said after Ross had spoken to him, "but I think it best. Her mother and father will be here soon. Enough powder kegs have blown up in our faces. There is sure to be another one if you're here when Alisdair and Anne arrive."

Ross left Seaforth. Annabella refused to see him before he went. Word came to Seaforth the following week that her family would not be coming. Her father had written that his wife had taken to her bed upon hearing the news of Gavin's death.

> *Your brother is buried now and nothing can be helped by my coming, and your mother is not up to taking such a journey. Don't worry about her. Her health is as good as can be expected. She has lost some weight, but the doctor feels this is all a part of her grieving. In time that, too, will pass, as the anguish of losing him gives way to the sadness of missing his smiling face. He was a bright light in all of our lives and his presence will be greatly missed. Of all my children, I know the two of you were closest. My grief is deeper in knowing your pain, too, is great. I cannot say you have acted wisely in all of this, Annabella, but neither can I condemn you for the way you have felt. To do so would blacken your brother's memory, for I know he would not want his death to come between us. Because he would have forgiven you, I can do no less. But I do think it best if you remain at Seaforth, at least for the time being. Lord Huntly still wants the marriage to take place, but understands that it will have to be postponed until after the mourning period for Gavin is over.*

Chapter
23

Ross had been back at Dunford three weeks the day he was arrested.

They had come out of the cloak of night, pounding on Dunford's doors, demanding Ross be brought down. Under armed guard he was taken to Edinburgh to await trial for the murder of the Marquess of Larrimore.

Annabella was feeding the chickens in the rain the day Allan rode home with the news of Ross Mackinnon's arrest. After Allan had told her, she dropped the bucket of chicken feed and cried, her tears running down her face and blending with the rain. She thought she had absorbed all the grief she could contain with Gavin's death, but she was wrong.

Only yesterday she had received a letter from Ross, telling her the things she would not listen to when he had been here. He had not killed Gavin, he said, but by the time she read it, that part was old news. Annabella knew as soon as her mind began to clear that Ross could not have killed Gavin. Only yesterday he had written her of his innocence, and today she heard of his arrest.

Some people were never meant to be happy.

Perhaps she was one of those.

Word of his arrest brought questions flooding into her still grief-numbed mind. Ross, she knew, was the one who found Gavin, the one who carried him into the house that night, his clothes stained with Gavin's blood. But there was a matter of motive. What would Ross stand to gain by killing Gavin?

"They dinna think it to be a murder of gain, lass, but one of emotion," Uncle Barra said. "His pockets were full. Robbery was not the motive. Huntly has been questioned and has verified that Gavin came to him, telling him he had come only to pacify you."

Annabella blanched. "What are you saying?"

"I'm saying, lass, that Huntly has sworn that Gavin told him he never intended to ask Huntly to agree to withdraw from the betrothal between the two of you. He swore that Gavin wanted the marriage as much as anyone, that he only pretended to be on your side to keep you quiet until the marriage, which had, by the way, been moved up to December twenty-first. Did Gavin tell you that?"

"No."

"The wedding was moved up, lass. Your father told me in the letter he sent with Gavin."

"Why didn't you tell me?"

"Because you told me Gavin said not to do anything until he returned. I felt it best to keep the letter secret until then."

"I don't care. It doesn't matter. I don't believe a word of Huntly's sworn statement. I know my brother. Gavin wasn't like that. He would have never played me false. Never."

"You will have to admit it does serve Huntly's purpose quite nicely, however."

"In what way?"

"Let's say—strictly for the sake of comparison—that Gavin had no intention of asking Huntly to withdraw. He goes to Huntly, tells him of the early wedding date. He leaves. On the way home he encounters Ross Mackinnon. The two of them talk. Gavin lets it be known that he is on Huntly's side in all of this. If Gavin tells Ross of the earlier marriage date, that adds more pressure to Ross. He and Ross argue. Ross stabs him."

"In the back?" she shouted, leaping to her feet. "If Ross killed anyone, he wouldn't stab him in the back. I know he wouldn't kill any man in such a cowardly way. I know it. And he would never kill my brother."

"I know that. You know that. But Mackinnon is a foreigner to these parts. Huntly is held in high esteem . . ."

"In only a few circles," Annabella reminded him.

"In only a few circles," Barra repeated, "but unfortunately those circles are the important ones. Huntly is a sly weasel. He's out to get Mackinnon. I feel it in my bones."

"Why would he be after Ross?"

"Because Ross made a fool of him by taking the woman he was to marry. Revenge runs hot in Huntly's blood. He's already obtained proof that Mackinnon is a wanted man in Texas. It doesna look too good for Mackinnon, lass."

"Wanted? For what?"

Barra paled. "Leave it be, lass."

"For what, Uncle? I have a right to know."

Barra sighed. "It seems the lad seduced a lass and promised to marry her, then left the country. But there are always two sides to every story," Barra went on to say, but Bella was not listening.

Dear God. Did he make a fool of me as well?

In her heart Bella didn't want to believe it, but her mind

was more shrewd. Too much evidence pointed at Ross, and she could think of nothing, not one point that could be declared in his favor, save the fact that she loved him.

Her hands trembling, she turned, her face pale, and looked at her uncle. "What will they do to him if . . . if he is found guilty?"

"Hang him."

A portion of her mind refused to believe it. Another part was full of doubt. For a moment she thought she might faint. She felt sick, sick beyond reasoning, beyond rational thought, even beyond speech. Gavin was dead. Murdered. And Ross would pay the price for it. Ross would hang. He would be no more. He would cease to exist as Gavin had, save in the dark, shadowy corners of her mind. He would die and she would never see him again.

Just like Gavin.

She would never again know the feel of his dark head held close to her breast, or know the whisper of his thoughts against her flesh. There would be no more moments of laughter, no more times when he would happen upon her and take her by surprise, no more times the sight of him would set her soul on fire. Never would she enter into the sweet, teasing banter with him, or know the pleasure of being loved and loving in return.

Annabella looked at her uncle and started from the room. She paused at the door. "Perhaps he will be spared," she said. "Perhaps he will find a way to save himself."

"Perhaps. Are you going to see him?"

"No."

"Why? Do you believe him guilty, then?"

"No . . . I . . . I don't know. I'm not certain of anything anymore. All I know is my brother is dead, and someone murdered him. So far, Ross is the only one with a motive."

"You don't think Huntly has a motive?"

"What could it be?"

"You."

"Me?" she retorted. "Me?" She laughed mockingly. "Why should he kill for me? I belonged to him already."

"Perhaps. Perhaps on paper. But in your heart, lass, you will always belong to Ross Mackinnon."

"What are you saying, Uncle?"

"I'm saying, don't be so quick to condemn the lad."

"I thought you were convinced of his guilt. You certainly sounded like it."

"I merely told you the facts, lass. Facts dinna make a man guilty."

She came back into the room and took a chair across from Barra's desk. "All right. Let's back up here. You mentioned that Huntly might have a reason for killing Gavin, and I was that reason. I don't understand."

"What if Gavin went to Huntly as he said he was going to? What if he asked Huntly to back off? What if Huntly refused?"

"What if Gavin got angry and told Huntly the wedding was off anyway," she finished.

"Exactly," Barra said. "What if Gavin left after that?"

"Huntly could have had him killed."

"Or he could have followed him and killed him himself. We know Huntly left that night for Edinburgh. He could have killed Gavin before he went to Edinburgh. Your brother was stabbed in the back. Dinna be forgetting that. That in itself smells of Huntly. I dinna think he's man enough to face a man down."

* * *

Over the next few weeks Annabella tried to pick up the pieces of her life that had been scattered like that bucket of chicken feed she had dropped that day in the rain. She found herself spending more time in the kitchen, bending over a quilting frame, or sitting in the parlor with Una and Ailie making lace or smocking. Her aim was to keep busy, but soon she learned the hands can work even while the mind stays idle. And whenever her mind was idle, the same thoughts would return.

Many thoughts were about Ross and the moments they had shared, but often she would find she relived and rethought the conversation she had with her uncle that day. What if he was right? What if Huntly was involved here? She had no way of knowing, and perhaps she never would. But she did know one thing. Ross was innocent. She would stake her life on that. She felt guilty for even doubting that for a moment.

She made her mind up to go to Edinburgh to see him. And then she thought of his grandfather. The old duke had to be taking this hard. *But Percy is there with him,* she told herself. *I know Percy wouldn't go back to England now, no matter how much he needed to return. He loves the Mackinnon. Loves him as much as I do.*

"I'm going to Dunford," she announced the next morning.

"Can I go with you?" Ailie asked.

"No," Barra replied. "This is something Bella must do alone."

It was past midnight when she arrived at Dunford two days later, but the old duke was still up, at least she thought him to be, since the light was on in the Mackinnon's study.

When a sleep-dazed Robert opened the door, Annabella

hurried through the door, her skirts swishing around her. "Is His Grace in his study?"

"He is, miss."

"Thank you, Robert. Will you have my things taken from the coach and placed in my old room?"

"Yes, miss." Robert watched her go. "Oh, miss?"

She paused and turned to look at him. "Yes?"

A wide grin split his face. "Glad to have you back, miss. The old duke is a broken man. Maybe you can do something for him."

"I'll try, Robert," she said. "That's why I've come."

She hurried down the hall, stopping at the duke's study and knocking softly on the door. No one answered, so Annabella opened the door and stepped inside. The Mackinnon was sitting in his chair behind the desk, his head resting on his chest. Stepping closer, she noticed a quill in his fingers. On closer inspection, she saw he had been writing a letter to his solicitor in Edinburgh. Tears welled in her eyes and she reached out and took the quill from his fingers.

He's been through so much, lost so much. He doesn't deserve this.

The duke snorted and shifted his position, his eyes opening slowly. "You came," he said. "I knew you would."

Winter settled in. Christmas came and went. But not even the cold weather could slow down progress. Percy and the Mackinnon made repeated trips to Edinburgh, talking with the solicitor and hiring investigators, always returning without much hope. Annabella remained behind at Ross's request. He had written his grandfather.

Don't bring her to Edinburgh. Things look grim for me. I don't want to put her through the pain of seeing

*me like this. Tell her—tell her to remember me as I was
that day I went hunting. She will know what I mean.*

March arrived, all blustery and windblown, as if Mother
Nature had decided to throw a tantrum. Perhaps it was the
temperamental weather that sparked it, perhaps it was the
agony of being kept away—whatever it was, this was
the month Annabella decided to accompany the duke and
Percy to Edinburgh. She couldn't let Ross go without seeing him at least once more.

Four days after she made her decision to go to Edinburgh, she was there, crossing Dean Bridge and the Water
of Leith into the city Robert Burns called *Edina, Scotia's
darling seat.*

She sat in the coach reading *Holyrood:*

*The moon passed out of Holyrood, white-lipped to open
    sky;
The night wind whimpered on the Crags to see the ghosts
    go by;
And stately, silent, sorrowful, the lonely lion lay,
Gaunt shoulder to the Capital and blind eyes to the Bay.*

Annabella closed the book and glanced out the window.
A sea of daffodils danced in the wind in front of the cold
stones of Charlotte Square as they passed, and she wondered if Ross would ever be free to see them.

It was two days before they allowed her to see him, but
the long, nerve-dangling wait was now over. She waited for
him in her black taffeta dress—for she was still in mourning
for Gavin—but she had thrown a Mackinnon plaid over her
shoulder.

Only an hour ago she had left the office of the duke's

solicitor, Lord Braxton. They had spent the better part of the morning there, discussing an earlier meeting Lord Braxton had had with the advocate. The case would be tried in the highest criminal court, the High Court of Justiciary. Their decision would be final, for there was no appeal, not even to the House of Lords from that court. The finality of the solicitor's words rang in her head like the echo of an iron gate closing.

And now she was here, where they kept Ross. Waiting. The chamber she waited in was small, sparse, and stifling. She moved to the window to open it, and noticed the bars. The shock of seeing them, of knowing Ross had spent weeks that were now turning into months behind bars such as these—was more than she could bear. She turned quickly away from the window, her mind, as always, on Ross. A jury of fifteen would decide his guilt or innocence. Fifteen people who would, by a simple majority, decide if Ross was to live or die.

The door opened and Ross was led into the tiny waiting room, which was furnished with only a small table and two chairs.

"Fifteen minutes," the guard said, then left, bolting the door behind him.

He looked the same, but tired. He was thinner, paler, and so tired; his face showing the deep, jagged lines of strain. But the beloved face, the inky blackness of his hair, were as she remembered. The fire and spirit of the man she had known still burned in his eyes, but the clothes he wore were strange, not his usual buckskin pants and blue denim shirt.

The moment he had entered, his eyes were upon her and she saw the bright flare of emotion quickly repressed. He loved her, but she knew he would do his best not to let it show.

He looked at the Mackinnon plaid draped over her shoulder and a lingering smile touched his mouth. "There was a time when you wouldn't have worn that plaid," he said softly.

She smiled at him. "There was a time you wouldn't have cared if I did."

His expression turned somber. "I didn't want you to see me like this, lass. It would have been easier for y—for us both if you had stayed away. It isn't very wise of you to be here. If you had given it more thought, you wouldn't have come."

"You told me once that a man who does everything with planning and forethought has very few memories worth keeping."

"Memories, is it? Is that why you came?"

"Oh, Ross," she said, rushing to him and throwing her arms around his waist. "I came because I love you. Surely you know that." She pressed her face against his chest and closed her eyes, pretending for a moment she was happy and never wanted the moment to end, pretending for a while the pain and grief that surrounded them was all a bad dream.

"Darling Annabella, I'm not clean. You'll leave your sweet smell with me and take my stench," he whispered, his words fluttering soft and gentle against her hair.

"I don't care. I don't care about anything except being with you. I had to see you. I wanted to see if you were as dear to me as the picture my memory holds. I had so many things I wanted to say to you. Only now . . . now that I'm with you, I don't seem to know what to say." Tears bubbled up from the hurt place inside and she couldn't go on.

"I know," he said, cradling her head, feeling the anguish of her tears, knowing she cried for both of them. "I know."

He didn't say anything more; he was content for a while to hold her and let her cry herself out. The only comfort he could offer her was to cradle her to him as if she was precisely what she was: the dearest thing in life to him.

When the tears gave way to jerky sobs that eased into an occasional shudder, he slipped one finger beneath her chin and lifted her head until she was looking at him, and as if it was the most natural thing in the world, he kissed her. It was a kiss not given in passion, or one to feed its hunger. It was a simple kiss, one of compassion, of understanding, because he cared for her and because he could not bear to see the suffering in those green, beautiful eyes.

"I didn't kill Gavin," he said.

"I know," she said slowly. She studied his face. "Oh, Ross. Why did you say that? Why did you even feel you had to tell me? Didn't you think I would know?"

"I didn't want you to wonder years from now, after I'm . . . I just wanted you to hear it straight from the horse's mouth."

She smiled sadly. "There you go again, using one of those odd expressions. At least I understand that one." Her arms slipped around him to hold him to her and she felt him flinch and stiffen as if her squeezing him had caused him pain.

"Why did you wince? Are you hurt? In pain?"

"Just a little bruising on my rib," he said. "Nothing to worry about."

"How did it happen?"

He sighed and looked off.

"They beat you, didn't they?"

"It was just a small disagreement."

"Over what?"

"My signing a confession."

"Oh, Ross . . ." her voice trailed off and she reached out and touched his rib gently. "This side?"

"Yes."

"Let me see it."

"It's nothing. Just a small bruise."

"I'll be the judge of that, you big bairn."

How wifely she sounded. How concerned. He did not miss the way she had used the Scots word for baby, or how it sounded so natural on her lips. He felt a flood of pride in her. She didn't cringe or cry, or wring her hands, or do any of the dozen other things an overprotected English lady would do. Scotland had changed her and she was his lass now. With a stab of regret he remembered where he was and what it meant that she was here.

She was his lass.

But it was a happiness that came too late. A happiness that was gone before it arrived.

She took his hand and led him to the table, pulling out one of the chairs. He sank into the welcome support, weariness heavy in his bones. She began unbuttoning his shirt with quick, capable hands, pulling the shirt from his breeches when she finished. "Oh, Ross," she said, seeing the inky bruise that fanned his ribs, her fingers touching him gently where the purpling gave way to blue. "Do you think it's broken?"

"Cracked, I believe. But it doesn't matter. I hardly notice it, since all I do is sit around waiting in a cell all . . . my God, Annabella . . . sweetheart . . . my God! . . ."

She had dropped down beside him in a billow of rustling black silk, her hands pushing the fabric of his shirt apart. Her head down, she was kissing his bruise with all the gentleness she had used when touching him with her fingers.

Again and again, she kissed him, her hands fanning out flat against his chest, her fingers woven into the hair that covered him there. Her touch, her kisses drove him wild. He wanted her. Here. Now. On this hard plank floor. He wanted her here, because he knew he did not have enough time left to have her anywhere else.

The weight of his future pressed down heavily upon him. He pushed her away, intending to bring her to her feet, but his weakness for her took over and he found that instead of pushing her away, he had drawn her face up to his. Whispering. Needing. He nuzzled her and searched for her face. Finding her mouth, he covered it with his own, forcing it wider, kissing her hungrily, unable to kiss her long enough or deep enough to give him ease. If he had the rest of his life to kiss her like this, it would never be enough. His feeling knew no bounds—none save those imposed upon him for the punishment of a crime he did not commit.

The weight of his own death pressed down heavily upon him, and he felt the last urging of desire fall away. *What are you doing, man? You're only making it harder for her. Don't give her false hope. Don't give her something you don't have.*

As quickly as he had pulled her to him, he put her away. He stood up, drawing her up to stand in front of him. His hands still holding hers, he looked her over, committing her to memory. "You must go now," he said. "Promise me you won't come back. Promise you will remember me as I was. Not like this."

"Don't say that, Ross. Please. I want to be here with you," she said. "I don't want you to go through this all alone."

"I won't be alone," he said. "I have too many memories of you to ever be alone."

"I can't bear the thought of not seeing you, not being with you when you need me."

"I don't want you here. I want you to forget me, starting now. I want you to put the past behind you and go forward. You were meant to be loved, Bella. Find someone who will love you. Find someone who will love you enough to make you forget." He knew what she was going to say, knew she was going to resist him. "Get away from me now. Get away and leave my memory behind when you go. Forget me, Annabella. Leave this place and don't ever look back."

"Will you kiss me before I go?"

"I can't," he said, and turned away. "Guard," he said, pounding on the door. "Open up. The lady is ready to leave."

She left the room without looking back.

Only when she had gone was he able to think of her as lost to him. Only when she had gone was he able to weep.

The old Annabella would have listened to Ross. The old Annabella would have returned to her life and grieved for his loss for a time.

The old Annabella would have.

The new Annabella did not. The new Annabella had no intention of forgetting him, of finding another man to help her forget. As long as there was a breath in his body she would not give up. As long as he lived, he was worth fighting for. For that reason, she hung on to hope, long after Ross had given up on his.

One week before his trial another letter arrived at Dunford, this one a short note reminding her not to come. *"It will be easier on me, if you don't come."*

It was cold and raining the next morning when Percy and the Mackinnon left for Edinburgh, and Annabella couldn't help wondering if she should look at that as a bad omen. Standing at her bedroom window as she watched the coach pull away from the house, she fought the urge to grab her cape and go running after them. *"It will be easier on me if you don't come,"* he had written.

Little did he know it was so much harder on her because she did not.

Chapter
24

She knew they had sentenced him to hang the moment she opened the door and saw his grandfather's face. Never had she seen a man go downhill so fast. He had aged ten years since that day she had met him a year ago.

Percy helped him inside.

"It's bad," she said to Percy, "isn't it?"

"Yes. As bad as can be. They've found him guilty," Percy said.

"They'll hang him?" she asked.

"In two weeks."

First Gavin, and now Ross. It couldn't be happening to her. Not again. Not a second time. Surely she couldn't be losing another so dear to her. She wanted to scream and smash things, she wanted to run out the door and keep running until the heath swallowed her up and ended her misery. But she looked at the old duke, and she knew she couldn't break down.

"I haven't given up," the Mackinnon said. "Help me up-stairs, Percy." Then to Annabella he said, "I'm too travel-weary to think clearly tonight, lass, but tomorrow we'll set to work, you and I." With his old, wrinkled hand he squeezed her arm, a gesture all the more dear to her because she knew how much the old duke suffered, how much that one act of comfort had cost him. She stepped into his arms, feeling this old man was a part of Ross. "Dinna fret," he said, patting her back. "We'll free our lad. We'll free him if I have to sell my soul to the devil to do it."

Percy came back downstairs after the Mackinnon had been put to bed. Annabella shared a glass of Drambuie with him in the library and listened for two hours as Percy told her about the trial.

"Was Huntly there? Did he testify?"

"Yes, briefly." Percy paused a moment, deep in thought. "Something struck me as strange."

"What was that?"

"I talked to Huntly for a moment. He told me he went to England and talked with your father. He still plans on going through with the marriage, after the period of mourning, of course. He said the circumstances of your brother's death were unfortunate, but nothing more than a temporary setback."

"I know," she said. "My father wrote me." She turned her head away and stared into the empty fireplace. "I won't marry him. I would rather be dead like Gavin than go through with that marriage, but I don't want to deal with that now. I need my wits and my strength for the Mackinnon, and Ross. For now, I'm safe—safe from that man's clutches for as long as I mourn."

"If you marry Huntly, that mourning period may go on indefinitely."

"I know that too," she said softly. "Percy, why do you think he is so obsessed with having this marriage?"

"It's reported—nothing proven, mind you, just hearsay—that Huntly has grossly mismanaged his lands and his fortune since receiving his title and inheritance. I've heard from a few reliable sources that he squandered his first wife's fortune as well. If this is true, that in itself could drive a man to obsessive lengths to marry a rich woman."

"My father knew nothing of this. I'm sure of that."

"Then tell him."

"I shall, but it won't do any good. My father is a proud, stubborn man, a man of honor, a man of his word. He would stand by his word. And he would, more than likely, tell me that men have had good, strong marriages for hundreds of years, even when they have married for the very same reason." She shook her head. "He would probably find it even honorable—that a man would put his obligations before his own personal feelings." She sighed and turned a weary face to Percy. "What should I do?"

Percy stood. "I wouldn't want to answer that now. I'm afraid I'm not capable of making much sense right now. I'm tired as a gamecock after the fight." He started from the room but paused beside a leather satchel on the Mackinnon's desk, then placed his hand on the satchel and said, "These are the records from the trial, if you'd like to see them. The Mackinnon hired scribes to record as much of the proceedings as possible."

Annabella carried the stack of papers to her room and stayed up for the rest of the night reading. It was half-past six when she read something that struck her memory, but she didn't know why. She backed up and read the sentence again. "Deceased was stabbed in the upper quadrant of his back, near the right shoulder blade." She shook her head, not understanding why this sentence jogged her memory.

I'm too tired to think right now. Tomorrow, she thought. *I'll read it again tomorrow.*

She did read it the next morning, but the words didn't seem all that unusual, so she went on. Once she had finished reading, she had lunch with Percy and the duke. After lunch they met in the library and began combing through the reports from the trial. Over and over they read and reread, each time coming up with nothing.

Over the passage of time, she had begun to realize that having her thoughts occupied with securing Ross's freedom had enabled her to go on after Gavin's death. It had become a reason to keep living, a reason to get up and face each morning, a reason to step into the dark unknown. She still grieved for her brother, and not a day went by that she didn't think of him more than once. But she was able to put things in perspective. Gavin was dead, and one couldn't live with the dead, or change the finality of that circumstance. She could let his death destroy her, or give her the strength to go on. She chose the latter.

Thinking about Ross brought her only pain, but even the pain could not keep his memory away. It was all she had now. Many times she found herself staring off into space, reliving the times she had been with him, the times he had molded her to the long, hard length of his body, the times he had held her as if he wanted to absorb the very substance of her. Thoughts such as this made her clench her fists in anguish, for she knew and feared what they would do to him in a matter of days. And as always, the distress of thinking that she would never see him again made her yearn to see him one more time, to feel his strength and patience plunging into her, to feel the strong assurance of his arms, to know that he was.

Nights were the worst; they were the times she missed

him most. Often she would awaken in a cold sweat, the need inside her like a bright, spreading flame sharply edged with desperation. She would roll to her side, her hands clutching her middle as she rocked back and forth. *Don't let him die. Please don't let him die.* It reverberated in her head like a litany, until the tears burned and blurred her vision, and she would cry until her throat ached and her mind was fogged with remembered passion.

A week before Ross was scheduled to hang, Annabella walked up the trail with the Mackinnon as she had done that day so long ago. They walked for over two hours before returning to Dunford.

Seeing how tired the old duke was, almost to the point of exhaustion, she went with him into the library, asking Robert to build a fire for them. As Robert laid the fire, they discussed the hanging, both of them deciding not to go. "It's strange," the Mackinnon said, "how I seem to be outliving them all—my children and my grandchildren."

"Don't give up now," she said. "Remember what you told me. We have to keep the faith, keep on hoping and praying."

"I'm all prayed out, lass. If God won't give me the lad back, then I pray he will give me the strength to live with his loss." He shook his white head and she thought he looked like an old shaggy lion. "You know, I think Ross knew he wouldn't come out of this thing alive. I remember the day we left, when Percy and I went to talk to him that last time. He had been in another fight. His right hand was bandaged. When I asked about it, he laughed and said, *'Well, I guess that's one good thing about my hanging. It's a cinch this hand won't be bothering me for long.'* He told me not to worry for him, that he had always gotten by. After we left him and started out of town, I glanced up to see him watching us from the window, his face smiling down at me from behind those bars. He lifted his hand and waved at us. The sun glared off of that bandage as if it was a mirror . . ."

"My God!" Annabella sprang to her feet. "Oh, my God!" Her hands clamped over her mouth. Tears were streaming down her face. She opened her arms wide and looked heavenward and dropped to her knees in thanks. "Oh, dear, sweet, loving God! Thank you! Thank you!" she said.

Turning to the Mackinnon, she rose to her feet. "Prayer changes things. It does! It does!" She grabbed the Mackinnon on each side of his face and kissed him. "You did it! You did it! You wonderful, adorable, beautiful man. You did it! With the help of God, you did it!"

"What's going on in here?" Percy said, running into the room. "Are you all right?"

"I am," the Mackinnon said, "but I dinna think I can say the same about her."

When Annabella calmed down, she rushed to the table and began shuffling through the papers from the trial. "Here it is," she said. "Listen to this. 'Deceased was stabbed in the upper quadrant of his back, near the right shoulder blade.'"

"We've all read that, Annabella," Percy said. "And it was brought out at the trial."

"I know that. But I never really understood what it meant until now." She looked at the Mackinnon. "Not until you mentioned that bandage. Don't you see? You mentioned that it glared like a mirror, and in a way it was—a mirror into my mind. The minute you made that comparison, this passage flashed into my consciousness. I had a vivid picture of Ross waving to you . . . waving with his right hand. His *right* hand. Don't you understand what I mean?"

The Mackinnon looked at Percy. They both shook their heads. "It doesn't matter, as long as I understand. Just believe me when I say, it was no accident that this has been revealed to us, Your Grace. It was divine intervention." She paused and looked at them.

"Go on," the Mackinnon said, and Bella would have sworn the weariness dropped away from him, right before her very eyes.

"Gavin was stabbed near his *right* shoulder blade. Ross is right-handed." She went to Percy and turned him around, putting his back to her. "Gavin was stabbed here," she said, making imaginary markings to show the upper right quarter of Percy's back. Then she made a fist with her right hand and stabbed his back. "If a right-handed person comes up behind his victim and stabs him, where does the knife go? Here?" She stabbed Percy again. The natural swing of her arm went, not to the upper right portion of Percy's back, but to the left.

"To the left side," the Mackinnon said, his eyes blazing to life.

"And what would you guess to be the angle of the slant?"

"I suppose it would angle down somewhat, and a little to the left," the Mackinnon said.

"Exactly. It would go toward the left shoulder blade, while a left-handed person"—she clenched her left hand and stabbed Percy again—"Would stab in an altogether different direction, angling toward the right," she said.

"Perhaps you're right. It would go to the right. But, I don't think it's enough evidence," the Mackinnon said.

"It is. I know it is . . . and more importantly, it's all we've got. Read this," she said. "See how it tells the angle of the knife wound. I'm no expert, of course, but from reading this, it sounds to me as if the man who stabbed Gavin would have to be a left-handed person."

She handed the paper to Percy. He read a few sentences and lifted his head in sudden enlightenment. "Huntly is left-handed," he said.

"Huntly," Annabella said.

"Are you sure?" asked the Mackinnon. "Think, man, this is important."

"I'm sure. I remember, because before he testified at the trial I saw him write something and hand the paper to the advocate. And he wrote it with his left hand. I'm sure of it."

The Mackinnon rang for Robert. "Order my coach. We leave for Edinburgh immediately," he said.

"Tonight, Your Grace?"

"Right this minute," the Mackinnon replied.

"But dinner, Your Grace. It's ready to be . . ."

"We haven't time for dinner. Order the coach."

"Very well, Your Grace."

By the time they reached the ferry, there had been a change of plans. "I've been thinking one of us should go to Seaforth. In order to prove our claim that Gavin was murdered by a left-handed man, we'll need the doctor who examined your brother's body," Percy said.

"I suppose you're right," the Mackinnon replied. "When we reach Kyleakin we'll hire another carriage to take the two of you to Seaforth. I'll go on to Edinburgh to meet with my solicitor to set everything in motion."

"I want to go to Edinburgh with you," Annabella said, but Percy vetoed that idea.

"You'd better come with me. Gavin was your brother. You would have to authorize the doctor to give us access to the information we need."

Even though it was decided Annabella would not go to Edinburgh, but would continue on to Seaforth with Percy, she couldn't help the feeling of elation that lifted her spirits. She had not felt so good since before that terrible day at Seaforth when she had come downstairs and seen Ross standing in the doorway with her brother in his arms, his clothes covered with Gavin's blood.

They reached the mainland and the Mackinnon went on to Edinburgh alone, Percy and Annabella heading north. After another day of travel, they arrived at Dr. MacTarver's. He was away on a call, so Percy left word they would return the next day. They spent the night at Seaforth.

True to their word, Annabella accompanied Barra and Percy to Dr. MacTarver's office the next day. The pungent fumes of formaldehyde wafted over her the moment they stepped inside, bringing with it all the painful memories of Gavin's death. It was Saturday morning, and a woman was sweeping the floor. Otherwise, the office was empty.

"Is Dr. MacTarver here?" asked Percy.

A door opened and Dr. MacTarver came out, drying his hands. "Ahhh, Lady Annabella, isn't it?" Annabella nodded. "I heard you were looking for me."

"Yes," she said. "This is Lord Percival and my uncle, Barra Mackenzie, you know."

Dr. MacTarver shook hands with each of them.

"It is most urgent that we talk to you," Annabella said. "It's a matter of life or death."

Dr. MacTarver knitted his white bushy brows and began rolling down his sleeves. "Why don't you go clean in the other room, Elspeth?"

The woman left and Dr. MacTarver motioned for them to take the two chairs opposite his. He sat behind the desk. "What can I do for you?" he asked.

Percy leaned forward. "A few months ago you examined the body of Lady Annabella's brother, the Marquess of Larrimore, shortly after his death."

"Yes. I remember the puir lad. Knifed in the back, he was."

"It's concerning the report you made after your examination of the body that we're here."

Dr. MacTarver leaned back, his leather chair creaking. "I'm afraid I can't give you any more information than I included on my report. I am a very thorough man. When I fill out my report, I leave nothing out."

"We aren't questioning that," Percy said. "We would like further clarification."

"Clarification on what?"

"The study you made of my brother, Dr. MacTarver. How extensive was it?" Annabella asked.

"What do you mean by extensive?"

"When you examined him, was it to determine the cause and conditions of his death, or simply to certify that he was knifed?"

"Young woman, I'll have you know conducting an autopsy has been around since the Middle Ages. I knew what I was about. I have a medical degree from Edinburgh University and I studied at the Great Windmill Street School of Anatomy. I know how to determine cause of death."

Percy looked at Annabella. "Lady Annabella did not mean to imply you didn't know what you were about, Doctor. She read something from your report that caught her attention. It might prove the innocence of the man due to hang for her brother's murder." Percy removed a leather envelope from his pocket, taking out several sheets of paper. "It was brought out in the trial that the fatal wound to Lord Larrimore was in the upper right quadrant of his back, near the right shoulder blade."

"Let me get my report," Dr. MacTarver said, "before I confirm or deny that." A few minutes later he had located the file and returned to his desk. It took only a moment for him to find what he was looking for. "Yes . . . here it is. Yes, that's correct—I did say the upper right quadrant. I've drawn a diagram," he said, turning the paper so they could all see it.

"Lady Annabella believes from further statements you made concerning the angle of the knife that her brother had to be stabbed by someone who was left-handed."

Dr. MacTarver looked thoughtful, as if he were carefully weighing and considering what Percy had just said. Without speaking, he referred to his papers once again, reading what he had written, studying his sketches. He made several sweeping motions with his arm—first his right, and then his left.

The agony they had all been through, waiting for Dr. MacTarver to reach a decision was worth every precious moment of it when Dr. MacTarver looked at them and said, "I agree." He slammed his hand down and spoke with great emphasis.

Annabella jumped a foot when he slammed his hand down, then gave him an astonished look that gave way to one of great joy. "You do? You really do? You mean you agree with what we said?"

"I do, and I'll show you why." He took a clean piece of paper and began sketching a diagram of a back. He laid his pen down and picked up a letter opener, holding it in his right hand as if it were a knife. He stabbed it forward. "Now, watch the swing of my hand as it moves in an arc." He stabbed the letter opener again. "You see how the natu-

ral swing is from right to left?" Percy and Annabella nodded. "Now watch." He changed hands, holding the letter
opener in his left hand and going through the same motions.
"You see the difference? In the left hand the arc swings at a
different angle. If your brother had been stabbed by a right-
handed man, Lady Annabella, the wound left by the knife
would have angled downward, going from right to left. On
the other hand, a left-handed person would have stabbed
the knife at a left-to-right angle. These sketches I've made
of the wound coincide with what you've said." He closed his
file and stood up. "It is my professional opinion that your
brother was murdered by someone who had a marked pref-
erence for his left hand."

"Thank God," Annabella said, rising to her feet. "You
don't know what this means."

"A man's life, I would guess," Dr. MacTarver said.

"And we don't have much time left to save it," Percy said.
"He's scheduled to hang in Edinburgh on Monday."

"Holy heather!" Dr. MacTarver said. "That's the day after
tomorrow. You'd best be getting under way." He reflected a
moment. "I suppose you'll be needing me to come with
you?"

Percy grinned. "Yes—it would be much easier to have
you volunteer than to drag you there by force—chloro-
formed, if necessary."

"Chloroform? I see you've kept up to date on your reading," Dr. MacTarver said.

Dr. MacTarver's offer to accompany them seemed to be
the end of their good fortune, for the trip to Edinburgh was
besieged with unfortunate delays. It rained during their entire journey, making travel slow and difficult. One of the
coach horses came up lame near Ft. William, causing a delay in acquiring another one. Near Stirling they lost a wheel

and had to continue the journey on horseback. They reached Edinburgh early Monday morning, going straight to the hotel. With the Mackinnon in tow, they went first to the solicitor's, then to the advocate. Less than an hour before Ross was scheduled to hang, they had the proper papers to secure his release.

As they left the advocate's office, Annabella said, "We haven't much time. Why don't you take the horses and go on. I'll follow in the coach."

She watched Percy and the Mackinnon take off at a gallop, then climbed into the coach. If anyone had ever prayed their way across Edinburgh, Annabella did.

She saw no sign of Percy or the Mackinnon when she arrived and was shown into a small waiting room. She paced the floor, anxiously waiting, wondering. The sound of drums rolling drew her to the window. *No,* her mind screamed. *It can't be happening. They can't hang him. They can't.*

But they were.

She watched in horror as the tall, dark-haired man she loved above life itself walked slowly across the yard toward the gallows. She began screaming, pounding her fists against the window, pulling at the bars—doing everything she could think of to stop this madness. He was a free man, released to his grandfather's care until they could schedule a hearing. The advocate and the judge had said so. They couldn't hang him.

When he put his foot on the first step, she knew she could endure no more and turned away.

Ross would be dead before she left the building. He would be as dead as Gavin. Nothing seemed to matter any more. The future stretched before her like a long black ribbon with Lord Huntly waiting like a jailer at the end. Nothing could save her from Huntly now. Proving Ross's innocence was not the same thing as implicating Huntly. Huntly would go free, unless he confessed, something she could not see a man like him doing. There was only one chance. If she confronted Huntly and made him think they had proof against him, she might be able to use that as leverage to get him to agree to dissolving the marriage agreement between them.

She didn't remember much after that, except that it was like a nightmare, where she saw dark, shadowy visions of herself leaving the room, stopping for a moment to ask a guard how long it would take to go to a place near Aberdeen called Stonehaven, and telling the driver of the coach to take her there.

Chapter
25

"Surely you're going after her," Percy said. "If she confronts him with the truth about Gavin's death, her life might be at stake."

Ross opened the wooden shutters over the window and looked out into the courtyard of the inn. "She's safe as long as she agrees to marry him," he said. "That tasty little tidbit you uncovered at the solicitor's about his near financial ruin proves that. He will have to start selling off the Huntly lands soon, unless he makes this marriage." He turned away from the window. "He needs her fortune, even if he doesn't need her."

"God's breath! You can't mean to leave her there," Percy said, frowning at Ross's shrug. "You can do what you want, but I'm going after the lass."

"Dinna fash yourself," the Mackinnon said, putting a calming hand on Percy's shoulder. "The lad is trying his hand at baffling us with a bit of Scots craft. He thinks to rescue his lass all by himself and be the sole recipient of her gratitude." The Mackinnon looked at Ross. "If the guard

was right and she did go to Stonehaven, you're going to
need a plan to get her out."

"Just because you were snatched from the jaws of death
once today, doesn't mean you'll be so lucky next time,"
Percy said. "You saw them hang that other poor fool. Be
careful lad, so you don't end up back in prison."

"I'll be careful."

"What are you going to do?" asked Percy.

"I don't know my plans as yet," Ross said. "I'll have to
see what I'm up against once I reach Stonehaven and find
this Mercat Castle of his."

"I can tell you now what you'll find," the Mackinnon said.
"A well-built castle set on a promontory with three sides
protected by steep cliffs that go more than a hundred feet
down into the North Sea."

"Then I'll go in the same way Huntly does."

The Mackinnon shook his head. "I don't know. Getting
out is impossible. Getting in won't be much easier. You
can't very walk through the gates on your good looks."

Ross grinned and ruffled his grandfather's white mane of
hair. "That's exactly what I plan to do," he said. "Even
Huntly can't run a castle without a lass or two about."

The wind was a flood of blackness weaving through lofty
trees as three riders galloped by. They kept to the screen of
trees as the full moon shone like a ghost ship sailing
through clouds that churned wild as the sea. At last the
horsemen dismounted and looked at the great hulking
shape of Mercat Castle sitting at the end of a road that
gleamed like a ribbon of moonlight lost upon a lavender
heath.

"Here you are, lad," the Mackinnon said. "Don't you
think we should go back for the sheriff?"

"No," Ross said, "I've got my way in already planned."

"How about a way *out?*" said Percy.

"I'll worry about that once I'm in and have my lass," he said.

"Then what?"

"As soon as we reach safety, I'm going to wring that lovely neck of hers for leaving. I don't know what in the hell she was thinking of—chasing off after Huntly. Why couldn't she wait until you had me released?"

"Maybe she thought you wouldn't let her go to confront Huntly," Percy said.

"You're damn right, I wouldn't have," replied Ross.

"Or perhaps she thought it was too late, that you were already dead," the Mackinnon said. "That other miserable soul did resemble you a great deal—from a distance, that is. I found myself believing it was you at first, until I saw you with Percy."

They heard noises in the distance—conflicting notes of disharmony on the road behind them. A few minutes later the laughter of bad singing voices and creaking wheels reached a near-painful level. They turned and saw a cart loaded with young people—they had passed it half a mile back—making its way slowly up the road. The night was young, and so were the cart's occupants, their blood running thin with whisky as they sang off-key a verse of "Open Your Bodice, Leonore."

"Hide yourself," Ross said. "And take the horses. My ride has come." Seeing his grandfather's anxious face, he said, "I may be awhile. If I'm not back by daybreak, go for the sheriff."

Hiding in the shadows, their hands over the horses' noses to prevent their nickering, the Mackinnon and Percy watched as Ross turned and started walking up the road.

A few minutes later the cart drew alongside him. From the midst of the revelry came a cheerful greeting. "Are you lost?"

"No," Ross said with a laugh. "I'm not, but my horse is."

That brought a round of laughter. "Are you going to Mercat?" a girl of sixteen or so asked.

"As fast as my tired legs will carry me," replied Ross.

"Hop on, then," the girl said, "we're going that way ourselves."

Ross hopped, seating himself between the two girls who had yanked him into the back of the cart. "Do you live at Mercat?" he asked.

"We work there," one of the girls answered, kissing his ear.

"Lord Huntly must be a love to work for if he gives his help a night off during the week."

"Oh, he don't usually," the other girl said. "Only today he had a visitor. A *lady* visitor. "Open Your Bodice, Leonore," she sang with a laugh and fell back into the cart, pulling Ross with her.

By the time they reached Mercat, Ross knew two verses.

Annabella stood beside the grand piano in a gown of claret velvet, rearranging a bowl of roses. The Earl of Huntly sat on the corner of a French writing desk swinging one foot, his two spaniels at his feet. In his left hand he twirled a small silver dirk.

Her heart pounded beneath the gown of claret velvet, but she fought to keep her breathing even and her voice steady. Across the room from her, Huntly looked as though he was fighting his own battles with rage. He took another sip of burgundy wine. She knew he was walking on eggs, that he had to remain calm.

He looked her over, taking in her pristine innocent appearance. She was a beauty. It angered him, knowing she probably wasn't as pure as she looked. That drove him mad.

"You can't be that stupid," he said. Then he mimicked her, "I don't wish to marry you, sir." He pushed away from the desk and came toward her. "As God is my witness, I can't imagine why not. You'll not get a better offer. You have ruined yourself, you know. No decent man will offer for you when word of your time with Mackinnon leaks out. Only my decision to honor my word and my signature on that betrothal contract stands between you and ruin."

"In that case, I'll take ruin." He slapped her then, knocking her backward. She righted herself quickly. She felt her lip burn and tasted blood in her mouth, but she did not speak. She kept telling herself that even if he killed her it would all be worth it, as long as he was convicted of Gavin's death. She had decided to remain quiet, hoping he, like her father, would bluster for a while and then wear himself out. She hadn't expected him to strike her, but even that didn't deter her from her determination to deal with him.

"Your behavior at Seaforth was scandalous. Even my good name may not completely erase the stench of that folly."

"Then don't give me your *good* name. If you try, I'll only refuse it."

He was still close enough to strike her and she thought he might, but instead he touched the dirk to her throat and lightly drew a snake shape that ended at the lace across her breasts. "You are in no position to bargain, my sweet little slut. You are nothing more than Mackinnon's leftover."

"I'd rather be his leftover than your wife."

He threw the dirk across the room and backhanded her on the return swing. Her head snapped around as she was driven back against the piano. She clapped her hand on the stinging welt on her cheek, her eyes glittery and hard. But she did not cry, nor did she say one word.

"Don't provoke me again," he said. He was about to say something more when he heard her gasp, saw where she was looking. Her face was white, her eyes overly large. He turned around.

Ross Mackinnon stood in the doorway, his eyes dark blue and filled with rage. He stepped into the room and Annabella saw the sword in his hand.

"That sword was on the wall for a reason. It is over four hundred years old," Huntly said. "It's priceless. It was last used in the battle of Culloden."

"Then it should serve my purpose well. Get out of here, Annabella," Ross said in a controlled voice. "Wait for me outside the door."

"But how . . . how are you here? I saw you climb the gallows."

"I came close, lass, but that wasn't me. Percy reached me in time."

She almost swooned, but she knew Ross needed her to be level-headed now. He had told her to leave. She started toward the door.

"Have you told him yet?" he asked.

"No," she said. "You came before I had the chance."

"Told me what?" Huntly asked.

Ross waited until she had left the room. "That the sheriff is on his way here to arrest you for Gavin's murder."

"You've already been convicted of that crime, and although it's apparent you've slipped the noose this time, they'll be hanging you soon enough."

"I'm a free man, Huntly. It's your neck the noose awaits. You had this planned out pretty well, but you forgot one thing. I'm not left-handed. It's too bad. You write with your left hand. You threw that dirk with your left hand—I saw you. You should have stabbed Gavin with your right hand, but you didn't."

Huntly stood motionless in the center of the great room, his jaw working, his fists clenched. "You bastard! If you think to trick me . . ."

"It's no trick. The sheriff will prove that soon enough."

"Why wait for that?" Huntly said. "You came here to kill me, didn't you? What are you waiting for? Get it over with."

"I wouldn't want to deny you the pleasure of going to trial, Huntly. I came here for one reason only. Because you had something of mine," Ross said. "The lass. As for the other, I'll leave that to the high court. I'll not kill you and leave the way open for doubt."

Huntly lunged at him and Ross slapped him across the chest with the flat side of the sword. Then with a mocking salute he lifted the sword to his face and turned toward the door, slicing the rope that held the chandelier in its place. It fell to the floor with a crash, the candles rolling onto Huntly's priceless Persian carpet. The carpet burst into flames.

While Huntly stomped the candles out and screamed for help, Ross slipped through the door, scanning the hallway for Annabella. He saw her standing in the shadows, her petticoats piled beside her on the floor. She had pulled her skirts between her legs and tucked them in front of her, cossack fashion.

"Don't laugh," she said. "I thought you might be leaving in a hurry and I would need leg room—to run."

"That's my lass," he said, grinning as he crossed the hall to her and took her in his arms for a quick kiss.

"I can't believe you're here. I was so sure you were dead," she said.

"I know, and remind me to paddle your backside for running off like that. Now, let's go before Huntly gets his fire put out."

Taking Annabella's hand, Ross started down the hall. Huntly's frantic shouts for help rang after them. Running now, they turned down another corridor and sped through two rooms, pausing only long enough to shove a chest in front of one of the doors. Annabella felt a thrill of joy when she saw the balcony. But once they were outside, her joy faded quickly. They looked over the edge and saw that the ground fell away to a steep descent. Moonlight sparkled like spangles upon a sea as black as midnight. Ross stood beside her, looking at the long drop to the water below.

Huntly's men broke through the door behind them.

"There they are!" one of them shouted.

Ross looked at Annabella. "Are you game, lass?"

"Aye," she said with a twinkle in her eye. "Are you?" Before he could reply, she took his hand and jumped, pulling him over the edge with her.

The sound of Ross Mackinnon's laughter followed them as they went over the side. Down, down, down, they went, dropping at last into the sea.

Epilogue

Texas, 1880

Stewart Mackinnon rode his horse hard down the dry Texas road, stirring up a cloud of dust that seemed in no hurry to settle behind him. A minute later he pulled to a stop in front of his uncle Alexander Mackinnon's house.

He found his mother sitting on the back porch with a fan in her hand, her eyes drifting closed.

Breathing hard, he sat down on the top step. "I really do like Tess Delaney," he said.

"I'm glad. I think she's a lovely girl," Annabella said.

"We've gotten to be friends . . . good friends, while we've been here."

"I thought so. You spend a great deal of time together."

"I told her we'd be going back to Scotland in less than a month."

"It will be three weeks tomorrow," Annabella said. "Our six months have passed awfully fast this time."

"I surely do hate to leave here."

"I know you do," Annabella said. "Of all my children, you seem to enjoy Texas the most. You're a lot like your father in that respect. It's always hard for him to leave when it's time to go back."

"That's what I've been thinking. It's *awfully* hard for me to leave."

Annabella opened one eye. "It will pass and you'll be glad to get home, just as your father is, once we're on our way."

Stewart rose to his feet. "I'm not going back, Mother."

She opened the other eye. "When did you make that decision, Stewart?"

"Last night. Mother, I asked Tess to marry me."

"I see. Has she given you her answer?"

"Yes. Just now. I've just come from her place."

Annabella swatted at him with her fan. "Well? Don't leave me in the dark, Gavin Stewart Mackinnon. You're a fine-looking lad. I'm sure she said yes."

Stewart grinned. "In a roundabout way."

"You either agree to marry someone or you don't, Stewart. What exactly did Tess say?"

"That it would make her as happy as a pig with its head in a slop bucket."

Before his mother could respond, Stewart kissed her on the cheek and leaped over the railing of the porch. "Where are you going?" she called after him.

"To find my father."

Annabella smiled and started fanning herself again. The sun was on the horizon now, its golden-red glow touching the world and setting it afire. In the cottonwood tree beside the back gate, a mockingbird found something happy to sing about, and Annabella thought about Stewart, her baby, the youngest of her seven children.

She was thinking that years from now, when she was an old woman, she would probably remember this gentle, gold-washed evening when she lost the youngest of her brood to the land of his father's birth. She closed her eyes, thinking of her loss. *Out of three girls and four boys, it isn't so bad to lose one to Texas.* Faith! In the beginning, she had expected to lose more.

She heard someone come up the steps and opened her eyes to see Ross standing there, looking as splendid as he had that day so long ago when she had hit him in the head with a croquet ball. She smiled in remembrance of how handsome he had looked in his kilt on the day of their wedding, and how proud the old duke had been.

Ross was standing before her, wearing the clothes he had always preferred; a blue cambric shirt, buckskin pants, a sweat-stained hat, and a pair of run-down boots. There was nothing of the Scottish duke in the way he looked now—but inside, in his heart, she knew he was every inch the laird of Clan Mackinnon.

He dropped down into the rocking chair next to hers and removed his hat, wiping the sweat from his forehead with his arm. "Stewart said he spoke with you."

"Yes, he did."

Ross stretched his legs out in front of him and gave the rocker a push. "Did he tell you what Tess said?"

Annabella smiled. "He said something about her being as happy as a pig with its head in slops."

"That's a mighty strange way to respond to a proposal."

"Oh, I don't know. I seem to remember something similar that you said to me when I accepted your offer."

"What was that?"

"You said, *My love, I wouldn't trade you for an acre of pregnant red hogs.*"

At the astonished look on her husband's face, she began to laugh.

The sound of Annabella Mackinnon's laughter drifted over the yard and across the white picket fence. It whispered through the green glossy leaves of the orchard and over the rusting remains of an old moldboard plow. It was caught up in a little whirlwind that came out of nowhere, and riding on the current, was dropped in the barnyard, where a contented old sow lay with her head resting blissfully in a bucket of fragrant, cool slops.